DOMINATING WOMEN

ALAN GOLDFEIN

There's no answer,
And that's the answer.

> Gertrude Stein

Sometimes I think she was right.
Sometimes I guess she was wrong.

> Alan Goldfein

'It is the best of all possible worlds'.

> Voltaire misunderstanding Leibniz
> (and thus mocking him) in *Candide*

It is the best of all *possible* worlds.

> Leibniz

.

to Ute

About the Author

Alan Goldfein has written for *Time, New York, The Village Voice, Commentary, Playboy, Oui, Satire, Beyond Baroque, Cimarron Review, Colorado Quarterly, Forum, Florida Quarterly*, and *The San Francisco Chronicle*. He is the author of *Heads*, and has been anthologized in a Random House Collection, *On the Job: Fiction About Work*. In the 1970s, Alan Goldfein received the Mark Twain Society Award and a New York State Council of the Arts award for fiction.

During an extended stay in Germany, the novels *Jews and Germans/Germans and Jews, Europe's Macadam/America's Tar, Let Us Now Praise America, The Black Wife*, and *The Guidance Counselor* were created.

Alan Goldfein has taught economics at the University of Maryland, history at Carnegie-Mellon-University, and writing at Berkeley. He has also written numerous episodes for television series, such as *Knots Landing, Perfect Couples, Bodies of Evidence*, and *Paradise*.

ALAN GOLDFEIN

VERSO

Like your average squirrel speed-footing breakneck across a street, then stopping dead-cold halfway and (for some reason inexplicable to non-squirrels) turning back and speeding the opposite way, I debated the doubl'entendre of Domination in this book's title, I rejected it and then, frustrated, feeling dishonesty closing in on both sides, I hesitantly brought it back. Such wordwork is a kind of cowardice, but it's also the crispest mapping of my Iliad: my ways with women and their ways come back at me. Sieges. Atonements. Contentments. Relish. Satisfactions. Sieges. As one of "my" women once said to me, "Alan, you are a guy, and guys, at bottom you are so *cold*. You, they, you, you do not like to be hugged, unless it's for the sex-prospect. You do not like to tell your inner secrets, you *Feiglings*.[1] You cannot *bear* true adoring, true *companionship*—the joy of having a *soul*-mate in the world—and Lord knows we *need* these, *all* we people.

---

[1] 'Cowards': she was German.

1

Alan, in a word, you—and all your men—you are perverse. And your perversion, it is unjustifiable—as *any* perversion is." And this woman, she held to her opinion even as I had replied, "*Bullshit!*—I *want* to hold and I want to be *held*, I *want* to reveal deep secrets, my *deepest* wants—even with *men* I want that, if I could find one, a *man*, one who made me comfortable—a *soul*-mate, not that this rules out *women*, even slightly—I'm not *gay*." "But," this woman had replied (and with quite the primal smirk), "Alan, with that gay-fright you have just proven my point, don't you *see* that! Alan, you only *think* you want what you *say* you want: *soul*, hah!—but no, you do *not* want. 'Wanting' is cheap, it's a failure, of self. And *saying* 'wanting' is even cheaper. You, and your *men*, you are born exclusive *ids,* your egos are all *ids*." (And she had expressed those 'ids' of hers with her upper lip snarled-up as if growling 'shits'). . . But something has just come to me—and I hesitate to name-drop just as I have admitted the male-aleckiness of my "Dominating" title: Montaigne, he had a deep friend, male, to whom he'd revealed his soul. A butcher, yet, in his little home town. The butcher died; then Montaigne started writing.

By the way, I exaggerate, a bit. For perversion, it *is* justifiable.

As I will freely admit here that I find myself to be a character without a plot—at least an easily discernible one—I do believe that I have got to start-out here, for honesty's sake, mortifying as it may be, with mention of the following: There is (or was) this woman, Eugenia, who loved me and who taught me (such tidbits as the little known item that even Plato had a female teacher, Diotima), and who came, eventually, to be belting my ass with a belt—my own (irony, it was an olive-drab military one with a copper buckle [I'd been in the Army's hurried Six-Month Wonder program, when the Berlin wall went up]); there is the woman, my ex-wife Linda, who I once pushed against a lamppost, and not so lightly either (she went to a chiropractor, then she thought that he, with his own ["professional"] pushings, was "total incredible horseshit and making-his-own-play"); there are women who have put up their dukes at me—and not jokingly (and who seemed to have real talent for the old one-two); there is one who mime-thrust a knife at my belly in plausible attack, and then, in guilt or self-disbelief, stared at her own knife wielded by her own hand as if it were a harmless thing, a rubber replica, a flashlight, a spatula, and then evidence of a psychotic break that had put it there, and handed it over to me with her eyes both threatening and apologizing and (really, I'm serious) demanding punishment—her swollen eyes happening to be, pretty much, similar to the coal-black saucer-orbs of sarid-up Suddha Rao, the indignant daughter of India's Minister of Economics ('68), whose right breast I had gained ungranted access to over the Scrabble board between us (she'd been winning), wherefore I'd had to explain feverishly my "it-was-nothing, I swear, I'm so sorry, it's just *play*" to both Suddha and to the two uniformed 911 policemen she'd called. And, although it was not the last event, or experiment, there was my sex-identi-fying, or shoring-up, or devastating, my onetime recip-rocated fellatio with my buddy Shel Sevenecker, my (or our) Hey, let's-take-a-chance-on-the-strength-of-our-man-selves-by-seeing-what-being-a-woman's-self-is-like (e.g. does sucking a cock register as dominance or submission or both?), *and* by chancing seeing what being Gay is like, i.e.—if we *like* it and we don't throw-up and then give-up-the-ghost and kill ourselves. . . And before these more contemporaneous events, there was Annetta Barron who at age seven (we were in second grade) perceived some kind of psychic-dawning pre-sex-sex daylight-opening and directed me to go down on my hands and knees in the brick schoolyard (in Baltimore—inner city, '47), whereby she straddled and slapped my ass while hollering *"Gallop, Man O'War!"*. . . Then there came the episodes, of an older-younger man, of a Fifties Boy-Man. Here's the most memorable and most shameful: There was me, I, nice-boy Alan Geist, aged seventeen, and my harsh-cold-callous "affair" with poor Sally Asher: In the Mission District of San Francisco, where I had cruised ('54 Plymouth ex-taxi: 250,000 odometered: "It's gone farther than the moon," I'd bragged), I'd scouted, sniffing for "available" females, which usually meant Hispanics. And I had spotted a wander-lost girl who was clearly not Hispanic, not with that pale skin of hers—it was really ghost pallid—and her hair so scraggly but lightish brown; she who clearly had no destination in mind—she'd sit on a stoop confounded, she'd stand, or half-stand and change her mind and sit again confounded, as if figuring a sad what-next? if there was a 'what next' in existence. And I'd gone cruising round the block a few times for nerve and best pavement-pullover opportunity, and as she was good-looking, or, well, nice-looking, which you could see through the ragged hangdog poverty of her clothing—she had on a too-large navy peacoat on this warm evening, and so she seemed as downtrodden-used as any gamin child of coal-miners given to us by Zola (school assigned), if Zola had ever described a girl with a country overbite like June Carter Cash's and Loretta Lynn's—I offered her a ride, which she, destinationless, was glad to accept. I had then re-crossed the Bay Bridge—which was not in those days a traffic-gorged nightmare—and I ferreted her into my dorm room at Cal, where I had kept her custody, a secret for an entire week, bringing her Big Macs, fries, tuna salads, tacos, and imploring her (more like ordering) to not go out onto campus (the magnificent sight of which from my narrow dorm window had astonished her, it really stunned her); and she had obeyed—my closet of a room did seem fine refuge for her—I guess in her mind it said 'steady', it said *Life-might-yet-get-to-be-Okay*. Sally Asher was from West Virginia or Somewhere Around There (I didn't pay much [any] attention to "empty-benighted" regions where I just *"knew"* they hated Jews, scientists, atheists, niggers, "goodie-goodies", etc., and where [Sally had proudly apprized me, as if she were tutoring me on basic American History 101] the Hatfields "still feuded" with the McCoys with "Civil Warry" rifles, and where I pictured Buddy Ebsen parodying the whole deal on *The Beverly Hillbillies*). So, no surprise then that Sally was tottering on illiterate's edge (which I found disgusting and cute-appealing); and who couldn't miss that she had been abused quite bad and quite as often shown the rocky road—God, I couldn't shrug-off her reactive winces at other students' footsteps in the dorm hall (did she hear them as the jailers' treads?); and so she so often (too often) would go clinging (to a fellow, me, who, again, found girl-clinging disgusting and cute-appealing—callow creep that I was). But she was sweet—oh so sweet a girl. In Sally's huge brown eyes (so big they near obliterated the whites), those eyes staring so righteous-patient, in her questioning fright-looks, this pretty, and tender-soft-hurt-girl-with-warm-reserve (the last sort of tranquility that you would expect from someone who had been subjected to so glaringly miserable and unfair a life: lord, "sweet" is a calumny, a miscoloring), Sally went so far beyond mere "sweet". And such sensitivity did affect me greatly—I swear it!—as much as it could soften-up a juvenile seventeen-year-old who had been on-the-lookout for sex sex sex and who had never given shit-one about "The Wretched of the Earth". So, incredibly, our entries into each other were perfect, perfect as could be; inexperienced as I was I just *knew* this was perfection (I even feel that trueness now at age forty-four): we were equals, no bed-hard-driving, no sex-carpentry hammerings and plungings, no fancy slips-and-twists-and-slams, no "sophisticated" hand-to-hand combat, certainly no affected Zen or Yoga with heads hung exotic-backwards. What we'd had was, you could say, *I will say*, rose-petal-sex, flower-bloom-sex, cared-caresses slow, considerate—maybe this wasn't even SEX. "I love you," Sally said and Sally said—weakly and strongly. "I love you," I'd said, and I'd meant it (in my young-boy weak-meaning way), I'd said LOVE to this girl who had obviously been junked and trashed-away all of her life and was, after all, street soot (which "chestnut" I also could never allow myself to forget). Yes, both of us did mean that "love", as much as we comprehended it—until I got slapped up-back (once too many times) by what had been my unbaked love-standards and my teen-boy love-hopes (blonde-goddesses) and my love-coldnesses. And, yes, I kicked her out, I booted Sally out, and sure she'd cried—that was instinct, that was her life-treatment in its long-learned battered breaths. She in her love-begging was the very loyal attached opposite of a French woman, Hélène, I had later known and "loved" (she would have had to have been French, no?), Hélène who'd demanded, actually stone-cold *demanded* in her best unflappable sangfroid (which had of course bewitched me), if I were to win *her* "love", "*Make me jealous.*" Well, French-woman antithesis Sally Asher had, yes, started-to cry when I let her go, but then she'd caught-back onto her street-earned dignity and her own street-wise expectations (or *non*-expectations), she could handle what she, lost-she, was used-to; and watching her control herself with her gripping breaths had me hating myself—though not near-enough to let Sally stay. Here we were, Baby Bluebeard and his Beaten Baby, who he ferried back over the (never-ending then) seven-mile Bay Bridge in jumble-worded embarrassment (I'm fucking *making-conversation*) while his forsaken girl now stayed silent, with a glinting squint to her eyes that meant, that meant, well, I-don't-know-what—a last ditch attempt to *understand*? to draw out from me my meaning, why I was intent on rendering this act that really had no meaning *("You swore you Loved me!")*; and I vowed never, ever, *never*, to cruise the streets again—which vow I of course violated within one month (of acute masturbation), even less. But no, I never saw Sally Asher in the streets again—I'd even feared that she was dead or beaten-close-to and in hospital (if hospitals would take her and keep her), and of course I felt regret—that's such a lame-weak nothing word, so cheap—okay-then, sorrow; but so what: here I was just a middle-class *boy* in process of gaining his (entitled) college education, and resuming his scrip-tured quest for The Perfect (non-Jewish) Girl who could, what? read Kerouac and Mailer (who indeed wrote about what Sally Asher lived and *knew*), a girl who could Yeats as well, and eagerly raise her hand in class and talk-talk-talk with crisp (falsified) authority, and, by the way, who—in my experience at Cal—could never equal "my" Sally Asher in any of her senses and intuitions (even "my" Linda, my eventual [and ex, by now] wife, could never match sweet Sally's sensitivi-ty—dependant-independent-authentic as it was). Needy can be very authentic, you must know.

Do you hear remorse? You should.

But truth is truth: My behavior with Sally had been immoral, granted, but clearly we were not fate-aimed. What might then have altered how I had ultimately comported myself by—call a spade a spade—imprison-ing the resourceless girl (just by my ordering words, no props nor implements like cuffs: she would have been happily spellbound by traipsing about the majestic otherworld of "her boyfriend's" Cal campus), what might then have altered my then kicking the girl out? And, in the first place, in picking her up? What would have made horny 'Fifties-decade Alan Geist a different *boy*? Had there been an easier way for Sally and myself, these two plain samplings of American-life-polarity?—had there been a nonchalant "no-biggie" way to begin and to end, or to begin at all? Well, sorry to say, No—I think not. And yet there we were, or had been: we liking each other. We liking each other a goddamned lot. I'd told Sally I loved her—I said that to you before, and I want it remembered by you. I told Sally I loved her more than once, so much more. I wasn't even lying—I felt no internal cringes—although I knew that I was lying, in some way I was. But the girl was—a spade a spade again—well, scum. She even knew she was and she'd blurt it—*"I'm scum!"*—she hoping I would say, 'No Sally, no you're not, you have a future, you have a Life, you have *Me*.' But Sally didn't have a life—she knew it, *I* knew it! Dwight Eisenhower knew it! We people, we're like amputees, no leg, yet suffering those damned phantom-leg knife-stabs—*how damned cruel is that!* . . . . Except, some-times the pain feels good. Tourists will pay to go to a swamp—The Everglades! Bayous. Haiti. Miserable Other Places too. Pictures they will take—and then jet home.

Thus this book.

ALAN GOLDFEIN

AH ME ME ME ME ME!

The Fifties, tail-end—a tale oft-told, even more than those of paper-millionaires jumping from the top of the Flatiron Building in the Depression twenties—and, what-can-I-say?—my beginning: Oh those "sorry-assed" Fifties—I'll be dispensing with them here with super-speed-dispatch, I swear it; but a guy's got to say what a guy's got to say: The Fifties, with its "mind-forg'd manacles", when a posse of deluded sex-deprived "good" boys (deprived from sex by sorry deluded sex-deprived "good" girls) "collaborated" to have a mischievous go and a go and a go at some non-deprived Fifties girl—a "gang-bang", original (non-gun) term. Us Fifties boys, we justified ourselves by considering our attacked girl a "whore", because with her colossal-sized confessional grin she'd seemed super-willing to go helpless-prone and too teasing in the bargain. But Us Fifties Boys, we didn't quite get it—and here is the lesson we could have taken from us Now Boys: "The Whores", they were not bad girls, they were horny girls, they were smart girls, as eager as were their attacking boys—only in their defying of dumb convention they were the wise ones: they made it appear as if *they* were the victims while really the boys held that distinction, having had their "peer-group" ethics led down a contrived corridor, they to don the sackcloth of atonement: Instead of *The Taming of the Shrew* it was *The Shrew Tames You.*

But seriously, I-am-a-good-man—I do believe that about myself, I'd bet anything it's not delusion.

This book shows why and how I managed to get to good.

Everyman, even a hater, believes that he is a lover, if even of some concocted-twisted, hate-evading (and embracing) sort. And if not a lover of a Woman, then of some quixotic Dream: a utopian society that is not futopian; a religion which is pure as poetry; a sunrise and a sunset. And by Everyman here you bet I include Everywoman. It's second nature, this inveterate lover-upholsterizing of the Self. . . No, it's *first* nature, our rawest fabric, it beats-out the bodily organs—"The Heart" beats out the heart. . . Even with me—especially with me, who had been The Chameleon of the Heart. I was a guy who had intended to attend Medical School (UCSF) and become a neurologist or cardiologist—head or heart (as an undergrad I'd passed the ominous-repped Organics—they weren't so bad), and I laid claim as well to an English minor (which actually tottered on the cuff of major). But what I did do was not Medicine nor Literature (your educated hunch might now be that I did not have the self-confidence required for telling people what was wrong with them and what they should do [*or what I would do with them!*], nor for telling people what literary things meant beyond the narrow dryish literary, and this while up there priest-poised, pulpit become podium: I just did not have blazing within me that strong-enough American Dream, and Russian Dream [at least in Russian Lit] of the heroic Prince Myshkins, that beating soul-greed of us groundlings rising uplands). So what I did do was I borrowed bigtime (after working two years as a baggage-loader at Oakland Airport) and I opened a bike store, GEIST'S BIKES—and why that? Well, because I anticipated that such proprietorship (and fake-ish expertise) would earn for me The Great Worthwhile-able, fame locally. And lest you see me as an execrable faddist, this was long before the scandal that came attached to "The Great" Lance Armstrong (a pseudo-nym if I ever heard one). And, sonofagun I was cor-rect—bikes are sexy stuff. Here follows an inventory of what at first naming was AL'S BIKES but became, as I say, GEIST'S BIKES (I put great faith in the seductive powers of comic rhyme with [pretentious] spirit in there too). I still own the place. I "carry":

Merck—the gray, elegant line, but fragile: deep
    pothole-iffy
BMC—a beautiful bright red: always suspicious and
    accident prone
Trek—speaks for itself, especially when outfitted with
    the deep treaders
Giant—better than its over-compensatory name
Raleigh—excellent for commuting, such as riding to
    campus and around it
Focus—a dreamy blue, can't take your eyes off it
Canondale—elegant, with its slightly further-slanted
    front wheelbase
Felt—a sharp black devil bike, unfortunately named
Cervello—fast and light

Jamis—translucentish, pedals pastel blue—a Wonder
  Woman bike
Surly—green, goes well in nature routings—again,
  unfortunately named
Birdy—a folder-upper; some women like it, a man
  wouldn't be caught dead
Cube—light with sturdy frame

Now, a number of these "selling points" are crucial
inside-expert hokum that I've made up, as I've learned
that, well, pulling the rug from under, well, suckers'
eyes (or, okay, the honed-in noses of the uninformed
[acting informed]), is more and more what "business-
men" do in these-days-America—and once you start-
out doing it, immoral as it is (*and once was not*) you
can't exactly stop—hustling (well, that is what it is) can
be (I'm sorry, what can I say!) fun. Fulfilling, some
would say. . . And also, I should (actually) warn you,
bicycles are and are not like people. Many bikes with
brand names are blatant (unapologetic) rebranders.
Chameleons. They may, through their shipping-travels
from China to Singapore to India to South Africa, have
had their names and colors changed: An Indian Poona
may well not provide the origins of but actually *be* the
internal-workings of an English Raleigh—twice-the-
price, *watch out, sucker!* Bikes though are *things*—they
are not human—do I actually have to come out with a
self-evidentiary like this?—yes I do: Over forty years
ago a man wrote a book comparing the motorcycle and
the Self—and, being a Zen-blended book it became a
hot faddistic, it did very well. But its basic theory was
ridiculous, a stretcheroo. There is no viable metaphor
between man and bike, motor or pedal, there is no
analogy. Repeat: A bike is a THING—it's linear, while

you (and I) are scrambleds, we're all over the place. But
pleasure though—I will accede to pleasure, that's the
link-up: I often love to sit on many of my bikes' seats in
my Geist's, recollecting how delirious with unmitigated
joy even broke-down skeletal rental bikes had made me
when I was a boy and riding with my dad Moe
(Morris), who was quite depressed—except when on a
bike. By the way, I don't believe fucking did all that
much for Moe—so, to not be like a Raleigh sonofa
Poona (you'll see why) I have fought-to-fuck. . . .
Upshot: I know more about women than I do about
Raleighs and BMCs (etc.), and about that creature aka
myself. Arrogant, schmucky, delusive—but true.

False too.

As a kid I had gone riding so often with my dad—
around Lake Merritt, up the hills of Berkeley and
Oakland and in through Tilden Park, then down along
the Bay, and halfway (maybe three-quarters the way)
up the two thousand feet of Mount Tamalpais in Marin
and on-down to the ocean, watching it spread and
spread-out to meet me (and swallow me welcomely) as
I descended; and I had loved what seemed the mys-
tique, the quiet roar of thin tires (you really had to
listen), the rolling past pedestrians, the twin lurches of
pumping-pumping-pumping as if we, dad and son, were
not-so-large Jewish men but headlong thoroughbreds,
Seabiscuits and Secretariats with giant-determined
equine hearts. No exaggerations here: By way of that
mate-riding, that pedaling side-by-side, even leaning
forward and racing as if nothing else in the world had
mattered I had been brought closer to my dad—but too
much happiness, the bigtime Zarathustra quote, that

happiness is hazard: my father was a man who seldom spoke and who too often, too too often, seemed uncomfortable in my presence—as if I had been a bad mistake just deposited on our front doorstep in my infancy: an ironic "joke", a poor substitute, a booby-prize, as he had just been cut from even the Orioles, the Phillies farm-club then in the Minor Leagues, Triple A. . . Biking though, hadn't it brought us to be brothers? . . . Wellsure, sometimes, like I've said, I saw that brethren resin—when I wasn't seeing Moe as cordoned-off with mild-ravaged face within "the heart of darkness" (before I knew any clichéd-up words of Conrad). . . So I saw us as rivals too, peddle-edgy ones, just as dad saw us. . . Near-to-deadly twins, considering what befell my dad—or, rather, what he had chosen to have befall. . . The thing worst possible.

You might guess.

Now, my clients at GEIST'S BIKES are young men mostly, they who buy all the extra gear and gizmos, the professional-sleek slipperlike bike shoes (with subtle collapsible soccer-shoe-ish cleats), the ballet-esque tights, the Tour de France jerseys (in various flash-colors), the protective helmets with those bee-antler rearviews (on my trips to Europe I have noticed an interesting thing: the Euro bike-riders, of which there are many, do *not* wear helmets—as a rule—while the Euro *motorcycle* riders *do* wear helmets [fancy BMW jobs] and the American cycle riders [like on Harley "hogs"] tend to not—a societal macho-question here that might warrant serious analysis for more global understandings?); and my clients are also young women who purchase none of that excessive abovementioned glut, while (I've got to say) some do go for all that shit

(some even have requested visors: "Visors are for
motorcycles," I've said, and with my most pleased-wry
smile I often cannot resist a hairy-chested "Visors are
for sissies"—to which some girls grin amused, and
others scowl at me the male chauvinist pig proprietor
who doesn't care about sunlight's damage to the eyes).
But, as if they have some serious savvy from uniquely
female-research (that bestseller *The Lady Biker*?), the
girls do also ask smart questions: mudguards-pedals-
pumps-racks-rims, and spokes-seats (saddles or "stool-
ies"[2])-shocks-frames and stems-tools-best, wheels dura-
ble for street or mountain—even proper-prep quadri-
cep-hamstring-calve-knee workouts and (you'd better
bet) *nutrition* ("Is absolute veganism inimical to all-day
endurance?") (I don't give a shit, but I answer Yes [it's
what they want to hear].). In any case, with all such
interest in bicycles never ending, always growing, I find
myself to have achieved a recession-proofness and
indeed a recession-surmountation that would impress
the satraps of Stanford's "rightish" Hoover Institute
with their (aptly-named, and eponymous yet) Laffer
Curve. (Except, me being weird, and "left", my in-
vulnerability fucking does annoy me). And by the way,
the girl riders oft-times wear flouncing-loose skirts and
dresses when they go about swiveling their legs for
testing-out bikes in my showroom (they think they're
being Dutch or Danish or Swedish or *Parisian*), and
GEIST'S BIKES approaches becoming a boutique of
(acceptable) rotatory pole dancing (in my mind anyway). Needless to say then I meet in my trade many

---

[2] I always refrain from telling them that these small tight saddle-
mounts can cause hemorrhoids if one rides too much; and when
men ask, I never tell about the possible prostate problems.

many young women, but "women-of-a-certain-age" also seem nowadays to be availing themselves of bikes too—for shopping and (that illusion of) health maintenance—which I (unscrupulously; sometimes) stoop to foster. One might even describe me as (as I have described me as) in loco transportationis.

But myself these days, I've got to admit, I don't ride a bike—not so often: as I say (or don't say) seats will crunch the aging prostate, the necessitated bar-lean-forward on uphills can be murder on the lumbar and (surprisingly) the triceps (I don't tell customers), and those nifty shoes (it's been speculated) may well effectuate the gout and even squeeze the nerve-endings that lead up to the penis, thus causing erection pain, not to mention cruel and unusual punishment upon ejaculation—which is perhaps the most counterjust phenomenon in the world (and, tell the truth: have you ever seen a bike rider [*of any age*] whose expression was other than a crunching teeth-gritted frown?). . . Oh sure, I used to ride: I won a race or two (localwide and state), but I'm now "a-man-of-a-certain-age", with the requisite one divorce packed in my back-pocket too. Paradoxically, regretfully, tauntingly, fate's payback, it's that I can't but meet what my ex-wife Linda (*who does not ride*) has tabbed "a sorry shitload of bike-struck women who you can't lay your better-days' peter on—haha". (Well-bred Linda never used to talk in that indecorous way until the last days before our divorce). And Linda is right—and Linda is wrong: I have earned (yes, that's a good word, *earned*, although it may not go down so well), I have *earned* what you might call a "shitload" of lovers. Like Hugh Grant, a man may have (had) as his the most beautiful woman in the world, an

Elizabeth Hurley, and yet go on-hunt along Santa Monica Boulevard for the funkiest of ten dollar hookers, with (yet could be) the syph. ("You want your blow job, jim, with dominance or submission?"). Go figure (And I have). For men Ugly can just (magically?) become beauty, or at least it transforms to Hot Desire. Perversion, what can I say? it's at our base (in both meanings)—doesn't the Bible tell us this. . . But anyway: because women always do contain (somewhere within) A Good Way (which men do not), with women I always Diogenes-it for The Good. I still try to tie together and smooth-out that Möbius Strip of love-and-sex. . . Which is why, looks like, I'll have to begin at The Ground Floor. A Good Girl.

Suzanne?

MY GOOD WIFE LINDA INADVERTENTLY LEADS ME TO A DIFFERENTLY GOOD SUZANNE

I had only owned GEIST'S BIKES for little more than six months, and I had only been married to my Linda for little more than seven. We had met at Cal in 19th Century American Lit, and I had been drawn to her for her very first remark in class: characteristic of her (although I couldn't have known it was characteristic at the time) she had asked the professor if he believed that Melville had been "harkening" to "the biblical Jonah" and had he read many books about whales or had just "read-*in*", say, one, and used that singular information to make up the "usable" remainder—and she did have startling-snide recourse to that utilitarian word "usable". The young professor—I forget his name (although I do recall his "theory" that Moby Dick represented "man's deepest search for his phallic

21

consciousness"—which he himself may have read in just one "usable" book about the American classic)— the young professor looked astounded at Linda, he looked insulted, wounded: Herman Melville was a god who had "sailed the seas" and who had labored in far greater universes than we "spoiled children" could imagine, and also in lowly clerical jobs for his survival—he was no (and I do remember the professor having snide recourse equal to Linda's snide questioning of Melville), he was no (two sneers here) *Thomas Pynchon*, who was all the (unread) vogue and "a spoiled rich brat" who was just "egotistically relying on his fanciful-vile world-view 'concoctions' of likes and hates." But sharp Linda had actually read Pynchon, and she then countered the young professor with scholars and authorities from whom she had gleaned knowledge (or decided that she had gleaned it) from Pynchon's work—C. Wright Mills, Mircea Eliade, Irving Howe, Robert Hofstadter, and even Robert McNamara. She was determined, she was intense, her interrogation of our young prof (really just a lowly Instructor) had been accompanied by a left-hook-double-jab into the classroom air—she was "cruisin'for a bruisin" (a Fifties expression which would have sickened her), her voice had screeched on Eliade, as if she'd been hollering-out for a snubbing taxi; but the professor, in contempt had simply exhibited his distaste by amateurishly turning away from this bumptious dirty-blonde girl with stiff backbone and incisive prepossessing upper-class accent and (inappropriate for her well-aimed brain) pucker-bowed lips—she from whom I myself, a nobody's nobody, could not turn away. But yet, yet: Linda Miller had come to remind me, once I came to know her, of

that sweet lost Sally Asher—and this despite that there
was no good reason for that reminder, real or otherwise
. . . No surprise, Linda Miller became a lawyer; she
worked for the Alameda County Public Defender's
office, which was headquartered down in Central
Oakland across the street from Hearst's *Tribune*.
Linda's most frequent gripe was the limited time and
resources she had to work at "saving" (or "protecting")
her unmoneyed clients ("in this super-moneyed George
F. Babbitt land of ours where grinning Chaplinesque
lobotomite clowns clap and cheer from the Wall Street
podium at the startout of each day's Super-Bucks
Stakes, the New York Stock Exchange"), Linda trying
hard as hell to rescue her "clients" from the considerable railroading resources (*money-money-money!*) of
the Alameda County Prosecutor's office. For the accusations of rape, robbery, battery—"*accusations*, Alan,
accusations—but really for just *being*", street people
went to jail and then to prison. In prison their lives,
"human *lives*, Alan, these are *over*, done, *kaput*. *R*ehab
is *d*ehab. Three strikes and you're *out*, our obscene state
law, except the 'out' is not just one at-bat, it's the
ballgame—your *life*." California was Republican-run at
that time. As a Public Defender, Linda had little or no
access to exonerations by way of DNA—she had no
O.J. Simpsons to defend. She wore no schmatas but
special-fit suits to work, oftentimes pinstripes with the
broadest of lapels, as if those spreadout mantles were
the kinds of badges of jurisprudence that Katherine
Hepburn might have buttoned herself into for tooth-
and-nail court-fighting onscreen against her offscreen
lover and opposing smooth attorney (for the rich)
Spencer Tracy; and as Linda seemed to (indignantly)

enjoy revealing, her power-suits were mostly a parody of her powerless power—but she'd thought such overdress might impress a judge who might happen to be (like so many were) "arrogant social-climbing snobs who might well be 'into' affected flaunting when off-duty." Despite all, and certainly weirdly, Linda was yet the least ironic person I had ever known, while she yet admired irony—the main reason why she stuck it out so long with me, Alan Geist, Mister Jew Irony?—seven years; no, ten years—this protraction chock full of my infidelities (which I rationalized, when I could rationalize, with the "justifier" that my philanderings kept me in a steady state so that I might "love" my (sexless-pretty-much after one year) Linda, who I did so admire. Uncomfortable to say, truly so, but I had never been overwhelmed by sex with my Good Linda, not even remotely near to the radioactive realms where I had been groinally-galvanized and "spiritually united" with poor loser illiterate homeless (even bodily filthy) Sally Asher. When we'd first got married, with the colossal exception of poor deprived Sally (and a trio [or so] of gang-bangs[3]), I was no Mister Experience, so what constituted Linda's rote "moves" and somber "mellow-nesses" in bed had started out fine with me, hesitant as they were. And anyway, I had so admired her kind-nesses, her decency, her attempts to be always bent on Truth, her extraordinary rushes to help anyone in trouble, her seeming absence of envy or hostility (pretty much), her belief in everyone's best residing some-where within everyone (again why she stayed with *me* as her "man"?), such that I felt blessed (and sort-of glittery) to be *her* "man" (She had actually taken-to

---

[3] Again, that "boyscout" Fifties meaning: penises, not guns.

sacrificing her needed night-rest, sitting-up in bed and reading insomniac me to sleep: "*aesthetic* fiction that's *real*, Alan, it's *virtuous* writing": Elizabeth Hardwick, Joan Didion, Annie Dillard, other *women* [I did not complain, for then I wouldn't sleep.]). But I shouldn't sell myself short, or too short—which is a behavior I'd picked-up as the son of Moe-and-Ida (more of this later): The so-youthful Linda Miller, she had started-out seeing me as a-good-person, and I had started out my adult life in the attempt to be just that (okay, despite the felonious "jailing" of poor Sally, who I'd "loved"): I too had wanted to liberate the Negroes ("blacks" came later), free them from their poverty and their shut-outs from the perks of democracy, like good schools and voting and serving-in-the government; I wanted us out of Vietnam; I read books and couldn't plumb what the hell was wrong with true communism—I mean, *sharing, it's Sharing, no?* (In economic history class I'd read the astute phrase of the anthropologist they unembarrassedly called "the great Karl Polanyi " that "Capitalism was planned, reciprocity was not"—and if 'reciprocity' was as natural as had been hunting and tilling [and screwing], what more could you say). . . Now Linda Miller was from Racine, Wisconsin (Lake Avenue, if memory serves—such details of your True First [well, in some most-important ways she was] you just don't forget), Linda with that long straight pointed Euro-nose that said "*listen*-to-me", like a person holding forth their eyeglasses to accent their opinion, and her straight wheat-grained Anglo-Saxon hair that fell (intentionally) over that pin-striped charcoal double-breasted lawyer suit of hers; Linda out of, first, Mount Holyoke College (which I'd located as precisely as I could by imagining one of those Northeastern States I would have no business ever visiting); Linda who, just by playing her many CDs (and vinyl records!) in her many (culture) raptures, taught me as much as anyone possibly could teach me about classical music—such as that there were seven modes, one didn't always have to start on C as the root, that's why there could be so many sharps and flats needed to keep the do-re-me-fa-so-la in accord (or something): so we listened and we listened to Stockhausen and Reich and Glass and Cage and whoever. She: "Alan, it's like astro*physics*—listen to the noises of the *spaces*." Spaces got noises?—and who wants noises anyway? "And listen to the dis*locations*." (Duh?). So Me: I listened, unlistening—while (well) trying honestly to *listen*. But Me, I listenened-*listening* to the sweetest beauty of, say, Strayhorn and Ellington—say, "Sophisticated Lady", its first two low-linked downbeat notes, G flat, F (so they tell me) all you needed for your mood's capturing, your mood's attendance, its waiting for the lush of more. And then there were Linda's stacks of small-taut-torn back-pocket paperbacks; and here, unlike with her sleep-readings to me, there *were* some men included: there was Borges, with Colette, and Doris Lessing hooked somehow to that pomperoo Anthony Powell ("His name is pronounced *Poole*, Alan. Listen, Alan, to the *elegance*, it makes the formality *in*formal." But Chrissakes, why did the informality have to be fucking *jerry-rigged* to be informal?). And by the way: This tutorializing by Linda, I have just now realized as I write this, it put me in somewhat the same position in which I would find myself years-years later with this woman, Eugenia, who, call-a-spade-a-spade, dominated me (stern words, cock-rings, cock-spankings [god her backhand hurt], panties (only pinks and whites for Mister Me), asshole-lickings [and deep too], "strap-on play" [okay, not so deep], the whole mishpucha—and Eugenia's sex *still* resonates, the bizarre respect it bore, damnit [more of this on-later]). . .

Now here's Suzanne. It sounds like a cliché because it is a cliché, and a very disturbing one, but I noticed this young Suzanne girl right off, and I mean right-off, no more than one month after my marriage to the girl-woman I (supposedly) revered: The girl—and she was a girl, hardly even remotely a woman—was Suzanne Thalbrucker—who about eight-to-ten years later I saw acting (and still as a girl) in *Dog Day Afternoon* (three short lines, tops). But now was now, with Suzanne come bursting into GEIST'S BIKES, mouth agape in girl-horror-mode, verdant eyes in dire accord, as if she were being chased by, what? a pissed-off human-sized cockroach with its feelers out, or a menacing Cyclops-ian miscreant kept heretofore in the back wings of Cal State Hospital—or as if she had been for weeks re-hearsed her thrusting entrance from the wings of an overly wide Cal-theatre stage. Turns out Suzanne was a "Dramat" student at "The University", a *grande amoureuse* in training (without quite even knowing it) and boy could she exude—faith-pains-frights-loves with deepest intensity (albeit with her paradoxically stark eyes she could even exude that most difficult of simplistic emotions—indifference) (and barely bear-ably, for me, she was the most "a*maz*ing"-ridden girl I had ever known: near everything earned the laudation of "amazing")—all such that I came to call her "The

Exudatious Suzanne". And she did love that sobriquet, I'm not exaggerating nor patting myself on the back when I report that Suzanne was brought to spanning eye-roll and eye-swell shimmy-shakes by my mention of my nickname for her; but I suspect (no, I know) that Suzanne could be brought to ecstaticish conniptions (which looked phony, if you did not know her, phony as an actor as in-patient at a mental hospital being readied for electric shock treatment and fighting-off the five muscular hairy-forearmed actor-attendants), this authentic jump-down-up exuberance of Suzanne's could be triggered as well by even a moderately huge J.C. Penny sale (I *witnessed* that: She worked part-time on part-commission at Penny, and I gave her credit for that honest labor—most white girls of that day wouldn't have stooped to the menial hunkering over a cash register hour after hour, all her "colleagues" black or Hispanic—and *she being nice and sisterly*—nice as nice could be.). Okay, I exaggerate about the, what? conniptious exudations?—no, well no, not really, I'm not going overboard. For Suzanne's paroxysms really were not fatuous: they had to do with, not just girlish enthusiasm, but with what seemed a spiritual breathing, a taking-in and giving-out, a shuddering absorption that was as non-mutable as a strong addiction, and so was overwhelming; and it wasn't even clear that she preferred being saddled by such idiosyncrasies—they must have hurt as much as they helped—I'm sure other students mocked her. Let me put it this way: ecstasies are a going out from one's body; Suzanne experienced *instasies*. She just could not control her feelings—to myself I'd joke that she might be on the road to Parkinson's or some other spastic neuropathy (and then

I'd feel guilty for the "joke" and change my description to something literary [and beautiful?], like "Suzanne's equatorial sieges"). As my wife Linda (of too short a time my wife then—as I miserably said above), Linda never would have made-it as a flaunting, exhibitionistic actress, so Suzanne would have flunked-out laughably-cold as a cool-spined lawyer (she'd never have passed the Bar exam anyway [different shapes and warps of brain?].). One ought to control one's emotions—as wise as that admonition sounds, as undeniable, believe me it can be a naïve rule in certain singular cases and pretty damn closet-mind stupid and off-the-mark—one such case being Suzanne Thalbrucker. Years later, in that famous Pacino movie, arguably his best, Suzanne played the Puerto Rican hostage in the Brooklyn bank when "Sonny" (Pacino) got tackled outside (while negotiating with the FBI) by her Latino boyfriend. But now, some years earlier, this movie-hopeful was just a Junior working at school at being a terrified-in-love Desdemona in her Cyprus-royal robes murdered by her mad-in-love *schwartze* Othello (I saw her performance—she'd invited me: her eyes did do their moral storm-burst perfectly, Suzanne style, she in knife-wielding husband dread—and for a moment I wouldn't have been shocked had the big black kid who played Othello gone breaking from script, tossing away his long-blade and whining to Suzanne-Desdemona, "Jeez girl, shit I'm sorry, I didn't *mean* but nuthin'.").

But when she wind-swept herself into GEIST'S BIKES, Suzanne was not dressed in a royal robe; she wore short-shorts, and they were plastered-on rounded hips so perfectly wasp-waist hourglass that one might have conceived that she had spent the previous ten years inside a shaping mould—nothing was left to the imagination but the potential Venus mound of hair or shaved-baldness in the hippie fashion of the times. Suzanne's green eyes were—or were acted—so bowled-over by my omnibus-rows of glittering two-wheel riding paraphernalia that they appeared to have converted at the rims to a Martian Red as vivid as the Cinzano sun shields by which Italian restaurants protect their outdoor tables (and I protected the loss-leader bikes that I kept out-of-Geist's-doors, when it did not rain); her eyes could go as cry-shiny as those new (mostly imported) bikes themselves; her hair was loosely curly and long, a surprising waterfall of a rasp-berry-strawberry (had she colored it in this beautifully nutty way?—was it some sort of compensation for the child-inadequacies she felt, a compensation that only seemed to magnify those youth-bloom inadequacies?); her nose was quite short and it was upturned in that disregarded way that Europeans have come to sneering-ly call "so American" (yet we Americans dumbly label as snooty), and her mouth was naturally rather narrow (except when it was exploding with her [also natural] dramatics), so that you might, if you looked too quickly, see her as a colorful puppet, or a giant parrot—however a parrot with a voice that was full, guttural, deep-sympathetic, and strong, which I came to learn reflected the tempered-tenor that "dramats" were taught to display as "natural"; but paradoxically, her cheeks were pale, as if the other, rambunctious, colors of her face had intimidated them into obedience. In short, Suzanne was striking but no beauty, not quite exactly. And I'd already seen her outside the GEIST'S show window looking in so many times, trailing and peering like a child before the lions' cage—and in fact I'd clocked her peering-times (classes ended) and I waited (never looking over, which might have prevented her ever returning, much less entering). As she wasn't a starlet then (and truth is she never became one full-fledged: a few more gigs, all TV), she hadn't yet changed her given name, as she ultimately did, from the ethnic Suzanne Thalbrucker (bridger over a valley?) to the far more American (and meaningless, bridger over nothing), Sue Brooke. But this Sue, Thalbrucker or Brooke, just seemed too intimidated (or too something) by the rows and queues of bikes (and heaps too—used ones traded-in) to bring herself into GEIST'S BIKES— *an embarrasse du riche*?—but one of the embarrassee. That Suzanne-entrance did take time, considerable time, but finally it did take place. Perhaps acting classes had helped her to eventually burst in as if Gene Hackman or John Malkovich (or that Cyclopsian miscreant cock-roach) had been about to strangle her.

"I'd like to see a nice bike, but," were her first haltingly nervous words, as if I were also dealing-in the best of watches and the cheapest, or the latest in the complicated hi-fi equipment of that ancient day (twin woofers and tweeters!); I suppose Suzanne couldn't just then see herself confronting in one cinemascopic take my entire stock of at least two hundred, plus color photographs, of others to come. "But I don't know anything, I'm serious, I'm sorry. . . . *Any*-thing."

This young lady who could speak-the-speech on-stage was barely audible now that she'd found herself actually shopping in Al Geist's humble five hundred square foot GEIST'S BIKES (which had previously been the only failed wine shop in radical-gourmand-bullshit Berkeley: location-location-*location*!)

"Any type bike in mind?" I'd asked.

"Well, one, I mean, this sounds silly (she smirked at her own smirk), one that rides, like, you know, a*maz*ing, and steers . . . sharp?—I-don't-know, re-*sponsive*?—and doesn't bounce so much so you can't fall off of from every strewn-out crack-in-the-street and, you know"—disgusted roll-eyed sneer—"*gar*bage?"

Along with Suzanne's fallback-default 'a*maz*ing', and as comically paradoxical, were those 'likes' 'you knows' 'I means' of hers, for she enunciated them with the kind of precise emphases that (I didn't know this then) had been drilled into her in her "advanced thespian" classes. (*I pray thee, Speak the word "y'know" trippingly on the tongue.*).

"I know, I'm a jerk," she then whooshed out the corner of her mouth, hands aflap, as if she were imitating Diane Keaton in *Annie Hall* when "Annie" happily volunteers to drive Woody downtown "on her way" although she was heading uptown.

Suzanne smiled, but, again paradoxically, with a collapsed cringe; such amalgam having her mouth widen while its corners hooked down, beneath her risen eyebrows, which were, by the way, especially furry—tender, you could say. The upshot: an inescapable stage-shock coupled-with, playing-on, self-bemusement. And the confident nature of her embarrassment did seem authentic, natural—and sure I was drawn to the paradox. (I didn't even realize until years later that my own MO worked in precisely the same way: ricocheting—mediating—"cover-all-your-faulty-bases".).

*   *   *

In order to free myself for an evening get-together with this anomalous (and oxymoronic) Suzanne (not to mention the begging question of why-in-the-hell-would-I-want to?), I called Linda at the Public Defender office and told her a bike shipment would be coming-in late, as Schwinn, the first American producer, had gone out of business with their dopey big-body bicycles from the Forties (which resembled motorcycles—intentionally), and they were now getting themselves organized to produce and deliver a supposedly decent-skeletal modern product—and there were, "as always" (frustrated spleen-voice here) "routing disconnections due to amateurish planning". Linda said No problem, she'd be working late anyway for some poor soul's innocence (she tended to believe that all the poor souls of ghetto Oakland were black and innocent), such laboring of hers was turning-into not at all a rare event (but I do not blame it for the ending of our marriage—I don't think I do. How can you blame a woman's noble charity?—even as it races to become obsessive—as one moment's contemplation cannot help but tip-you-off that *you* are the considerable cause of that escapist obsession, even as it goes sweatily compulsive, even as it may save lives.).

Anyway: Suzanne Thalbrucker already: First came weed, Suzanne expert-rolled (accurate as a jeweler two-fingering his loupe—while modestly claiming that she was "all thumbs"); then, after we inhaled she topped-off with "dessert", some "quickie-shakes of cocaine-frosting"—"It's the spice, sir, like parmesan."—this "parmesan" she'd rolled into a torn-out page of *The* (infamous) *Berkeley Barb*. I hadn't smoked or sniffed in years (and "my" Linda never had). This prelim took place in Suzanne's dorm room (coed building, a try-out innovation in the "progressive" days following that insipid pop-book *The Harrad Experiment*): I'd asked, "How do you all handle the, you know, toilet?"—and to be hip I added "scene" to toilet. Suzanne's answer: "We pee and we shit, *trala,* boys and girls together—isn't it, like, a*maz*ing!" Me: "And the . . . (I should have held my peace) smells?" She, cavernously grinning: "Smells are smells, *tada!*—you're anti-*smell*? What are you, Mister Prissy Squeamish Anti*septic*?" And then (after one quickie giggle), "I'm sorry for my mockery, I really truly *am,* it's in my DNA."—and it appeared in her swollen actress eyes gone to sweet that her next words would be the hammy, "I'm sorry because I do love you." But instead, then came Suzanne's ultimate in child-libertarian sophistry: "But, you know, there *are* no bad smells, Alsy. Pee-*u's* are just pee-*u's*"—which was of course as annoying as it was wrong, as much as was the "Alsy" abbreviation which I hated, as it reeked of a crummy plumber fixing a toilet. "Don't call me Alsy," I said in a guttural mumble, which actually had Suzanne assuming a perceptive adulthood (acted-out, likely) with her sympathetic "Oh I understand." . . . But I now tried to quash any and all gestures, all kneejerkly pathetic ripostes—and we toked again; and then, again, we snorted. Suzanne's room overlooked the empty but magnificent and sunken Cal stadium, which from Suzanne's one dormer window (no pun intended) now appeared to stoned me as a quicksand update of the Roman Coliseum where gladiators were about to be delivered to victory or dispatched to death—thumbs-up or thumbs tauntingly up-then-down (as they sometimes do [to appear ancient Roman?] in the U.S. Senate): (And yes, yes, as this was my first affair [of many, many to be coming] I felt great guilt regarding Linda, the thumbs were more drooping-down than dropping). Thus there was that Cal stadium which, well-stoned, Suzanne Thalbrucker and I then, super-speedy, dope-speedy, rider-speedy, biked all-round—on two of my well-used but decent best reliable GEIST'S rentals (she hadn't yet purchased a bike, so damned if I was going to waste polished-perfect newness, and unscraped brakes, and never-once shifted derailleurs, on an un-tested and quite possible nut-case, even if (and because) that lovely case exuded beautifully at even a butterfly's flittering (she near flittered herself, by way of her shoulder-quakery). . . And it was all such then, until *I*—not fervent *she*—*I* the bike mavin/maven? crashed, into a warped jut-out part of the surrounding fence of the stadium (which Suzanne had adeptly skirted), I skinning my knee but no big deal—and stoned Suzanne neither laughed nor appeared, in the least, worried. She smiled softly, as at a child, and helped me up—her tugging hand had me realizing that she was quite strong, more animating than were most women—I ought have realized that a certain type of actress, or one in-training, might have been built in that powerful unisex way, or had worked hard to be so (and, inter-nally embarrassed, for a moment I was reminded of my mother Ida, I saw the determined, willful mom in my bike mate, she who had protected me from my neck-chop-wielding father who had grown beaten by his 'Jew-failure' at pro-ball. "Don't say anything, anything funny or shaming," I now said to Suzanne Thalbrucker about my fall—and she said, "Why in the world *would* I?—Alan. *Shame?*—I won't, remotely, I won't *anything*: all you did was *fall*." "You didn't have to even say *that*," I'd said, and this stoned-crazyish girl, this rapturous-gush exuder, this aura-swallower, she regarded stoned-me as if I were doubly, chauvinistically, outmoded and insane. But the big deal was a Big Deal: the stoned BikeMeister had fallen off his bike— failed as had his dad—because (he decided) his girl bike-mate had such an all-devouring-diverting All.

Sure, we slept together, but how does one write about what was, essentially, nothing?—while knowing that that "Nothing" was immensely powerful. Realistic writing doesn't work (I've tried it); imaginative writing comes off "airy-fairy". Anyway, here goes: We were in her narrow cell of a dorm room which was hardly different from the constricting chamber in which I had held captive poor life-deprived Sally Asher some twelve years before; that collegiate-cell with the squeaky narrow bed-springs (it took us a passionate ten minutes or so to realize the " genius brainstorm" that we could lift the narrow mattress from the bed and lay it on the narrow floor and just quietly rumble). But if you're in the market for prurience, please forget it: I can't tell you how the sex was. This is not gentlemanliness, nor is it, in any way, forgetfulness—sex being sex being sex (and with this carnal identity in mind one can accept how seven foot Wilt the Stilt Chamberlain could have claimed in his autobio recollection every one of his lascivious "billions" of five-foot fivers, while I am trying here merely [merely?] to work and analyze my way into some good woman-knowledge, and therefore some good woman-future.). No Wilt-ish toting-ups, no records set—not even remotely close—but an Alan Geistesque delving-in: Here I'm beginning with Suzanne Thalbrucker's being Suzanne Thalbrucker being Suzanne Thalbrucker and not a logged-in number. However, okay, sure, details are still necessary or you've got nothing (but your prejudiced projections), so I will let you in on this—you may do your best with it: Suzanne was the proud proprietress of such a magnificent strawberry-orange bush that I couldn't but dive into it lips-first before we had even begun our more standard sexual introductories, and I was put in mind then of—believe it or not—sad life-deprived John Ruskin, the handsome nineteenth century critic and essayist of whom, it is said, he never consummated his marriage because he was shocked by the considerable, same, female attribute that I was—except in the opposite way: Brilliant, art expert, knowledge-knower and great appreciator of (painted) beauty, Ruskin hadn't believed that women were embellished by pubic hair, with which, once he learned firsthand that they did grow such what?—evil-corruptness? perverse jungle-filth advertisement? (as did a *man*!)—he wanted nothing to do, not with *that* shrubbery, even that of his new young wife—those demonic pubes spoiled the idealist's ideal portrait of what a perfect (or even imperfect) female should have been. . . And when I dove into Suzanne's wild auburnian (Golden Retriever hued) thicket I couldn't muzzle my outcries of *I love you! I love you!* (surely the residents of the neighboring dorm rooms heard my insane forswearings). But no, as magnificent as it was, as taking-aback as it was, it was not solely Suzanne's aforesaid chaparral that launched me abawling and blubbering. Again, it was that Exudation of hers: It was spontaneous. It was silent. It was organic and unstoppable. It had gone sweeping-on to (and through) my determined viewpoint when she undressed, and when she closed the dormer window blinds (not school-provided, "no way, José": she had bought the pastel blues at Bed Bath and Beyond); and the Great Exudations had even accompanied her brushing of her teeth (yes she took time out to accomplish that pro-active task—although at least she did not mess around with stringy unsexual flossing [although I might have pictured her flossing as circumrotatory as a belly-dancer might have done the job]), and she had made the usual commonplace proactive dental-scouring maneu-ver seem to contain the wholesome dedicated (and sin-gular, as protracted) the self-sanctity of a religious act—perhaps all actress hopefuls were well-advised to tooth polish-up real real good, I don't know—I do know that that operation was no tease; and the Exuda-tions were certainly in play as she approached me, un-doing my tight bike togs (which effort required, as had the pulling-me-up after my bike crash into the Cal Stadium fencing, serious determined strength; so that, before I even, as they said in the Fifties [so I hear] "muff-dove" I was experiencing the emanations of what I came to realize was [I was pretty goddamn sure] an ongoing standup Suzanne orgasm—her knees locked.). And, unfortunately, I did realize that, as wonderful as it was, as sui generic with its vertically precocious (and maybe even preconscious?) tollings (not toilings), it was all, also, unavoidably, pathology—it was extreme, it was *too* extreme—I was frightened. Sure, you could intone, *Vive la Pathologie*—but, you know, something

was wrong with Suzanne Thalbrucker, and it might well
have been beyond the plain old everyman (woman)
neuro-normal sex-tics. Yes, I realized that, but with my
mouth well-baptized into that mélange of strawberry-
orange soufflé between her legs, that pubescent graini-
ness, and my ears set-upon the soft motions of the
insides of her thighs (so that I heard a sex-rustle [which
might well have been my own eardrums brush-fizzing
like a jazz drummer's]), and with her Exudations being
(or threatening to be) so seriously osmotic, I found, or
feared, that I was possessed of them myself—or on the
verge of them, and quite wanting to be. I was *learning*:
I was within Suzanne's within-ness, Suzanne's
Suzanneness, I was *her*—really, I mean this, and she
was within me of course—as she likely had been with
many other me's (she was, afterall, a leading lady in
college-training, a *jeune première*, who couldn't not be,
while being a what-she-was, *what-the-Other-was*), and
while I knew that this "communication" of ours was in
a way absurd, was in a way way-beyond (as it had gone
through nothing but silent air and the barest of physical
touchings), it really was nonetheless unstoppable—I
just damn knew it! I just damned feared it. For nothing
like this attachment had ever happened with my wife!—
and while it had happened (kind-of) with sad dispensable Sally Asher, I had always known that Sally was
sad and temporary, so dispensable, so I was not, never,
her—that was impossible. But here, in this crumby-thin
darkened humid dorm room with my head between her
legs (and still, in my mind, seeing her face), I was
Suzanne and she was me (I really could really *feel* that),
and this with—I had no doubt—she being used-to such
transferences. Suzanne, I realized, I reflected-upon, no,

I embodied, no *I was*, the frightened child I had been as
a child, the boy who feared his frustrated-failed pitcher
dad's beatings (and who had wanted to similarly,
physically, beat his dad—belt that skinny ass, backhand
across the scary tough-guy face, stiffarm-up that
arrowed stubble-chin); and I was yet the boy who had
feared the neighborhood bully's taunts and beatings
too—and so I saw that Suzanne was as isolated and
alone as I was (married as I was or not). And so, because she was so trapped in her own battle of compensation for her frailties (whatever they were: how the
hell could *I* know?—but why else become an *actress*,
an everybody-nobody?) Suzanne could see me trapped
and frail, more deeply than could anyone (except, I'm
sorry to say it and say it, poor-sad derelict Sally
Asher)—and yes this deep-seeing surpassed by far that
of my own wife Linda (whose true empathy rushed
rather downhill towards the ghetto folk—I couldn't
blame her [though, yes, I did blame her]). Just as they
teach actors, grilling them, over over over, Suzanne reflected by way of instinct, strict-taught-instinct
("taught-instinct"?—*was this possible!?*), so she now
understood not by understanding but by that queer
(insidious) taught instinct, and she sympathized (if you
can call it that) by way of that taught-instinct—no
damned thought involved. Suzanne just felt me. The
artificial was the real was the artificial was the—oh the
spinning etc etc etc etc etc of it. And so, thoughtless,
mindless, a handball bouncing back to the handballer
off the enclosed brick wall, I felt Suzanne, I compen-
sated my way into her own compensating love. And I
knew that Suzanne could swallow me. . . Except: "Hey,
it would be a*ma*zing, like put me in your *pocket*,

Alan"—Suzanne did say that, and she said it in squeaky little girl pitch—and this unexpectedness (and expectedness, sort-of) was startling as well: For that phrase, I had heard it before. Twice: Unattainable Grace Kelly had asked it of Frank Sinatra in *High Society* (and then she had rejected him!); and the other time, that was a real life one: A woman I had seen some time before (and after), Eugenia, a firebrand who had, well, put *me* in *her* pocket—she had dominated me. My first time too. And though I won't describe it now (*I will get to it*), I had loved it, that pocket-put, and hated that I had—did it make of me a freak? I mean, a homosexual can nowadays come out, it's acceptable behavior, it's admired. But a man admitting that a woman taking full charge, *full*, gives him a hardon, a *hard* hardon, that is just not manly in-the-least—you can never come out and holler from the rooftops *"I got Submission Disease!"* So, until Suzanne Thalbrucker had bridged the valley and come out with that *put-me-in-your-pocket, Alan*, I had thought there had been no bosses here, I was "taken" but I still had the male prerogative of "taking", whatever that might have been—bring my knees up towards her beautiful (exuding) face and go shoving-in my dick; bend her over the naked coiled springs that were now the remainder of her dorm bed, or over her little kiddie-dorm rolltop desk, and, as we said in the Fifties, "go for the glory" up her ass (even with no K-Y Jelly [I hadn't even yet heard of that saving salve]); *or, yes,* be put in *Suzanne's* pocket (which I already was, and I knew it!) and get beneath her and lick her "exuding" asshole—what-the-hell, *taste-her-shit!*—as if it's chocolate—ain't *that* Love!? So, with Suzanne I (a married man of "experience") was learning, finally, that sex was a mystery, a mystery's mystery, a ricochet wild-card, and I was packeted in the mid-dark of the card pack—what was happening wasn't necessarily what was really happening. What hinted wasn't even what was hinted. Sex required an instantaneous interpreter, who you did not have, and *who was never there*—once the forensic laparoscopic-dude arrived sex would become Xs, Os. . . . Well: Sex then you ask?—*give us already the real deal, its nimbus at least—at least of it what you can.* But I don't know what to say (try honesty?)—for all I know I might well have been impotent with this instinctive thespian, and dramatizing Suzanne might well not have even known I was (for in my impotence I would have been well-potent; and/or she wouldn't have known too that *she* was all that too. As wife-Linda once said to me: "A woman has to get-it-up too, you know, big boy."). God, trances are trances, they are so powerful—just look at the wobble-prey of the tongue-talk evangelists, just imagine how Nothing Billy Graham would have been had he not looked like God. I mean, how do you tell an orgasm when The Other is so orgasmic that she is living within her orgasm even when she is brushing her teeth or bending to take off her constraining socks and shoes?—and the orgasm continues within her within-ness even afterwards. And *you*, once you have been sucked-in and are now alone, or on a bike, or even with wife Linda (at rarest moments) you wonder if *you* can be that Suzanne-way as well. *Ever. . . And* if you really *want* to sad-wallow "happily" within that (natural?) achievement. . . Sort of, you do want it—as do want most men. . . So they'll say. . . As so they will believe... No one ever wails, *Oh Please God, give me detumes-*

cence! . . . No one, except for the great wisest of the (Exudatious) actors.

No you don't want it: As there was something else: How do I say this? It was almost as if Suzanne went and became beyond, or counter-to, all that I have heretofore been saying: she'd become too, not an out-pouring thermos but a greater vessel to be poured-*into*, as if any motion on her part beyond the swell of those oblique green eyes and her seeming to resonate (but *not resonating!*), any further-active Suzanne motion, would deny, would despoil, her Great Exudation—which had so drawn you in; it would just negate it by its own activating, its own invigoration: Embrace, thee and thus dissolve. Suzanne, whoever she was, would no longer be Suzanne Thalbrucker, The Great Exuder. There was, for example, the one time weeks later when I had to lay on Suzanne a Valium, a placid-blue five milligramer, to chill-out those ever-ready far-flung Exudations, those great sweating vibratory nothingnesses, when they went way too far, miles deep beneath the horizon of her flesh. (I, an insomniac that I have always been since my father's suicide, always kept these benzodiazepams at the nite-table ready for the baddest of bad nights). And Suzanne Thalbrucker had never before in her life im-bibed a Valium, her liver was a neophyte at absorbing tranqs, and a good twenty minutes after the swallowing she slept for one entire afternoon and well-on into the evening—not one super-loving exudation in the air. A few seep-out fartings, if you must know. . . Which I, kind-of, liked. Appreciated for their normalcy.

*　　　*　　　*

So how did what began with its rectal-exudish ending end? Certainly not by my Linda's doing, for obsessive-social-helpmate-for-all that my wife was, she was ever-working, ever nite-hunched over her home desk, and damned if, although my attitude was coming to be (in defensiveness) politically incorrect, I had been growing for some time to resent Linda's poor-folk, falsely indicted as they might have been with their police-forced confessions; it was as if my fate, little-bike-boy that I was, was more important than theirs (well, to me it was), and, in life's tricky-sour-life-way, they'd become doubles for my failed dad Moe who—I know I keep repeating it (I can't help it)—dad who'd never made the goddamned fucking Majors (and who mocked himself by wearing about the house his Minors Baltimore Orioles cap, red-black it was, as was that eponymous bird perched on its beak.). Anyway Linda never did find out about Suzanne. Although, for God's sake, all she'd had to do during those six weeks of Suzanne would have been to look at me—perhaps caught-up in a simulacrum (albeit weakly) of the riveting way in which Suzanne had looked at me. . . No, Suzanne and I ended things as things tend to end. The girl wanted most of all to be an actress (which she was already, no doubt there with her daily Method Work, quite natural as her breathing was)—and she'd never even heard of Lee Strasburg or Susan Strasburg or Una O'Neill or (I'm just guessing here since she was after all a Drama major) Stanislavski, and there she was having come close as rubbing shoulders with all of them—only in her real life! She was a female James

Dean or Monty Clift, and as such there was only one place to head for—i.e. some agent's office on La Cienega, in L.A. Where I imagined her exuding her ass off and sweat-struggling and sleeping with those agents and the rest of *"those people"* for whom I had contempt while not even knowing a one of them. . . And sure, we did telephone for a while until The Big Drift Off happened and we telephoned no more, and I never saw Suzanne again until I went to a movie theatre (with Linda yet) and saw "Suzanne Brooke" portraying a hostage of sympathetic failed-but-decent bank-robber Al Pacino in sweaty-summer Brooklyn, with hundreds of extras as sympathetic locals-in-the-streets hollering *"Attica! Attica!"* at hundreds of extras as un-sympathetic guns-out police—all re the prison where Governor Nelson Rockefeller had had rioting inmates shot and killed (you can imagine how "my" Linda'd felt about all that). . . On the very next day however I did call Suzanne—she still had her first (L.A.) Los Felix number from the days when we'd dragged-on our weak and weakening communication, she certainly hadn't made the-big-bucks with her small role, so she hadn't moved up from Lower Hollywood—but she couldn't talk to me beyond a few words of Hi-Hello, wonderful-to-hear-from-you: she was in a hurry for "a meeting", an audition, a couch-cast, a job at MacDonald's, whatever. Or perhaps to have "a larger, important, role" in a new TV show, which I never caught: exudations, they just worked best on "the small screen", she'd once wised-me-up on that, on those yards-wide theatre screens too-much emotion tended to blow the audience away. Reality in grossest reality was too artificial. Too unbearable. Oh, sweet now Suzanne Brooke. . . Had her exudations dominated me, or bounced-back to destroy her? Or made both of us, in our natures, artificial?

And perhaps I had seen Suzanne on TV—I'm one of those liars who do not like to admit that I watch the small screen (and way way too much, without even Streaming)—but it was hard to tell if the woman I thought might be Suzanne was Suzanne: the face, the toning-down, the gestures limited, imprisoned-seeming, and her aging age. The sadnesses that seemed to have grown of their own beyond the role? . . . Same story with this movie I once watched on an obscure channel—and this was even years later: Suzanne (or a Suzannish actress) was playing a part in this parody designed I guess for nincompoops who'd not have known it was a parody—of *The Postman Always Rings Twice* (whether the old John Garfield one or the "more recent" Jack Nicholson, it didn't matter). The "movie was called *The Postman Never Rings* (a play on the post-modern truth that the postman does never ring— why bother? your neighbors never talk—why bother? your bills never request checks—too much bother), and this woman, this Suzannish woman—or (a reduced) Suzanne herself—was, what triteness!—being e-mailed his dream-loves by her lover (they never even spoke on the telephone). Ah the diffident coldness—absolute because unrecognized, unacknowledged, unknown as Earth's inner core of universe. So Suzanne (or whoever), she did *not* leave her drabbish husband, or have him murdered, because the e-mail she received from her new lover was just tamped-out words on a screen, functionarial—and she responded to those electro-words in kind. The "words" had said (no, read) 'I love you'. No clout to such silent love.

Maybe it was a good movie.

But I'm lying through my teeth: There is a truth here which I have avoided—I'm not even sure why, more than ego is involved. Before Suzanne and I "drifted off off and away" there had been a stronger push "off off and away". The Great Exuder had exuded herself onto a fellow whom her spirit guided towards redirected and improved (and more soulful) exudation: Cadeau Courir (an elegant international-ish show-biz alias if I ever heard one: he had a southern accent, maybe coastal: Savannah or Charleston?), "Cadeau" was "generously donating his time" (supplementing his income? adding to his prestige performance-resume a highly regarded touch of academics?) by teaching for a semester at Cal: Advanced Mime, I suppose. Well it was true that he was internationally known as an entertainer, he was often seen on PBS and the German channel DW; he was slender as Marcel Marceau (does mime even work with the rotund?—it can only convey comedy when projected by the fat [Suzanne told me this, as undoubtedly Cadeau had told her]), he was a gracious glider and soft-speaker when he lectured on mime publicly (I attended once) while demonstrating such "basics" as strain-faced rope-pulling against an imaginary adversary's pull—perhaps if not the most trite certainly the most symbolic of the struggle of the individual; and I do have to say that he was a projector of decency and a lack of arrogance (this annoyed me); and this calm soul-eyed fellow—a Montgomery Clift if there ever was one (superimposed upon a Daniel Day Lewis, as I see it)—he stole The Exuder away from me, him with his own accomplished brand of Inner-Exudicism. And he did this, I suspect, without his even trying—and perhaps to his eventual regret: I'd see Suzanne following this Cadeau character about Berkeley, especially in what has come to be known as The Gourmet Ghetto (him in his precisely rolled-up workshirtsleeves and his white jeans [ass-taut-tight of course, no slack)—and she appearing to have absorbed that perfect subtle-unsubtle mime-walk (likely without the slightest conscious effort), she was just so thoroughly hooked: Exuder Trailing Mimer, a queer marriage reflected in a queerer mirror. And of course I then, despite all I have said here, and thought, and feared, and imagined, I wanted her back.

Not the slightest dice.

And I've often wondered how Cadeau eventually managed to extrude himself from the exuder and their perfect-oppositional picture of duality.

He'd certainly never helped her get much work in Hollywood.

GEORGIE AND THE IRA

The gnawing question that ought to have gnawed but that did not gnaw—not nearly enough: Why was I, Mister Unfaithful, looking looking looking?—faithfully *looking*, and to be *more* Mister Unfaithful, and not, *within my marriage*, trying-trying-*trying*—to be *less*, of course, until I made my uphill rock-strewn way to decency? A reliable husband. *Or:* facing the spirit's mirror and accepting who I was, as honest as was that dishonesty, and therefore *from* the marriage just being consistent with myself (and perversely dependable)— and with Linda—and simply done-the-right-thing: *splitting*? Paul Simon's *There Must be Fifty Ways to Leave Your Lover* was repetitively popular at around that time *("just get on the bus, Gus, no need to discuss much")*—and even the hearing hearing *hearing* of that supercilious song had me feeling guilty guilty *guilty*. Though not guilty enough to quit my being the rotten character who I was (I sure called myself by that adjective often enough—and then tried, somehow, to deny it: *I-am-a-good person!*). What the hell was I, this "good person", looking *for*?

I've given hints. But these haven't even satisfied my (rotten) self.

"Irish" Georgie Lee? New infatuation. And new type infatuation. She was born in a foreign land ridiculously romantic to me (I knew that the exotic romance was ridiculous—Henry Miller had been born there; Burt Lancaster; Tony Bennett; all the Jewish intellectuals— so it seemed). Brooklyn, "the crab-apple-scrapple-pit of America"—Georgie's self-pleased borough words. Georgie was no Suzanne, hardly; she was actually closer to being "my" upper-class Linda's lower-class alter-ego—her toughness, appealing as hell to me, was hardnose in a blatant, alley kind-of way. Georgie was Irish Catholic, her father was—you guessed it—a New York cop (I couldn't or wouldn't make that up). She had spent her childhood and adolescence in what is now the expensive "shit-gentrified" Prospect Park neighborhood loftily called Park Slope, but was back-then an in-the-streets redoubt, an atmosphere carnival-loud and "ball-busting"—to hear Georgie enjoy her telling of "my super wellspring of a human zoo." She had grown to become a pal of Pete Hamill's, of Jimmy Breslin's and of Norman Mailer, etc. More accurate to say, she'd been a tagalong (she admitted this), for she was at least a decade or two younger than those hotshot writer-guys. Georgie too was a writer, at one time for *The Village Voice*, and when I met her she wrote a political column for *The San Francisco Chronicle*. She was, not surprisingly, when one entertains the rowdy-brainy picture of who her early-years friends had been (and still were), a later-year friend of the (once) great fighter (and now flabster) Roberto Duran (they would mime body punches at parties), and she was a fan of boxing in general. Or perhaps I should way, fighting (or, I should say, killing)—for she tended to put up IRA warriors hotfooting-it away from the British. The one I recall, Jimmy "X", had surreptitiously avoided M-5 (or M-somenumber) and made his way across the Atlantic and was as big as that movie-ish character they call The Rock (although "Jimmy" was not exactly muscular [except maybe his rocks rested beneath his prideful blubber]), and he was as back-slap friendly as Bill Clinton had been. To paint a picture: Georgie's nick-name in her younger years had been Kim (although Georgie was itself a nickname; Josephine was the bap-tismal.). She was "Kim" because she'd bore (she said) an uncanny resemblance to Kim Novak. Nuff said? Maybe not: Straight blonde hair (but roots black), dark eyebrows (but thin), intelligent-shy blue eyes that glinted when no glinting was necessary, full lips that communicated vulnerability and honesty, and ready explosiveness. A generalized look of bravery yet on the familiar edge (it was like my own) of self-doubt, and secret warning—*layoff!*—to anyone who cared to inspect (not the best, I considered, for a delving jour-nalist who must inspire trust.). And a huge eruptive smile that said, *Despite all, I want to have a good time, I want LOVE, and no disaster nor tragedy, nor false morality, can keep me from what I should have and am owed in spades.* Amusing also was Georgie's insistence on holding onto certain Brooklynisms: For extra money she was always writing a "blockbusta" screenplay that would be a *"kaypah"* (a caper); she ordered out *"bits"* (pizza); and for a story that would be a one-in-a-million shocker she continued to employ the two words "a *pissah"*. But for the Brooklyn Bridge she did reserve a unique and countervailing specialness: "It's so bleak and intricate and plain."

And, turns out, having been a New Yorker from birth, Georgie happened to be an avid biker: From Flatbush to Coney, from The Village to The Cloisters, Georgie had hunched and pumped her way, with Hamill even ("the pot-belly buckie was trying to stay in shape"), and with others her own age, telling me of her near-misses from borough boys running stop signs and driving haphazard-crooked, and even once or twice she chasing after vehicles that had, out of childish playfulness, tried to accost and-or injure her: "Ahmagacha," one idiot had hollered out his window in Brooklynese (*"Almost gotcha"*). So, with this wild journalist-woman entering Geist's Bikes (but walking-in pleasantly and observantly as if she the most normal of persons), a match was about to be made in two-wheeler heaven; and my love, or sex, or romance, with Georgie Lee (what words are left?) was probably the most carefree of my life. To this day, I'm talking. Georgie did not smooch, she did not smother like a bereft mother, nor did she wait for smothering like a bereft girl-child; no, she attacked like a guerilla, a guiltless and guileless freedom fighter—and the effect of her efforts, or effortlessness, was usually "a pissa". Georgie Lee was a friend-by-love, or a love-by-friend; not, like Suzanne, a wished-for spiritual-acting alter ego.

Except, of course, I'm lying-by-delusion.

The oddest thing—although comforting at the time—is that I met Georgie through my wife Linda: Georgie was at work on a series of articles for *The*

Chron ("pieces", as journalists liked to humbly describe them), these reports and analyses and disclosures were on unjust juridical decisions as the newest-evil form of Jim Crow, and the consequent incarceration of far more blacks (and Hispanics) than their share of the population might indicate—and Linda had invited the energetic-smart and even pugilistic Brooklynite to our house, or more accurately our apartment above Geist's Bikes, whereby over dinner, stats would be given to this stat-chasing writer, who would in turn be able to help publicize the socially legal but immoral wrongnesses for lawyer Linda, and especially for the residents of our majority liberal Bay Area. . . The evidences were delivered by my wife, however, in the formal-edited fashion that was her customary use:

> The U.S. faces a crisis of mass incarceration—the per capita rate of imprisonment has increased six-fold since '72, from 93 per 100,000 to 536 per 100,000.

> There are about 2.3 million people in our jails and prisons—overall we lock up more citizens than does any other nation in the world. As a consequence we have moved towards the proliferation of private prisons, some owned by nations even more unjust than ourselves, notably China.

> Blacks and Hispanics are vastly overrepresented in this lock-up inordinance; they make up 31 percent of the general U.S. population.

> African Americans are six times more likely to be incarcerated than whites. If current trends coninue, one of every three black American males born today can expect to go to prison in his lifetime, compared to one of every seventeen white males.

Tough drug sentencing laws have been a means to sustain the social control of the black population previously maintained by segregation, which links the disproportionate numbers of blacks behind bars to nothing other than a form of slavery.

In recent decades prosecutors have become more aggressive in their indicting decisions, charging those arrested with felonies rather than dropping charges or seeking only misdemeanor con-victions—this is hardly the justice and mercy emphasized in our Constitution.

Prosecutors act behind a veil of secrecy that even the President cannot enjoy; they are the most powerful actors in the criminal justice system. They are immune from damage suits even when they act unconstitutionally.

Funds ought to be increased dramatically for Public Defenders, so that they might be able to forestall coerced or ill-informed guilty pleas.

"Good Americans" seem to be especially fond of the system-as-it-is.

And of course, me being me being me, during the litany delivered by my much admired wife in her much admired courtroom factuality, with face frozen into that righteous grounding with but the merest dose of observ-able (but not actor-augmented) indignation, I had become an up-back/up-back observer at Wimbledon watching the Scandinavian(ish) Bjorne Borg (Linda) volleying with precision at the natural rawbone recept-ivity of the Brooklyn-born John McEnroe (Georgie) who is nodding, smiling, even laughing, even receptive-ly shouting her agreements and swearing her disdain-fuls at her native American indecencies (It would not

have surprised me terrifically had Georgie suddenly
blurted-out an indignant *"Are you blind!?"* at the
imaginary line-judge which was the United States
Supreme Court)—and, you bet, I "loved" her, this
explosively hammy Georgie (Josephine) Lee.

Not surprisingly, Georgie and Linda became friends.
No, surprisingly too: My wife could not have missed
those failed-at-furtive admirations of mine for the
exotic to me New Yorker (I didn't know at that time
that this Manhattan-origin implication was an insult to a
confirmed Brooklynite), she a bone-fide product of that
mysterious anti-Shangri-La across the just as exotic
Brooklyn Bridge and the (equal and oppositely) fabled
"East Ribba". Ah this wisecracking Georgie with her
Kim Novak looks and her slurred and rakish accent—
why, despite the well-placed crudenesses, mightn't a
man be super-happy with this direct opposite of his
wife who was in the bargain quite as intelligent as his
wife? Well, a sick man, a needy-man, an immature
man, *he* might be so happy—if he did not ask of
himself the obvious question: *why in the world would
this SUPER-FLAMBOYANT SHE want me!?* And
additionally: *why in the world anyway, and <u>really</u>
anyway, do I want to want her?. . . But Chrissakes, you
schmaggie, you have just not so unrecently married-up
with THE WOMAN, your Linda, the mature Oakland
ombudswoman (by now even locally famous—a trifle)
with whom you have foresworn that you've wished to
spend the remainder of your life, haven't you! Yes,
but—say it!—okay, your foreswearing was in-your-
childish heart a half-the-time promissorial, when you
were not (attempting to) philander (to save your soul)*

55

because half-the-time, truth is, your heart still has been living its life a zillion miles from the—well, call a spade a spade—the factual-precise pedantry, the well-clipped (and well-meant) precision annoyingness, the "that's casual" of your Others-Saver wife, who has even metastasized her "that's casual" routine off-over-into the marriage bed—your fault or not, even should you take only half-blame. . . Then why—again for the ump-teenth time!—did I MARRY Linda?—Why why why why Why? Because, well, I LOVE HER, think I. Because I RESPECT HER. Because she is the nicest-person-in-the-world! Because THERE IS NO OTHER WOMAN IN THE WORLD LIKE HER! Other men, like me—they are Not like Me! . . . Or are they?

I am not a bad man. I am a Good man!

Think I.

I am a Good Man.

And sonofagun: In Georgie's articles, and by way of Linda's persistence with the county attorney's office, prosecutors came to be curtailed (semi) in their unjust (legally-illegal and sub-rosa) efforts, such as the with-holding of exonerating evidence, and they were "advised" to seek milder penalties for milder crimes such as the possession of marijuana—these would be reduced to misdemeanors, if indeed to anything at all if it was the first-time arrest. As a consequence, the lockup of blacks and Hispanics was reduced in Alameda and Contra Costa counties by nearly one-third. ("Not enough!"—both women). Additionally, and this bears repeating, with their new doubles act Linda and Georgie did become fast friends—and I did become a jealous man (and doubly, of both women), even though Georgie and I managed to access what we

considered our own, as individuals, rightful freedoms—
from conventional moralities. . . Georgie and I went
biking. Same general hill and bayside routes as those
Exuder Suzanne and I had taken. Georgie and I took
however far more frequent stops—such as for upright-
humping (clothed) against a live-oak (in Live Oak
Park), Georgie sometimes laugh-calling out TILT! as if
her body were an old-time Bally pinball machine:
Georgie did tend to come like a temblor—this after I
did what she taught me: that of rising-up underneath her
with my (clothed) belly so as to gain full swollen
abdominal access to her clitoris—this even as she
continued to wear her own biker-tights. . . So, we,
Linda-Georgie-myself, we were a foursome in our own
intimate trio way, Al the Biker the proud (self-deluded)
fulcrum and hypotenuse.

Except, now, along came Jim—to make the imaginary foursome a (I think) reality three-and-a-halfsome.
Jimmy X (not that I'm trying to protect a terrorist or
Freedom Fighter for Northern Ireland, but I just never
knew his last name). Jim (or Jimbo, or Jimmy, as he
preferred) X—although I doubt that he had ever heard
of that much more famous X, Malcolm—he was hiding
out, or "being put up" in Georgie's apartment way out
in what San Franciscans refer to as The Avenues—
these streets border Golden Gate Park and end where
the city ends, at the ocean—at, I believe, Forty Eighth
and The Cliff House (Georgie's flat sat on Thirty-
Third). Jimmy X from Belfast was not so tall but he
was big (what first came to mind was Mastodon)—and
of course I was scared of him. He had the sort of
muscular wide at the shoulder, narrow at the hip

physique of Mike Tyson, or if we include the face for accuracy's sake, Mickey Rourke in his build-up boxing years between his two separated acting careers. Jimmy X, once he arrived for his hiding-out hole-up at Georgie's, assumed my lover-role (except for a few sneaky-Pete skulky slip-ins of mine [after which, *twice*, Georgie had the ridiculous reassurance for the nice [unreassurable] Jewboy to tell me: "Alan, we fit perfectly, you and I: Jimmy's, his is too-much the gallows-churl, it's too *big*—it hurts." And this confiding revelation, this faux-complaint, it was supposed to make me feel proud and happy about my "comfortable" jejune penis?). Anyway, this replacement of the paltry bike-diddler by Jimmy X the fearless freedom-fighter took place without one word being uttered in tandem by any of us three participants—it was fully assumed as right and proper and even, I think, hospitable—the courteous (and Irishly patriotic) thing-to-do. My abandoned role was however sans the bike riding partnership, which Jimmy regarded as "Jessie", which was, I presumed, Irish slang for pussyesque—and which I had been coming to see as prettymuch Jessie too. Although Jimmy did edge me out—to some (way past considerable) extent as Georgie's lover, he and I became, sonofagun, friends, and to tell the truth I felt rather proud to be the buddy of an escapee-hero and fugitive from the British Police—and, as with my knuckle-down belter dad Moe, he was a man who frightened me; and, yes, who I admired. The Irish being "Pony-lovers," (as was my dad) Jimmy dragged me at least a half-dozen times to Golden Gate Fields (as had my dad) where he cadged my money, "for betting purposes only, m'boy"; and to get even I dragged Jimbo to shooting pool, and—you could have bowled me over with an eightball—I was better at every game (straight, 8-ball, 9-ball)—and bowl-over again—the stalwart Gaelic knight didn't give a shit, pool just provided him with another activity beyond that of the ponies and fucking the woman I was (lesserly now, but by way of a greater accommodating fit) fucking—which was by way of the sneaky-creepy-crawly, for Jimmy would not have appreciated his being cuckolded, especially by a "Jessie"—and in the bargain "a little bike-boy Jew"— although truth is I was of a height slightly more extended than that of your average low-to-midsize Jew.). As Irish writer Georgie would certainly have been a prime suspect for harboring an Irish murderer (she bragged this killer tidbit to me; who knows if it were true) Jimmy hung-out (or hid-out) at GEIST'S BIKES—and being a rather nice guy (in his way), and equipped with a "cool" clipped accent, offbeat and even gurgle-sweet, he was actually able to help out in a few sales—to, of course, a few girls: whom, I assumed, he did manage to sleep with. He and I even went to "the moving flickeroos" together when Georgie was busy with writing her deadlined articles—and she had balls, she was not intimidated by "The X-treme Man"—she called him that, and not without a sort of affectionate diminishment. She might just bellow, "Jessie, get your bluddy fat rump the fucko *out!*" . . . But life being life, I grew bored of this Bibulous of Belfast who did do-up the Irish earmark a bit beyond-the-top ("I'll have a bit of the Guinesses, if you please—and do not spare the whoresies—it's now arunnin' like a gusto through the cloister of me mind."), he who incessantly referred to "The Trubbles" as if these were the squalid-sad-hellish origins of all the human race, and which were well-known throughout the human race—the *Irish Trubbles*, I'm talking, as if Northern Ireland were on the tip of the tongue of every citizen of North Borneo, and which might be, with a few more "shootings and blowups and such", "done-with in total rightful and absolved". No doubt "The Jimbo" was blowing-up in his mind not only his "invading" Brits but his performance-status for us idiot-citizens of the "clot-wit" U.S.A; and I hoped that Georgie, as Irishish as she was, would soon grow bored with all this hokey "errorful Joyce" crap of his ("the swoon of sin")—despite her being "native to the bluddy spirit-soul". Jimmy's presence, and his edging me out with "the loverly lady herself", did (of course, as with the exuding mime Cadeau Courir with the exuding Suzanne Thalbrucker) at first magnify my desire for Georgie and my diminishment of my own 'unloverly' self; but hey: if I could defeat "this clod" at the subtleties and sharp sight required of pool (but in imitation of whom I had begun speaking [and loving it as much as hating it]) why not defeat him at another racket which required "the old stickety-wick and 'ate'-balls"?—slighter-"fit" as mine were. And certainly Jimmy suspected my turncoat ruminations, his "crooked-eyes" showed that—my excuse of my wife Linda's obsessive working at the office for blacks and Hispanics, that wore thin: Jimmy didn't give one "frowsy damn" about the American underclass, but they did seem to him to "put up a good and honorable back-fight—"I'd be with'em were I a dumb-depriven nigger-boy as well." But, as I say, after my initial competitive urge for "sex-and-love", which in a way was neither—and might well have been described by any good shrinker as my way of having sex with Big Jim as a substitute for having sex with my dead athlete father Moe (who'd rejected me?)—I tired of the whole deal—just as, sonofagun, did Georgie ("me body is tiring of this outer skin I'll peel"); and as did Jimmy, who took off for lord knows where: there were obviously thousands of Northern Irish "rebelists" and sympathizers in our nation of three hundred million—maybe he had a packed black book or a back-pocket list (this was before computer printouts). . . As I've implied then, with Jim's departure so did my erotic urge for Georgie, and likely hers for me (or whatever had remained of it throughout Jimmy's "clobbering" reign). . . But, she was such an interesting and bold person I do suspect that, Home Sod Loyalties aside, and Jimbo's potency aside, she was likely the giver-of-the-boot which sent this mockup Stephen Dedalus aflying (I even suspect that he was scared of her, she could glower, he could wince)—and as she was one multilateral character through whom I might meet local bigtimers (I never did, almost)—we did hang onto our friendliness.

Big Example: Pete Hamill and Shirley MacLaine—they were in town (I don't know why). As I've said, Georgie was an old pal of Pete's, who was now Editor-in-Chief of *The New York Post* (I think it was that paper) and a famous novelist of the cry-in-your-beer genre (had Jimmy the Terrorist Rebel had brains he'd have been Pete Hamill); and Pete was also the current-then live-with guy of the best-known American actress (and rebel-actress) of that time—she who was not so big herself on theatrical folk, preferring instead the more muscular political and the political watchdogs. I had called Georgie one Sunday afternoon, as GEIST'S BIKES was closed (not religion, just flagging-to-lost interest and a growing contempt for shoppers and even buyers, and, even, it was coming to look like, bikes— they were becoming more and more the go-to-thing for confirmed vegans and scrupulous enemies of glutin) and wife Linda was fully engrossed at her desk in the composition of some argument aimed at preserving a ghetto-guy's out-of-jailness (which the prosecuting attorney would wrist-flick back straight to jail-damnation): "Whatcha doing?" I asked Georgie. "I'm meeting Pete and Shirley, they're in town." *Pete and Shirley, holy mackaroli!* As I've already implied—and admitted—I was not not a sucker for the infamous nor for the famous, nor, for that matter, the near-famous (I didn't even draw the line at the near-infamous and the hangers-on of hangers-on of hangers-on [of which clique, I'm sure it is in your mind that I was one [sort of]), so I answered Georgie (who hadn't asked), "Sure, I'd love to come." And she answered me, "Somehow I figured you wouldn't mind. And don't be goin' and embarrassin' me arse."

"No way."

"Way. Just you recognize and acknowledge here my generosity."

"I recognize and I acknowledge."

I heard a histrionic-but-muffled-comic harrumph. "God," Georgie went, "I pray I don't regret this—too much."

"Come on, I'll be good. You won't regret nuttin'."

"Talk normal."

Her harrumph had grown volume, containing this time a feather of a threat.

We four met-up at the center of San Francisco's Union Square (I'd had to rush to catch the next BART train to get there on time from Berkeley); a few heads turned at Shirley MacLaine, but not as many as I'd expected (and planned to look down upon with superior indifference, as if I myself were "in the movies", of the status of, say, the relative newcomers John Travolta or Richard Gere.). But I learned a truth of life's expected anonymity or really its nothingness: If one does not expect to see a star walking the street, as everyone does-not, one does not see a star, at best what you see is a star lookalike. But Ms. MacLaine, underneath that patented pixie-cut orange marmalade hair of hers, aided by her threaten-penetration eyes (I have no recollection of their color—I'll go with green), she came out at first with a non-everyone comment—or what I regarded as such (and was disappointed-in): "Georgie I just *love* your earrings." Which sounded to me like Hollywood going Hollywood when it definitely should not; but then again if a woman likes a woman's earrings what else is she going to say but that she likes the woman's earrings?—which I hadn't even noticed. . . As they were old pals, Pete and Georgie walked off ahead for this walking hangout, Pete's overhang belly (this did surprise me) leading the way, and I was relegated to a version of the American Everymale dream: I was, in effect, the *date* of Shirley MacLaine—a walking date, but a date is a date. True, Ms. MacLaine might have elected to stay with Pete and Georgie, but she was being polite to me, and I recognized and admired that consideration. However: I was also inebriated by finding myself teamed with the biggest female star in Hollywood at that point in time, or for that matter in the world.

I looked about, for I could not look at her. Our reflections stared back at us (or rather at me) from the window-mirrors of Macy's and some Britlike haberdashery. I would rather have been paired at that moment with the reflections that said *couple, comfort, compatibility*, than with the so real awkward thing: with reflections can come fantasy.

What conceivable things was she thinking? Was she an intellectual?—even a bit of one? A "policy wonk"? A reader of the current Greats? After all, unlike most movie figures—except for Jane Fonda who had hitched her wagon to the leftist-leader Tom Hayden—Shirley MacLaine seemed to have little truck with folks who boasted stars on Hollywood or Vine. Perhaps her penetrating expressions and their seeming preparedness to confront—what? phonies? idiots? buffoons? (all characteristics of a fellow I was quite prepared to consider attached to myself) were the consequence of a twisted angriness at the pop-celebrity she had become and was having impossibilities escaping. . . Why else choose to live with a writer/editor like Pete Hamill?

What to say? What to do?—especially when you, Mister Nobody, discover it welling-up in your less than sane mind the conception that this "date", if conducted right, just might lead to, not necessarily a Thing, but Something—a friendship?—between you and Shirley MacLaine, where you might come to enjoy the latitude of calling her up on some other Sunday and going, 'What's up?—whatcha doing?' . . . . I tried the following:

"I saw you a few days ago on *Dinah*."

Shirley nodded opaquely, with the slowest and most

grave reluctance one might have imagined. As if in a movie she were playing a character who had just that moment been asked, 'Is it true you have been diagnosed with bone cancer and have only one more month to live?' As the song goes, she now had "Bette Davis eyes".

At that time the singer Dinah Shore had a talk show, which I had seen (only a few times—I swear it), so I continued within the only direction I had made available:

"You know, maybe I shouldn't say but you seemed . . . hostile?—to Dinah."

Ms. MacLaine regarded me now, not as if I were inquiring about her screenplay cancer but as if I were the most presumptuous, bumptious schmuck afloat in the universe. I saw her weighing answers, and then came her, "Shit, I should have been fifty times *more* hostile."

Well, you might have thought that such a response would have unnerved me and sent me running to catch up with Pete and Georgie, now at least thirty yards ahead, way over by the windows of Esprit. But no: I felt elevated, highly regarded. One of the most famous women in the world had just taken nobody Al Geist of what was at one time AL'S BIKES into her confidence, as if we were intimate pals dating back together as far and as close as did Pete and Georgie. And so, what did I do? . . . Without a moment's pause, I 'the long-time intimate and advisor to Shirley MacLaine', placed my right arm around her shoulder, brought her to me yet— well, slightly, more like a lean-to—and administered a dollop from my vast show-biz directorial savvy: "Aw, Shirley (yes, I "enjoyed" the brazen justified insolence of calling her Shirley), you know that kind of stuff doesn't work on TV. TV's an in-your-home family . . ."

I pulled-up short, as this one-time Broadway dancer not so gracefully—but rather muscularly—squirmed out from beneath Al Geist's "protective", presumptive, embracing arm:

Must I describe the belittling bullet-hostility with which she regarded me?

Must I mention the horrific knot forming in my stomach and my confusion over what to do with my abandoned dangling arm?

Must I admit that my bladder had begun begging "pee" and my lower intestines were in a quiet intimating rumble not so far behind?

"Dinah *Shore*," went Shirley MacLaine, "I try to talk 'the-glass-ceiling', that's why I came onto her pathetic show, and she cuts me off to introduce that incredible stiff David Niven."

I knew who David Niven was, certainly, but although I did also know what "the glass ceiling" was (my god, Linda spoke of it at least three days every week), just now The Women's Movement for top jobs in American industry had escaped my cortex and my concerns—and my hesitant narrowed-nostril-eye-blinking face showed it.

And Ms. MacLaine did not miss my befuddlement. Her levelled eyes said Who am I being condemned to talk to here?—a rube on-loan from The Redneck Riviera?

I was about to try redeeming myself from exhibited ignorance by repeating the phrase "the glass ceiling" with all the fake-authoritarian braininess I could muster (*'Well, the-glass-ceiling, sure, but one has to consider, don't-you-think? the architectural expediencies along with the pitfalls involved, and then, and only then, perform a cost-benefit analysis, which might yield . . . ').*

Where was the nearest toilet?

"Look at that *building*!"

It was Pete Hamill saving the day, and without even being aware of it.

At first I actually believed that he was speaking of a building's glass ceiling.

He and Georgie had walked back to Shirley and myself, he the ultimate Brooklynite equipped with what was apparently a startling note of post-fire San Francisco interest, and he was pointing to the intricate and undulating cornrow-like narrow columns supporting and decorating the top floor of a not-so-tall building—the sort of feature I would not have regarded as of architectural insignificance, assuming that I would have even noticed it at all: "It's a pre-*fire*," said Pete Hamill, factually, not as if he had discovered anything quite rare. "Amazingly there's still some frames around after, whatsit? *seventy* years, and showing their old damage, like museum pieces. You can tell its vintage by the large number of beams and the struts strung between them like the sort of Renaissance armature daVinci would have used, along with a few gargoyle-figures, they're small, *see* them!? (and now I did)—ironically they're also made to look like a kind of soldiery, knights without their shields, there's a great number of them scattered all over southern Europe, but they're falling apart, crumbling." When Pete Hamill said 'falling apart, crumbling' I, being me, identified, experiencing once again that pee-and-shit insistence. Pete added: "The concrete used in those early days here on the west coast was feared unreliable, and it was—for some reason. In earthquake country they had to be confident of stability, and they disguised their uncertainty with architectural density. Pretty smart and pretty dumb. Amazing those columns have lasted."

Still the illiterate jerk, I volunteered a "Right" so phony that even *I* couldn't bear to hear my desperate idiot-giveaway.

"And who the hell is *that* miscreant!?"

Georgie later told me—when we were alone—that Shirley MacLaine had taken her aside to ask of me—as Pete had been architecturalizing.

I told Georgie that I was sorry, and she nodded, as if she'd more than half-expected something of the like from me—and perhaps even, in her perverse way (her jealous way regarding Shirley MacLaine's "theft" of adored Pete from her, for that may well have been how she saw it—it's how immature *I* would have) Georgie had wished for, waited-for, even cultivated, a not unexpected Al the Biker faux pas with her "rival". With flying schmuck colors, I'd come through. How could I have failed?

"You're still my friend?" I asked.

"You have other qualities."

I damn did. Have other qualities, that is ('good' implied). Without arrogance (which was of course not one of my good qualities [as I did have a shit-load of it, arrogance]) I will still admit, and demonstrably too, of that having of good qualities—although sometimes when I am trying hard to come up with some demonstrable Al Geist admirables it keeps me up at least one-fifth the night (and I have to go for my buddy a Valium—a yellow fiver, so I do then drop-off to slumberland without ever having struck a rich vein of the-gold-of-the-good Al Geistness—there's so much personality fool's-gold laying about eager to preserve [and pump-up] a guy on-the-weaker-side's personality: say, here's one: *I try, as if I am Immanuel Kant, never to hurt any asshole's feelings.*[4]). One quality though, I must say, is (and was) my awareness of my failures, in the desiring and in the not-desiring (of what I *ought be* desiring—and/or of what I ought be *not*-desiring)—but that is not to say achieving much degree of success in my correcting those found desire-perplexities and loop-de-loops. (But here we are confronted with the oh-so-human stumper of a good quality ferreting out a bad, and the bad negating the originating good—and thusly making you angry at yourself precisely because you were trying to be good-to-yourself; and others. [I'm serious, just as Maxim Gorky was serious when he created, and *isolated*, such straining catercorner characters]). . . One peculiar, and trying, thing was that I was driven to sleep with outwardly exciting Georgie

---

[4] But that philosopher of the Categorical Imperative never in his whole life took leave of his native Königsberg (now Russian Kaliningrad), so he had a very limited number of people who might have offended him in some way and therefore whose feelings, in return, despite his Goodness, it might have been possible to hurt. Is the best solution to this feelings-hurt problem then never to leave town; or, better yet, your neighborhood? Or your apartment? Thus, hermitting: which word in Cantonese does translate to 'wise man'. . . Except: The Unabomber was a hermit in that shack in Wyoming. . . Idaho? . . . About all this, I am, though joking (a bit) seriously serious.

Lee for precisely the (*supposed*) opposite reason as to why I had slept with the inwardly exciting exudatious Suzanne Thalbrucker—and my reasons were (no, not were: *seemed*) far closer to why I had years before taken-up with my wife Linda, whose brilliance and drivenness and morality put her in the Georgie category, and indeed this was why they two did ultimately become fast friends—which Linda never could have done with Suzanne, although Suzanne did derive from the same upperish class as had "my" Linda. . . Confused? Well, confusion can amount to non-confusion, if looked-at right, just like Gorky did. Anyway, here's the answer to my sleeping-withs—as close—and honest—as I can get to it—which honesty is at least an Al Geist "good" thing: I was scared, I felt no identity that I could catch and hold onto in my hand, it just wavered all-over, my Me, so how could there be love-passion, real true love-passion for another, and not just floundering-self-fooling—leading to a whole messy bunch of oxymorons like *onanisms a deux*. And so then in the case of Georgie there had come my way a rushing-out of the strong-woman spirit, like Linda's but not, that for its rawness; it come to meet and fill-up my (dwindled) own spirit, which was threatening-bad to become a vacuum—but a turbulent unvacuum vacuum (a black hole?) fighting to scramble its way out of that admitted vacuum. . . Georgie, I'll say this: she'd taught me to love someone I did not love, to philander (although a word derived from the Greek-guy skirt-chaser Philander sounds to me in modernity so ugly, accusatory, silly-small and empty). But Georgie's teaching-without-teaching, that taught me to do my, yuch, philandering with, I believe, a decency and respect for the philander-provoker, *and* (her new friend) Al the philanderer and philander*ee*. *And*, to crave, but without obsession-craving (as in the case of young actress-Suzanne); and so in my confused-but-somehow-earnest mind I'd picked-up-on how to be a betrayer without betrayal (okay, serious, meaningful betrayal). Decent "good" hypocrisy.

But the joke, the final joke: My wife Linda and my "friend" Georgie were enjoying each other, minds and moralities, and learning from each other's passions in far greater ways than I was. Not I, as I wrote before, but we three, we were fulcrum and hypotenuse. And so, we remained. Although, inevitably, my sleeping with either woman—*friends!*—that fell to next to naught.

And in truth I have to admit that I was too impressed by Georgie Lee, and in a way that was obviously so adolescent: I wanted to be accepted by Georgie as both lover and close respected friend (respected for what?—owning GEIST'S BIKES, which was repression proof [in Berkeley anyway], which quality had never occurred to me when I'd bought out the only failed wine-dispensary in town). And this Bothness of connection, I have been beating it over the head, but, still, alas, whatever did and does it mean? What did (and does) lover mean? What means friend? Might just one exist without the other, that is after one has existed *before* the other or even simultaneous with it? Re Georgie Lee I was that most ridiculed of social animals, a climber. I asked myself, 'Do I *truly* love my wife?' I've admitted that (like everyone) I didn't know what love was—it had a zillion meanings: and, for that matter, I didn't even know what 'like' was. Had Georgie Lee written for the Garden Section of *The San Francisco Chronicle* I would no doubt not have even bothered with such a conventional domestic scribe—unless of course it had come to my attention that she was harboring a dangerous IRA fugitive who belonged to a romanticized cabal of killers, and that she was "close" to Shirley MacLaine, who loved her earrings. . . And she really wasn't even "close" to Shirley. Shirley, who—bad-person, I—told and told and told to guys, that I had, "for-a-while", get this, "dated".

MOE'N'IDA
IDA'N'MOE

THEY caused it all, right? Parents, they screw and out-you-come holding the goddamn bag. What's a sap to do?

No, it's not fashionable to blame your folks. You blame them, you ain't gotta chance to change.

But I'm fucking blaming. I'll chance changing, damnit.

Who was it who called me, with her sharp immigrant accent, milquetoast, she who got me falsely reaching to contest her with a rumbling cantorial bass-baritone, like my dad's—at which voice I miserably failed? Intellect Wanda it was who did that, but she is pages down the line.

And I am not no milquetoast: It can take pretty good balls to blame.

So: It's about time, it's well past time, for a fuller,

more comprehensive, appearance of my dad Moe and my mom Ida. . . So, Morris, Mister I'm a Man, I'll go straight-off with dad. I loved Moe, I'd wanted to be like Moe (or not too unlike him as for the resemblance to be dangerously irresemblable—considering his fate.). This Moe who, by the way, I could never kiss. The Glass Wall. I'd come close to my father's cheeks and feel the scrape of his Remington electric shaver's poor (and grindingly noisy) work roughing-up my young smooth cheeks and I'd sense wrongness—a plough upon a lake. Some something, natural or not, was out-of-whack: Man on Man? Or Boy on Man? This should not be done (maybe attempted, surely *attempted* for God's sake— *he's your father!*—but caught at the brink-of-cheeks and then not-done, mission abandoned), it carried with it too many possibilities, although I guess (I never asked) any number of my friends of late adolescence kissed their dads, as, say, when they were going out to play ball or they had a date, or—or anything. Millions of possibilities, I imagined in distant dad-son-kissing envy. So Moe, no. And it wasn't just me caught-up in that warding wince: I could feel that my dad himself did not want that pressing touching-touch coming from his nice-boy (too nice?) Alan. The very improper scrape of it would be our undoing—not that we had, to begin with, much super-doing. Moe was a unique Jew—if unique is the proper word for what he was. 'Unusual' might have done, but that word (although obviously it did come to me) can imply "strange", as it did for Shakespeare, he used it all the time. My father Moe played ball, *pro* ball—and I do not mean simple sandlot, although he did play with us kids at times on neighborhood vacant lots (and once he showed his top-dad-toughness by with his left hand sweeping-off the glasses of another boy's father who was playing and had mocked my father for not having made the Majors, and with dad's right hand he had landed a haymaker square on the other, mocking, dad's jaw, causing that other father to be rushed to Emergency)—and so my dad was easily, without question, the best father-player around: but it's just baseball I'm talking. For, as I said, and I so often think-about, my father had played *pro* ball. *Pro*-ball. For the Baltimore Orioles—before I was born. The 'O's, as they were known (and still are), had once been a major league team, but they had lost their bigtime franchise to Saint Louis, the Browns. Now they were the farm club of the Philadelphia Phillies who played in magnificent palatial Philly Stadium, while the O's languished in B-moh's (what the local blacks called Baltimore) Memorial Stadium, which wasn't even large and round enough to complete a stadium O. At best, it was a U. In the lesser-kempt grounds of Memorial, and on the mound, my father Moe was a pitcher—he'd walk from the dugout to that mound with this lope-gait that began at the hip, not the knees (were his knees bad?—I never learned). His specialty was "slow-slower-slowest," like the old Yankees great Whitey Ford. My dad Moe had taught me how to throw a "slip pitch" which was a version of slow—a change-up, so I usually befuddled neighborhood kid-batters. (I will not divulge any pitcher secrets as to how to hold the baseball and then let loose with a slip pitch, which maintains the arm-speed motions of a fastball, thus fooling the anticipating batter.). Still, equipped with his respected change-up, dad just didn't quite—still!—have IT for "The Show" (occasionally he had been known to complain "anti-Semitism", but the glorious existence [and successes] of Hank Greenberg and Sandy Koufax among others [a handful of] couldn't but demolish his argument) so he'd worked on a knuckler a la the incredible technician-magician Hoyt Wilhelm (of the Fifties)—but Moe could seldom get that "wobbly butterfly-mother" to flitter its way anywhere near home plate, it flit-gazonkled between pitcher and batter like, well like what they called it, a "butterfly". So Moe remained honkered down in The Minors, in old Baltimore, "the biggest pig-town in America"—self-named with weird oinker pride. . . When I was born, dad was driving a taxi for the G.I. Veterans Company, although he had never been a Vet: too old, and too with a child. God dad despised driving that cab. He—we—moved to San Francisco. . . Where he drove a cab.

It fits, I guess, all considered—*it's dad's fault!*—that I never wished to dominate a man, not in any way (sort of)—and I'm not talking Sex—I mean not dominate in brains or argument or employment or whatnot. Or, rather, let-me-say, I *do* wish to dominate, and I mean *all* men. Best fighter. Best quarterback (in touch games). Best (latent) cerebral cortex in the coffee-house clique. Best features of handsomeness such that all girls and women—well, you know. Just be top dog, while living in portrayal, active-passive pussy noblesse-oblige, of a bottom-feeder (and therefore, you betcha, building up resentments mountainous, against all-involved, especially the *gemuetlich* diners at the summit). What I've wanted was (and is) to just be looked-up-to, by even those who wish to look down on me or ignore me (and why now did I bother to write that last?—simple, I still feel that I'm being looked down upon, and *I cannot stand it!*—I'm the un-named "hero" of Dostoyevsky's *Notes From Underground*). Anyway, it appears—and it has always appeared (despite how it has always looked to appear, and how absurd my wanting does even appear to me), I the Peasant wish to be fucking I-Royalty—and I feel (Lord knows why!) I *deserve* it—*Bow down! you commoners, you populi minissimmi, you hoi polloi!* . . . But as soon as I do dominate (or think that I do [self-delusion can be a positive pathology that has been given a bad name]), as soon as I do dominate in political argument let's say, or even in arm-wrestling (I *love* arm wrestling—you really can't get hurt [I have gone to the World Championships held each year in Petaluma, Cal.), as soon as I win, I feel guilt, that uprising retaliator, I feel sorrow—for the other guy—and I apologize, or if apology seems too extreme-emotional (and wimpesque), I simply go submissive—I knuckle-under to the will or intellect or power of the other guy, which may not amount to much (which again then renders me all resentment-guilt again: this cockamamie bullshit was what I did with Irish Jimmy X—even though, in his case, with his girth and his patriotic will, he would have dominated me in any case physical.). Truth is, what I do is I-go-submissive. To blame by not-blaming I'll go with saying that Guilt is the pull of my fucking gravity.

Go fight The Ultimate.

Dad, Moe, he committed suicide. Probably the only time he had fired a '38, or any gun (I picture a '38, it has a certain coolish TV ring, it sounds romantic, no?). Dad had strutted into a telephone booth on Berkeley's Bancroft Avenue at 5AM, just after finishing-up his night's shift (I'm picturing this) as if he were Clark Kent intent on quick-changing to his big red-blue **S** shirt and taking-off skyward to save Metropolis—and *Kablooie!*—and as I write this (semi) concocted memory—I was what? twelve? thirteen? (and never Jew bar mitzvah either)—my stomach rumbles with the so-real (so-falsified) memory, it reverberates like the earth beneath your feet at an earthquake in its first sundering (Northern Californian, I know), it growls-down to my intestines and it blows up there with the gunshot of-and-by dad Moe, and my neck aches up to my eyes and through my eyes to I-don't-know-where, all with that one '38 gunshot, and I see Moe scowling at my horror-memory, made-up and not made-up, and my brave-cowardice at my telling it to you. *It's all My Fault!* My Revelation Guilt.

I never saw Moe lay-one on my mom, Ida (kiss I'm talking, kiss, not fist [and why do I even think of anything so grossly primitive as a marriage punch?]), although word was that when they were young and in love they had, kissing all the way, eloped to some town in northeastern Maryland—ah, Elkton, at the tip of the Chesapeake Bay, where you could get hitched as quickly as you can today in Las Vegas or Mexico. Lots of New Yorkers used to drive down to Elkton for that romantic reason. And up from as far away as at least Norfolk, I imagine. There were no Interstates in those days (when, as the Republicans swear, "it was a Great America"—forget Jim Crow and the National Guard beating union men, and etc.).

*   *   *

So, love, we were talking about that all gathering, all-inclusive, all-functionally capable word. What did Moe and Ida know of love? They had had sex in the (armrest unencumbered) back bench-seat of my father's green Nash (or was it a Hudson Hornet?—they'd looked the same, like an oldtimey bathtub without the bear's claw feet), and they'd taken-to their love-work from there. Considering who I am and how I've turned–out, I picture their love-work as a passionate-fervent-hidden-guilt-clumsiness as they were parked on some low grass hillock in Baltimore's Druid Hill Park, they with their eyes (and ears and necks) snapping to alert at every outside rustle, not just of possible police or skunks or rats or bats but of "schwartzes" and "hic-hillbillies" (ironically the "hic-hillbilles" happened to be of the same ilk of those who had become my father's Orioles ball-mates)—I seem to just have to have such a picture hyper-impressed into my origins. . . I also (again, considering who I am) can't resist stating that, naturally, there were no bumper-stickers in those days that might have delivered the bumptious unclever warning IF THIS CAR'S A'ROCKIN' DON'T COME A'KNOCKIN. . . Anyway, my father Moe wouldn't have had the forwardness to have plastered-on such an advisory Achtung.

Love. For one deep syllable such a difficult high-pitched word (Actually that's like lots of things, as if maybe The Universe intended the paradox.). Right off, what you've got is you've got sex. Religion, you might put that one in the love-instinct category as well; and then there's your children, your grandchildren, your nation (I really am not so sure about that one), your job (another iffy compartment, unless your job is your dream, your calling), and there is yourself—the most complicated love of all. And the most simple one: there is sports. You do not wish to lose-out on *any* of these 'loves'—and in the relatively rare case where your job (baseball for a while) happens to also be your calling, your sports-love, your breath, wellthen, loss of such a fortunate-rare god's-blending (dreamed-of by most men, and boys—though most men and boys do recognize dream from real), that loss of dream can become unbearable: You see the world and you *don't* see it, that injustice-Void, that "you ain't quite good enough." "But," you demand, "I'm *great*, can't you *see*." "But," counters your manager, "Scottie Dummer, look-at-'eem, 'ee's got-it-*all*, 'ee's *better*." You watch Scottie Dummer pitch and you can't see it, his stupid betterness—but everyone else can. And that's your second baseball loss: you can't even fucking *see*. . . But bearable The Loss for my dad Moe was made, I decided, I had to, I forced myself to, make things bearable for my Orioles-dropped dad (as bad as earth-dropped? god-dropped?) by dad's bike-riding with me—except that, sure-enough, dad couldn't help but turn such a dad-son twosome into a dad-son competition—who's first? who's the loser?: Rounding Oakland's Lake Merritt we'd start out okay, pumping easily, ogling what talent was ogleable, dad even letting me get ahead—slightly (like in the first few seconds of our arm-wrestling at the kitchen table); but in no time the urge to win at any cost would take over and Morris Geist (who had just lost-out to that oaf Scottie Dummer) would just about stand and lean into his bars, and even on-over them, grinding-down like a city worker drilling his way into a street's hard tar—and he'd push his way ahead of me, and then farther ahead, and then farther, and then he'd turn his head and crane back to witness his poor son falling back, way back, way back, into the diminished distance, while his son's fear grew that his father no longer even saw his son as his son but rather as an enemy or an opposing batter who had better know his place, and so he might even try to lap his boy Alan on that lake, just to show that biking was little different from being on the mound and brushing-back a batter with an intentional inside pitch, or even beaning the motherfucker. Yes, Moe Geist got into his fights on the ballfield, win some/lose some— maybe his quick spurts to pugilism had at least a modicum to do, a force-draining, with his never making the Majors, *he must have been good enough!*—and all along, those fights, maybe *he'd wanted to lose*, not the fights, but his Majors-making—*why!?*—I could think this for instances even at age eight. . . . But, even now, how could *I* know which was what was which?—when dad Moe, he likely did not know himself. . . And of course it occurs to me that, with my not wishing to dominate a man, any man, nor to submit, I was in the lost-act of copycatting my dad. . . And, sonofagun, the only way to defeat another man without defeating him, and to submit without submitting, was to sidetrack: girls girls girls girls *girls*!).

One thing though that my father Moe did *not* do, which I did do (it will become apparent later—with Eugenia—why I cannot today write *do* do), was mess around. With other women, other girls, I'm talking. Moe did not engage in such—the word that quick comes to mind for that 'such stuff' is *'shit'*. Moe would never have cheated on my mom Ida—I doubt if seeking-for and hunting-down some other woman ever even occurred to him, and this I bet includes in the contents of his dreams. Baseball and horse-racing occupied surely the gist and thrust of his dreams— which was why he went so often, alone, just Him, to Bay Meadows, to Santa Anita, to Golden Gate Fields (and I picture him at those tracks, standing alone, and silent—even when his chosen nag won, which was Jolly Cholly, a galloper so inappropriately-named, con- sidering my father's grim personality: God I hated horse-racing.). Actually dad-Moe was quite the-shy- guy, and one who all my aunts and girl-cousins found to be the nicest and most desirable (my word) of all my uncles. Well, for one thing, he was built: A middle- weight at five foot ten he was narrow at the waist and broad at the shoulders and so he resembled, I thought, Sugar Ray Robinson, who was of course black—except Sugar Ray could dance and my dad couldn't, he'd stumble all over himself at wedding and bar mitzvah parties (As I've said, I was not bar mitzvah: the fact that my cousins were bar mitzvah into Jewish manhood carried no weight with my dad—to him, and for me, such a ritual was primitive and hypocritical, as none of our extended family's participants understood either the meaning of the event [becoming a Man at age *thirteen*, that was "stupid and smartass cocky"], nor did any of my relatives comprehend any of the ancient Hebrew words—not that they would have understood modern Israeli Hebrew either). But getting back to my father's body, man was I envious—I being slender not just at the waist, which was fine, but at the shoulders as well;

and, unlike my dad I had no remarkable calve muscles that looked like living slabs of leaping liver and likely had been developed from years of twists, arcs, hurls and balancings on the pitcher's mound. So, like I say, I couldn't kiss my dad—and it now occurs to me that that (failing?) was because I was envious of his man-body as well as of his sports skills. Sure this sounds ridiculous, I know it, but I do believe that there is some smidgeon of something to this stretched conjecture, this boy-contortion: I mean, I was no dad-disappointing schlepper like poor-sad Quoyle in *The Shipping News*—I had *balls*, I *did*. Problem was, I'd wanted Moe-brand balls (I'd glimpsed them once at the Berkeley Y—and then I'd turned away as I hadn't wanted him to catch me latching-onto an eyeful, as dad was a screwball at jumping-to-weird-conclusions [that he already might have had]). Anyway, as I've said, or intimated, I'd felt that I was a physical disappointment who, although he was better at it than most of his buddies, he (me, I) could not pitch a baseball with any super-speed or dead-on accuracy, and therefore I did not deserve the right to kiss this father-of-mine who was—to this adolescent's way of considering—more manly, plain superior—to Alan the Disappointment. I've said it before, but I'll say it again: when cheek scratched cheek, the older cheek was rougher-tougher-leaner, just as the older body was more rawboned, more ideal. . . What to do? As compensation then?—I got funnier. I got myself un-shy. I got my brain going, not my muscles, I got wit. Also as my method for obliterating in my mind (or heart) my father's depression—which kept growing, which anybody could see, just as the way with the soles of his shoes drilling-in harshly he'd bore down on the bike-pedals more and more, leaving his kid—me—way back in the dust path round Lake Merritt—and him staring back at his growing smaller kid. And me watching my father Moe pump away away away, me perceiving rightly—and wrongly too (I now know)—that dad, growing smaller too (but in the opposite way, the "victorious" speeding-away way) was rejecting me, was leaving Me, not He, to rot down in the gray dust uncheering people-spotty trailer-park stadiums of the Minors. Wheeling; Steubenville; Wilmington; Bethlehem. *All aboaaard!*

Do I mean this?—I'm not sure.

Neither probably did my dad.

An overload of happiness is a threat to happiness—thus said Zarathustra. My dad did not have to worry about the Z-man's incisive warning.

And did my mom Ida see what I saw, or I thought I saw? Yes is my guess, a guess not needing much education but educated anyway by my years of watching people, analyzing people (out of jealousy or to dominate or just to reject or avoid rejection, or to save somebody from the consequences of what he was always doing and couldn't stop doing even when he was told to STOP.). My mom: I was a kid but I could tell she was beautiful, or that she had been so; and she told me herself that when she was young and hadn't yet met my father she was the-belle-of-the-ball. Well, maybe she had been and maybe she hadn't, but she sure could dance fantastically—I saw her Terpsichore going through its stuff at those post bar mitzvah dances and wedding celebrations (that my dad came close to the edge of reviling and refusing—especially when my mom Ida, to save dad any ridicule [she figured wrongly], led him as her [stumblebum] partner in the easiest of fox-trots [I recollect—or I think I do—*I Could Have Danced All Night*, as I'd pictured heaven-voiced Julie Andrews]: and dad, the great rhythmic pitcher couldn't even manage the stiffest of box-steps); and at those affairs my mom also took her young son Alan into her arms and again she did the leading (of course—habit derives from personality) and I could feel her grace, I could feel how natural it was, that ice-skate glide of hers, she couldn't have stopped and broken it had she wanted to (she even took a few primadonna moments to segue perfectly into the Charleston, a witchy-watchy cross-leg arabesque that hadn't been around, even in ancient 1955, for a third of a century— while I'd at moments crane my neck to see my father on the sidelines with that determined forlorn [yanked-from-the-mound] beat-pitcher expression of his which said I'm gonna strike out this showboat *some day*, he [*she?*] ain't got a shitload of nuthin: *But was he mind-swearing at My Mom?*). . . But my mother Ida had sumthin': To me this Jewish lady with her high cheekbones and her shy but somehow delighted eyes, wide but ready to go downcast on a dime, then only to rise again, she resembled the actress Joan Fontaine, who I'd seen in some movie and caught the resemblance straight-off—otherwise I would never have remembered Joan Fontaine, who was the sister of Olivia de Havilland and wasn't in her own-right much of any big star at all.

So, as I was an only child (had my mom psyched-up the resolute need for a hysterectomy? or had my dad's being-who-he-was led her to doing, in that case, the-right-thing?) they fought over me, their only Alan, those two—and it was plain as their matched noses that no ref was required; they knew completely what they were up to, using what talent-tools they had in their vastly different (and oppositional) repertoires. Dad Moe took me to the track, Golden Gate Fields, which was quickly becoming a serious alternative to taxi-hacking (how he avoided being fired I'll never know) and he'd holler-on his chosen pony—only his hollering was a rally-whoop that took place solely within that quiet hollow echoless cave of that shy man, no vocal chords permitted—except, well, once-or-twice when his long-shot was ahead near the finish; yes, then he would allow the escapement of a short-barked Hey Hey or three; but the quiet man's yells and spur-ons felt to me so wrong, so out-of-place, like a whale flying like an eagle, that I certainly couldn't copy them, those rah-rare jubilations, as dad made out he wanted me to do; no, I just stood silent, and I would be lying if I didn't admit to feeling sorry for my father and his forcing himself to be a gallut-loudmouth—and as I've said I never took to the goddamn track. . . So dad took me to a place that I had requested, even begged-for: the local camera store; and knowing nothing about such equipment he bought me an 8-millimeter projector. It was made of a smooth burnished and well-rounded composite that felt irresist-ibly professional to a child—and to a man who knew what a child knew: appropriately-but-disappointingly, it was made for only silent films—or rather, films with talk that my dad-projector-gift could not fulfill. But hadn't the salesman explained such a blatant incapabil-ity?—he'd likely assumed we weren't so stupid as to not know (and that maybe my dad had figured it and

had his paternal reasons for wanting it, the soundlessness). In any case, we had such little money, the
weak-talented projector filled the budget-bill, and so we
made do: we watched Abbot and Costello and honed in
on the mouthed-out yells of Lou Costello as he fell
overboard from an ocean liner and called-out to Bud,
"Toss me a lifesaver!" (the words were, flimsily, on the
screen) and Bud obediently lobbing a Lifesaver candy
(with that tiny doughnut hole) to a supposedly
drowning Lou. I laughed, my dad gave his knowing
grin. Same as when Bud and Lou found themselves in
the capacious cannibals' pot in "darkest Africa". And
then I became an impresario for my friends, showing
also Martin and Lewis and some dumb-ass Jack Benny
movie where the famously deadpan comedian comes
down from heaven to save somebody, *The Horn Blows
at Midnight*—until my friends soured on that whole
silent deal, I showing the movie on the back side of our
white kitchen door—and then it was just me and my
dad watching alone movies we had seen a dozen times,
both of us decently afraid to admit, Hey, I'm *bored. . .*
But my mom: aside from her being a magnificent(ish)
dancer, how could mom-Ida compete for the affections
of her good son-Alan?—he who was our triangle's
hypotenuse? Well, she couldn't—and mom, despite
herself, went and turned mean. Jealous-mean. She'd hit
me, on the arm, when she thought I was being too
"wisenheimer". She told me "You may be smart in
school, Alan, (I was, I even skipped the second grade)
but you're losing your common sense." That was a big
sine qua non, common-sense. . . Then, guilty for her
unmeant meanness, she'd tell me "I love you, my
darling," and she'd embrace me, and she'd hover over

me when I had pains, as in my fallen arches (today they still hurt like hell)—and mom would give me her motherly arch-massages that went on and on and on, better than anything a podiatrist could do. . . . A mother with an only son, truth is, try as she might, she is stuck with less resources than is a father. And I believe that my mom could see, in my countenance, a kind of understanding for her dilemma, and a sympathy—and no way in my boyish sack of woe and joy to make-up for what, for my mom, I felt. And I'm pretty sure I did have for her those felt things.

And then my parents would fight, my depressed dad enduring, my mom grieving-plaintive, gritting her teeth at dad's showboat hostile endurance (which was his own gritting of his teeth—fences and gates went facing fencing, gates), mom just about covering her regretted words as one would a persistent cough, until the cover-by-palm became a shouted fist and not so all-regretted. Well, dad was a slacker hackie-taxi guy, wasn't he, now that's what he was, that's *all* he was (he believed this, finally, and so, fully); and so he deserved, after a few year's of mom's attempted understandings, he *deserved* mom's relenting give-way to attacks, he felt this, I know it, it showed in his amethyst Tartar-like eyes (from honed-focus on the target of a catcher's mitt some million miles away), slittened eyes of not vengeance but (now) of internal hemorrhage—neither one of them, my perplexed parents, argued about dad's just-bad-deserts as even he did believe he deserved them, and that belief was of course the worst: Dad would now even park his cab, his unearning cab, at the racetrack lot, he didn't care who noticed—hell, he probably hoped people did and would tell his bosses (which they did), and then he'd have more pulsing ammo for the loading of that gun that was first a trigger and barrel in the picturings of his brain, but as he couldn't stop the doing of what he was doing—I suppose that's how suicide begins—that ammo would become real metallic cartridges placed into the real bolt for the chamber, of his brain.

And one day, I believe I was about eight or nine or ten, mom took me aside as I was heading off to Hebrew School (dad was likely at Golden Gate Fields being his patented silent, which he was when *I* wasn't around him at the track to be shown the possibly-wonderful-but-crude benefits of occasional loudmouth boisterism, even if it was so sadly artificial in dad's case when he tried it for his boy Alan, and he hated it.)—and mom-Ida confided to me: "Alan, I'm going to get a divorce. How would you feel about that?" She hadn't held or hugged me when she said it.

Divorce was unknown in those days among Jewish people. Almost unknown.

And, contrary to what, dear reader, you might think, I *did* have at least an inkling as to how divorce would make me feel: *I'm going to be real screwed-up when I get older.* Yes, that was my brilliant second-grade-skipper-boy psychoanalysis that, maybe, predicted myself going in for what I did (*and did not do*) with this uninhibited woman named Eugenia, whom I keep saying saying that you'll get to meet.

I certainly did not, at that early stage, imagine anything, or anyone, like Eugenia. And it was also when with this Eugenia that I experienced the most guilt—guilt for not being what I should have been, or not being it more of the time than I did. For, once with that woman, that self-justified amoral-moral woman, and feeling that I was doing the most benighted thing that I could do, the most passive thing, I recollected how, when I was a late-teenager and had a girl in the house, my parents' house (an apartment in low-class "niggerland" East Oakland), and was unsure what I was going to do with that girl, it was then that my dad Moe had come home, early, from hacking (I guess he'd been hacking—his suddenly oblique face bore hacking-sweat) and instead of his usual—heading straight for shit-and-showers after first pouring the contents of his cabbie pee-bottle into the toilet—he had avoided me and the girl (I forget her name, it might have been Allison, I had a crush on her), and dad had gone on down to our semi-cellar (okay, apartment locker), where he never went—nor I nor my mother—and I could hear him rearranging boxes and then restacking them and generally sliding a bunch of our old stuff down there all around—and I thought nothing of it. Until years later, that is, when I realized that on that day, which was but two weeks before Moe did-the-deed that ended his life with a gun blast to the temple in that telephone booth (they had doors then), on that day when I was with Allison and preparing to launch a questionable (unworthy?) smooch, dad had come home and dead-headed straight towards the hiding of the gun. As, six months before, he had tried with sleeping pills and failed—and no doubt this had furthered in his mind that sense of loserliness—No Majors Success, no Death Success—I ought have had at least an inkling of the meaning of that clunky-shoving noise downstairs and then, when dad was again out hacking oughtn't I have gone downstairs and proceeded to go counter-shoving-about those boxes, and finally found The Gun. . . And then? *Then what!?* Then what would a father-loving-fearing eighteen-year-old have done? Gone to mommy mom? Gone to dad and acted as his juvenile psychiatrist?—a pumped-up phony man-to-man? Played the youthful gun expert and warned this man who really could do little in life but pitch (as I, *I, I*, am a Man, a Successful Man [in this land impoverished by the Religion of Success], *I* now a Man who can ride and sell a *bike!*—a fucking *Boy's* thing!)? No, trying to come up with a choice as to which dad-saving route to pursue, I would have felt the isolating tentacles of Failure too—isolating while muting and then strangling, voice strangling. . . And suppose, it occurs to me now, suppose that I had succeeded with my father in prevention of his offing of himself. *Then* what would have gone down? *We*, that's who—*We* would have gone down: Instead of Moe not existing, or Moe regaling me with tales of pro-pitching and how the chess game of batter and opposing thrower went through its intricacies and subtleties that few people know (or care) about, my dad Moe, prevented by me, convinced by me, that Suicide-is-not-the-Answer, why he would have gone hunching about the house—for *years*?—he averting his eyes at his son's presence, probably not speaking except to ask about dinner and such worthless such, watching my own watching of him like a sentry—and perhaps even, rather than thanking, *he hating me!* . . . And certainly never, never again, reliving for me his victories on the mound. These strikeouts would have disappeared. These never would have happened. These would have existed now as if they had taken place in a Hollywood encomium. Moe would have transmigrated his soul into that of Jimmy Stewart or Henry Fonda—or rather some Super slip-pitch ace they had portrayed—and who had *Made-The-Majors.*

That Delusion, THAT would have been The Answer!?

And I do doubt that he himself, old Moe, had gone into a gun store and bought the '38 (wrong weapon: the police had corrected my imagination of the gun type, it happened to have been a powerful '357 Magnum snub-nose which could not have missed it's barrel-to-temple target unless an earthquake had just then hit—had hit what was a personal earthquake in itself). No, dad Moe was too nervous-anxious (and paranoid) a guy for the strict straight-ahead strut into a gun emporium (*'emporium'*? well, these do exist in our land, don't they?). Dad certainly had enough lowlife "colleagues" at the taxi garage, guys who had variously failed at so many various cop-jobs ("I'm tired of beating niggers!"), firemen jobs ("I flunked the blood-pressure test"), post-high-school quarterback let-goes at colleges ("I fuckin' wasn't *tall* enough"), and kumsches (schmuck spelled backwards [almost], as jokey Jews often do—for what reason, clan-clannery?), and guys who just liked hacking ("You meet so many interesting *people*"—who happen to regard you as a failure-kumsche and rob-bait), so dad had likely arranged a walk-in and weapon-choice by way of one of those "helpful" guys, who wouldn't have inquired as to why Moe'd wanted the implement—so many hackies carried "the equalizers" under their seats, meaning dad's excuse for asking for the gun was easy and pro-forma: it's a dangerous world of taxi-hailers out there in Success America where you (and they) happen to, pro-forma, not Succeed.

But you will have to wait for that wild Eugenia I mentioned, and her break-the-mold doings, and my doings and not-doings with her—these recollections above are what-they-are, and they are also I think the causations of my remembering that Eugenia.

Yes we shall have to wait for some precise juncture which seems unquestionably ripe by either being tearful to the eyes or, funny-rageful and get-even non-tearful at all.

MORE "MY" LINDA

Poor Linda, Great Linda. My ex-wife Linda—who I betrayed so often it might have seemed as if betrayal was fate's order, or, perversely (yet understandably) survival's order. Linda, she hasn't received anywhere near the accolades she deserves. Nor have I, by way of Linda and my once-fortunate love for her. I mean to say, accolades for me from me, myself—and I do deserve them, damnit. So far I've been too ironic in my descriptions of my onetime wife, way too ironic—and in my descriptions of myself. How caddish-cold and myopic of me to merely attach my once-upon-a-time wife Linda to portions of chapters on other women who really couldn't have held—to use the perfect medieval phrase—"a candle to her". Despite myself, I had acquired a need for virtue from Linda, what need could be greater than that?—it was a need I really had never absorbed in my childhood, and now I really couldn't lose it. . . But I did lose it. . . Or I came close. . . and without Linda now, with other women or with none, emptiness is what I feel, so often anyway. . . But I have been known to exaggerate.

Linda-Linda-Linda: Marriage-marriage-marriage:
How do you ready yourself for that imprisonment?—
which you've wished for, because in your youth you
haven't understood what prison might involve and then
evolve-to—enclosure was not even a question in the
watery eyes of sought and found romance, commitment
could not possibly devolve to incarceration; so there
was no need for anything so prosaic as "conflict resolution", no anticipation of the dangers lurking in the
faceoff between the honest impulses of two full-fledged
opinionated human beings; there was no appreciation of
the oldtimey comedian's phrase, "the old ball-and-
chain." "Take my wife, please"—my parents' cherished
one-liner Henny Youngman was a facile schmuck to
my young me. *But*: when I went to a movie it was with
"my" Linda; when I watched TV it was with "my"
Linda; when I went to a Raiders game (Linda went and
tolerated the "crude barbarian caveman boredom");
when I did nothing, I did that too with "my" Linda
eyeballing my do-nothingness (which I oft-enjoyed, one
leg hooked-over the back of the couch, just as my
depressed father had "relaxed"); and Linda was always
aware that my silences were growing translucent to
spotty-opaque to cavern-dark, as if I were faking them
as my "solitary wisdom" (which she certainly saw
through). Ten billion dollar question then (and most
boring one, as it has been asked ten billion times): Can
one in marriage have love—not sex, nor not really Sex
even when it technically *is* sex?; how can you have that
Sex that at age, say, twenty-nine, your entire being still
craves and keeps up its dogging-away at you with its

nipping and its maneuvering and so keeps up maintaining that stupid CRAVE?—can one just do away with such a lit-to-burning fire that still has your neck your eyes aspinning in the streets when you see—*you animal!*—an anonymous *ass* being assish, a pair of perfect tits bouncing just a perfect little (*and for you*, you married hornball, you dumbly tell yourself!), and your amygdala is thus telling you *CHASE IT*, GO *GET IT, BOY!* and at the same time you just still love your wife and you wish to carry-on with your decent-upright *marrying*?—to a woman, with a woman with whom you have sex (small S) who is now your partner, your (supposedly) *higher* love—which is not (remotely) the hornball sex you yet, goddamnit, CRAVE? Apparently, such can happen, such *does* happen, a decent peace for two (I know, it sounds like a Mel Tormé song—*Nevertheless [I'm in Love With You]*), and it can happen not just to an ironic draggy Chekhov character or to a determined Turgenev. It happened, to *me*—in my own way, but which was not my wife's own way: she wanted the CRAVE as well. . . But I am talking about Me: You (I) love the person, you (I) respect and honor her, you (I) even dream of her, even as you *have* her own dreaming-self right there in bed beside you. This girl, this woman, she is all you want, or rather all you wish to want, and therefore all you've *ever* wanted (you dissemble such to yourself, meaning well), except for this One-Little-Minute-*Thing*—That CRAVE: Your wife's tits and ass are just by now human-lady tits and ass—as she has said, "they're functional"—the dermatologist has gone over them for psoriasis while you've waited in the waiting room; the breast surgeon has palped her palp while you've turned the TIME pages in

the gynecologist waiting room at the hospital. After this
monthly that ("I think I've just arisen my first liver
spot, can you *see* it?")—and you, with your complain-
ings about constipation (and other shit, haha), how can
you go on getting *hot*!? *That's perverse!—no?* And
after all, turning-you-on is not a thing, *the* be-and-end-
all, that "my" Linda Miller is about (or really ever
was)—"it's so one-track-fixated and ulterior and sad-
exploitative—and *male*." My response: "Women can be
like that too." Her response: "Yes, I admit it, but it's
brief and rare." My response (internal, unvocalized):
"Bullshit." Anyway, what I am is, I'm just hindered:
Hamstrung: even when—or especially when, naked (or
not), equipped with her slight-curled Dietrich hair and
her aqua-green Bergman eyes that are not love-slave-
like (and never were) and her Dunaway-sharp cheekbones, even when she sits atop me and she is faintly
smiling (because her wise eyes are both demanding and
reproaching [and awaiting] [and even understanding]),
and she is faintly raising her eyebrows (in a taunt or in a
gnawing chronic ouch from hemorrhoids or unathlet-
icism or in yet another love-dubious forensic she can't
help but have, considering who she's married-to), I'm,
how not? held-back, shackles-city; and yet, because we
are Us, she is also expanding her nostrils in this gathering love-hope breath that she has always done (and that,
despite all, she still *feels*—because she understands
love's evolving, because she is an ADULT), and then
slowly, as with a curtain drawn across a proscenium,
she is leaning forward and tracing her slender fingers
across her (smallish) nipples, revealing them to lucky
me, lucky me who knows that he must now go the
thespian route and act as if The Eighth Wonder of the

World has just been brought before my naïve eyes, only mine mine *mine!*—while The Wonders, they have, in real reality, *not* been brought, for they are no longer Wonders. They're tissue, breast tissue, when she's in a sweatshirt they're nothing, they've dissolved—she might as well be trammeled in the walking body-box of a black burka. They're FUNCTIONAL. And yet I wonder, still, certainly, why I am not reacting *as-a-Man-would,* brimming over, with delight, with growing expressive noises, even those once holy guy-grunts. . . As if my wife is not beautiful by comparison with The Others?—*all* the others. As if she is not *more* beautiful? . . . And you (I) turn her own individual grace, again slowly, again watchfully, again over the routine years, six of them (*and you are still in your twenties*), you turn your Linda's grace now into a thing part cynical, part zombie-melancholy—and then your kiss cannot stop its own, slow, turn to—well not superficial, no, never that, but just—too tranquil, too *excuse-my-lips-for pucker-ing.* Too pacified are they. Too disappointing—even for yourself. Especially for yourself. (*I can do better. No, damnit, I can't!*). Your (my) marriage has become this swirl of slowness, this (forgive me, but it fits) Charyb-dis: A warm urge to be together, *because you are together*, while yet the urge is also to be not—*because you are not*. The urge is to be far away, while yet not— you wouldn't last one week with Linda gone (so you think *before she is gone for the eternal weeks*). Marriage: the onetime key to your wife's sweet face, strong face, that crucial key is lost, you didn't even see it slip through your fingers and fall through the floor, it's supernatural this loss, you heard no noise, and so the soul of it goes translucent, goes murky—and then it goes withdrawn? . . . And who can blame it? . . . And then, once you have searched down all round the marriage basement and found it—a semblance any-way—you try to piece it together, jigsaw pick-up-sticks; and you fail—because you are trying with your trained-old trying fingers.

Marriage.

Whew!—and I ain't finished yet.

More questions: A six-year marriage gone kaput deserves more questions, and at risk of total excusing and alibi-ing myself I've got to go with every possible possible. Is it the awkward, well-slightly bumbly way, she, your *wife*, damn you! *your wife!* she has tended to cross her legs so that calves and ankles cover the more erotic (in this situation anyway) upper thighs (which, to tell the truth—and why is this so?—women's thighs, in truth they ain't much just as-themselves—they're *thighs! [everybody's gotta have thighs!]),* so due to the Linda calve-and-ankle configuration the Linda vaginal V is not in that taunting position that all men can waste hours plagiarizing-about in their reveries but rather that V ends up *thewy* behind those thighs; and Linda was no muscle-woman, no gymnast—farthest occupations *ever* from her mind—those thigh-endings of hers were just the inherited off-gift of DNA, it was birth-sent, not her fault. But they were not a gift to the yet horny (while yet wife-loving [in his way]) proprietor of GEIST'S BIKES who was blessed? (tormented?) with his being able to observe (and even innocently [seeming] correct-by-handling other women and their asses on a Schwinn seat or a Merck's or a Raleigh's, etc.), that placement of female thighs and rumps gone-on all day long—on spade-shaped seats too (wonderfully) small for their ample and wriggling bottoms (and, you bet, as soon as Linda and I broke-up those great asses did lose their greatnesses for me, they became as much paraphernalia as did the bikes' seats themselves, and I handled them less and less). . . And! Plus! Let me say! Linda and I, we could walk arm-in-arm in Golden Gate Park and up Mount Tamalpais; we could talk for hours (I'm not exaggerating here) about whether or not Beckett was "a one-trick pony" or had far subtly deeper intentions than even those who granted and praised him for his deeper intentions could dredge-up; and/or was ill-fated trumpeter and singer Chet Baker just a wee-bit too girlish-falsetto in his voice?—it was, though more lyrical, more altoesque too than was, say even tonselly Anita O'Day's; or we worked-on whether the skyrocketing prices of pharmaceuticals in America (*and only in America!*) was more the consequence of the greed of the Pharmaceuticals or of the non-paying Insurance companies, and the consequent national disgrace of a forty percent American poverty rate—which few Americans could even believe was the case, *but was!* I mean, about all that, for crappy fuckers, we sure could fucking *talk!—serious stuff*—we could embrace-ourselves into the illusion that we were one-person, and at peace, a good mental peace, and so then even our silences could do the same for us (sometimes), and as the wise men say (I'm thinking now of little Mickey Rooney, who'd married-'em-all, from Rita to Ava to etc.), you marry a *friend*, Mickey Rooney said (once he'd got old), a *friend*, he said, if you're smart, not a lover. (You learn to *love the liver spots*—you become a Mensch-Man). Anyway, Linda and I, we did kiss a lot, and we *meant* those kisses, as I said, even weak as they were as sex-kisses (if there were such a thing as a kisso-meter we'd have crapped-out), we kissed even when reaching at the same moment for the same Bic pen— our kisses, they were *love*—although again, goddamnit, they never approached the kiss-erotic of what love-kiss-erotic is held-out to *be*. Love, a wall a person builds for beauty and then foolishly (*unconsciously!*) chips away at while trying to build a stronger wall and even more beauteous.

So, what really was the problem? Was it that Linda's intelligence intimidated me? that and her magnanimous societal concerns annoyed me?—or they finally came to? ("Alan, did you know that in Europe, in general, the poverty line, which qualifies you for many benefits, far greater than America's, that poverty line is a full sixty percent of average disposable income? and that *America's* poverty line is *now* a niggling *thirty* percent? No, of course, you did *not* know that, *not* with your bikes' gears and chains and precious hand-worked *Italian balances*." "Or I don't much *care*?" I came back, "you're implying—me and society?" "I guess I'm implying, yes—you just talk-the-talk, that's it, you don't *do*—I'm sorry." And I was sorry I'd made her sorry, and I'd say it—and she'd answer "I'm *so sorry,* I just get carried away."). That steep gravity of Linda's would be the conventional shrinker explanation for our love-flat-nesses, that and my (compared to *her*) shortfall *lack* of The Gravitas, that snowballing societal earnestness of hers—and in fact I've already laid that out, haven't I, and my guilt for that lack, that growing growing lack (*I was starting to not-give-a-shit!*)—*and*, here's something new, my suspicion that Linda's ethnic "care" was a rebound—partly, a double-dip doubling-up on political correctness like one boxer hitting harder-harder because his opponent was, frustratingly, hitting softer-softer-softer (as a mental way of hitting harder). . . And I've hinted at Linda's upbringing—which she had to hit back on: her private The Unitas School in Madison (pronounced with a heavily accentuated "U", not a fortissimo "i", as was the surname of that great quarter-back Johnny Unitas, who I'd wished *I'd* been like [and of whom of course Linda had never heard]), this youth-propriety of hers already established before she at-tended the admired "Seven Sisters" Mount Holyoke College; her family home located on Lake Avenue, on the more serene shores of Lake Michigan, far north of hectic ("low-class immigrant-stuffed Chicago"—Linda joy-rebelliously mocked her Lake Avenue street as *"La plage du Conservatisme"*), her "castle" was a double-lot Victorian her grandfather, the admired (on the Right, of course) near-Senator Jurgen Miller (he never won his three election tries, Wisconsin being then a "decent farm-laborer's Democratic state"—but he was still referred to, in his circles as "The Senator"—and *out of his circles*, with cheerful irony), he, "The Senator", he had had that multi-colonnaded Victorian beauty of theirs built. And now, here at this juncture we come to take a super-sharp turnaround from Linda's upright activities Linda's family knew about: her obsessive grocery-shoplifting (of avocadoes for neighborhood raccoons; and black lace panties for herself), her "bad boyfriend" Spence—the one who'd taught her to steal—Spence who'd hitch up to Racine from "grungy" Chicago and, she swore to me, "He gave me a climax when I was *sixteen*—I'm pretty sure it was what it was was happening down there" (she was superior-demurely pointing to her 'down there'—as she'd been taught such honey-refined reference at Mount 'Holy-hoke'?); her— "to see what it was like, Alan, it was no bigger, like Negro-boys always say '*they*' are"—her jerking-off Spence's black buddy Earl—"who didn't even go to *school*—and he *stunk*, they *do* smell different, it's *true*—you have got to be decent and get *over* that, until it actually in your mind stops *smelling*." And, far worse than these previous three: As a Sophomore and a Junior at The Unitas School, Linda had been a member of DADAR: the Daughters of the Daughters of the American Revolution—she'd been a convinced and staunch defender of the "Rights of 'our Founders' ", which were being "slowly but inevitably overtaken and overcome, inch by inch by inch". "I mean," she told me after we were married, "I by all rights *couldn't and shouldn't* have been a DAR heir as my family hadn't even *arrived* in the U.S. until fifteen or so years *before* the Civil War, and from Braunschweig, *Germany*." . . . I'd laughed at Linda's confused and confusing past, and this mockery was along with Linda's modern prompting of course, she being now "a Progressive's Progressive"—I had after all only met her because she had come to Oakland/Berkeley after law school (Georgetown) "for some freedom, Alan, and in a region well-known for its proclaimed *Leftism* and its needing badly some more lawyering social work" (hearing such explanation, her mother [also a Linda] had done little but, like a perplexed maltreated cat, stare at a corner of their huge ancient kitchen for hours [folks thought she'd had a semi-stroke]). . . So: I've had time to think more rigorously over these intervening forty pages and I've decided that Linda's growing moral intimidation of myself as we got older, "it just ain't necessarily true". Men have to rebel, as do women—*more* than do women, I'm serious, because what men are rebelling against for themselves, those expectations, they are more dug-long-deep. Sure, women have had it tough, trying to be too many things in order to be equal to their men, respected by their men (and by their [old-fashioned] moms.). But men, they have to live up to their falsely-gained beyond-equalities, even when these were even so *religiously* gained—*vide Abraham.*

But how much "living-up" is living-up? Linda had once pointed-out to me an anthropoidal fact (that I already knew): "Do you know of the bonobos, Alan?".

"Yes," I'd answered, aware of the mammalian discovery that I was also aware that she was now determined to reveal to me (I'd seen it on TV):

"Well, the bonobos are a species of chimpan*zee, Alan,* and they are famous for *two,* call them *"idiosyncrasies"*: *One,* they comprise a *female*-dominant society; and *two,* they screw all the time, day and night—and so, unlike their male-dominant cousins, the chimpanzees, they do not fight at all, they do not kill each other off or the offspring of their rivals—as they have within themselves, *no* rivals, just *lovers*—so they just have *good government.*"

I did not irritate and then aggravate Linda by answering, 'I know all that.' And adding, 'A bonobo is a bonobo, not a humanabo. Their behavior, for us, means nothing.'

I did not answer such flip-wise as she would have certainly counter-answered on the order of: 'Bonobos *prove* that *female* rule is both possible and more equable—and happier, and *successful*. And *intelligent*.'

But bonobos aside, I did not, I simply could not, live up to Linda's best beliefs and hopes (but not expectations) regarding modern society and the human male. Even my guilt—and it was considerable (and it got worse yet)—my guilt did not deter me. . . Actually, the only time (or times) when the mature Linda Miller cracked and broke-out from her modern-times shell of Goodness and Mercy to All was when I so infuriated her with my Al Geist-selfishnesses ("GEIST'S BIKES, a pile of inadequate *things*, it has become more important to you than THE HOMELESS!") that she would become (or revert to) the "bad" shicksa that my mother Ida had so always warned me off: Linda hurling dishes (really!) as I stayed huddled downstairs repairing bent handlebars and installing new spokes and hammering dented fenders to a microscopic even-smooth: Linda breaking glasses and then stomping on the dangerous shards and slivers (in shoes, of course), Linda slamming doors so loud that the convicted badasses in the penitentiaries she generously visited would have been set on edge. I had finally met that "bad schicksa" that, in a way, she had been before she had even been DADAR (and under those false Braunschweig credentials); and that "bad schicksa", of course, of course, no longer Lady Pacifism, that "bad schicksa" now having reverted to the other resident of her soul (as duplexed-up as is just about any American's), Lady Frustrated Violent; and *she* (unbonobo-like) (and *whadayaknow!*) gave me then the hardest of hardons (which then pleased her and also did its [expected] displeasing—afterwards.). . . Funny, Linda Miller Geist might as well have been having sex by then with another Spence-the-hitchhiker-up-from-Chicago-in-'66 or with one of the out-on-bail incarcerees she was working with so dedicatedly hard to Save—and had worked so hard for to raise big bail (meaning only about one thousand dollars). . . No, again I'm exaggerating—to maintain some Male-ish Power and Right, and Justifiability. . . And self-respect that was just as much its opposite.

But don't get me wrong: I *was* grateful to Linda Miller Geist (now Linda Geist Miller) for my having acquired that one-half of one-quarter knowledge of the local living evils handed out in the name of local Justice that did (and do) persist in The Bay Area—and elsewhere in the good old USA—and righteous-comically in the names of Freedom and the Founding Fathers. (Why anything social-political should be held aloft as the "ideal legacy" of "Enlightenment Slaver Men", pre-Darwinians who'd believed that the chaotic universe was as right-regular as a clock and that the ways of government ought not change as men *did* change—and all those founding-fellows were really *farmers*—face it!—all that believing in those provincials as gods is beyond me. [No it isn't]). And hell, through Linda I did indeed at times "get involved" in at least what one might label a mini-activism. I who years before had laughingly quipped re Louis Farrakhan's Million Man March that it should have been tagged The Million Mugger March, I now, on occasion, did wear a Black Lives Matter T-shirt (I drew the line at a banner or a wall-sign in GEIST'S BIKES). . . And I relented from my (usual and unconscious—sort of) policy of the exclusive hiring of white salesmen (blacks, I had observed, did not ride bikes, so what was the point?) and I took-on Jamil Wilkes, a parolee from no less a frightening penal institution than San Quentin (by-the-Bay). Jamal had been convicted of manslaughter—the beating to death with his bare hands—*"unintentionally! unintentionally!"*—a guy, a lawyer yet (Jewish yet; an "acquaintance" of Linda's yet) who had called Jamil an "illiterate nigger" (which he was—at the time) as they had faced-off as a consequence of Jamil's '72 Merc (a patriotic red-white-blue) having been T-boned by attorney Louis Salzman's polished-up black Beamer 325i as Salzman was engaged in the remunerative process of ambulance-chasing and thereby in the process of running a Stop sign. In any case Jamil Wilkes had served his time (for being a model prisoner [he'd taken courses—one, on Social Responsibility, taught weekly by none other than my wife], he'd done the minimum of nine years of a quite possible thirty-three), and Jamil was indeed hired by me—after, okay, Linda's having sweatily worked-on me until I (nervous-ly) came through with the hiring. To my professional credit, by the way (and personal balls), I did not payroll Jamil until he proved to my satisfaction that he possessed some mechanical talent to go with his talky-talk shpiel-abilities, and actually turned-out to care-for the work (he said he loved it, and he was not gaming-me, I could tell [I thought]); and re the sales part, aside from his "glib-naturals" bronze Jamil was handsome as hell. But to get to the point already: Jamil became—for me, who is not the greatest male-friend-maker in the universe (you can surmise that one, can't you)—he became my best friend, my new Jimmy X from Belfast. We biked, we shot pool (I was better, as with Irish

Jimmy), we played one-on-one "roundball" (basket-ball), and we confided in each other over our woman problems (he lamenting that white women often expected him to "do and talk somekinda roughhouse shit so that they could 'teach me the sensitivities' "), and he talked too over just living life when no one—except Linda and the Linda-ishers of this world—seemed to give a damn:

Me: "I'm with that. I can dig it."

Jamil: "Al, don't talk that black shit—or should I say 'id-ee-um'."

Me: "Sorry. It's just, by talking to you . . ."

Jamil: (mocking) "I'm with that. I can dig it—you hate and so you're in awe. And reverse of that too. But you know what more than that I *hate*?"

I hesitated to take any kind of stab.

Jamil: "I hate when the TV commentator assholes—even *black* ones—on sports, *all* sports—on ESPN they do their *White-jive* hypers. Like calling an okay *White* player like Larry Bird or Joe Montana 'The Greatest', just because he is *White*—and even though he's *slow* as shit and he can't *jump* for shit, that shit don't matter, as the *TV Commentator fuckhead,* he goes round *that truth* by giving-out *white-praise-shit* like, 'He knows The Game real-well, he's *smart*, he *studies*, he's got *Heart*.' As if a black player *don't do all that*, as if the-black-man, *he* ain't *smart* enough and *he don't study*, as if *he's* runnin' on *the* black instinctives *alone*. His *nay-chur*."

Me: "I know what you mean. (And I did—although it did not bother me; it had never even occurred to me.)."

And then came worked-up Jamil's coup-de-grâce.

"O.J.—you see that news booking-shot of him at the *po*-lice?—he's in his Jockeys, nothing else; and you can see on the front view the dick-swell, and it does not jibe with the white man's—and *woman's*—black-dick-scared-and-wanted conception: That O.J. dick-swell, counter-to-you-*all*, it is *small*."

I wasn't sure then whether to convey sympathy for O.J. Simpson for his small penis or to agree with Jamil unracistically that a dick is a dick is a dick and that's all there is to it; for I too had seen the cop booking-shot, and like most white men—and women—I had been surprised by the shrunken-up littleness—and not relieved (actually *disappointed*, go figure!) at that super halfback Heisman Trophy winner's unthreatening small-normal "tool".

I'd wanted to feel threatened by black men!?
Interesting what men and women want!

In any case, our true friendship graduation, I think, I *know*, was when I got allowed to call Ja*mil Jam*-ill (the sharp *eee* diminished, dispensed-with, the slurred-drawled-faux Middle East name become thus farcical-sounding as pajamas and, I hoped, buddy-buddy-palsy-walsy—he giving white me latitude, and Jew me yet), and Jamil had taught me the fancy-tumble fistwork required in mastering the finger-wrist conniptions of the black-brother handshake-bumpshake (this accomplishment took me no little time); it was then that I knew that I had "made it" *with a black*, such that Jamil now called me nigger by compliment and even "wigger", which was a put-down for a white who wants to be, and acts like, a "nigger"—when Jamil called me wigger I knew it was likewise a close-compliment: I was accepted—which got me to venturing, "Hey, *Jam*-ill, how come lots of black guys and girls are pre-named 'La'?—like La-David or (and here I really took lati-tude) La-Muvvah? or La Toiletta" (He laughed). Okay-yes-sure, I see your thinking: What with Jimmy-from-Belfast, a robust possible killer, and now with smooth black Jamil (also a killer), I seemed to have an affinity for tough guys, and a copycat sympathy, and—I dread the phrase—a proclivity for the old suck-up. And I know you know precisely without doubt from whence came those on-your-knees sense-urges: me and old tough daddy Moe. Of myself and all three of these characters one might have said like Jacob to his angel, "I will not let thee go before thou bless me." (this always a losing proposition) . . . Now: I think, by the way, that handsome Jamil (six/one—two shakes of a shade over me—medium complexion, caramellish, snub nose but a slender one for a black, thinnish lips—thus no moustache required—close-cropped hair only semi-kinky, no tattoos [visible] and a predilection for T-shirts that boasted pictures of black boxers with gloves raised before chest in mode of attack-protect), handsome Jamil may have become "my" Linda's lover—about which I tried in vain to wangle wordage out of him (never *HER, never*), whereby he'd do a fancy-dance off the subject, off off and awayyyy, usually to some Republican politician he wouldn't mind 38' ing or pulling the balls off. Actually it did occur to me that Jamil might well have been more embarrassed if he'd had to admit that he was *not* Linda's lover than that he was; but even if he was screwing my wife that wouldn't have ruined our friendship—I don't think: By then "my" Linda and I were pretty far gone and beyond, our fingertips seldom touched upon the occasional stretched out-reachings. . . And actually, come to think of it, just as when my wife had morphed for moments to become my mother's "bad schicksa" (whether this change was my fault or not), this liaison of those two, Linda and Jamil, limb-locked—with my own pinion variations that my imagination could not control (I even awaited my brain's directorship providing clever deviations, Ghetto Sutra carousels that Linda and I could never have chanced upon), such new black-white moves might well have gone quite-a-ways towards galvanizing me even more (*but to whom? Linda or Jamil?—God we are such a super-perverse species!—it can't just be only Me.* . . But then again, as everyone knows, such things are hard to figure about oneself: I might have got quite totally torn-up rather than excited by painting those mental pictures—*even at the same moment as when I remained equally dug-in galva-nized—by painting those mental pictures!* . . . And another point, in my defense, sort of: I might well have imagined Linda's sucking on the black man's (uncircumcised) dick at a very unideal time in her day: I seeing that industrious-earnest pursing of her lips, and worse, her just *kissing* Him, and worse, she staring into his eyes searching for the true-heaven-meaning that she wished from men, while earlier in the day she might have so morally in court, so powerfully and indignantly, defended some other, and similar, Jamil—who might well have been a black man rapist and conscienceless as-hell. The Hypocrisy of Good Intentions. The Goodness of Hypocritical Intentions. . . But then: the truth is, *the real truth: I still wanted Linda back,* even as she hadn't quite yet (fully) gone. I did not wish to be ALONE—the universe was not made for solitude, just look! But I also feared what would have been my deep pleadings to swear-off other women, I distrusted such Al-pleadings (this distrust another form, actually, of self-trust): I feared Linda's eyes become iron-grey filings, not the blue-green winsomes of onetime, and these eye-filings facing me and drilling-in and never-stopping drilling, and her ears gone to hardened close-fisted shells—shells through which you could not work-up a yell. Had I spoken out, my own true intentions would have turned to lies, the lies they had always been. . .

But I'm good, damnit, *I-am-Good*: At the very least, I could have fired my Jamil—and I did not.

Good thing too, because through him I met black Marie Smith, who impressed me firstoff because she did not have a black first name like Latrina or La Whatnot—and secondly because she *did* have one of those terrific ski-jump black girl rumps that I did want myself to be very familiar with, no matter how racist that sex-wish might have proven me (and I still do *not* believe that, sex-racistwise, it proves one damn thing—except that a-man-is-a-man and that black women are damned proud that they boast such "booties" that are *any* man's desire [except, okay, for "aristocrats" who *claim* that they prefer the backsides of the skinny-assed white princesses who can easily pronounce the word Ask as if it is not a cleaving instrument]). And Marie (ass and all), she did become my woman of the next chapter.

MARIE

Marie attended the local Laney College, which was
mostly a black-attended junior college (or, the faux-
neighborly-named "community college"), the minor
tuition for which she was able to satisfy, not by any
local "community" scholarship (although by way of
Jamil's exertions, Linda had tried to get her one), but by
hooking. I.e., by planting herself at the well-known
hooker-corner of San Pablo Avenue and Dwight Streets
or sashaying thereabouts down as far as Alcatraz Avenue, Oakland's borderline (sheer gumption that work-
ing-girl station and parade required, as a hip [white]
café affectedly named Dizzy's [jazz trios nightly,
except Mondays] was located just dead-center of
Marie's promenade, and was not the sort of establish-
ment that, on the face of it, might cater to patrons who
catered to prostitutes [even quarter-timer ones, ones
with their hard hopes upcasting their hopeless ways
towards an Associate of Arts degree which might then
lead them to be accepted at [Cal?—forget it] Hayward
State or San Jose State or such). Marie, it turned out,

aimed to become, eventually, fate amenable against all fate-less odds, a *dentist—a dentist!?*—and sure I pictured her hunkering over my bicuspids (and penis) with her dental whitecoat's top three buttons un-buttoned and her white lace bra all the narcotic I required, and stimulant in the bargain. But, Marie said, "For *blacks*, Jack—Blacks Only—no White Chops allowed. They're different." She was being cute, of course, but she did happen once to say to me: "Just like in those Hollyweird *'Step'nfetchit'* movies of 'the day', just like how those Jew directors had 'our'—and she stared at me as if she had ferreted-out every racist opinion I had ever had, and/or cherished—"how Holly-weirdwood had 'our' walks *different*, and our *smells* different, and our boldnesses differed-down into cow-ardice, as with our bullshittedly swelled-up eyes, well Jackson, OUR *teeth <u>are</u>* truly different, so different techniques *are* required—you didn't know that, did you?—well maybe you *did*—that racism can sometimes reveal a *true* and *honest* 'thang' people are afraid to *say* as because of where they will be *leading-on*—to their disbenefit. And a *non*-white girl's got to be wholly liberated to accept *that* kind of science 'disco-ver-*eee*'." No, I didn't know if she'd meant that, any morsel of it, or was just mocking this whitebread me who obviously, from the first, wanted her. Marie had been grinning super-stretch-wide when she'd claimed that total teeth deal, her "smile" couldn't sound the knell of any alloy but play mixed with (and maybe overwhelmed by) hate—and now, to me, her teeth did look different. . . And, as I came to learn, she did not speak so "Black-lishical" when she spoke in her Marie Smith Everyday.

"Al," said Jamil, "meet Marie Smith."

He'd had the buddy-buddy effrontery to bring her into my GEIST'S BIKES. Which sort of struck me as like your cat might bring to your living room a token: a rat (okay, a nice squirrel, a gopher, a wounded sparrow, a rabbit), this poor broken animal as a gift for your cat's being taken care of (him, i.e.)—meaning not having to pounce outside in the wilds, eating such animals.

"It's my real name," Marie said to me, bowing and semi-kneeling to mock all deference. "The Smith, I mean. Slavemaster name, jim."

And the Marie, that's a normal name—a white name. It's not La Marietta or La Marilloguina or...?

Such my thought, obviously drowned, unsaid. Another thought—

I love you for this gift, Jamil—if it is a gift. And I had taken as well to Marie's usage of the 'jim'. That was very hip, so very hip: it dated way back to early jazz-talk, when a hipster was "a cat" hanging outside Birdland and scuffling to stay alive and was not a today's "hipster" in hedge-funds and the like with a million dollar condo in Pacific Heights and a ruiner of Greenwich Village. The 'jim" was also way groovier than the timeworn 'jack' that even a schmucky accountant might use by this creepy 'day-and-age'.

I suppose to appear interested, to seem off-the-bat as white-normal as any GEIST customer in North Berkeley (she wasn't as black-confident-cocky as she put-on), Marie punctiliously walked the line of bikes in my store, bending to scrutinize the shiny wares as if she had some amateur expertise. And also, no doubt, to show herself off, arches, curves and all, but by way of utmost innocence. As I've already indicated, Marie's ass was a definite-decided thing to behold; and I tried to keep myself from too much beholding of it. Thus its beholdable surroundings: Marie was slightly more caramel than was my "buddy" Jamil (okay, she was dark); she had long and seriously straightened hair—was it that day not a process but a Cher-hair wig?, such coif of course was necessary in her quarter-time (or so) profession of currency (but of course that self-employ-ment had been enjoined so that she might become, eventually, a professional dentist—and what a perfect name for her eventual practice: *Different Dentals*.). Marie's Cher-hair, or whatever it was, was long, shoul-der length, managing thus to effect a narrowing of her face, not that Marie Smith's face was so broad that it required narrowing (it was a kind-of sensual-strong Eartha Kitt face)—and really her "natural" indicated more of a hiding, a smart sensual concealment. Her eyes were brown of course, black-brown, and large (contacts?), so that they seemed by their very nature ascertaining and estimating, sloe-eyes; her cheekbones were so sharp that I considered native-American blood; her chin and jaw were advantaged by a slightly chal-lenging jut (*is this a built-in ready-aimed defiance? is she instinctively paranoid?*); and her lips, which were Black Woman full, presented another certainty of attitude to accompany her jaw-jut—the whole deal made it impossible to not occupy one's mind with a sexuality that could deal with any, well, "comers". And she smiled a lot (which retracted her threatening chin). Marie smiled almost as much as she scowled.

Perhaps a black man can easily ken the subtle differ-ence between a black woman's fake and real smiles when she wishes to render herself opaque. A white man cannot tell what's what—not for the most part anyway.

I don't believe that even a white shrinker could.

Is the above a racist-justifying statement? Or a sexist. I do though believe that it is true, and I'll stick with it. . . I'll go with the That's Being a Man.

Of course, as I said, I wanted Marie Smith. And of course I hoped that she liked me (out of respect for a black woman—and fear of—I did not handily adjust her ass on any of the bike seats she tried out)—although how does one tell such things as a woman's liking you if she is a hooker? (even one who is also a collegiate and but a hooker-quarter-timer)—there's just too much ulteriority racing round, dipping in and out. . . I suppose that, sex aside, woman-ness aside, my desire to be liked by a black female was not so very dissimilar from my aspirations with Jamil. To be a pal of a Black, I am embarrassed to admit, can be bizarrely exhilarating (even for a White who might otherwise see Blacks as inferior [I am admitting nothing, while admitting, in that Nothing, Everything]), and so what you do is you begin to become roused-up by goosebumpily patriotic Americana notions of goodness and fairness even though when you are alone—or with other friends (assuming one has such) you can hear in your head and speak-out your prejudices full force—the lower IQ; the (supposed) bronchial-voiced uncouthness; those twist-round wrist-fist bump greetings (that you envy [and screw-up every time you venture one with [smirking] Jamil); the sloppy-slow hunch-walks of contrariness, especially with the underwear perking out, usually white; the fabricated words and phrases of low-uneducated "quality" such as the pointless, stubborn imbecility of insisting-on "axe" for "ask" [I even had a black professor, of sociology, who "axed" folks while doing his political opinion surveys]); the essential multifarious double-negatives. Yes there was just that entire textbook, or rulebook, or guidebook, or Black Bible, of obstinate-ubiquity Black gestures meant to give mock to the White proprieties. And damn, these "tics" can make a white man angry, even if he craves black-friendship (and *because* of those black-tics all the more), and his own White tics notwithstanding (like giving a too hard brittle handshake when you are less than five foot six, and enunciating—*over*enunciating—"*muvvah*"—which would be the hip-right way of saying "moth-er-fuck-er"—if only you could articulate it right. And lots of other things, I'm sure.

But when a woman is being brought to you—white or black—and she is regaled in a casualized overdone-ness, a misconceived White daytime soigné, such that it has been so obviously planned-out—and maybe for meeting-up with the likes of *You* (you hope)—then, sex or no, you take far more than the casual sex-notice: Notice of: A cape, green plaid, covering shoulders already covered by a red blouse filled with frills at the sleeve-endings; a militaryesque (navy) belt (two-incher) with large golden buckle (three-incher) like an award of some kind, holding up black slacks pleated all the way high to said belt, those slacks not obscuring green (turquoise-jade) tennis shoes (women's, high-girl heel) with the Michael Jordan swipe (it wasn't outmoded then).

"Marie," said Jamil, "she is not interested in bicycles."

I said, "I can see that."

She said, "What?—you got some-way somekinda X-ray eyes?"

"In a way, yes."

"Hey, I am *too* interested, *damn*. Can't a girl take her *time*!"

Theatrically, Marie was doing her jaw-jut while clamping her fisted hands onto her perfect-proportional male-magnetizing hips—while balancing herself on a beauty of a red BMC (she could sense the bikes she looked best on).

And why had Jamil brought her to GEIST'S? Was Jamil reciprocating then for his having slept with "my" Linda?—whether he'd really slept with my wife or not. Did he simply want to show me, his "good-buddy-bruhtha", that he was cool enough to know on-intimates the unique likes of this Marie? Was "my" Jamil, prospectively, bringing Marie to conjectured *business*?—a way of tying us more together.

When the clock's hands indicated five, Jamil abruptly left us and, instead of leaving with Marie he went upstairs to the apartment of "my" Linda and myself. Being a clever soul, and a man who knew the streets, Jamil had become Linda's new, informal, unofficial, assistant, and they two were "working on this "new difficult case", as they also had come to do down in Linda's office on Fourteenth Street in Central Oakland ("Alan, I'm eating takeout sweet-and-sour Chinatown fourth day in a row"—and was she also being "worked-on" [and eaten] by Jamil for the fourth day in a row? But look: I certainly can't blame my wife: I knew that from her many days of working in his defense she had developed feelings for Jamil, and respect for him—and by now feelings *against* me, which were justified—I hoped she still had *some* respect.). . . Anyhow, as the old typewriter test line goes, "Now is the time.": I approached Marie Smith who had not blinked an eye when Jamil took off upstairs (*I* had—although he had done the same a few times before), Marie just continued her counterfeit test-around of my congeries of bicycle seats with her stand-up left-right-left-right potent-pumping—the most provocative in-store peddling (and thus phony) I had ever lain an eye on.

"Made any decisions yet?" I asked. "Need my help?"

"Help to pump and peddle. What'you think I am?—some kind of a *handi*cap *footi*cap?"

I grinned as if she had just uttered the most witty retort I had ever heard, and then my spirit went what-the-hell and I put the bumptious Big Al moves on so obviously now bumptious Marie: I'd analyzed and debated the brazen *('she's inviting that, and she is after all just a schwartze, so anything goes'*—that's how my thinking went, at least I'm being honest, give me that), but I, being a temperate Jewish guy, I only merely tentatively reached up under her green plaid cape and just as tentatively cupped her nearest breast, the right; and she swiveled-round, crouched, and popped-me-one-good-one in the groin, a hard punch as dead-on as con-trolled in force, she grinning with her well-wrought evil-dead-eye friendliness. "You've been wanting to feel me up since you've met me," she said delightedly. "Have you not. Ad*mit*."

"Guilty as charged."

"Guilty as sin, I'd say."

As I intimated before, I loved her—you know what I mean by 'loved': The looks, forbidding and forbidden. That damned distant blackness. The liberal-correct American A-Racial Brotherhood which is all lie and self-delusion. And her wit, I loved that too, she being in this case way ahead-of-me. And of course her idiom— which I learned later she had been just putting on. All that jive black talk: Hell, Marie could talk as well as most any white woman.

"Now-sir," she said, "with my boy upstairs with your wife, and me dropped-down to diversion-behavior—*Man, don't you know what's going on!?*—I have done my deed and I have got to go."

As an excusing joke—and an intended cool-appeal-ing one, and one bent on showing I was not bothered by Jamil's being upstairs—I said: "I believe I love you."

And she said, "I believe you believe you do."

I picked Marie up at Laney College the next after-noon for our first date. I didn't exactly trust Jamil to handle GEIST'S BIKES, but my desire to start some-thing with this black woman—my first ever—can-celled-out my reservations about starting something like full trust with Jamil; except of course it did not cancel them out and I spent my entire Marie-date with the back of my mind fighting it out with the front—which was Marie; or was it the reverse? . . . But it was poignant, I've got to say, all those black students pouring out of the sadly few college buildings bordering where I sat cooling my heels, which must have been the un-scrubbed steps of the Student Union. And the kids poured-out towards what?—how many jobs could be available for them in this our land of diminishing GDP and increasing racism (You don't believe me?) and the ever-rising need for expert-techno?—how many "positions" for a squadron of "Negro" hopefuls with minimalist Associate of Arts degrees? The Triple

Handicap. . . But for a hooker-dentist maybe it would be different? The self-employment gambit. The blatant fact that this double-professional was a knockout, who was today adorned in coed (is this still a word?) duds (is this still a word?): knit sweater, jeans, low heel well-scuffed semi-hikers. And the jeans were casual-baggy, as if she did not wish to show-off her magnificently sculpted rear end.

Perhaps because she considered that "a walk" was a boy-girl activity that normal people participated in if they did not go to clubs or ballgames or dinner-and-a-movie, Marie suggested—

"What say we make-for a walk, old boy?"

The (outmoded) Brit-upperism, accompanied by her wry grin, showed no pretense—rather, play. And perhaps it was to impress me that she was just no plain-damn-U.S.-nigger. I think that because I was duly impressed that she was just-no plain-damn-U.S.-nigger. I responded in what I considered kind—

"Tally ho."

"That's for foxes, you schmozo."

Schmozo? Had the majority of her regular tricks been Hebrews?

Lake Merritt was nearby, so that was where we 'made-for'. Bumping shoulders as if neither of us had ever walked any distance beside another person (Linda and I were so linear in mind and motion, and in the unity of such, that we never walk-bumped), we continued all round the two mile circumference, where everyone else, almost, was black—and most were engaged in stern-faced steadfast running. A lake is a lake is a lake, urbanwise, but Lake Merritt was unique. It was surrounded by architectural artifacts from, I'd say, as far back as the Teens and Twenties: I imagined that at one time these colonnaded red brick apartments with their sculpted characters over the doorways and abutting the roofs, and even some constructs that appeared to be onetime mansions with their greenhouse-windows and iron-gated terraces, these must have been the residences of the local rich before such folks had hightailed-it up into the East Bay hills—away from encroaching negroes, no doubt (and maybe even rich ones—there must have been one or two of such); now all was rundown, well almost all, not unlike Lower East Side Manhattan tenements. Some even had fire-escapes attached to their fronts, like rusty teeth that might tumble-off from their clamps at any moment—so they appeared as full-scale skeletons. Zombies from the Greatness Americana. Land of Opportunity.

"You embarrassed?" Marie asked.

"Of what?"

" 'Of *what*?' Now come on, give me $\bar{a}$ break." She'd pronounced the 'a' hard, a sharpened 'aiyy'. Now she had taken-to being Southern, American Southern, or Brit Cockney. Marie might have made of herself a better actress than "my" long-gone Suzanne Thalbrucker.

"You embarrassed of bein' locked-in by-the-side of a *black* woman?"

"No. I've been with other black women."

"You're lyin', jim."

"Okay-well, a little bit."

"A lot."

I was also frightened that some black guy or guys might be offended by the togetherness of Marie-and-me (especially the shoulder bumping and its possible couple-love interpretations) and they might decide to beat the—no other way to convey this—the everloving shit out of me.

Of course that did not happen.

What did happen was that, for me, and in little time, Marie lost what one might call her erosis. She lost that gigantic darkly sensual and animal—but mostly human—pull precisely *because* in short order (approximately one quarter mile, I'd say), Marie became, not a dangerously wild inscrutable *schwartze*, but a human, full-fledged (aren't I nice). And Marie saw the transformation (or 'loss', if one wishes) take place in my eyes—and I saw her recognition of such in her own eyes, which shown, I've got say, a strange combination of disappointment and understanding—there was a distinct fall-down in those large brown eyes of hers (as if they were no longer needed); yet, most obvious of all, a triumph: at my own flat-ironed disenchantment, in my losing my own concoction and hoped-for (longed-for?) "brown sugar". Marie had defeated me, but weirdly she too had lost something, a victimized specialness—The Bigot Bubble Burst. The Fourth Dimension backed-down to the equal-but-sorrowful (and realistic) Three, which, if one is honest, is all there should have been in the first place. . . We had been "making conversation"—an activity about which I hadn't been quite so sure how to progress with a black woman who obviously hadn't been blessed with the advantages that I had had, even with my small nuclear family that had been so damaged and cut off, in a way White-Jewish-Trash. Now, wait—no misunderstandings here: Sure I knew that there were intelligent black women, intelligent blacks, scientists, novelists, often great orators (although this last, the oratory, having mentioned it makes me uneasy, falling again to the-easy-bigotry, as "oratory" is so close to song, to "the mellow throat", to music, even to dance, and to The Minstrelsy—and these constitute the ambiguous "compliments" that we, in our liberalism, in our generosity, feel free to lay upon blacks: as long as they are diminished by us in a thousand subtle ways we allow ourselves the one "compliment" [that we respect and we disdain]). And years before, at the urgings of "my" Linda I had read smatterings of Toni Morrison, who would later win the Nobel—although to tell the truth I did feel that she had made of herself a Faulkner ripoff, and that her Nobel was a form of Affirmative Action, like that "super-oration" compliment; I knew too of Alice Walker and certainly the poet Maya Angelou, but I could never rid myself of the horrid charity opinion that these women were exceptions, and major exceptions, bright wolves among the dumbest dopey dogs. My feeling had stubbornly, embarrassingly, remained that with most white women (I only knew college grads) you could, say, mention Sisyphus (Camus', not the real one) as an allegory for fate's-nature over man's struggling repeated efforts and it would be understood, whereas with most black women—deprived, *as we all know*, by our American racism and capitalism (and sexism)—if you brought up Sisyphus they'd probably think that you were calling someone a sissy—sissyism. Funny, this bigotry of mine is not easy to admit-of—especially as it is so common among my kind, which then makes it very easy to admit-of. . . So, I was surprised, more than surprised then, flabbergasted, when Marie, although not presenting any pretentious phony familiarity with ancient Greek lit or modern French philosophy, was miles ahead of me in speaking of the finer, detailed examples of corruption in the political worlds of Oakland and San Francisco, naming names of which I had never heard, including that of our local congressman (even had my wife Linda once mentioned them they would slide through my indifferent cortex like melted butter or grease for a bicycle.). And Marie did not simply name names: she went into cases, complicated ones (that I did not follow, that I could not follow [because I did not care?]), and then she presented to me her support for "the honorable stand-up men and women" who might be rivals to the "vile amoral thieves now running our own guhvament down-deep-in-the-ground for their own cheap-ass benefit." And as she spoke this way—what can I say?—I went, sort of, numb and dumb—the moron dog compared to the calculating wolf. And so I could think of no way, as I might have with an alluring white woman, to invite Marie Smith to cap off our walk with a short "stopover" at a local hotel. For one thing, that goddamned main thing, Marie, hooker-student Marie, while gaining my respect, my overwhelming regard, had punctured my desire for sexual liaison. A white woman talking the intricacies of local politics (of which even most "educated" people tended to know little) would have been, yes, still, an accepted thing, and one from which I might then have been able to finesse a smooth(ish) transition into a more horizontal proposition. A post-politic inner-course as a cap-off to an intercourse on politics—hardly a metamorphosis unknown to even the nicest of men. But this black woman, as physically galvanizing as she had earlier been (especially to this racist, me), was now, not just "a woman", but an object of awe, of admiration—even, absurdly, of inscrutability, and thus intimidation: she was in short, a woman I did not deserve, as she was—there is no other way to put this—better-than-me. This prostitute with dental goals had become for me a saint, or at the very least another Linda. One time on our walk about the lake (and I remember it especially as we were staring at a giant lakeside cage, about five stories high, which was a sort of quarantine hospital for sick birds, most of which stood on the ground and did not flutter-about), Marie turned to me and said: "Alan, my life's shit, by any objective standard, I know that, but, y'know I don't *feel* that, not so much. I feel good and I feel positive with hope—I don't know wherefrom it's even coming from; but when you feel stuff like that you *feel*, you really *feel*—and part of that feeling is feeling for *other* folks, which even when that feeling's bad because *their* life's shit, maybe, that feeling's feeling-bad, that is one *good* feeling, and you can't let yourself *go* of it—or you *ain't* you, you understand?" And, truthfully (I swear it) I did understand—for about ten seconds, that's the length of it: I was just too privileged and selfish, even though my brought-up life had not been so great, that's for goddamn sure. And weirdly, I even felt scared of Marie, of her depth, of her plain being-in-the-world. . . And Marie, I know, saw every sad bit of that (white-guy) fear, of my-being-me. . . *Every* sad bit? That with a white woman who had spoken of the things she had (and I do not here mean "my" Linda, she hadn't the emotional arm-spread that Marie did), with such a *white*-woman I would have (well, I might have) fallen within that expanse of a broad-smart (no, *wise*) heart.

But insanely (and sanely?), reactively, I saw no possibilities with Marie Smith of intimacies, of sex. . . Perhaps of "love". . . Well, in any case it would have been a love built on awe—the Idol Love? Such, from-self-to-self, my piddling consolation.

Despite all my fantasies of how she and I might have contorted in bed, of how she might be "different", "more flexible" "more bed-clever", of how erotic might be the unique (I guessed) purplish-black hue of her nipples and vagina, the cropped tightness of her pubic hair, Marie and I never slept together—and it is not my imagination-in-remembrance that pictures our walk speeding up to sad end at its sad starting point where my Golf was parked at Lake Merritt. . . And when I described to my black pal (and cuckolder?) Jamil what had taken place and what had not, he had—I guess the best right-on word is sneered. Whether he was sleeping with my wife or not was irrelevant; Jamil was now working for a white man who was a "wigger" un-possessed of the values that would have made wigger-ism at least acceptable and viable and (sure I do mean the following word) worthwhile.

MARLIES

A cast of inconsequentialitiers, these came then: To ease, I think, the embarrassment and the loss of black Marie, and the recognition of a bigoted self residing within me far more monumental and defensive (and touchy) than the bigoted self that I had always recognized in the mirror (which actually wasn't so touchy)— and that I had often come near to seeing as a social sighting that was normal and acceptable for any (white) man in his mirror (I'm serious)—but that now I just wished to deny (despite all contrary evidence) and do a for-safety's-sake out-fade. Total, not just blacks. . . And, considering that I was I, the fadeout was not of much duration either: the fade-out quickly became a partial: One woman for one month I did manage to hang-in-and-out with; to be honest, because aside from being a wicked wit she was a growing success as a book-jacket photographer of authors who had come to rival that woman named Nabokov who had photoed just about every novelist in the universe and who I guessed was related to Vladimir, but maybe she wasn't—I've (determinedly) never even bothered to look up her first name (that I do know, but it escapes me—I mean, who gives a shit.). This photographer I locked-up-with was last-named Hammerbeck (just look on the hardback back covers of some novels where that meretricious name was scribbled over usually the shoulder or gut of the snapshot of the "genius author" in question), and by way of Hammerbeck's indefatigable self-sales striving and hustling and emailing of publishers and telephoning and retelephoning and never-taking-no-for-an-answer I learned to despise her ambition, her lack of taste, her crude (and so oft-praised) American go-getterism, and her "ability to capture the essence of Writer X's inherent depths"—this whether the praise was performed by a man or woman (so my contempt was not sexism, *I'm sure of it*). And, to be honest, I despised Hammerbeck's commercial-way also for its reminder to me—unstated but obvious—that I was by contrast a laxity, a lay-back programmee-for-failure, she being on the ugly climb to her back-jacket portrait-snapping way to fame—which eventually of course had her dumping nobody-no-ambition-me with his pathetic boyish environmentalistic paltry "save-the-air" *bicycles* (that he [me, I] no longer even gave a shit about, for that time-period anyway). . . But this energetic scrambling roughrider Hammerbeck photo-phenom did not throw me over until *after* she had thrown–me-over—I'll explain: she had shown me how, into sex, her ever-ready occupation-hustling could be transmogrified, which meant her sitting-on-top and riding me rapid-intense, as if she were slapping leather for her steeple-chaser's leap over hedges-after-hedges after the skittery fox or rabbit, she leaving every other horse behind—

and I learning by repetition-after-repetition-after-repetition just how psychogenically overturned the male-female ratio could be when the one who is most commonly on-top is without question (and without even one "reversal-of-fortune") the lesser-powered "object" "taking-it" on the bottom—so that he comes to quit even attempting the sex-carpenter-plumber drill-in position, nevermore even expecting it for himself. Or wanting it, I'm afraid (Hammerbeck actually *complained* that I didn't have the "gumption" to throw her over!). Man thus not the plougher but the ploughed—and man learning, after first loving it (or her), to despise the plougherette—while thirsting-for that overturning plough of hers—sure I'd done it this way before, but never with anyone so grindingly charged, so dug-in. . . And I will repeat: It was this supercharged Hammerbeck woman who did the affair-quitting, not the Alan Geist (who should have done that quitting—*he should have? Why!?*)

What came about then (some two weeks later) happened to be a turn away from hard-drive-woman towards the curved or skewed-drive, towards Europe, which Prayer—yes I'll call Marlies a prayer—arrived at GEIST'S BIKES with *no efforting whatsoever on any part of my own* (this last italicized sounded good, but it's only true when I decide it is, for wishing and yearning can amount to willing, as they direct one's attention and their aim):

"As I am here, sadly, for a year or more," the woman said. "I am in your market. I am here to outright buy." (She'd said that firmly, as if no one else who entered my store was ever there to "outright buy".).

She stood there in goldenish wire-rim shades, her light brown hair crowned by one of those black ribbon scrunchies; and she was smoking away with that arch regality which she must have been enjoying and perfecting for years; and *smoking*: this was unlike any Berkeley woman in sight for, say, the previous two decades. Men tend to Bogie their cigarettes, vacuuming greedily, possessively, like divers about to go under. This woman Bette Davised hers, drawing-and-puffing so elegantly as to be not quite real, as if it were a cho-reographed dance-step, her fingertipping was with a tender precision to and from her lips.

"Well, buy away, please," I said. "Do not let me stop you."

"Stop me? I do not understand. You wish to *stop* me from buying one of your bicycles? 'Buy away' means buy somewhere else?"

She was squinting at me as if I had just spoken in Lower Cantonese:

"You do work here?"

"I own the joint. I can't just leave it."

"You would like to *leave* it?"

"Honestly, yes. But that's another story."

"You are a Berkeley weirdo."

Her accent seemed Germanic, yet it didn't, not quite—there was a choppy sort of twang to it, and to her voice, as if my grandmother's Yiddish had super-imposed itself on the mumble-pie Bavarian dialect and turned it into a kind of Donald Duckish quack quack quack.

I thought that, in addition to the Middle-European origin she might have been suffering from a generalized speech defect, and so I did mean the sympathy with which I stared at her—which I could see immediately she did not appreciate, as if I were reducing her.

"I'm Swiss," this woman said. "*Zoo*-reesch."

Not being a total moron I did get that that meant Zurich.

She said: "Many people find the manner we speak an object of the ridiculous—especially Germans do; they believe that we have persevered their language."

'Perverted', obviously she'd meant that?

And I was wise (and strategic) enough to not correct her—as she was smiling now as if her linguistic and societal explanation constituted a victorious mockery of the entire German nation for their parochiality, their poor taste, and their false superiority in the face of her people's clackety-cluckish Zurich coo. "Swiss is Swiss," she said. "The mountains have made us, from eons. Our voice of speech is normal, it is not our *fault*. And it's lyrical, like the Austrian yodel of their *own* mountains; but *ours,* it is quite the nicer, less arrogant—if you listen and you grant it. And I love it too."

"It is beautiful," I lied.

And yes, what can I say, she was beautiful too—I'm not lying about that. In my depressed mood I wouldn't have even spoken with her beyond gears and brakes had she not been at least in the beauty neighborhood. For looks such as these one could easily tolerate the rattle-snap *Zoo*-reech tympani of Donald or Huey or Louie— that beloved family Duck. Beauty-description in the offing.

And I should say that even laden with that strangle-gargled click-clack, her congeniality did come through—along with an ingrained certainty, a sort-of high-toned cloud-riding evenness—an I-know-who-I-am.

Consummate American schlemiel, so easily impressed by *any* European accent, and *any* unchagrined European style, I loved her—you know what I mean by that: the nervous, superficial jumpy-tingling in the nerve-endings that make your heart do its swollen drummings in your ears (that even insipid *you* know well will fade). But I loved just now too how with a surprising sophistication this Marlies Amram trundled round my rows of bikes, touching, squeezing, petting, bending and inspecting—and naming names: Compagnolo and Shimano for gear "derailleurs" (and admiring yet how Shimano had had the genius to integrate shift levers with brake levers: "it allows, no? we riders to do our shiftings with not the need to reach down, away from the braking needs"); she actually named Avid, Truvativ, RockShox for drivetrains (she must have just read-up, that *had* to be—*a woman could not know such things*), all this while admitting that she did not know which was best for her ("my legs are so long for me" [I throttled myself into not-looking]), while with head-turnings back my way she questioned, and softly (as if not to intimidate this provincial?) about "bearings which are ceramic" and—can you believe this!?—*axel* configurations; and then she unembarrassedly took hold of and massaged her rear end as she compared "saddle-fits" and "sit-bone widths", while revealing without the slightest smile, "my behind, you can see, it is quite narrow".

Not my favorite in the 'behind' department, but Yes, I still 'loved' her. This bike super-savvy super-Swiss woman from, she'd said, Zurich, which, of all the un-romantic-sounding cities of Europe, had always sounded to me of ultimate unromance with its well-known aura of financial czars and un-named bank accounts and fund-launderings in the multi-billions—business-corruption-business. Obscene, especially to a run-of-the-mill (proud) pauper. But, this Marlies, she who had come to GEIST'S BIKES in long black tights (but topped by a jacket that didn't look cotton—maybe it was muslin? what-the-hell do *I* know about such feminine-expensivities?), her tights being such that a ballet dancer might have worn for daily practice, but which, I later learned, she had donned for bike-testing (having dispensed with her routine shiny black leather pants which in America was indicative of fancy street-hookerism), she had her gliding walk and her so sincere eyes—and this look of decent concern for "strange-sad-weirdo" me—while outside GEIST'S BIKES she did have along the curb her white Mercedes 190 SL Corniche (top up). And I do want to emphasize, emphasize: when I report my 'love' here, it is to be assumed (as if you haven't already assumed) that you recognize this over-used Geist-verb as a stylistic MO, not to be confused with, well "love", with anything mature, or spiritual, or even adult—or even intelligent. So, again, captivated—and fully explained—I'll repeat: *I loved her*, this Marlies Amram, who while in the process of introducing herself had corrected my naïve American monolingual emphasis on the second syllable of "lees" rather than the European—and obviously correct—"*Mar*", which made the entire name, when pronounced, sound, if nothing else, less American Jewish-routine suburban: less a Brooklynonian Mar*lene*.

"Have you ever seen me?" she asked.

"No." I assumed she meant in-the-neighborhood.

"I ask because I am a model and cover-girl. Or, was. Famous in certain circles."

And obviously not very modest about it—although she did self-mockingly crinkle her nose and forehead— many lines did appear.

I went with a low-key "Ah."

The impressed Mister Unimpressed.

She: "I do not like to mention what I am, or in reality I *was*, I know such immediate boasting upon meeting a person is a distasteful mannerism, but otherwise, I think, you would think me, seeing how I am now, which is a habitual with me, so they tell me in my sessions of Scientology, you would think me exhibitionist, and unearned so—and thus disgustable."

"Ah. I see. I understand."

Well, what she'd said was, despite its being con- fusing, reasonable (or not too 'un')—but *Scientology?!* Just what I needed, right?—that agora-booth of Ameri- can New World perfectabilianisms; that walk into a reality as forcefully baroque as the "deeply-perceptive illuminations" of a Mondrian or Balthus. A skewed reality that she apparently lived within, or, worse, was trying to achieve. Make a pretzel of yourself and call it straight. Was a film crew about to show up at my store and do a publicity shoot with this *Mar*-lees (on order) posing on and about drivetrains, shift-levers, handlebars and seats?—the title:

SCIENTOLOGISTS CAN BE PLAIN
EVERYDAY NORMAL PEOPLE TOO.

Of course I was beginning to lose grasp on my blind infatuation: *Won't I ever learn!?*

Probably not. As I said I was only *beginning* to lose

infatuation. Beginning is not Being.

Okay, it's past time now that I describe *Mar*-lies:
She was tall and she was thin, her form descended
straight-on-down—no arching sweep of hips; she was
just about my height, perhaps slightly taller (facing her,
I'd oftentimes stiffen myself to gain imaginary height);
under a sweep of that pulled-back hair (scrunchie-tied
for speed-driving that "Corniche"?), ochre-blonde that
hair, a high forehead which insisted-on a kind of sturdy
substantiality to shape her face, an unworked-on (and
probably unreal) gravitas, especially as the sides of her
face slanted rapidly inwards, her cheeks becoming then,
like her hips, nonexistent, and her basic expression one
of—need I even write it?—poise. Major super poise.
Too much poise for a lost bike-boy. But that poise came
also with a hint yet of tenderness, its origin her soft
eyebrows; but the tenderness was only a hint because
one could see only the roof of her eyebrows, the
remainder blacked-out by her (everworn) sunglasses,
those golden-rimmed barricades, which seemed to
cause no impediment to her examination of my bike
collection; I suppose these were expensive shades of the
sort that perhaps even illuminated the view from within
while blocking-out others' views from without, especially when indoors: models' and movie stars' (and
goddesses') sunglasses was what I (in my joyous un-
sophistication) imagined. And these sure did work well
with her.

"You are a model and cover girl and expert bike
rider," I said; or was that asked?

"No, Mister BikeMeister, I am a phoney-baloney."

Huh? Did the unassailable Scientologist Leader (or
whatever you called him—I'm not interested in

Googling-it-up), did he tell her such put-down things about herself at her intensive sessions?—where, I had "learned" (a documentary: no good sports on the tube), The Oppositional was the first step towards The Real, which was only the next step towards the next step, etc., towards *THE* REAL, which was the cosmos deeming you worth answering . . .

"I mean," said *Mar*-lies, "I ride bikes in Europe, yes, but I know nothing about their outsides and insides, it's *com*plicated, no? But this is Berkeley, yes?—where the people are so smart and they *know*—so I studied bikes on The Google before I came to you, preser*ver*ing."

Again I let slide the malaprop.

"As I say," she said, "I do not wish to look like what I am until I am not what I am and I am The Other Higher, or many Others brought within—and then, absorbing, My-New-Self—and then rising . . ."

Jesus Christ Almighty! So that too I let slide—what in the world could I do with it!? I had indeed guessed that about bikes she had just read-up, it was endearing to see her now owning-up—but *to be not unimpressive in Berkeley!?*—a misguided notion if there ever was one, as, face-it, if Berkeley is full of anything it is full-up with the most pretentious of idiots and failures who maybe could even use, what-the-hell, *Scientology?*

"So why really are you here?" I asked. "I mean, in my store. I mean, I'm glad to have you, sure; but you have a bike already, bought in *Zoo*-reech, and probably a good one."

"I did not ship any of my bikes to here from"—she grinned at my simplicity—"*Zoo*-reech."

"How come?"

"I am foul."

"Huh? *What!?*" (I smelled nothing bad).

She laughed a near-silent hissy laugh and then, like a schoolgirl she covered-up her offending mouth. "Oh, I am sorry. I fell into the Deutsch. In German, or Swiss, 'foul' means lazy."

I felt relieved. I said—

"Well, you do have a Mercedes sitting there outside. A magnificent one. You don't really need—"

"But, as I said to you, I do not want to look like what I am and am not—the magnificence. It is phony and a problem. I hate it."

Scientology again working its creatively improving wonders?

"But ," I said, "you do look"—shoulder-shrug—"magnificent." I'd tried to say it casual-like, not as if I were thunderstruck.

She said: "I wish you would not say that thing of me, of the magnificence. Surely, certainly, it is true, but it is impolite your saying—and also it is arrogant that I know it. So I do not like to *hear* it—so often-times. Or too to know it, so much often—but I cannot help it, because I *feel* it, the magnificence—and I *want* it. It's a torment, it's terrible. To like and want what you hate. Or feel you should."

"So this, not wishing to be 'magnificent', again it has to do with your, you know, Scientology?"

"No. Absolutely not, it doesn't. Not. It-has-to-do-with-*Me*. I *do* have principles."

She avoided my scrutinizing look by 'inspecting' the sunburst spokes of the, well, magnificent, Canondale, and then 'expertly' moving along the bike row, while then saying, "Sir, I'm lying—but I'm not. Lies, you know, they are truths, in telling and in hiding, and they are the opposite of themselves. So, The Scientology, it is the sine-qua-non: Yes, I admit, it does have to do with me, and my changing trying-to—if I can."

Oh boy.

She took her hand from the Compagnolo gearshift that she had now been especially fiddling with (which annoyed me—endless shifting not the best for a stationary bicycle) and she leveled my way her slightly-soft-transmitting top-of-the-eyebrows but mostly sun-shaded eyes (the effect of which was to convey a surprise that was immutably also suspicious): "I am here in the U.S. not for modeling nor to be on a cover of a *Zeitschrift* nor a magazine of any sort but because my husband Fritz"—if I was not mistaken her shades rose on the 'Fritz' because of a distinct cringe-loaded wince—"Fritz, he has been brought here to be the CEO, of, oh what *is* the name?—of the name I really could care less I have to say to be honest and not impressive falsely—which has so oft-times been my very wont—and this shows on the *e*-meters too, Scientology has these *e*-meters, very *sensitive*, and they show my phoniness along with my indifference to Fritz's position—the *top* position—at this so big company; you do know, I suppose, our Scientology uses the *e*-meters (this time she enunciated the gadget's name as if it were the world's greatest innovation since the wheel or the frypan), it is done with-by our listening auditors so—"

"I did not know about the *e*-meters."

I did know, but I wasn't much curious.

"Oh, *ah*," she went—and, indeed as if she had just realized how great was the universe and the universes beyond it—"and *now* it *does* come!—I must tell my *e*-auditor of this, how Fritzie's 'big-job' comes to me when I think of the Scientology—Fritz is now the CEO of the big evergrowing international"—that eyelid explosion once again—"EmeryTech?"

I had never heard of the joint. Which meant, considering me and my local interests or my lack of them, and my technological disabilities, more rule than exception: the name Emery Tech meant zip. It might as well have been a college with a football fight song.

"Is Fritz too a Scientologist?" I'd had this comical urge to join with this *Mar*-lies and say 'Fritzie'. Competition, contempt, ridicule, diminishment.

"No. Fritz is *not* Scientologist—hah, the very *thought*. Fritz believes it is a fool's game, a fool's paradise, Scientology."

As I say, I knew nothing about that psycho-religion, except that when it was mentioned everyone, including "my" Linda, sneered as if it were the Moonies or some illiterate evangelical nut-faith arisen from the swamps of Mississippi to fill stadiums (and its own coffers). . .

Again, this *Mar*-lies, she went "*No! Fritz, He is No scientologist!*"

So adamant, so final—so angry. I could imagine their stubborn dinner dialogues over her beloved "therapy". And their solid-extenuated silences.

"Fritz," she said, "he is as I say a CEO of a 'very-important-company'. He is *not* a Scientologist and he will never *be* a Scientologist. He is not so intent on the *spiritual* awareness of our living lives. These, they mean *nothing* to him. He does not believe a person can become *Clear*—we call it *Clear* when you have thrown-off your engrams."

I assumed that these 'engrams'—although they sounded like they were pills, like say aspirin ("Take two engrams and call me in the morning.")—were "units" of neurosis, of the numericalized delusions of one's ego.

As I've said, knowing little (meaning nothing) of hi-tech I had never heard of this EmeryTech of *Mar*-lies's husband who was apparently so highly regarded that he had been brought-in from Europe to head-up this burgeoning outfit that was well-beyond the level of start-up. Obviously EmeryTech was based in Emery-ville, which had until recently been known as a Poker Casino warren for Texas Hold'Em habitués and a small hothouse for streetwalkers and auto-body repair garages. Emeryville was midway between Berkeley and Oakland—it had only recently become that tech rival to Silicon Valley across the bay. Semi-high-risers of sun-reflecting glass like shining eyes were now up or going-so, sprouting as quickly as those of the emirates like Dubai.

Mar-lies had taken off her glasses, apparently in aid of her memory for the name EmeryTech, she revealing the most sensitive and harsh-cold and frightened and hurt and yet sympathetic (and generous) blue eyes I had ever seen; they were just now more of a grayish Mala-mut blue. But eyes are magnets for variety and hyper-bole. And lies.

After gymnastically bending round and pedal-pumping a few bikes and posing (unconsciously?—I mean, posing was her stock-in-trade) and she exam-ining and reexamining (or acting it?), she bought a Truvativ (I wondered if the purchase had anything to do with her simply liking the bike's name), she using a stark blue Lufthansa credit card and informing me that she could not recall her "secret code number", and I (while picturing her stretched-out luxuriously in her "cabin" in Lufthansa First Class) allowing, "Oh, just slide the damn thing, it'll be all right."

I hardly expected it, but she kept "dropping by" GEIST'S BIKES, now not by way of her fashionably old 190SL from the efficient *Fabrik* of Daimler outside Stuttgart (I could not help but think of Grace Kelly rounding the sharp-winding Monaco hills in her "gull-wing" until that daredevil driving habit destroyed her), but *Mar*-lies was now traveling on her new Truvativ— and so often to GEIST'S BIKES: To have me adjust this "*Apparat*", to inquire if the tread on her expensive-ly thin Pirelli tires were not too "mountain-speed-oriented with their deepset treads "almost rolling round the tires in their entirety and fullnesses rather than to advantage me (her) on these chockablock-broken streets of urban Berkeley;" or she came to have the handlebars "down-turned in slight to accommodate my body-length, the upper, which is not so longish due to the longwise nature of my legs—or otherwise I would be so tall as an Amazon."

When she said that she was not smiling.

And she was not kidding.

Although I should have (and I certainly considered that she needed much more "engram" work), I did not find these bikework excuses to be excuses: After all, what would such a privileged beauty—even if she turned out to be a solitary bird in a solitary gilded cage somewhere in the oh-so-academic Berkeley Hills— which was likely not true at all but was how I featured her in my masturbation fantasies—what would *Mar*-lies want with me but routine, tedious bike adjustments and pointless bike inquiries? By now in my life I was just trying to accommodate myself to the grim self-regard of a Mister Anonymous Nobody. (I had considered anti-depressants, I had even had my Internist write me a script, which I filled; but after reading of all the possible side-effects which did seem worse than the depression [or at least the effects of *my* depression], I took not a one [while keeping the tinted plastic container close-by on my side night-table.]).

Well, what *Mar*-lies wanted from me was Companionship, as it turns out. For outside of a literary reading group across the bay in opulent Mill Valley, where she labored for "a communing-like community" over the impossible to her but au courante "brilliancies" of David Foster Wallace ("I do not get the jests of *Invisible Jest*, it is not so funny—and he *did* commit suicide, so how can it be a *jest*?") and Paul Auster (and someone whose first name was Richard but whose surname she could not dredge up) *Mar*-lies had no one in Northern California with whom to attach herself but her pretentiously-named Scientological Associates of Berkeley ("I know that they are seen as creepsy in the U.S., this is not so in Europe, I swear it" [she lied or was misinformed—more of this later]), this absence of "closeby souls of closeby people" leaving then her own brilliant and apparently powerful husband Fritz Amram, who I was coming to sense was coming to see her as a growing albatross; thus then, well, there was *my-own-(depressed) self*.

So I loved her (I've already explained that callow-sappy—but on the well-worn road to overwhelming—"love"). I wanted to spend time with her. I knew that, knowing what I knew about Mar-lies there was no reason, absolutely no intelligent reason in existence that would justify such "fantasial" wanting, just as there was, knowing what I knew about myself, absolutely no intelligent reason in existence to deny its being "fantasial"—and *every* intelligent reason to comprehend why I would challenge the "fantasial" and thusly "make-it-real"—knowing what I knew about myself.

Sure I will call myself fatuous here—how could I not?—and making the call in order to not appear so fatuous—well, quite so fatuous; but I "loved" her. I've already said that She was Me (magnificent looks aside, Euroness aside, limited literariness aside, exhibitionism aside, sex-identity aside, wealth not even close). And, as I've honestly admitted, I was well the-Infinite Jest-side-of borderline-depressed.

I was Mister Perfect.

Okay, what I mean is, I made so much, so incredibly more of *Mar*-lies's "predicament" of loneliness (and abandonment?) than anyone should have (including any psychiatrist observing—even sans the fabulous *e*-meter [which sounded to me like little more than a lie-detector, a fucking fancified doodlewhopped polygraph]): I mean, would I have offered my services to a guy, any guy, or to a plain average-looking woman?—perhaps Mellors would have, as he did with Lady Chatterley, but he was the ultimate in deadly striving boors: granted I was a romantic, and granted a childish one, but damned if I was an unimaginative *boor* (I'm pretty sure of that.) Nonetheless to spend time with *Mar*-lies, I began taking valuable time away from moneymaking: I had to close up shop after Jamil quit me (my confusing behavior [unracistically racist?] with his friend Marie Smith? and/or some rupture in his connection to "my"

Linda?—if there was a connection; if there was a rupture), and *Mar*-lies and I went riding: Geist's Tour. She in cutoff Levi's jeans (I told her that this was a bad idea for biking—falls, bloody scrapes, torn knee-caps, torn ligaments—but she hadn't worn the jeans to show-off her perfect ass, rather to "blend-in" with what she viewed as "casual-adventurous Berserkeley"), she also cocooned in a denim jacket (that was not Levi's but Esprit), and with not even a T-shirt beneath, only a "conventional-normal-basic-athletic-bra"—luminous lemon-toned, also from Esprit (but fronted by this golden-looking symbol, an S interposed with some suspicious triangles, obviously The Sign of The Scientologist?—I was sure that privileged-she hadn't herself woven it, but had she ordered it?—Scientology had such regalia on sale?). On our first trip we made the rounds of what had made this really quite nothing-much town become an American Something: We cruised the Cal campus, I pointing-out the infamous Sather Gate which allowed entrance to the equally infamous Sproul Plaza where the Students for a Democratic Society, led by Mario Savio (the name meant nothing to her of course), they had taken over the "undemocratic" administration in Sixty-Eight (she looked quizzically: what-in-the-world was I blathering about?); we rode to the top of the Berkeley Hills where, from one especial spot, you could actually see the Sierras; we rode past Brothers Bagels, almost equally as famous as (the now unknown) Mario Savio—Brothers Bagels where the Jewish radicals of yore bought bushels for all the demonstrators, along with of course rashers of the requisite cream cheese and lox. *Mar*-lies went "Yuch" at the mention of such "delicacy", with the most engaging conspiratorial smile, meant for my implicating agreement—and which I returned, although I of course loved bagels and lox—and then I recollected how my father Moe, proud solitary Jew stuck in the Minor League town (then) of the Baltimore Orioles, how my father Moe had bragged to me that he had once treated his goyim pals on "The O's" (Babe Barna, Al Yogi Syhocki, Gus "Tremendous" Triandos—an idolizing kid-son-of-a kid-man never forgets such names), dad "treated" those redneck ballplayers to tastes of Baltimore's Lombard Street deli lox, and pastrami-Russian dressing too on corned-beef, and they had arm-wrestled, grunting away, right there at the sacrosanct Jewish deli—Moe's real Yiddish name, by the way, was Maish, and the Hebrew Moses (and although it was said "Describe a dream, lose a reader" by no less a readable page-turner-man than John le Carré, I ought to mention [quick] that I'd once had a dream where my father Moe and I had stood naked-and-earnest before a mirror and compared/competed with the relative sizes of our gonads, neither of us smiling, neither able to walk away from that sight). *Mar*-lies and I, we then cruised on down to the bay, we rested our bikes on the grass beside the inveterate kite fliers and doggie-trainers and unsmiling-grimacing joggers and we sat staring at the triangular Trans-America Building and the old 'Twentiesish Coit Tower of the city—where, finally, she went now sweeping-off her shades; and weeping.

Weeping!? Such wet eyes all aglisten, such complicated miserable histrionic eyes. Aimed at me, Alan Geist, as if she understood and paired-up with my apparent emptiness and longing (was it so *visible*?)—

just as I was supposed to "understand" (and join-in with?) *her* taste for loony-credulous Aesopian-phrased Scientology and distaste for any food so thoroughly Yiddish and unsophisticated as shtetlish bagels and lox. But even in obvious misery, inescapable misery—or at least drawn-down sadness—*Mar*-lies continued to display such poise, it was in-her-bones: it struck in what appeared (to me) to be elegant, twin talismans (talismen?)—this perfect-rounded dimension for any woman in her pouted lips, they so balanced and pursed in a sensitive contemplation (it definitely appeared 'sensitive'—to mawkish *me*). At such attributes as those swollen lips *(and not the god-damn dumb-looking Clara Bow "bee-stung"!),* at this fortunate for *Mar*-lies birth-given jewelry-of-nature, I could have stared forever—except the forever I was then imagining was now sullied by that stupid dolt-ass Scientology; and because she had in me *a friend, a trustable companion* (apparently), she suddenly had to talk through those perfect-jeweled lips of hers all about "the Practice" as if dissemination, The Big Proselytize, were the absolutest goodwill decree of the head maven Barnums of whom she had "studied" under: "Our Dianetics, it can have us go *Galactic*, Alan—I am *serious*: it is in its method a control and a redirection of the more lethal and venal and egotistic of our impulses, Alan, the *reactive* mind— which we all have—which for me is I want to be gracious and I am *not* gracious, not yet—even while I *appear* to be gracious, and appearances which are empty are so ugly. I take hold of the *e*-meter grippings, Alan, and I become aware, and immediately aware, of "The Me", my electricities that are criss-cross and even *double-back* in that criss-cross, that unfocus of myself that I am plagued with, in my case, *because* I am so fine a specimen—I *know* it—and so I cannot *help* but *expect*—it is an ugly thing, so to be so beautiful, it can hinder the up-spiring to *Galactic—beauty,* it is not a goal in The Galactic, except the beauty that is in the peace and rest, in the comfort-of-one's-own-skin, as the French say, *'elle est bien dans sa peau,'* and Genevans too in Switzerland. But I listen to Randolph, Alan, my auditor and my guide, and, although it is not so correct to say in a liberalism as is Berkeley, I am *taught* to do as is his bidding—*because I wish to, because he is my guide,* and it is *the* first step, that—because exactly that it is *not my* bidding or *my* want or *my* expectation of myself come natural, but a focus on the ME-who-is-to-be-*told* until that ME needs to be *not* told, and maybe precisely, the opposite, direct, of the *what-I-am*—as the *what-I-am* is certainly *not* the What-I-Am, but it is, in its way, The Enemy, *not* The Friend—of which, with the aid, the *forceful* aid—as it *should* be—of Randolph—and my *e*-meters for my *progress,* well . . . "

So: As the perceptive and informed and analytic talk of the black demi-hooker Marie Smith had so turned me off from her as a sex partner, or even as a funky love-partner, so the Scientobabble of the elegant well-favored Swiss cover girl *Mar*-lies served only to have me finding myself (and, really, *despite* myself [I'll give myself a tad of credit here]) wanting her more and more and more. *I'll talk to her, I'll help combat the nuthouse Scientological dictatorship, we'll read, who?—Marcuse was too old hat, Norman O. Brown the same, what say Richard Dawkins?—he may be too tough going for her, and his atheism wouldn't help one bit; then Who?* I had convinced myself that *Mar*-lies's immersion in Scientology reflected not only her urge to improve herself but her passion in the face of her intellectual ignorance—which *I*, a reader (at one-time) could redirect. A purpose in my life. And unlike with black Marie Smith, the oh-so-White-and-Euro *Mar*-lies Amram was in her lack of education only a challenge and not a fighting (defeating?) threat.

The *Mar*-lies threat would-could come in other ways.

And then *Mar*-lies, the beauteous *Mar*-lies, as we lay upon the bayside grass and—believe this—*not* touching, for I was not quite sure how to begin anything sexual with a confirmed and obsessive Scientologist (she might well see my overture as an "engram", a spillout from the stubborn-selfish "reactive" mind—which I guess it was), *Mar*-lies lay into me on the subject of her other health obsession: Homeopathy. "It is European, Alan, much moreso than it is in the U.S., even in educated Berkeley, and that is sad. Sad. That America is so naïve. Homeopathy, it fits so well with Scientology if you think—and you really don't even have to think, they are so close—it is the magic of the minimum dose, Homeopathy, the faintest dollop of what had caused your illness in a greater amount, to now be in-taken, which is so *healthy*. As one bad person has said, probably American"—and now she did venture to touch my arm at the bicep (but she did not stroke)—"it is, haha, the hair of the dog that *bit* you. As is Scientology—when you think."

Nineteenth century Euro-romanticism! Proudly, she told me too that it had been developed in "our *Bergland* of Switzerland."—and then came such an obvious history-twist of the history-benighted: she said that no lesser a genius that Jean Jacques Rousseau had approved Homeopathy, "Over two hundred years before."

I despised myself.

Mar-lies, I'd joked to myself—in obvious despair at having "loved" what I decided was really, in plain fact, in her beauty and her "grace" and her "taste", kind-of, well, what can I say? a "reactive" idiot.

Like me.

I decided then to never see her again.

And then, after thinking about her—and she did still come to GEIST'S BIKES, as she was still lonely-lost in a foreign land—I did what I was most proud of: I let fall-away, or rather I pushed-away, or rather I did not answer-to, my continuing desire for her. I would not exploit this deluded woman. I would not. From where in my psyche did this sudden decency come? From my history, from my fatigue with myself. Still, god this abstention was not easy. But beyond a kiss on the cheek (once or twice on the lips, but friendly-like), beyond what *Mar*-lies herself would have wanted and not-wanted, beyond what her Scientology would have told her and told herself to tell herself, and perhaps repri-manded her for had she gone beyond, we only bike-rode. That was it. I will admit to the pride involved in showing-off my companion when we passed-by some-one I knew, the implied and bolstering untruth, com-mon to this showoff, that I was sleeping with this Euro-model, that was the sum total of my falsity. And that pride, which was after all the artificial self-sustainment of a man who had not distinguished himself in life (or even found A-GREAT-INTEREST), and who was lost because of that failure, that twisted rebounding pride I could deal with (I told myself). . . I was A-Good-Person by way of simply accompanying this lost beauty of a woman, and holding-off the great ulterior. (Although I will admit to fantasizing at times that *Mar*-lies found my good behavior attracting, and desirable—and so wished to sleep with me. Unique ME.).

DALE

So: what a man wants in a woman is not necessarily what a man wants in a woman. Conversely (of course): what a man does *not* want in a woman may well prove to be what a man wants in a woman. . . . Until he realizes he definitely does not want that either. *Wider and wide in the gyre.* I can certainly imagine, say, Kafka, as a perfect representative of this ambiguity, he turning tail at the very moment when his desire for his girlfriend Milena had reached—well, reached beyond what he could not believe it could reach, and seeing in that a frightening (and absurd) Life Requirement in which he could not see himself alive and living in perpetuity: Herr Paterfamilias. Responsibility. Time taken from his scribbled brilliancies?—"brilliancies" which he did not believe were very brilliant and worth the abandonment of all, of everything. Except, alternately, he did believe that they, his life allegories and metaphors, were very brilliant and worth much life abandonment. . . And this life's backward-forward was what his stories were about too, weren't they?

*　　　*　　　*

You'll see this now by-way-of Dale—who, through no fault of her own had got me to considering that I might be, or be better as—well, this sounds ridiculous—a transsexual:

This Dale, this whatever-she-was (you'll see what I mean), she does this absolutely unique scissors-gait-with-a-cowboy-hitch into GEIST'S BIKES. And, this Dale, she is some ensemble—you really don't get glimpses of put-together Dale-types much, not in the places where you go or I go—or anyone goes, almost. And I'm not talking beauty—not in any sense the agreed-conventional of such. Dale was like a movemade fade-in-fade-out, like maybe that earnest dweeby nerd who could become, lickety-split, The Hulk—and there's a reason why I should be so what-you-may-think is caddish-crude employing the apish musclebound Hulk as a descriptive—however distant—in reference to Dale. As I said, you'll see. I don't believe I've mentioned that my bike "emporium" was situated just the other side of The Checkmate Café from the Berkeley-Oakland branch of Gold's Gym—where both Arnold Schwarzenegger and (believe it or not) Oliver Sacks had been known to "lift and press", as "spot-buddies", when they were in town. . . and they with this Dale Lorenzo too—she knew the both of them (not that that impressed me, right?), and she had indeed "spotted" for both weightlifters, and they for her. She who I'd seen many many times in The Checkmate (and once or twice in my favorite café, The Depresso, which was downbeat-anonymous-readerish-retreaderish and situated across the street [and *never* frequented by

Arnold nor Oliver: Last I heard, the Berserkeley old-timer frequenters of The Depresso were [supposedly] working on *The Berkeley Book of the Dead: From Mario Savio to Tom Haydn*]), and Dale never said word one to me nor I to her. Not one real word anyway, nothing "meaningful" beyond the inescapable excuse-me type things (these "hip" cafes were small). It was the Dale-formidability that kept me at my distance. And I don't mean exactly in Dale's case beauty-formidable nor stand-off-hostile-formidable nor surrounded-by-other-guys-formidable. What it was was the change-able-flex-flexible-formidable: Dale Lorenzo's physical-ity was caterpillar-chameleonlike, a totally undulant element upon which you just couldn't get one straight certain fix while you awaited the emerging butterfly or the steady monitor color, both constituted Dale's isness, she just went up-and-back, even while—and this was obvious—not trying to. Muscularity, I'm talking, and unconscious motion—and I believe, I sincerely believe that she was the kind of gal my dad Moe, who was the same way (sort of) might have gone for (and who poor *Mar*-lies would have found confused by her "debili-tational engrams"). Anyway: Once, when The Check-mate was all-tables-taken I'd asked Dale if I could share her table if I didn't say anything to her, and I said it very nicely-low-key, and Dale just nodded—so the both of us coffeed together and the-neither-of-us had shared word one. But now here she was striding into GEIST'S BIKES, my bailiwick.

"I've got a stationary at home," she said, while looking round, "but I do need an outside job."

"We had coffee together once," I said.

She once-overed me: "I guess I don't remember. I'm

sorry."

"It was your table. You were gracious. You shared it."

"That gets me a discount?"

I'd laughed of course, at myself—and also at the changeability in this woman's voice, and at how the wry crackling descent of it was so natural yet un-expected. Her first words had come out weakish, questioning, almost apologetic, but her second had dropped to a deep-hoarse, as a comedian's might out the-side-of-his-mouth on his unexpected punch-line. This transformation happened within, I'd say, twenty seconds. It reminded me too of how you used to hear happening with old black quartets like The Ink Spots harmonizing falsetto on that classic *If I Didn't Care*, or the Mills Brothers on *Glow Worm*, the middle guy going drama-down, and playfully, baritone then bass. But Dale was one-person. It was weird. But not unattractive.

I spread my arms about my bikery: well, check'em out.

She was in her Gold's Gym tights, which were a blackish-gray, so as she checked, leaning, bending, sitting forward on some bike seats, and lifting the red BMC in particular (with one hand), then lowering it and hoisting it again again (I supposed that she expected to be carrying the bike a lot—maybe she lived on the fifth floor of some non-elevator building) I had the opportu-nity to observe the incredible hallmarks that were Dale Lorenzo. She was what, in a man, one would call raw-boned, slender-muscular with veins arisen like piping as if she were wired on the outside of her flesh—you could see this latent potency not just in her biceps and forearms but also in her neck—I suppose a physician might have taken Dale's pulse by just looking at the beat bouncing-out the skin, no need to go feeling for it.

"I like to bike to my workouts—and they're all day," she said. "The prep biking tones me ready for the lifting."

I went with my Ah. Then, an inspiration: "You lift weights *all day*, do you? Then how do you do your job? whatever it is." But I had already guessed the story.

"I'm a body builder," she said. "That *is* my job."

"Ah."

"I hate to brag, but I guess I will: I've won Pose-Downs."

She said that matter-of-fact. No boasting smile, no chin-lifting, no drilling-in of eyes.

Pose-Downs? I'd never heard the phrase before. It sounded, at once, so countrified and so obscene, like some term used only at The Grand Ol'Opry—a dosie-doh. . . Or something dirty.

To clarify for me, she did a Pose. Before that bright red BMC bike, and smiling broadly, all bright white monument teeth, as if for a magazine photo, she semi-squatted, triangulating-out with her arms like a woman imitating a Balinese dancer, and of course flexing all over like you would not believe (she could even flex her jaw, which made her ears rise up alertly): even though her gym-pants were long, I could see her calve and hamstring muscles bulging from that, I repeat, Dale-slenderness; and beneath her slender-strap-top there rippled that washboard gut, almost in seeming antagonism to her breasts just above—which were, true, not large, but on the order of, I don't know, small biscuits or muffin tops? Could they have been rolled-up

Kleenexes? I'd wondered, as girls packed onto their chests (for dances and proms) in the early Fifties when they also wore crinolines—but I dismissed the wonder: a female body-builder might not forsake breasts if she had them, but she wouldn't feel the need to have them if she didn't have them: they might amount to self-deniers, giveaways, in a way. But again, what the hell did *I* know? Like *Mar*-lies, Dale was about my height—five eleven—although tallness was certainly the only similarity shared-by these two representatives of womanhood: from a distance an observer of the two of us might have taken *me* (macho-wishing *me*) for the woman. . . Yet, somehow, with her thick dark eyebrows and her looming eyes, with her wrinkly-cute child-nose containing but the slightest of bumps as if she were somewhat life-frightened or life-confused (or she also boxed?) she seemed like at base a soft person. A head-shot photo or a selfie would present to you a nice pretty girl standing perhaps in front of the monkey-bars of a playground rather than the rising bars and wheel spokes and intimidating (for some females) gears and grip-demanding brake-clamps; so, a soft-cheeked girl was Dale—a nice girl—with (however) her cheeks supported-by twin-jaws that were (sad-to-say) lantern-ish (but at least her jaws' chin was not indented by any threatening Kirk Douglas cleft—I'd wondered if she were glad of that, or to her such cosmetic prejudices—well that's what they were—did not matter in the least). Dale was a woman you saw as but a girl, and one you had to protect; but one you could rely-upon; and trust—if *you* needed protection—from tough guys.

Weird.

Not-weird.

She bought. "You want to ride it home?" I asked. As if she were a child and the bright red new BMC were a pair of fancy buckle shoes.

"I do want. That would be my test of it, riding home—oh I know it's fine. Don't worry, I won't return it back on you."

"I wasn't worried."

Her smile was, I think, the most endearingly innocent, and appreciative; it was a smile I had never seen before on a woman (except for that stigmatic grimace of poor street-fated Sally Asher, remember her?—Sally who I had, years before, lifted from the grime-gutter lands of The Mission and then, after my campus-use, one week later dropped back down into The Mission's reliably grubby depths again [*what a nice guy I was!*]). But, believe this: This Dale's smile also managed to be now one of the assurance of a modern woman, one thoroughly confident of herself, or acting so. The kind such Modern Woman would force herself to present, if need be, while facing-off against the self-conceit of a Modern Man—like say the challenging eyeball-dominion of Arnold Schwarzenegger or even the curious perspicuity of the famous intellectual (*and body builder at Gold's!?*) Oliver Sacks.

If ever a person's physical appearance and psychical projection did not jibe, it was this twin sharing of existence that carried-on—and seemingly with ease—within the double-persona of this Dale Lorenzo.

Did the two share such bifurcation as easily as displayed?

Were "the two" really, triumphantly, but one?

"Those Pose Downs you won," I went with because I was a body-build idiot, "You beat all the *men*?"

Most women would have answered with some line on the order of indicating what I have just called myself—an idiot. Not Dale. She eyed me poutingly as if I were a stray dog or a pre-kindergarten child and said, "You're silly, don't you get out too much? How could I beat *the men*! First to say, the criteria are different. Second to say, well, you know, men are *men*."

But I had that night persisted: alone, I had actually tried to imagine such a competition, with Dale aligned in counter-pose to some male mega-monsters, like the determined weight-lifters that come these days from China and Mongolia. Why had I even worked-on picturing such ludicrous pair-ups? Even an imbecile wouldn't have—despite that these days you see on TV some girls wrestling boys in highschool competitions (and you sympathize with the internalizing battles going on with the boys: *What if I lose!? I won't be able to live with it!*) . . . But now, before Dale, as she wheeled her bike out of GEIST'S BIKES, I simply shrugged.

"And no-no," she added, and sweetly, to make sure I fully understood The Pose Down: "Hey, it's just bodies-competition—not pounds *lifted*. God, I just beat out all the *women*."

"Ah, I knew that," I lied (sort-of), and earned for myself another Dale-innocent megachild-sympathetic smile-grin.

I've got to say now—and I'm pretty total damn sure of it—more than I was repulsed by Dale's wiry brawn, and confused by it, far more was I drawn to her sweet lovely face and temperament—and we went out. The movies, downtown Berkeley, summertime, she in short togs and tight T-shirt, and naïve-happy so to be (it appeared), as that shirt of hers presented the large full-front drawing on red backdrop of a fat black boxer with his gloved dukes up and his tongue stuck out (amusingly)—and I cannot deny my distress at that goofy shirt as we walked down Shattuck Avenue (might it not be regarded by some of the blacks who dominated downtown as hostile-mockery of their own kind?), and I cannot deny my discomfort and absurdity in the wrapping of my right arm—not Flab City but not Muscle City either when compared to even her staunch-sturdy left, which enfolded my ribcage (tightly, of course)—I wrapping my nothing-much arm about her super shoulder, doing that To-Be-a-Man (here against all contrary odds and evidence), and this one man acting undistressed and undiscomfitted by "his girl's" not needing "her Man's" Protector Superfluous Nonsense.

Just walking together was thus so damned complicated—one might say it was, itself, a Pose-Down.

We saw—as she'd suggested it—Anthony Hopkins, as Hannibal Lecter in *Silence of the Lambs*, he being got the better of (or the equal of) by FBI lady (lowly *recruit* really) Jody Foster. Interesting, Dale's movie choice—Jody Foster, although in perfect FBI shape, was hardly a great body-specimen—but this was a film-popular. But more interesting was strong-built Dale's cuddling-curdling-up for security within her "sturdy" Alan's (nothing much) form as Lecter bit and ate the face of his unsuspecting cage guard.

Oh I will protect you, my poor frightened little girl. I can see by your rolling-small within my "iron" shell that you are not Gay, not Lesby-likely anyway, but it would be great if you would only but just ease up on the crushing envelopment of my midsection by your Jaws of Life forearms by which it's usually the Fire Department rescuing victims trapped in their cars after bone-crushing accidents.

As I *recollect*, I'd gasped, and Dale, huddling, movie-fearful Dale, asked, "What's wrong?"

I'd *shrugged. . .* And that shrug, considering Dale's envelopment, was not easy.

We did not sleep together, not that night. Maybe I could have led this confusing (but not-confused) woman-girl to the bed and done my very best, all things considered. And all things, after-all, could not but *be* considered—and it's not that I was, well, not exactly scared: I was, foreglimpsing our lovemaking and its, for me, psychical uniqueness, I was concerned-worried-apprehensive, and calculating, as if nagging-at a problem in arcane human architecture or geometry.

And I believe that Dale sensed that. Like as not she had run into such ambiguities before. . . And, I stress, she was a woman who was, if anything, sensitive.

Dale was simply Dale: she certainly was not going to change her makeup.

And by now I had had enough experience with girls and women to know, and know deeply, that such change was neither to be refreshing nor rewarding—nor, really, to be reached-for. A man wishes for a woman to change and when she does—*if she does*—he gets a woman who is not the woman he visualized as her changing-to; and that changed-woman no longer wants this man who had prompted her changing. . . Not that he now wants this changed-woman anyway.

*   *   *

In the misguided interests of, call it good equality, which would in turn be in the interests of good Sex chemistry, what I could do—and this kept occurring to me—was, say, challenge Dale to some contest that I might be sure to win and thus feel myself, while with her, more of a Man. Excluding the ludicrous, such as nine-ball pool (the gambler's game) or poker, where even if I won (and I would have won, *I would have won!*), I would have won a quite nothing, and ruling-out the sporting events where I most definitely would have lost, and lost bigtime (lifting weights; clambering up one of those majestic Berkeley rocks, where Dale's superior legs and arms would have had her shooting to the peak in nothing flat, and excluding arm-wrestling [how humiliating *that loss* would be!—especially if experienced out in the open at the wornout-retread radical Café Depresso], and excluding even bike racing—Christ that pumping-action of which her calves and hamstrings and quadriceps [which put me in mind of baguettes] were capable), I came up with a very simple answer: sports themselves, by which I meant what the average Bozo of an American male meant when he talked-of sports: pitching a baseball; batting-about a tennis ball; tossing a football in perfect spiral; maneuvering shake'n'bake moves on a court in basket-ball—I was quite sure that I could "take" Dale at these. Strength was certainly necessary in these activities too, but infinite bodily *skill* was the thing in the main. Fucking *Man Skill*. My daddy Moe Geist skill. Why hadn't I thought of those Real sports firstoff? *Ball* Sports.

Dale, being a game person, and an eager-to-please one, and one eager to learn, was game.

I defeated her, I outclassed her, at every goddamn *real sports* game.

I reveled in it. Internally of course.

It made no difference. Firstoff, her admiring smiles said that she was glad that I had beat her (although I didn't trust those smiles—they were just too kind); and second, all I had to do was just *look* at this muscle woman who I liked so much for the prettiness and sweetness and amenability which obliterated the musculature, but which sinew I seemed to not be able to do without—nor, for that matter, *with*—well, *staring at that Musculature* that I was pulled forward to and pushed back from, and then pulled forward and pushed back, so constantly and immediately and spontaneously of-a-piece, that I couldn't but feel schizophrenic and childish—I had to question, no, not my sanity, but my own sexual identity. My erotic limbo? My loving limbo too. What in the world did I *want*—or *could* I want!?—without questioning that wanting.

The making of love?

Dale made dinner at her flat, which was, indeed, on the fifth floor, the top floor of her building on Cedar Street, only three blocks from GEIST'S BIKES and the famous Gold's Gym. A tofu and shrimp mélange on a hefty heap of Spanish tomato rice—whereas I'd suspected that from the dinner preparations of a determined full-time body-builder such as Dale I would be sitting down to at best a burger and fries—and perhaps a protein-loaded bottle of ENSURE PLUS (my dad Moe, he drank'em); this all the while my thought-engagement was fully beyond food (of any kind) but about what would be coming—and I don't mean desert, I mean The Bedlified Bifurcation of the unlikely she and I. . . . But then again there was still the alternative, the possible exodus: I could have taken off, thanked her for dinner, suggested maybe a nice easy bike ride in the nearest future, maybe up the two-thousand foot high Mount Tamalpais, and let that "fun" be the ball game.

I couldn't.

I wanted to go to bed with "my" Dale.

I really did want that. For, even if I did not "love" her, as I had already "loved" just about every girl or woman who had had the fortunate-unfortunateness to have entered GEIST'S BIKES, I admired her. And sure, I wanted to know what such union between us, such mentally complicated togetherness, would be like.

It might constitute an awakening greater than that mumbo-jumbo promised by Scientology. It might even serve to mature me.

But once Dale and I got ourselves naked and she lay herself down on her (quite narrow) singlish bed (I thought of my old dorm bed and, again, my poorly treated Sally Asher), her small breasts fell to the sides and I couldn't but perceive her chest, now deprived of what femininity it did possess, as, not a boy's chest— because of all that well-developed muscle—but of course as a man's chest, although, thankfully, without any trace of filament. A Scandinavian man (but with dark brown hair—short-cut) laying there before me.

"Are you alright?" she asked, her eyes descending to discs as in one encompassing swoop they looked her own self over—and my own lifelessness between my own legs.

I was, I wasn't—so I nodded.

I lay down on top of her, as that was of course de rigeur and it obscured my limpid noodle of a penis from her sightings—her speculating sightings?

Once on top, staring down into Dale's sheerly-unmistakable woman-eyes, questioning eyes, even supporting eyes (I'm pretty sure of this), those large brown marbles that she must have had swelling monumentally when she had sought succor from evil Anthony Hopkins in my arms, my penis did announce itself as if called to the rescue with a choral fanfare (this did surprise even me), and I saw Dale smile—it looked like reassurance. And accomplishment?

I kissed her and damned if I didn't find myself getting harder.

We had sex. I did not plough hard into Dale, although I imagined that her powerful presence must have evoked such a contending urge among most men, assuming there was such a thing for Dale as "most men".

From the apartment underneath I heard a bossa nova, of an old song that I had always loved, even before it had been arranged into a Brazilian beat: *Change Partners*. Certain jazz numbers had always had me wishing that I had taken up music—why had I not? Moe, thinking that was effete and reservedly (and deservedly) girlish? (Moe had once beaned a batter who had girlishly wriggled his hips at Moe up there on the pitcher's mound—trying to unnerve him, the [in Moe's mind, no doubt] pussy-ass Jewboy). . . I tried again with Dale (what a sad word, "try", in this circumstance); this time the bossa rhythm from below was helping, sonofagun—and I know that she felt that, it was as if we were dancing, our mutual rhythms fit. . . But the song, with its sinuous melody and then its trans-formative long note bridge-change like a plea, also had a negative effect (*why does this always have to be!?*)*:* it had me wishing that, just then, with the singer im-ploring to the girl, *"Must you daance/ ev'ry dance/with the same/ fortunate maaan?"*, that song had me wishing that I too could change partners, perhaps to the exudatious-dream-ridden-actressy Suzanne of long gone-by.

Good old me, I went and got myself depressed, and I know that Dale couldn't avoid seeing that falling-in that happened to my face just as if her breasts, unlike those of old Suzanne's, or any girl's since, had just decided to let go of themselves, give-up, go-away, and collapse, dispensed-with to the sides—exhibiting what had remained as foundation, the true-deep-hard-hidden?: the *manliness. Her manliness.* . . At sex with Dale, as her musculature and her tendons went taut and then relaxed, at least to a semblance of softness, an imitation of female-softness, I had felt so transported, up-and-back, from dreamworld to realworld and return, from fight to struggle-to-dance-away-the-fight, and back, not knowing which was the more substantial and lasting, which was—at moments anyway—the more exhila-rating (as if I had conquered all genderish prejudices as to how man-and-woman should always be!) and which transportation was the more defeating and repelling and escapist and, worst, *and worst*, the most appropriate for myself, the more fitting or the more drowning, and how could this not be extraordinarily upsetting! I would approach Dale's soft-sweetnesses and as I did get nearer to her a voice, *my* voice, would pull at the reins of my being, yelling NO! I was learning, or accruing a taste of learning, who this mixture called Alan Geist was and how many varied people he was—and even, and this is the most difficult to admit, if I were even of a male dispensation or some half-drifted-off one, one which was written in basic blood, substantial, or one which was written in the form that flowed and changed. It seems unnecessary to say this, but I'll say it: this was the most confusing, the most dizzying sexual experi- ence of my life—to that date, anyway. And what that means is that it was the most unsettling *experience*, sexual or not: even the suicide of my father could not compete with this gyroscopical spinning of my identity. (Does that sound insensitive? Well, I should say, I have to say in defense, the self-death of my father, with its built-in message of rejection of myself [Moe'd left no note], that was a monument, a gravestone, that had not clobbered me full and immediate until, as I lived through my thirties and well into the true perceptive adulthood that should have come with one's forties, had had its growing, overwhelming, effect.]).

In bed beside Dale now (unaware I think that I was not even thinking of *her,* how she felt, fulfillment? Dis- appointment? embarrassment?—and that this indiffer- ence of mine to a lover of mine was *because of the lover herself, the sexual mixture that she was, the PHYSICAL mixture that she was*)—I was pressed and shoved-at hard by the question that I had always had, and nurtured, and stifled—and now that we had ex- perienced sex (sex?) with each other, now that we had achieved some level of intimacy which was (at least) greater than infinitesimal, I could ask it:

"Why do you do this?"

"Why what? Do what?"

"You know."

"No, I don't. I do not."

I couldn't further press it.

But of course she knew what I'd meant. The rigidly non-expressive angling-in of her face showed that, a sort-of forced, conscious, anaesthesia, as if she'd been caught shoplifting. She knew what images and realities had troubled most of the men she had been with, if not all—if there were such of any. She might well have been waiting and waiting for the inevitable: my voicing of The Question. Or maybe she had decided that this fellow, the nice bike man Alan Geist, was different (a judgment I was certainly guilty of myself, albeit in a different category), that even if he, I, was disturbed by doubts he, I, had managed to still those doubts until, just conceivably, they had diminished and dissolved—that would be a girl's wish held by *this girl, damnit,* Dale, who was a girl through and through and had "chosen" to be, nonetheless (*Why!?*), not "a normal-looking girl". . . And who, in our void now, no, our bed-furlough, was now staring blank-eyed at some photos and painting-prints on her wall, one an innocuous David Hockney(like) repro of a pale-drawn swimming pool before the modernish pillars of a white house, two bathing suits draped over the water's entry railings, one that of a suited man standing in a cocked straw hat who, with his jaded blue eyes downcast and cynical, appeared to be considering some act dissolute—or indifferent (even if the act might be drowning); the other bathing suit that of a woman muscular not unlike herself, Dale, smiling as if advised-to by the photo-taker—she naked (as if readying for a Pose-Down?). But, as I said, Dale was staring blank-eyed.

"Why shouldn't I do what I do?" she said, "it's a real thing. It's *normal*."

I was sorry I had asked: I said, "I know it's a real thing."

"Then what is with your *asking*?—as if I had committed *murder*. Alan, I'm not a Lesbian, you know."

"I know it well." I trying for even a catch at humor.

"I tried it once though. I'll admit it. Why not?"

And so now we were getting somewhere?

"But I didn't inhale."

I went with, "Haha,"—as she was grinning.

"Look, Alan. Men do it," Dale said. "And I'm not talking the homosexual. I mean, men, they build their bodies far bulkier-up than do we women—those of us who body-build. People may or may not like it, to their taste, but it's okey-dokes with them, as regards the men. It's *normal*, as regards the *men*. It's just another way to *be*. But with us *women*, well . . . "

"Life's unfair. I know."

" 'You know'. You keep saying that. As if you're telling me *you-don't know*."

I caught my next 'I know' before it could make its dull cowardly escape from frontal cortex to vocal chords and the end-of-a-relationship (such as it was).

"Alan, I love it," Dale said.

Again my wise blockade of cynical cortex and vocal chords. My substitute was—

"I do understand how you feel."

"Oh Alan, thank you for saying that, but, you know, you have not a clue."

I was staring at her, now with hesitance—she

seemed on the verge of either crying or further lashing out. Or both. It was obvious that she could beat the shit out of me if it ever came to such a pass, although I knew she didn't have that sort of aggressive (Moe-ish) male stuff bulked-up within her. I just closed my eyes—to transmit I knew not what, except maybe sympathy and passivity. . . And acceptance?

"I love it"—her arms had spread out in the narrow bed as if she were standing on a pulpit, explaining to follower congregants who toiled in the fields all day and never had much leisure time to think and care and connect—"I love it because it is my *life* saver, Alan, my way of *being*, in a way, I don't know; a painter, like, or a writer who confesses and then builds herself *out* from so *within* from her confession—does that make sense?—and she builds herself out in a way that, say, what? a dress designer couldn't, or a woman social worker or even a woman psy*chiatrist*. It's vain, it's *savior* vain, *self*-savior, and why not?" And then, she actually, tenderly, with her index fingers, slipped-open the closed lids of my eyes so that I had no option but to absorb her, all of her (which had me feeling feminine): *look at me,* she was instructing, she was pleading— *damn you!* "I love *do* it, what-I-do, because I love to, myself, *look-at-me.*"

I continued my looking and I continued my sensation of feeling feminine—and not knowing of course what that feeling was.

And walking home, I thought: what would be her male corollary?—a man starving himself to be weak and rail thin? A man going Gay?—no that is not a parallel. And then I thought: No, the whole thing, that is different, as men and women, they are so different. A man starving himself to become a skeleton is a man who is wishing himself, driving himself, to invisibility, to oblivion and to death—not to becoming a woman. . . And a man going Gay, well, that is just a man going Gay. Not even of the vaguest relationship to Dale and how she'd chosen to live. . . Except in that vaguest of relationships we cannot quite ken because it is comprised of so many human elements that are possible we are relegated, in a sort of decent fairness, to simplistically label the-whole-deal "choice".

And now, before continuing-on with Dale I find for honesty's sake (and living-with-myself's sake) that I must intrude with The Experiment, as here is certainly the best place in which to place it, the instance most relevant, although from other angles, from most angles, it is nothing but chocked-with batches of that beggardly word "choice", which means that it is, while relevant, of quite no relevance at all (you'll see what I mean)— and that even includes that encompassing word "sex"... The Experiment I'm hinting about happened with Shel Sevenecker—I had mentioned it briefly in the very first chapter—and about which now, considering Dale Lorenzo and her (call them) peculiarities and my mixing-in with them, I now bring-out for you all my most (call it) peculiar peculiarity: it would no doubt be *the* embarrassment for most men, that is most men who were not Gay—for with them it would hardly constitute a peculiarity at all. Rather, a normality—such prologue will of course put you now way ahead of me; although your anticipation will be headed-off wrong: I am about to confess a Sex-somersault, yes indeedy, but the somersault was not driven by any eros-need, *I swear it, I swear it!*—it was, what? intellectual? scientific? adventurous? curious? childish too. Elaboration: Stout Shel Sevenecker (he resembled the actor John Goodman) and I were best friends—it was easy to be my best as I had few friends. Male ones, as might be imagined by anyone annoyed (or bored) by my obsessions being glommed onto the female—or, even more annoying (I know it) my hankering after the-good-bad-male-hero like my dad. . . But I did have Shel Sevenecker. Shel was a man who was admired by all (just about all) and belittled by all (the all of the all), as the impulse to admire (even someone justifiably admirable) is too often followed-up on by the compulsion to stifle that admiration, to bring-down the man-of-well-founded envy: Shel, for example, did not work for a living—he never did, never had. But he was a man well-occupied. Shel read the classics, and by The Classics I mean both "the classics", like Plato, etc., but also The Classics like Joyce and Proust, etc.—and by read I mean glutton-gorging, the great devour. (I once heard a Classics Professor—a childhood friend—admit that Shel knew more of "The Noble Greeks and Romans" than he did, that professor.). So, Shel did not survive on wages, how could he?, but as did Blanche DuBois (and Joe Cocker in song), he relied on "the generosity of friends"—like me—who would lend Shel both their sofas for sleep and reading, and their bucks for beer and eats. And Shel was not a miserable mooch, he was not a slovenly mooch's mooch—he was "a nice guy",[5] he felt for folks, he confided, he confessed, he congratulated, he

---

[5] You older readers, you might recall Fred Exley's perceptively hilarious "Journey on a Davenport" in his *A Fan's Notes*.

consoled (he stole—in a minor key—to give gifts), and women (some), they loved him too (Interesting thing about women and their insightful likes, their very canny likes—that old maxim, you know it, "whom women will embrace."[6]). . . So: As was the usual with Shel, we had become passionately and frustratedly worn-out with each other's talk (I especially with Shel's inability to *not* call forth Democritus or Tacitus or whoever), we were dragged-down by our rattling-on about our empty "commitments" (environment; wages; pharmaceuticals; universal insurance; anti-gerrymandering ["It ain't like that in Europe!"], which opinions were sincere but empty bullshit re our efforts to do anything like, say, organize), we were just wiped-out by our routine-rote (impotent and we knew it) analyses of "The Great American Injustices", which at least my "ex", Linda, and "my" Marie Smith were working against and we men weren't doing squat. Then, after our usual cadenza which was comprised of "the hopeless hope for eventual morality over profit once capitalism evolves— or devolves," we weren't sure which (remember, we were stoned), my pal Shel and I talked, what else?— Women. Sex—and not necessarily with morality. Only this one time, while we were doped-up on dope at Shel's house (we called it that, but of course it was but one of Shel's multitude of "crashes" [he kept a rotatory list]), we, as the illiterate (which is most people) now say, "took-it-to-the-next-level"—we, as the illiterate (which is most people) now say, went "awesome": "Let's see what it's like for chicks, the whole domination-submission thing. For starters, let's suck

---

[6] Infelicitous Wallace Shawn as Diane Keaton's greatest lover ever, in Woody Allen's *Manhattan*.

each other off." Did Shel suggest that?—did I? Remember, we were stoned—I have to keep repeating that proviso. . . But my best guess is that the promulgator here was the "holed-up mega-leach" (one of his host-benefactors called him that) who was also trying (on his host's sofa in his spare time [haha]) to reconcile Seneca's stoicism with his joy—Shel.

"You're kidding," I said, already picturing the mutual sucking-off of-and-by two buddies, our twin penises, possibly (probably?) erect, Vladimir and Estragon hanging on each other (and dodging each other) for salvation? My god!

"Nope," said Shel. "Not kidding."

"I'm not Gay."

"You think *I* am?"

"Nope. I've known you for thirty-five years. I would have known that by now."

"People can cover-up the nittiest-grittiest of themselves. It's the nittiest-grittiest that they *do* cover-up."

"What are you *saying*, man?"

"I just had to say that. Plotinus said it—maybe *he* was Gay; and a man has to say what a man has to say. I didn't mean *me*. . . Necessarily."

But you could tell from the supercilious repartee way we were carrying-on that the both of us were nervous:

"You'd better," I said, "not be Gay."

"You hate Gay? What would be the difference what we're doing if I were?"

"Honestly, I'm politically *in*correct. I mean, I don't *hate* them, but—I don't know what it is. It's just that they—their presence . . . the unsettling nature, it. . . unsettles."

"That's stupid."

"Screw you."

"Al, it's our guy-unsureness that's at the bottom. Of everything. It's so easy to fear the slightest trembling, waffling, the weak-knees at our bottoms, some dick-love might sneak in . . . we've all got that."

"So say the shrinks."

"And they're right. And, for some reason—it's just, well, I've never seen this done in lit before—I've never read any Arab lit—and I've never heard of anyone doing it in real life. Not when neither man was Gay. It seems to not have a point, but it *does* have a point—when *neither* man is Gay. Damn, I've thought a lot about it."

"Apparently."

"Haven't you?"

"Let's not do it. There's no need."

"Let's *do* do it. There's need. To be full-fledged, as human, to *know*. The unexamined life is not worth living."

"Somebody said that. Who said that? Rousseau? And you know, he wasn't the nicest in his personal—"

"Montaigne, he said it, okay?"

"You know, you can be an annoying pedant at some times—too often."

"I try. And you're trying to change the subject. The act that we're about to—"

"Shel, I'm asking again: you haven't been covering-up your . . . 'nittiest-grittiest'?"

Eyes shut for gravity, for drama, he slowly, profoundly, shook his head. Wordlessness can be so much stronger than mere words. Stronger, because the definite is most definite while it's unascertainable. It's potently indefinite.

"Women," Shel now said, "they do it all the time, with each other."

"No they don't. Only gay ones."

"No, man, I'm telling you. They do it all the time, women. They can all switch to lezzieness up and back fast as squirrels on a bannister—they're not like us men. They're different, women. We men, we've got to *be* queer, turned-on *queer*. Women don't have to be turned on. It's rational with them. It's decision, choice. It's their take on morality. On sensitivity, understanding, I'd say, being *inside* the Other. Women, they've got free-will."

"And that's why *we're* doing it, *if* we do it—free-will? To prove that we *choose* to choose, even though we men, we don't choose or *have* to choose or have to not? To do it. By-and-large, as we're not queers."

"Something like that, whatever you just said. Sans the female sensitivity."

"As we don't *want* to do it or *have* to do it—so we'll *do* it?"

"Again, whatever you just said. *R*esearch."

For the sake of our own identities we decided then to consider that what we were about to engage-in then was thusly a beyond-convention, a beyond-the-"correct"-right-and-wrong; an, as I said above, psycho-scientific investigation into you-could-say free-will, kind of—with maybe some dose of obsessive compulsion and soul-friendishness thrown-in, we subjecting ourselves to the inner-beings of The Other—haha, such nincompoops we were—we figuring our "inner beings" would be brought-out and filtered (and *changed*? and *improved*?) by way of the beings of Our Selves and our

Othernesses-of-Ourselves-and-of-The-Other and The Other's doing all the same. Holy Shit! Double-talk? Triple Talk? Well, we people, we humans, we are more than even Quadruple-Talk can ever come close to capturing—no? (and remember, we two were very very stoned [or am I just cowardly bringing that up just now?]): Okay, we would be—and I believe Shel quipped this out of an edgy-scared chagrin (although maybe, like the stoned-excuse, I've come up with this in years subsequent)—we would be Neil Armstrongs: ("Two small suckoffs sucking-off for two (unGay) men, one Great suckoff sucking-off for (unGay) mankind.") . . . Nervously, unlike how we would do were we in the locker room at the Y (we'd never go to the famous Gold's Gym just beside my Geist's Bikes, as we were too flimsy-bodied for that place with its Arnolds and its Dales), we took off our pants and Hanes Jockeys (Shel's were tents). We were standing by the sofa of Shel's benefactor *du moin*; we stared, not at our uncertain dipping eyes but at our midsections (which were fairly okay to be honed-in on); then even those, our stomachs, became too intimidating, too threatening, and we looked away—I at the piano of Shel's "crash-for-the-month", a stand-up studio job which had atop it a photograph of Shel's homeowner friend John Reid (another lawyer, but one who made real money), his wife Rachelle and their ten-year-old daughter Susan (who, I imagined, of course, was now comically smiling-down upon us from her gilt-edge photo).

"You go first," said Shel.

" 'Go. Whadayamean 'go'. *You* 'go' first."

"It's my house."

" '*Your*' house."

"Putting me *down*. See?—that's what this whole thing's about. Losing that crying put-down need; after we've done-the-deed we'll lose that sorta shittola, that's my hope. It's so *male,* y'know, that put-down crap. And so *Jew*-male, miserably so *kike*-ass—irony the last refuge of the impotent, don'cha'know. Cunt don't rag and word-smirk, not anywheres near where we *men* do—*Jew*boy men—haven't you *noticed* in your pathetic *life*? No, we *have-to* do it, what we're about to do. Anyway, *I* get to choose who starts the start. It was *my* idea."

"You are such a child."

"Your excuse for backing-out."

"I ain't backing-out."

Tent Haneses down, gone, Shel sat on "his" sofa. His thighs, which I'd never really noticed before (why should I have?), I noticed now—and they were hairy buggers—but maybe they weren't so hairy, I was just so on edge, each house crack (benefactor John Reid's house sat on the active-motion Berkeley Hills, just above the Hayward Fault), each little crepitation be-spoke potential temblor to me. Anyway they had that skinniness, those Shel thighs, that taut man-muscle devoid of the cushioning that women have, even sinewed women such as Dale with her magnificent national award-winning quadriceps. . . Deciding hesi-tation was vacillation was indecision was cowardice, was bourgeois, was lostness, I went bending my knees to the task. Shel began to spread his thighs—and yes, yes, they were hairy sonsofbitches. Shel (with a realist brainstorm I guess), he suddenly stopped spreading his thighs, which meant, as with a cagey sex-wise woman I would have to effort the widening, that entry-opening of my friend. But then I realized that as Shel was *not* a woman—there was no need for the thigh-spread (I actually had to *come to realize this*!?), I could lift-up my pal's penis and just blow him as is—a sort of drive-by fellatio; which did however put the kibosh on my aiding myself by imagining that my buddy here was a woman (which I couldn't have succeeded at doing anyway as the male scent is different, it's sweatier, more oniony—you realize that just as soon as you get your nostrils down there—you cannot learn this on your own as you cannot bend down onto your own groin, unless you are, I guess, a Chinese gymnast [on serious steroids].). . . Shel did not have an erection, and I was thankful, very thankful—what such hardon might have said about he-and-myself, and about his quite perhaps lying about his gayness, and that hardening of his might then have led me into a libido-interest that I (think) I did not wish for—i.e. a hardon-by-subconscious sympa-thetic copycatism (like a "referred pain" that doctors talk about, where your knee is injured but it makes your hip hurt) and thus Shel and I would not *not* be Gay and what we were up to would *not* be a "pure" "investiga-tion"—it would be ulterior, "compromised-by-engorge-ment" (I know, it sounds like a legal term), a sinister-shaky thing. (And maybe one that we had known would be coming-to-fruition all along—which being why I had my skittery-itchy troublings around Gay men.). But we two men, Shel and I, we were in search for "truth", we *were*, were-we-not?—except provided that that truth did not implicate, did not bang and resonate like a church bell and clang-away our old-established (solid foundation?) truths. We might really rue the day when we decided to be fucking seekers and iconoclasts. And by the way, Shel's penis was approximately my own size—except its being uncircumcised (he *was* Jewish—what was the deal here?), that uncutness gave the thing a hooded look, a bit like a monk's head hung-down to prayer in a monastery—so maybe in sheerest essence, in its guts (in a way) my penis was the bigger (I thought this and felt glad, and then I felt embarrassed and silly-absurd and [I guess] "unprofessional".). . . *Hey, do the damn thing and get it over with!* But such speed-attack attitude was counter to our intentions, wasn't it, our investigation into what this experience that we had submitted-to from women, or enforced-upon them, actually felt like to those women—I mean, the semi-clinical way we were going at it, or *about* to go *about* it, one might just as well have employed an EEG contraption to measure another's poetic sensibilities and enthusiastic flights: Nonetheless, (and/or *therefore*) I immediately found myself sinking into a kind of good-faith/bad-faith, drawing-upon my pictographic memory of my best-received blow-jobs from various women (of course), thus imagining that I-the-fellatioer might be a sort of prodigy of one of those best fellatioettes: As the girls had, I moved in slowly, and I felt Shel's body give with a slight tremor, a twitch, almost a premonitory buckling—not one of sexual excitement, I was sure of that (I think), but one of anxiety and discomfort—and perhaps of an incipient take at throwing my head like a football off-off-and-away from his, I'll call it, his centerpiece. . . As I said (and said and said and said), we were stoned, and I don't believe that my next move would have occurred to me were I not floating in my marijuana haze, but floating as I was, I licked. *I licked my buddy Shel's dick,* stalk of onion-salt, and then onto

183

foreskin with its basted-in redolence of urine and its scrunge from his having not much to do with more showerings than the normal weekly—and I occasionally now looking up to my pal's face, as women do when they are performing the act upon us, usually with what always seemed a many-faced questioning: to ferret-out our reactions, approval-or-dis, to quietly and subtly revel in their effect, to make it known to us that they were, while perhaps forced into the act, subjugated beyond the civilized, also in full control—they could even *bite*; while men, I know (well, I ought to know), tend to look toward the woman's long hair, her lips, her pointedly directed nose, her entire *womanliness*—we men marveling at the event that really seems so many miles beyond the allowable pleasures of this world— even beyond the imaginable (Did the devil-snake instruct Eve in this?—no other animals do it.). But Shel showed nothing in these varied realms, those of the woman or even those of the man—and he did not betray, as I expected he might, the slightest horror (perhaps while in the first stages of my "attack", coming to my own first-timer grips as it were, I'd missed what must have been the Shel-discombobulation and then the Shel-revulsion?, I coming in rather moments later with my up-gaze on the [what appeared to be] Shel-toleration and mild confusion and the lay-back waiting-it-out for friendship-agreement's sake [and to not hurt my feelings for my doing a neophyte rank-beginner's crumbum fumbly job?])—and Shel now followed-up with the shutting of his eyes, to, I suppose, *forget, blot-out,* that the cocksucker in question here laboring honestly at the-pride-of-his-groin was no marvel of femininity (*what's wrong with this pic-*

ture?!) but merely his card-player buddy, his 8-ball pool pal, his hiker and biker compadre, *and* his (as all we guy-liberals do, even "in this day and age", when we can trust our "auditors") his fellow mocker of homosexuals and homosexuality—and, with his eyes closed, Shel also imagined, I imagine, that my lips and tongue were those of his girl Susan (who certainly had her own distaff technique and therefore had to be galaxies beyond my rank guy-bumblings), his beloved Susan who was always pleading with him to put down the noble Greeks and Romans for a spell and "go get your pampered ass a *job*"—or maybe not, maybe there was smoothly swimming-along in Shel's fallen-back head on the sofa armrest a serenely different and unhenpecky sort of girl—maybe it was Angelina Jolie (*those lips!*) or Scarlett Johansson (*those lips!*): For, uh-oh: one way or the other Shel had begun the (dreaded, for me) penis-stiffening—not full but I guessed *on-that-rocky-route to no-return—and how will I handle that!?—goddamned if I'm gonna swallow it! (it might make me pregnant!*)—don't laugh, I actually did hear in my sorry head the echo of that old Miss Maiden fear—and the comicality of it did not one bit lessen the semen-in-my-mouth disgustingness: Nothing yet had come to squirt or seep from Shel's stiffening schlong but damned if I couldn't already taste it—how did women put-up-with such chlorinish spurt?—did they like it? want it? consider its drawn-up "geyser" a wo-manly accomplishment?). . . Which affected how I began then to, well, marvel at something else: I had begun to become aware of how from such a different anatomical perspective, a polaric one, which can be a tongue's perspective, how shoddy as crumpled tumbleweed is an erectless "weenie". Tonguewise, it is not experienced in any way as how your own hand handles your own potent penis; the lingual-eye (so-to-speak) is a perspective fully unintended by nature: your Golden Retriever may well sniff the rectum of some new-well-met Dalmatian—that is just a friendly psycho-alimentary inspection, a handshake if you will, but picture your Golden Retriever sucking-off the Dalmatian's *cock*—that is sick, doggie-sick, and it is "sick" because it makes your canine seem as perverse-human as if he had just barked-out from doggie-memory Lincoln's Gettysburg Address. So and thus, the tongue's perspective—getting-fucking-*on*-with-it—and remember, to emphasize: thisall observation comes by way of the viewpoint (unadulterated) of the (strictly) non-gay guy—and my lips did at first rebel, they refused the close-in, the touch-to-touch, *Chrissakes, not on an Erection!* This especially as Shel, being not a Jewish fellow, was as I've already said, not "cut", and thus the lack of circumcision and the consequent turtlish-blatant extension from undercover (like some rude-pert pushing-in on your nose with his finger) the *advancement*, out into the naked-wild (my gagging uvula in this case), it made me feel, or experience, at first a diminishment, and an indignation—*he's in my space!*—that gall sure was natural of course—but then a *motherishness*, I'm serious, an instinct of the protective, my mouth became a huddler, a comforter, an arm-about-the-shoulder, my mouth became (apologies to P. Roth) a breast, which went, perhaps by way of the sucking-motion itself, it went turning (partwise) (*part-wise*) to an *excitement* (*on my part!?*), a turn-on, *really?*, a desire that, I *swear* this, damnit! *was not*

sexual but was purely physical—sucking on a hard,
well—I have to be risible (and big-wordish) to save my
soul—dicksickle (just like your Retriever's sniffing that
Dalmatian's rectum with no ulteriority involved,
except, perhaps, potential friendship)—and so I learned
that these two, sex and the *act-of-sex*, the rub of it, the
Erection of it, *they are Not the same.* Necessarily. In
any case, this cock of Shel's, it just was not something
to go impolitely lifting-off-from like a woman de-
murring the request from a man for a dance, or just
crudely spitting out the damned thing—and, let me say
right here and now, as it almost seems standard accepted knowledge, that when a woman gives a blow-job, it
can make her wet, it can turn her on (so she can go at it
and go-go-go, head bobbing like at times—no
offense—not unlike a dribbled basketball [I've said
'can' here: I know that a woman doesn't *have* to go like
this, I mean no offense)—but me, I have to say, all said
that I have just said for the past pages, that I did not
have even an inkling of hardon (my own, I mean), not a
tremor—and I am, I don't think, neither bragging (of
my staunchest maley-maleness), nor am I complaining
(you can bet on that!). . . But, that inception by Shel's
"instrument", his "tool", towards a rocklike hardness, it
did scare me as I knew what was in the offing, what
was coming. Coming was fucking coming—if I did not
get away. So I did wish to slip-slide off from what was
fated; and that I did. And when I again looked up
towards my buddy's face what I saw, or what I inter-
preted, was a relief, but accompanied by a disappointment—and I feared (ridiculously-but-not-so) that he
might well have wished to "finish himself off", this as I
stood-up straight above him (and again in guilt-embar-

rassment got a gander of the photo on the piano of his host-house-donator-friend's wife and daughter); but Shel, he then stood too (he held IT in, he clamped-down and nipped-it-in-the-bud?—his penis at drooping-abandoned half-mast [and, Christ, I found myself feeling sorry for him, his having-to squeeze it back-up-in like that])—and then he told me to sit myself down with *my* penis exposed, while he kneeled to fulfill his side of the buddy *UNHOMOSEXUAL!*—I swear it!—bargain.

I'd had enough already of The Experiment, but I could not cop-out.

Of Shel Sevenecker's behavior, essentially what was in his mind while he was now engaged in sucking me off, I could not know, so, I imagined a this and a that (I wanted to feel in charge and dominant as I sat now on the sofa of his benefactor as if I were seated man-mightily on a throne, but sensations of submission and subjugation did keep creep-crawling in, never-ending—and I did hold back on any guesses about Shel's well-known moocher-mind, filled-up as it was with Greeks and Romans and early Christianity and early dictator-democracy and romantically idealized "friendship in the Athenian polis", which was a million miles deeper-better than Berkeley and its self-illusions", etc. [sorry]), so I certainly cannot accurately report on my friend's visions-of and speculations-on my penis. I can however add, re my own sucking-self, that I had experienced no penis-envy, as a woman or girl might have found charging-away within herself (and she despising such shallow emotion?)—and then her reacting in accordance (penal-tip biting until a touch of blood might become evident?), this depending of course upon the particular woman's personality and inclinations. I can say, nonetheless, that I (and perhaps Shel) had sustained what I might label a species of phalicism that ought also be labeled vagina-envy, or vaginacism, which I expect had to do with the various vaginas which I knew that this penis I had been engaged-in sucking (*like a man! a straight man!*—I did try to keep thinking that) had sucked. But not because Shel's penis was so great, nor because my sucking was so off-the-charts either. Does this all make sense?—I believe it does. In any case, this-all led then to the seesaw symptomatology of superiority verses inferiority, another jolt of the whirl-pool chaos that sex is and cannot not be if it is to (properly I think) do its natural work of sharp arousal: I'd begun, while sucking, musing over Shel as regards what was better in him, about him, than in and about myself, what was in life more successful (he knew literature up and back and sidewise), and, sure, what was in him, about him, lesser (the compulsive-annoy-ing-entitled-unconscionable moocher mishigas)—it was as if our two penises might have been two little men, and our mouths abusing, enveloping, weapons, but love-up devourers as well, while engaged-in their being abused. . . Thus and afterwards? We looked at each other, Shel and I, hesitantly then fixedly—and then we laughed, forced unreal laughs I have to say. And then, what did we do?: Well, in default I suppose, embar-rassed default, sex-escape default, we righteously swarmed towards talking capitalism once again, Ameri-can Capitalism, its juvenile unfairness, its corruption, its overpricing everything, its billionaire-worship (com-pared to Europe, really!), its desire to pointlessly keep set on adding-up, enlarging its GNP, its screwing The ("unambitious") Little Man—and for *what?!* . . . And unlike, dear reader, what you might expect, Shel and I did maintain our friendship—we did not avoid each other like a broken-up couple might. We shot pool, we played cards, and all the rest. We never did, however, mention our reciprocal suckings-off—we left that Experiment as if it had never taken-place, a dream, an informative surreal nightmare. Knowledge in the lock-box of the insecure male-made brain—like: *Who, what nitwits, who could participate in such sick tomfoolery?* the manly-men most male-secure or the boy-jerks the least?. . . So then, okay, what really have I learned? I suppose I have, in process of the process, already done-with my describing the personal knowledge gleaned. As much of it as I know. Or ever will.

Well, with a bit more information provided-you on my research into sexual identity, on sameness and dif-ference, I may now again return to sex-mixed Dale. I'm guessing that off my guy-guy experience you might never think that I would have asked Dale Lorenzo out again—Dale might have reminded me in bed of (ugh!) Shel. But, guilt, or interest, or identification, or lone-liness, or decency, or liking "the woman", or a new-found discovery of strong similarity (which is, after all, a form of Love)—all, these had me calling her. I fancied walking with "my" sweet (and she was *so* sweet) manly woman (or womanly man?) everywhere, parading her, My Gal—as if I knew what was in her soul and she knew what was in mine. Yes, I did think this possible at moments. And not out of pride either. Although I guess pride was in there too. I would not care, damnit, what people would think, how they would look at us *("Is He the man or is She?")*—even my friends, though as you may imagine (and I think I've admitted it) I had few friends, not real ones—guys I'm talking—friends to whom I might explain what I was doing and go-about trying to explain What I Was (as if I knew). . . Friends aside from Shel, that is.

In any case, Dale outright turned me down.

I guess she found me weird.

ALAN GOLDFEIN

WANDA

And I found Wanda weird (so what else is new?).
Example: One of the first declarations she made to me
was the honest one that she most preferred sex with
guys who had full-drive-muscle-power-asses, as the
strong bulk of these rumps could permit the men she
had sex with to drive hard up her ass, "like nobody's
business—whether it hurts or not." (I admitted nothing
here, as I did not [remotely] boast such an ass). Anyway, as you now might guess, for Wanda Hardesty I
needed no sporting contests, as I had felt I needed for
Dale Lorenzo (desperately contested bouts of pure
strength and agility like arm-wrestling or push-ups
beyond the bell-ringing kewpie-doll winning seventy-
five [guy push-ups, not girl push-ups], contests which I
would have had to have had rigged somehow in my
favor [*somehow?*] in order to later-on achieve the
confidence of erection); nor, as for the Euro-model-
beauteous Scientologist-neophyte *Mar*-lies Amram, I
would not need with Wanda Hardesty any semi-quasi-
horseshit-intellectual tutorials on "real philosopher"

Herbert Marcuse, him with his "polymorphous per-versity" (which I also would have had to have, *some-how*, dumbed-to-haute-bonehead [by way of *some-body's* crib notes?—there are no Marcuse Cliff Notes nor classic comics]), nor would I need any brain-strained comprehension of articles on the psycho-socio-politico physics of the brain, as appear at least quarter-regularly in *The New York Review of Books* (and faked by way of Shel Sevenecker's [own faked] explaining of them to me). In a way, Wanda Hardesty did not *need*— and that independence was of course what I, an admitted male-needer, "loved" about her. Wanda taught at Cal—joint appointment yet: History and Economics. The History was of Ideas—Wanda was not a details woman, she couldn't bear what they, awe-bloated, called the *Annales* School, established by some French-man who wanted to know, as in the sixteenth century, what people actually, daily, *did*, like how they *slept* (''They took two-hour midnight breaks, Alan'')—and with *what*, like, say, did they "utilize" in their "pre-soap-hygienics days", and who came up with that soap-sanction anyway? and where did said soap come from? did it come in bars or slushy (filthy) buckets?—and who got rich from whipping it up, *soap*—some fifteenth century huckster like *our* Trump with his steaks and his cheap-shit expensive wine? Well, there you are with your Academy; and well, there was Wanda, she was surrounded by the place, the coddled atmosphere of the land-of-learning—she loving it, she hating it, she mocking it.

Being in Economics, Wanda was ensconced with all men (there were no fashionable French-econ Christine Lagarde éléganteuses in her classrooms); and *why* was she ensconced with all men, and drab men at that—she never tired of contemptuously (and happily) calling them "philistines"—*why* did she choose *these* drab classrooms, as opposed to seminar rooms devoted to lit or history or psychology or any theme where real true human flesh and blood were the ingredients? One question, many answers? Especially as Wanda was—believe it or not—fun. Wanda was wit, super wit. She even enjoyed calling herself an "asshole"—I mean she actually *enjoyed* that, as she knew she wasn't one. (And not that labeling yourself an asshole is such a super-witty thing.). By the way, Wanda came to call me her "bike schmuck", and then she'd go on: "But, hey, Keynes, him with his wearying interest rates and his money supply drudgery, *he* married a *ballerina, he* knew beauty when he saw it, and he wanted a *beauty.*" "And geek-faced *schnozzola*-nosed Greenspan, in his twenties he played clarinet with an all black band, can you *believe* that!?—then, instead of becoming a Benny Goodman, Greenspan, *he* goes and takes himself wrongly into the *i* rate and money supply, that pathetic pig-of-a-*schnorer*—the brilliant musical Jew as dead-dolt, as idiot, as good-white-boy—no offense." Needless to say, Wanda loved her own talk and she was quite the intimidator employing it—even when only trying to be funny or just plain amusing; so it's a truism that she had her battles to fight, self-hatred railed within her, you could almost see the bubbles swell and pop: Like me, she was stuck. But not in the passive way I was. . . For, despite it all, Wanda did have a center, a main perspective and avenue to knowledge—which from all the evidence shown so far, I, Alan Geist, did not have, and did envy. What I had, and I had an excess of it, or them, were peripheries—oh did I have peripheries, thises, thats, overs, unders, none-at-alls. . . But, when you think of it, multi-peripheries could be an advantage, no?—like telescopes placed not just on a mountaintop in California but all over the world, catching our nightly dark-sights of the wonder spaces from so many oblique angles—lending possible oblique, and multi, meanings? . . . And hopes? . . . And theories? . . . And (being me, I have to say this) universal dreads. (But at least I just now did manage to say something [maybe] positive about myself. My own self.).

But, damn, one hint of a me-on-me and I sure do carry me away, I'm off to the Geist-boy races (to use a daddy Moe Geist obsession)—so back to Wanda Hardesty. Those Wanda physical modalities were wanting, I bet you've likely guessed at that: Wanda was definitely no *Mar*-lies Amram. Nor, say, any trace of a Suzanne Thalbrucker—or the others—*damn*, why did there have to be so many *Others*!?—not remotely did Wanda fill-the-meagrest-bill on beauty. (And for me there had to be a bill, that is until came this internally explosive Wanda). Intellectually she was closest amongst my repertoire, my Rolodexers, to Marie Smith and to my wife—but that's the mind, Wanda definitely was not near to those women in physique. In body type, Wanda was in the ballpark of, say, well, Linda Hunt ('ballpark', so I'm generalizing here, but the simile is still close-on: I'm talking the woman who played an awkward little man in *The Year of Living Dangerously*.). "I bare-hardly break the five foot mark," was Wanda's unabashed pronouncement, even proud, even smiling, a claimer-disclaimer, as if shortness were some

sort of rare genius accomplishment worthy of a Mac-
arthur Prize (she loved to observe men crouching to
meet her eyes when they were engaged in serious
conversation—she told me this: "It's as if I'm shrinking
them, bringing them *down* to where they do *belong*.").
And Wanda did know how to play other roles that went
with such a cramped-corky body like hers: Dangerously, that was her ticket; the attack-panache. She climbed
a tree, a high one, to retrieve a frightened, dog-chased
cat—I saw this; she actually joined-in with a group of
little girls playing jump-rope ("_A_ my name is Afghani-
stan!"—I saw this too.). And with, sonofagun, Sex—
and this eros-connection is *really* hard to explain.
Strutting like a toughass tomboy little girl, walking with
her amusing-happy non-leashed Pit Bull Mister Winston (so named because of his resemblance to Churchill), she'd entered GEIST'S BIKES proclaiming,
"You'd better not tell me to leave my dog outside—
he's got *feelings*." ("He's welcome," I'd said, aware
from what must have served as Mister Winston's smile
on his so spacious mouth—and his immediate jump-up
to the greet-lick-smothering of my face—he was an
inveterate sweetheart among Pit Bulls.). "And you
better not make any comments about my height as it
relates to bikes," Wanda said, "like 'I don't sell them
with training wheels.' "

"Actually," I'd admitted, "Being full-service I do
sell training wheels."

I had little three-wheelers in one corner. They sold
well.

But Wanda had appreciated my retort. Over-compet-
itive but over-enthusiastic, she spread her eyes wide (a
bit, it occurred to me, like little muscular Winston's

broad bay-mouth), her nostrils flared in an oxygen-devouring way, she bent at the hip (which was quite low-down, as she was afflicted by exceptionally short legs) and she held her belly (and she did have one, small, and unappealing as bellies might be on a woman—it really was as if she might explode with belly-laughter, or, more likely, with belly-fury—I, a few times, pictured sumo wrestlers sticking-out those dirigibles of theirs (I couldn't help it)—except I believe they did that in ginormous respect, not in any Wanda-like taunt; and: Wanda's pixie-cut pitch black hair, it was not "cute", it was not gamin, it was too full and wiry for that, too bird's-nesty for her small head, it appeared rather (I'm sorry about my allusions, but they are what they are), it appeared not so unlike a foot-baller's leather helmet from the 'Thirties, or even a World War I foxhole pot; and it appeared not so unlike the end-result of the "process" by which black women oft-times "do" their hair. With Wanda's bending-over I could look down her male button-down-collared shirt and feel not the slightest carnal twinge: no tits.

So why was I turned on?

Because I was turned on.

Why?

Wanda's smart-girl pugilism in its goofy-girl variety: her cock-of-the-roost walk (she had no ass to speak of: thus baggy-ass pants or jeans, no different than what a guy is usually stuck with [a white guy anyway—black guys, as we all know, do have serious muscle there]); so like a halfback she could walk (if she wanted) with a sort of back-to-the-huddle tiptoe and unbent knee that seemed to say, "You wanna *try* me?—you want *some-a Me*!?"; and she'd spin-round fast, a welterweight, a flyweight, to confront what-or-whoever confronted her or she believed just might be readying their confrontation. No counter-puncher was Wanda Hardesty—she led. . . And I? I was *interested?*—I being yet hitched-up to straight-worded, literal-linear and unexplosive and unbelligerent Linda Miller (*and we had*, get this! *we had just, unadvisedly, blindly, hopefully-and-hopelessly, purchased a small house on the ghetto border* [Linda had insisted on that precarious location as if it were on the edge of a seaside cliff, she would reside nowhere else but beside those folks she was helping])— *I* aware that Linda, social-sturdy Linda, "centered" Linda, was my bedrock, my—ironic to admit, pole (and she aware [by now for sure] that *I* was, what? comic relief but yet sweet potential while also being sheer psychiatric challenge?—which was, believe *this*, *her* bedrock?), and *I* telling myself therefore that I *did* love my Linda—and *I* aware that *I* was telling the truth as much as *I* was contriving and lying—for I also remained starved for the-shock-and-awe, for the *un*linear, for the messy-shredded mesh of life: as for this little-bellied-sumo flyweight Wanda who tossed that puny weight of hers around like a medicine ball (she with her mannish-narrow hips, yes, they did resemble weight-lifter Dale's). . . Except, come-on, hold-on, hold-on, hold-on: that tossed-punch way of Wanda's, it was betrayed a bit—by this slightest of draw-back retractions her mouth would make, these shadowing fears (and I had them too—it's how I could know them); yes it was fear, no doubt, hidden fear, covert fear, and (I think) it was also raveled-up real benevolence. Masked decency . . . But Black Marie, hooker Marie, she might have given me the same shock-and-awe I required (and hated requiring), along with the same decent goodness, had black Marie been the black Marie I'd first expected and I'd wanted (not an "intellectual", not an infernal *social activist*)—and, I guess, face it, not much black.

Thus, Wanda:

But, come on: I had no idea what Wanda wanted. Aside from a bike, that is. Which she'd only wanted for faster transport on Cal's many street-and-path campus.

I sold her an American-made Schwinn, which, in compensation for its many tech failures in comparison to most European brands (even Albanian ones), manu-factured small-size frames, for precisely those who had no interest in "thingamajiggy" tech innovations and probably would have not cared for them. Pre-adoles-cents who were post. Not training wheels—but close.

"Hey, it doesn't have a *bell* on the handlebars," Wanda had joked, or half-joked: "I could use a little dingaling warning bell when I ride straight-on through those goddamn student-pedestrian walkways. There's a few asshole students I wouldn't mind crashing-into, but, you know."

We rode, I comforting myself that were anyone I knew to see us, to see me accompanying what—tell the truth now—was such an example of female, well, insuf-ficiencies in the usually reckoned female departments, I could later explain to the observer that it (*oh how could I say of Wanda, even to myself, the dehumanizing 'it'?—I must have been referring to the peculiar situation of our "date", I must have been*—she was *she,* Wanda, *she*), I could have explained that she was my young niece, I could launch the blatant abject sheepish lie—or, considering Wanda's neutral double-gendered looks, I could say she was my nephew. And how then did I first explain it to *myself* that I had gone ahead and actually asked Wanda out? Answer: I could not explain it, and I did not: "It" was just what I, Alan Geist, *did*— you buy a bike, you buy Alan—Geist's Law—what an obsessive weirdo. . . No, I'm wrong: I felt sympathy for the woman, and this is both easy and hard to admit: that I was "a nice guy", for, as Leo Durocher once said (or many times), "nice guys finish last."—but, and you may laugh here, despite all that I have heretofore been saying of myself these past one-hundred pages, I do take some credit for being a better guy than most, and I do mean this—*how'bout'dem weirdo apples!*. . . Wanda's Schwinn had only three gears, so we kept our distance from the steeper Berkeley grades. However, even with hectic Wanda peddling that weak bike as maniacally as a "sinful" Jewess liberal hightailing it from a phalanx of West Virginia redneck "libertarian" evangelicals we could reach the woodsy hilltop forest known as Tilden Park by taking the long, only slight-inclined route up Spruce Street, and as it was such an extended, roundabout, tiring route, once we reached the densely-treed areas Wanda had needed badly to pee, and she dismounted, lay her Schwinn down, dropped her pants, turned away from me (and from any other nearby bikers and hikers) and squatted, so that I, behind her and watching (you bet), observed her urination coming out in a stream by way of illusion (and male dopeyness) from her rear end, not from her vagina— which natural act I had never ever before seen with a woman, not even "my" Linda, and it all-in-all—I'm sorry—revolted me, while impressing me and exciting me no end (Wanda joked: "I'm working on an innova-

tion whereby, like you men, I might just pee-stand."):
Wanda seemed wild as a thirty thousand year old
female from the days of the Lascaux Caves, she peeing
precisely as did then the lions and bears pictured on
those rocky walls. . . To the best of my recollection, we
only had two outings: Our riding was mere prelude, we
both knew that, and I did wonder if Wanda were
surprised, or even amazed (as was I), that I seemed, in
some way, to want her. She was hardly the type to look
gift horses in the mouth (not that I am, or was, so super-
narcissistic as to see myself as a gift-horse, but I do
expect that no one else was fucking her), and my
wanting her, I think, made her both more hostile and,
although not as sweet as her beloved Pit-Bull Winston
(who cheerfully ran alongside us), sweet and amenable.
I say this because on our second outing, almost immediately, no prelude, no fanfare, she'd detoured us to her
hills-house and changed from her riding gear (olive-
drab gabardine long-shorts, rolled-up to suit her short-
leg length) to a slip (I wouldn't call it lingerie, it had no
designs adorning it—I doubted that Wanda had much
experience, or truck, with lingerie); but this sight when
we first entered her house—a bachelorettesque redwood
and brick beauty with bedroom bay-view balcony (no
guestroom) in the Lower Hills: it was marred though, to
my mind, *oyoyoy*, by three of the relatively large prints
on her living-room walls: *Sick Mood*, by Edvard
Munch, and worse, by the same depressed-desperate
Norwegian—*The Scream*; both paintings by that artistic
genius depicting anguished hopeless men in twisted
Nordic nature; and then—comic cynicism I imagine—
there was also hung Max Ernst's opulent vest-dressed
man with a bewildered pernicious duckhead (I com-

mented nothing). . . Wanda's house was a fifteen minute walk or a five minute bike ride (uphill) from the nearby campus. On her double bed (not a queen, certainly not a king), in her "nightie", she lay back and stretched-out her elfin legs (for but an instant my perverse brain conjured an amputee veteran from Vietnam), this her reclination move which she must have witnessed some confident allurer perform in a movie (but it was obviously not in Linda Hunt's film repertoire).

Sonofagun: To not my amazement—but maybe amazingly close to that—I experienced my erection, the nerve-endings of which allowed the transformation of Wanda in my mind (and actually even in-my-eyes [sort-of]) from cut-short fierce pugilist to semi-long-leg seductive sensualist (my lie is not so big here, I'm serious)—and I do believe that this sea change (if you will) was *not* the result of the rather amazing feats which a plain old slip or, definitely, even an out-of-fashion skirt (or a bath- towel), can give-rise-to for a man that nakedness-baldfaced (if you will) may not alone have a shot at effecting. And I had been worried that a marshmallow-sponge-like non-galvanization (or even a determined anti-galvanization) would dead-set-itself-in here like a thousands-of-years-old Egyptian burial crypt that had long defied discovery, and be an unmitigated cause for, what? The Big Lie? ("I've got prostatitis, baby; it'll be gone in a few weeks."). But no, *Wanda just lay there—expectant!* And she had the (again baldfaced) bravado to stare at my penis as if it were the enemy, or (I considered) the twin-brother of some previous penis which had done her ill—maybe its owner had promised a return bout and had never shown.

And then, blatantly, unabashedly, as if it were an annoying impudent student who had scowled at her during one of her econ lectures on interest rate policy she did what she might have done in that case fantasized: she took hold of it. She reached-out and took charge of Al Geist's near-stupefied Mister Johnson. Which, despite all, did please Al Geist, of course it did, as he awaited this forty-one-year-old woman's further action—which however turned-out to be, not cuddling nor stroking, and not merely holding in approval—she squeezed it—and I mean she damn well *squeezed*—her clamp came near-to a strangle (I actually considered that my "squozen" boy there might well have developed a voice of its own and cried-out for female-pity). Wanda just did what a Wanda would do: she put-the-screws-on, while staring me straight-on in the eye: *No decamping now for You, my dear sir!*

Personally, I did zilch. Insanely, I enjoyed it. No, not insanely. I certainly did not believe that Wanda would now try to work on my organ as people do with those hand-pressers they use in repetition to build up hand-shake power to the crunching point. Although I was aware even then-and-there that such people were indeed little people like Wanda, they developing the one physical power skill they might lord over others who weren't so little. Tall strong folks don't crunch-shake-hands to kill. Nor penises, I'm pretty certain.

And Wanda, she saw my enjoyment play across my face—and it was enjoyment-within-the-pain, and antici-pation, no playacting.

A flaring spread her nostrils, as if they were the doors to her entire hidden being—and I liked the sensual promise in those two growing apertures—and she squeezed even harder, as swollen crease-lines formed an arc from beneath her nose to about her mouth—nasal-labial lines, I've later learned. . .

Her face was going fierce, sneering—but I expect she was scaring herself, for unfiercely she flat-said: "Why are you doing this to me?—this leading on?—as if I have no *feelings*. Just because a person looks a certain way does *not* mean they *are* that way."

I said, "I'm not, I mean, I know." *Doing this to HER!?* At this point, in this situation where it would have been obvious to any other human being but Wanda that now I *did* want sex with her, I hadn't the vaguest idea what she was talking about.

"I suppose," she said, "now you are going to laugh."

"No. *Laugh*? Of course not. No."

Clenched teeth had broken-out with her sneer, as if on their own. Worse, Winston Churchill the Pit Bull, who had been resting by the bed, had now adopted a slight growl of, I guess, confusion, or extra-sensory perception: *Do I destroy this oppressor of my mistress*?

"You'd damn sight *better* not laugh, mister."

"Wanda, I'm not going to laugh. . . Please stop Mister Winston from his growling."

She told the dog that all was okay, and she said it softly; but I was not relieved—I made to coil-up like a wounded animal, as if the dog were about-to take a massive bleeding nugget out of me: I think Mister Winston was way too smart for such cajolings as Wanda's—not in this woeful-odd (unprecedented?) situation. . . And I believe, for nuance, he also had to be way too dumb.

I had also begun to picture what I had, only for moments, imagined before: To be the startlingly aggressive woman that she was turning out to be, ill-dimensioned Wanda must have endured a difficult and probably humiliating life, from childhood until even now. The probable tauntings, the silent exclusions, even threats. And I hadn't even known the worst of it: For here was what I later learned, what she turned-out-to-be rather eager to tell, to let go of: Those demeaning mockeries and insults had not been merely because of Wanda's "unique" physique but because she had been a Polish Jew growing up in Krakow, perhaps, not ex-cluding any town in Germany, the most anti-Semitic city in the world. She had been born in Krakow in 1950, her father luckily escaping the Nazis by having been a traveling salesman of "shoes and socks and 'un-mentionables' " in "The Eastern Territories" of his Polish company (USSR-owned) just as war had broken out, and as he had always taken his wife Chava with him on these "business jaunts", this final time they had rushed all the way to the relative safety of the Eastern Caucasus, returning to Poland only years later ("There was no other out," Wanda had related to me, "but that onetime center of the Jewish Pale of Settlement—no land else would take us."), there in "the new-crowned Jew-hostile land now that Germany was defanged" to bring Wanda into the world—and into the new-old reality of children's vile-fun persecution—with Wanda warding off Polish spit and blows by making wretched faces that justified for Pole-kids further spit and blows. The small family of three had realized that a Polish surname for such a huddling-hunched clump of outsider-escapees who looked so awfully different was just about the worst bet in the world ("and an insult to 'illustrious' Poland" [Wanda had grinned maniacally when she had lain-on the 'illustrious']), so they had changed their last name from the German-Yiddish Handelmann to (Zev, her salesman-father's "genius") Hardesty, as Zev had heard that the Lord High Mayor of Dublin at that time was—*incredible! wonderful!*— Robert Briscoe, a beloved *Jew* ("apparently")—"oh those *Irishers*, they were so happy and so *generous!*" But such bizarre and ridiculous name replacement—"it sounded so goodly to us at the time"—it had obviously made for an understandable paranoia at every turn for young Wanda (I imagined that she had been mocked and sneered-at and jostled in school, and probably beaten, as she most certainly would have been the brightest and most mind-driven girl in her classes in [again, what my own Al Geist prejudices told me, was moronic Poland]). And "the little ugly, *Irish*, ha, *Jew*" had probably lived her early years, and maybe all her youthful years thereafter, pressured with an intense desire to get even, even when the persecutors, real or imagined, were no longer Polish, but American and British—and even when *they* happened-to-be, like *me*, Jewish. Driven then, determined, Wanda had published rather than perished—one-half-dozen books so far— and each one, although no doubt well-researched and painstakingly written was subconsciously a little bomb to be thrown back at "The Normal Ones", "The Life-Lucky Ones"—even if the academic tract encompassed such an "essential" theme as The Sixteenth Century Rice-Revolution (supposed) of Lord Halifax, "the Trimmer", overwhelming in economic importance the Contemporaneous Gold-Influx Revolution of Sir Francis Drake (I imagined Professor Wanda's col-leagues smirking at her cranky-antipathetic thesis behind her [rather Lilliputian and cranky] back—so they were "Poles" to her.). . . And there *I* was—I with Wanda's still-determined hand now squeezing my penis to kingdom come—I seeing her seeing my "instrument" as yet another academic hand grenade meant to explode her "novel theories" about The Industrial Revolution— or whatever. . . Except, this penis-clutch of Wanda's wasn't a Whatever. And I knew Wanda, in a way, because, in a way, I was she. No, I hadn't been the brightest kid in class—I was somewhere usually between fifth and third—but having been Moe's son, he who'd been the most athletic kid in class (especially for a Jewboy yet), I had taken-on by osmosis not so much of his physical prowess but too much of his misery-prowess at never having made the Majors—*and* my own misery at my disappointing Moe for not being the class best athlete; such that I had learned early-on to *feel*, to feel for self and to feel for a man who should have been my family-teacher, my looked-up-to and consoler, but who had spent so much of his time feeling for himself, and even being near to tears—*for himself.* I'd loved a silent stormy sullen man. I'd wanted to comfort the man who ought have been my comforter. I was the son, the loving son, of, by way of Moe, the son of the lost father of Wanda. And, also, by way of Moe, *I was Wanda.*

So, there lay Wanda now beside me, Wanda my dop-pelgänger (in a way, *in a way!*), she taking her life out (and incidentally *my* life out!) on my poor unsuspecting penis, and, suddenly, I found that I had rolled on top of her (while she still held on to that "manhood" that was by now aching pretty damn good and was likely pretty damn inflamed [yes I did fight-off considering seeing a urologist after this all was over]—such a determined, committed person Wanda was, in every venue), and, believe this, I was kissing her, and kissing her, and with—I believe it was a sort of—"love" (and penile pain-diverter)—even as I found myself, this just seemed to happen of its own (or it began as a kind of plea to "let my pee-pee go!"), abandoning that kissing in favor of another "kissing": And the cunnilingus I performed had never been my favorite (as verified especially by the many complaints of "my" Linda: "You don't get *into* it". "You're in the wrong place—move slightly to the *Left*." "Okay, hell, just forget it and use two *fingers*"); and the "eating-of-Wanda", as it went on, did mature into three rightful-reasons: One, a kind of balm and sacrament for the major life-miseries she had endured, my small compensation and my own self-redemption; two, a kind of balm and sacrament for the state of her vagina, it's shape appeared none so good—was this caused too by her hard life? (as if the genitalia can mirror on-their-own the forced distortions of the larger being that carries them!?); and/or was this malformation caused by her own masochistic self-abusing "It" as a nervous consequence *of* her mal-formed life—for Wanda's vagina was so purple-pro-lapsed as to imply that her insides seemed on the verge of disengaging-to-outside, or that she'd had a child by very difficult birth (a multi-rape in Poland?); and three, as my instincts had strategized before, by sliding down there to nicely-sweetly lick I might manage a genteel escape from the crunched-up beating my penis was enduring.

The Weirdness. The Weirdness.

And me hating myself for that, well, cruel (and

certainly self-reflective), thought of The Weirdness as
The Weirdness.

For no it wasn't weird.

I was weird; *she* was weird. But do two weirds make
a Weirdness?

Mightn't they actually, by accompanying each other,
*un*make that?

Or, okay, yes, it was weird—and I am aware, as I
write this, that my inclination, because of that weirdness, is to go, even if I fight it, for the relief of the
comic. Which tendency, however, makes it even more
uncomfortable. More weird.

"*Hit* me," she said.

"What?" Had I heard right?

"The 'going-down', good. But after your 'dinner',
then hit me. After you've finished."

"After I've finished? I'm finished when *you're*
finished."

Didn't she know how it worked?

Her core seemed to retract, as if her marrow were
pushing itself deeper into the mattress, away from my
determined glossal-work on her clitoris, with its lip-
pursings and releasings.

"Look. Okay Alan, you can stop. I won't come."

And her declaration did sound more like a resolution
than a historically-based diagnosis. But no great surprise there on the non-coming—I'd been employing
"my" Linda's guidelines, but, as you can already surmise, my heart was much not in it—never had been
(although, despite myself, I'd always tried to do my
best—which always did seem to elevate my reluctant
heart). The surprise was of course strongly otherwise:

"Wanda." I lifted my eyes from their resting spot just above her vagina, "When you said—did you really mean '*hit* me'?"

"I did. . . I did."

I had, due to her "hit" request, discontinued the fellatio and, blocking-out that "hit" proposal, and after a brief burial of a kissing pause within her pubic hair (why kiss there?—I'm not sure; maybe to show, once again, a kind of love; or at least the respect I believed she was owed by the thousands of sad events [and avoidance-events] she had endured by way of men: why not the experiencing of a man's lips and tongue emotionally pressed within that rather thick dark [but unmoist] brush of hers), I then began the relatively limited climb up over her strange cantaloupe of a stomach and chest to have our faces facing (and thinking of continuing my kisses along the way, but not doing it—it would have been too much and maybe even backfired sensitive-aggressive Wanda into a suspicious mockery).

"Yes, Alan," she'd continued saying, "*hit* me. *Then*, perhaps, what you *want*, I'll come."

Aw Jesus, Hit her? Obviously in a million years I couldn't. I had never hit a woman (and I did experience then a momentary vision of what might have happened to me had I tried such a "technique" with body-builder Dale).

"Alan, *damn* you, *hit* me already! I *do* want to come."

"Where?"

"What do you mean 'where'?"

Well, I was curious of the bodily areas in her mind.

"It is your call, alright? But not the features of the face."

211

I have to say that I did deliberate—while not deliberating. I think it was just natural to contemplate the what wheres—what would hurt the most and least—all while, again, not really contemplating the actual doing. It was, basically, an intellectual exercise. I swear it.

And the good side (I have to say in self-reassurance) was that, love or no-love, I had now been able to, in a positive (and agreeable; and obedient) way, abandon the uncomfortable "sacrament" of cunnilingus, especially on a prolapsed vagina with its so purplish-stretched-out labia. And yes, I'll say it again: Love or no love, sympathy in full flower, identification with Wanda blossoming into a deep-and deeper-knowledge, I had nonetheless not regretted the cutting-short of that "eating" gesture one bit. I'm sorry but I admit it and admit it. . . And, on further reflection, just as I was scaling Wanda's so short trunk to confront her on an equal level, I also came to this frightful question: Had it indeed been easier for me to suck the cock of my ne'r-do-well buddy Shel Sevenecker?—and my answer: It pains me to say that it had been easier and less-messier with the cock; but the psychic pain deriving from that dawning conclusion—*My God, I am Gay!*—was however lessened by the still further reflection (coming to me by the time that I'd reached up to Wanda's neck) that told me that genital-oral exchanges were a complicated matter involving such a subtle, manifold, array and changing-variety of human involvements (including that what pleasure I *had* "enjoyed" of sucking-*into* rather-warped-Wanda—and, okay, there *had* been *some* of that pleasure—it had been partially comprised of my having defeated my general longtime *dis*pleasure at such inner-bound vaginal spelunkings [that I have already mentioned and mentioned and mentioned: [I confess, goddamnit! that I had at times even thought of anteaters doing what they do—I'm sorry]), all such that sucking-off Shel Sevenecker had been, in addition to its being better and easier and less accessibly-complicated than "pussy-lapping" Wanda, it really had also been far far far gagging-worse as well.

Therefore, Thank God, I might have been male-scum, but in compensation to that recognition was the one that told me *I was Not Gay!* . . . Necessarily.

And, as I say, re Wanda's new request, when all is said and done, I just couldn't hit. I was no crude kike-despising Krakow Polack, and despite black Ja-*mil's* compliment of having called me both nigger and wigger, I was neither—I was not (what I envisioned as) a ghetto tough. I even imagined that had I, Wanda's doppelgänger, been the Jewboy surrounded in that yet uber-prejudiced Polish city, it was *I* who would have been the one who would have been hit and hit and hit.

So, with all this interpersonal, and intersexual, confusion in mind: What I'd now thought of giving a shot at was, and believe this, *lecturing* "my" poorly treated woman here: *Wanda, don't you know that your desire to be hit is a reflection of what you'd had to bear as a young girl, and as a woman. You'd learned to eroticize that punishment as a thing deserved, a thing to be absorbed, and embraced—almost as normal. I don't know about your previous sexual experiences, but I suppose you've reacted to them by then fighting back against life's unfairness in a battle that you cannot win, a battle that can only serve to—if it has not already—only . . .*

Only *what!?* Wanda was not poor deprived lost Sally Asher from Appalachian hic-land and the streets of San

Francisco's Mission. She was a full professor and a writer, highly regarded (at least as a professor and writer). No doubt she knew what and how she was, how she'd got there, and probably how she'd always be. One of the unfairnesses of life—surely the greatest unfairness—is that it keeps-on-keeping-on with its Original Unfair! *Because of its Original Unfair,* its grave gravity. 'Atlas Shrugged' all right, but not in the grandiose "objectivist" way that that "super-noble" Ayn Rand had meant him to be shrugging (I saw the Gary Cooper movie). No, life's quicksand stickiness sticks from jumpstreet. Too much the pity, I suppose. Wanda had read the books; she knew it all.

I kissed her and closed myself down upon her as if we were now welded.

Or even wedded.

She lunged-up into me, which raised me up off of her, only to fall back down again onto her, and I felt her stiff-shifting discomfort at my kisses and my falling back onto her, this woman bucking bronco—who, once I-the-rider was again hiked by her into the air, she thought better—I could *see* she did!—she thought better of what by her own nature she was doing, by force of self-dignity and self-protection and self-addiction and learned singularity (or call it loneliness) and queerest discomfort and sense of wrongness and even *lack-of-self-dignity*—and she pulled her rider, me, back down onto her (I felt the rippling contractions of her belly and the whiplash snapping-bucklings all along her, as if she had touched a hot-pot or frypan)—and she began pasting me all over my face with kisses kisses kisses, remorseful kisses? weapon-kisses? for her jaw felt clenched, desiring kisses? for her eyes kept opening-closing as if to adjust herself to herself, it was such that—and I truly believe this—it was all such that she had never quite done this before—and, what complicated emotions met for the two of us—I was disgusted and I was drawn, and I did, well, now, *want* her (or I wanted, maybe, my father Moe (*yes, Moe!*) who I could never kiss, this as I kissed Wanda back, did it hard too, like, well, a punch I guess (as her clench-punch-kisses were also that punch way)—and I even experienced my father's rough-shaved beard—it had rivaled Richard Nixon's raw dark facial murk and had been a family joke that dad had you bet hated)—and, guess what, I "loved" *her, Wanda,* I'm *serious,* and I kept-up kissing her during our, now, sonofagun—*fucking*—how'd *this* happen!?—and because I yet—being as weird as she—wanted to get away while wanting to remain within her—I felt the kisses were also a kind of oblivion as well, hiding-kisses, a somewhere-nowhere—so that it was impossible, it could never be determined I am sure, who would want to end it, leaving both she and me within that enforced cocoon of discomfort that we had inhabited for comfort for so much of our lives—no, for *all.* . . Then, you guessed it?—

I *hit* her! I did. It happened. Part slap, part (unintended?) knuckle, on one of my pull-backs from our passionate-confusing kissing. *It* thrust-out with *its* own brain and it happened—just to the right side of her cheek where her helmet of black glossy hair had slid down from our oscillating actions—and there was blood, just a scrape of it, and redness, the coarse blush of inflammation. And, of course, I *knew* this: I was hitting my father Moe. I was hitting other men I'd always feared to hit, as I'd dreaded the strong male back-hitting, the counterpunch return. But with a woman, well . . . Of course I came out with "I'm sorry."

"No. Thank you." She, touching the "wound" tenderly, with no Kleenex, just her fingers.

"Don't thank me." I'd gone to shaking my head fervidly, as if denying that I had killed someone (which maybe I had). "Wanda. It was a . . . a . . . "

"Slip of the hand?—like a slip of the tongue?"

She had actually *enjoyed* it; she could joke, and intellectually yet. She could smile. She was satisfied? She had succeeded: In a way, by my having punched her, she had found for herself that she had fucked *me* good, and she appreciated herself for that—her gratification was so visible . . . And (ought I mention this, re my own [and ever] self-involvement?) my middle knuckle ached some with the scrape and I was rubbing it.

"My father," I said, "somehow he . . . he intruded in the, I don't know, the picturing of it all, the idea of it all, and I . . . "

"The *devil* made you do it?"

With her astuteness, she could even *joke*? I stared down at her in amazement. And, I have to admit, I'd wanted then to chuckle, how about that?—but I stifled it. The chuckle was due to my then picturing Flip Wilson: Years before, likely earlier than Wanda's entry to America, there had been this comedian, a black guy, Flip Wilson. He had had a TV show, and on it he had always, invariably, done this bit where he had gotten himself up in drag, portraying this black ghetto bitch, Geraldine (I believe "her" name was—I'm too lazy [or self-righteous principled?] to go to Google), and she, this "Flip" Geraldine, he/she would have done something bad and then gone about swearing to white TV America in an indignant ghetto-lady's yodel of highest-harpy-dudgeon, *"The DEVIL made me do it!"*

On top of a satisfied Wanda what came out from me now was a limpid "Huh?"

"Alan, will you tell me, tell me, something good, about my goddamn-cursed body?"

Already, she was well past my punch. (Further past than was I). And, in case you are interested (and because I did not know what else to say—and because it might have lessened the gravity of the punch) I almost asked her if she had ever seen Flip Wilson— maybe in reruns? But she was surely not a TV gal.

I commenced the decent (and repentant) search for "something good" about Wanda's body, as she had requested. A good answer might well be sacrament as well as had been everything else, unsacramental, we had done. Better, I was hopeful.

She had by now pulled her head back from our kisses (and my hit), she was resting back on her pastel blue pillow, as if my involving myself in what would be (to her eyes) a grueling-but-decent pursuit for the physical Wanda-good, that effort might allow her some (well-earned?) lay-back lounging time.

"Okay-then: Not beauty about my *body*, Alan, let that go—I'm long past that shallow dream, that 'Alice in Wonderlander', but . . . but . . . well, look into your soul and tell me *something.*"

Actually, I did not have to work so hard. Having already seen us as doppelgängers I needed merely to imagine that I was looking in the mirror—and I do not mean that as purely narcissistic (although it certainly was narcissistic); I mean it as a form of, what?—

replication?, an understanding and (for sure) sympathy through our likenesses. Maybe this held Truth? Or more truth than not. . . Maybe.

"Your eyes, Wanda (which earlier I had seen, uncomplimentarilly, as counterparts of her Pit Bull Winston Churchill's humongous mouth), your eyes, they are gray-green oceans. They're so deep."

She scowled at the grade-school triteness.

But I did not mean the dunce-hollow poesy, I did not mean my triteness as a triteness—but then again what poetaster does. What I meant, and said:

"They are so wide, your eyes, you seem to not be opening them without your spreading them so wide and taking-in everything. Four-dimensional eyes. They have minds of their own, Wanda, your eyes—I mean that. They are frightening and they are like magnets, I can't *not* look away from them. They, and you, Wanda, your eyes, they always look to be pleading for the best, even though, as I know, you have seen the worst and you expect more of it; your eyes in their wisdom, yes they show their wisdom, they seem to be fighting your mind in *its* wisdom, in its *other* wisdom, its history—you have the most complicated eyes, Wanda, I have ever seen. What can I say?—they are *judges*." And an afterthought (which I wasn't so sure of): "And, they *hope*."

Wanda had shut her eyes while I had been busy digging into my brain to describe them (I'd left out that her eyes seemed also to be warding-off eyes), I non-poet-performing (I not even, alas, a *reader* of poetry), I struggling to anchor-up my best poetic versing-way— which, as I say and say (and say), I did also happen to mean. I had meant those words I'd said. And really I expect that Wanda had not closed her eyes: they had decided to close themselves.

"Will I see you again?"

She actually asked this twice: First, as I was dressing. And then when I was leaving her beautiful-small low-foothills house. Not liltingly she'd asked, but with a knowing—so as not to be disappointed—croak.

And me? Part of me, I wanted to laugh (as I'd wanted when she had reminded me of Flip Wilson's Geraldine)—she had pleaded, though roughly, with such a Hollywood line, from when, the Forties? Would Gene Tierney have uttered it to Dana Andrews? Would Jennifer Jones to Montgomery Clift? Perhaps Katherine Hepburn would have to Cary Grant, but she with a built-in mockery (I recollect that she [impossibly] broke his golf clubs over her thigh in *The Philadelphia Story*). But they, not a one of them, would then have been laughing-on with that Wanda-crying-laugh of self-mockery and throat-scratchy self-protective misery. Laughing-on with the bizarre lovelorn "love" that was and wasn't bizarre guilt and real-life eternal-waiting heavyheartedness. And reaching.

I saw Wanda again, again. It was what I'd like to call, with reservations, the most fitting thing to do. Although I didn't want the repeated "seeings", I wanted them, I might call our "meetings" the exchange which was, if anything, The Muddled Similar. . . Even as— and Wanda did "teach" me this, so she must have done it before—we hit each other: We did begin slowly at such a symbolic and palpable act: we struck shoulders, arms, ribs, genitals too (her backhand on my hardon I experienced as major, although she said she wasn't at all hitting hard), and we came to be squeezing necks, at first theatrically, a kind of loving gesture that might be photographed for comic memory; but this evolved, I believe, into a different photograph, the miming of the strangling of finality—and then we stopped. We had found each other. No supposing. *We had FOUND each other?*—Wanda quoting John Donne with his *'I wonder by my troth what thou and I DID till we loved. Were we but weaned till then?'* Me and "my little ugly Wanda"—and she liked my calling her that, she even told me to do it, and to continue at it, she just insisted. And she saw that, she perceived it easily, none of this was in the least, although it had begun so, The Al Geist Charity Sex Fund. Hell, had we considered it all as merely that we'd given up the haunting ghosts of our pasts and thus nothing untoward mattered, as we were about to take leave of each other, hoping to never run into each other again on the "Berserkely" streets? No, it definitely was not that. Sure, leaving each other, we did do, of course—but this leaving came only after the consequences of Wanda's, eventually, sadly, inevitably I guess, asking, "Must it only be about sex? Can't we go to, say, the movies or the symphony?" . . . And we did go, because her asking reflected, still, nonetheless, with all her brilliance and her learning, that remaining unrooted-outness of hers, that sense of exile, that irritated skin of any immigrant: what damned clung like a treed cat was an insistence that it was, *she* still was, after all, with no theatre and no concerts etc, to me "a Nothing"—"Alan, don't make me feel like a *whore.*" So, to keep those stuck-sadnesses at bay we went even to dumpy-small Art House on Telegraph, and to the Cal Art Museum (where I remembered Art Buchwald's droll story of the Army private breaking the record Four Minute Louvre—and of course I identified), and we watched Czech films, German films, French, Japanese, Russian, especially Postwar stuff (*Nostalghia, Drunken Angel, L'Amour Fou, Mouchette,* etc.), even Polish (*A Knife in the Water*: "It's okay, it was really done by Polanski, a *Jew*, Alan")—except usually all of these so literate films seemed to postulate, in one way or another, the lightness or heaviness of indifference *or* of caring, and if indeed there really was such an honest emotion as caring—there was the poignant sorrowful sadness of even laughter—forget tears, these were too obvious—such-all being the "perceptive" truest stuff of life-living in these films. The "genius" no-way-out of it all. And it might even be that these foreign movies, with Wanda and me side-by-side (in such narrow funky cinema "halls" which were in the American-progress-processes of dying [and turning into techie stores] because almost nobody but she and I went to them), these brilliantly-warped art-mirrors-and-interpretations of living-within with no choice, no hope, these movies became, I think, our way, our noblest possible way, of identifying who we were—*and* ignobly *defeating* who we were. So those hectic slambam hit-bouts of ours were *not* what had finished us.

No, it wasn't the movies which did us in—that kind of artificial, scapegoat blame is so insipid and coward-beggarly—and as transparently poor as were so many of those "genius" movies. The precarious identity that Wanda and I had both fallen into—no, frenetically leaped into—would not allow so quick or easy a dead-reckoning and finish-off as a few depressed-art-movies might accomplish. Come now. The truth is that Wanda and I stayed "together" for a considerable time (while I was still married, mind you, and telling my wife Linda that I loved her, which I swore to myself that I did). So what was it then that caused me, not to *be* with Wanda but to *remain* with Wanda? As I've mentioned, I had originally wanted to be either a scholar in lit or a doctor, but these worthy aims had been supplanted by my becoming the not-so-proud proprietor of GEIST'S BIKES! To be honest, by the time I had met Wanda Hardesty Handelmann I didn't even enjoy biking, it was coming to bore (and annoy) the hell out of me, all that stupid leaning-forward and pumping-down and street-hog traffic-blocking (sadistically enjoyable for more bikers than I care to mention)—and I was on the rocky road to hating it. Well, perhaps hating is too strong— but perhaps no it's not. I could look at my stock of glittering Italian brands and French brands and Japanese and, with a diffident sneer, decide that these instruments, all this functional and useful paraphernalia, represented a missing of life's mark, and an intentional one, by a juvenile man, a sidetrack that I had willfully, immaturely, rushed into, a sort of well-appointed and shiny vacuum of a lure that had succored me, away from what as a kid I might have called my-great-fate-appointments, awaiting, beckoning.

Because I was me and I wasn't me.

This seesaw not uncommon amongst our human types, nor not so dramatic as split-personality nor psy-chosis, I have come to learn. Actually, quite normal.

So why so?

Easy: Fear. To put it bluntly, I didn't believe that I had the stuff. To be neither a physician discerning

people's illnesses and then advising them, and certainly
not *operating* on them; nor to be a brilliant exegessizer
of any complex classics from Homer to Thomas Pynchon. The shiny bike vacuum was the alluring magnet-
in-default, the Alan Geist vacuity—what they now call
therapeutically "a low self-image". My dad Moe hadn't
helped—you know all about that; but there was that
other person living, struggling too, within the padded
walls of my small nuclear family. My mom Ida, who I
have mentioned only slightly so far, as when my
mothering mother had tried to help her too-son-ing boy,
Alan Geist, just too much, as when as a kid I'd been
afraid to go down an escalator in a department store
(going up I had as zero a problem as would an airlines
pilot). Of course I came to overcome that embarrassing
anxiety (and I do today go down escalators with
panache, without resorting-to even a piddling 2.5
Valium (the white ones)—you show me an escalator
anywhere, or even one of those forty-story all-glass
hotel outside elevators, and I'll go down or up it without tripping the Geist-switch of an atrial fibrillation or a
dizzying migraine (Although I do "suffer from" what is
known as—in the absence of really *knowing*—the
Migraine Equivalency Effect [the MEE Syndrome],
which does not cause pain but does cause the scenery
one sees before one's startled eyes to break up into the
piecemeal penumbrified chunks and lightning-lit
jaggedries characterized by Picasso and Braque in their
Cubist periods, or even those quadrangularly meaningless Mondrians]); but damnit I still do live with the
image of my mother worry-faced while energetically
hiking-up her skirt to scramble up those down-moving
escalator stairways as if she is a Master Sergeant bent

on saving her trapped platoon "grunt" from enemy gun-fire, thus to succor her quaking eight-year-old son and bolster him until he got the gumption to master that mysteriously moving (*and disappearing into the floor!*) slipslide-curling steel of Macy's etc. Little Al, the son of Big Moe yet, the same kid who in the schoolyard of Robert E. Lee Elementary #61 (this was in Baltimore ["the most northern of the southern cities, the most southern of the northern", proclaimed proudly by the self-dubbed 'Baltimorons'], this before we had moved out to California), this little boy who had been at Robert E. Lee the best athlete but had buckled and picked up the books that the school bully Sheldon Taubenfeld (another Shel, not Sevenecker my buddy who I came years later to suck-off—*this* book-drop-demanding Shel bastard became a bigtime ad exec), he had mockingly dropped that load of textbooks of his at my feet for my doglike retrieval—which I had, doglike, retrieved; I, one and the same kid who had won the school *hop-scotch* championship (only three boys had been pussy-enough to enter the contest, along with some twenty hopeful girls) and had then stayed home for one full school week out of omnivorous self-devouring shame-facedness at his own *win*—would I try next for the tiddlywinks crown? and then jump-rope? ("My name is *Al*an and I hail from Al*toona*"). And why had I been this way? Damned if I knew why I was a, face it, *face it*, coward?—even the word 'coward' (which I, brainy "pussyfooter", had had the curious-but-sniveling inter-est to look up: "coward" bore such an uncomfortable relationship to, well, "pussy"—I'm talking "pusil-lanimous".). So again I ask: *Why oh why* had I been this way, started-out life this way that had led, I suppose (I fucking *know*), to Wanda Hardesty Handelmann and my sticking-it-out for, at least not *years*, but (long enough) serious months? Because my mom Ida had in the middle of the night slippered herself into my little room and so fretfully massaged my fallen arches when I had cried at the foot-cracking pain down there?—she worried to death that I might in the future not be able to even *walk*? Because my mom Ida had encouraged me to, in counterpoint to my roughneck dad's by now jock-void, *read books*? Because she had shown me *her* library books—Carson McCullers, Flannery O'Connor, Harper Lee?—who I found, again that annoyingly adhesive word, pussyish. (Would it have helped had my "sensitive woman"-reading mom Ida introduced me to, say Katherine Ann Porter or Mary McCarthy? I do doubt it, I was too much in thrall to my muscle-dad (who did not read even Mailer or James Jones—or, for that matter, Mickey Spillane.). (And anyway, my mom Ida could not bear to "freethink" enough to read such female-muscle "intellectuals" as Mary McCarthy or Ms. Porter. ["My" wife Linda's mother read Ayn Rand]). And this brainstorm just now hurdles to mind: Had I "enjoyed" "castration anxiety" *before* my mother "helped" me, or was the "mommy help" the "castration anxiety" *cause*? Good question—no answer. And had I also become me because my dad Moe (who'd also fretted-over my hurt feet, but the worry was not that I might not be able to walk, but that [due to the afore-mentioned "pussyfeet"] I might not be able to be accepted into the Army, which would, as they said in those days, "make a *man* of me"). So dad Moe, he had, finally, after mulling it over (*No son-of-mine picks up a bully's schoolbooks! No son-of-mine is scared-stiff by a fuckass shitass* <u>*escalator!*</u>—<u>*that*</u> *son-of-mine is TRYING-TO-BE not-my-son!*), dad had gathered-up his own courage and in his own version of *L'Education Sentimentale*, asked me, when I was, I believe, four-teen, "Alan, are you *queer*?"—and *I* had been afraid to ask him, 'Dad, how come you didn't make the Majors?' And, say: 'Dad, how come you are not like my uncles, either my mom's brothers or your own? *They* talk and make jokes and lead *seders* on Passover and generally all-round make a lot of noise in life?' No, I hadn't been aware how much *they,* those uncles, had envied *my* father; I was too cowed in failed imitation of my "hero" dad to have embraced that envy. I was too damned *scared.* I was, if I say so myself, a goodlooking kid, but I was a goodlooker who felt himself ugly. In effect, I was "my" Wanda. In college, in discussion groups, I hardly talked—I was Moe in speech (or rather speech-lessness), if not in athletics, without the slightest trying. My college frat brothers had even dubbed me Sole. Not Soul—for some listeners did not get it—but *Sole.* Oh, true, this being of mine was yet mixed-in (somehow!) with a great deal of egotism—I saw that girls liked me, lord knows why. But when they did like me a certain part of me felt that they were shallow and unperceptive, and Wrong.

It was as if I had no center. Or if I *did* have a center it was more like a microscopic bullseye, and it dwelt deep down at the bottom of the psyche's slightly ever-shifting Grand Canyon. No, no as ifs: I was this-and-that-and-therefore, you guessed it, nothing. No as ifs.

Which made me, I think (I hope?) too hard on even Myself—and others. And too sympathetic soft on Wanda (even as she did deserve such sympathy-softness)—even as we, comradely, understandingly, beat at each other, *fists* for Chrissakes, *fists*—until we truly wised-up and gave out.

And that wising-up: it had to do with knowing that you took those sliders-curves-fastballs tossed by your parents, the bests for you that they could offer, they having been served-up their own parents' mixed-pitches some thirty years before. No blaming involved, might as well blame The Big Bang—which is just a theory anyway: But these personal whatsits are just natural to tell, and they're necessary to tell too. Even as they fall-away to become more historical, more fall-away vague and fuzzy, than contemporaneous. So, *I am Not Blaming*. . . At least, most of the time. Understanding is not BLAMING.

VERY APPROPRIATE ADDENDA:

1: Often, when strolling with Wanda I had found myself singing the apropos—

> We're two lost souls
> Oh the *Hi*-way of Life,
> One with no sail,
> One with no rud-*derrr*.
> (Yadda-yadda-yadda)
> We *got each Ud-der*.

The song was Us, to a T; and as hauntingly mean-ingful as it was to our life-warped duo, it was not from any musical slapped-together out of, say, Dreiser's *An American Tragedy* but rather from the keenly enter-taining *Damn Yankees,* which had been a Broadway hit in the Fifties (I'd loved Gwen Verdun, and, me being me, I'd loved the mid-cult/mass-cultness of such acerbic but sugar-poignant stuff—plus, it had been about my father's sport, baseball); and Wanda had smiled at my crooning the gloomy rhythms, and she'd loved it with a kind of a morose appreciation, and a pride in my spooky spontaneity, my seeming oblivious disregard of our disastrous Us. She not knowing that the song, and the hit show from which it came, had been based on none other than the Faust legend, which of course she (in her adopted haute couture) knew from various operas (perhaps belted-out from Berlin's great halls in Charlottenburg or Kreuzberg), not from the "lowly" Yid-chocked shtetled-up *brethren of hers* who inhabited New York's Tin Pan Alley—who had had their Yiddishkeit song talents nurtured by their parents in the dilapidated crumbum *shuls* of The Pale of Settlement, where Wanda had been raised and tormented, into her (unadmitted) Jewgirl self-hatred (and thus— think about it—self-love), she craving to be a John Maynard Keynes type economist, a courtly-goy Bloomsbury Groupee, and not a thorax-hunched, nose-doughy Alan (Allen?) Greenspan.

2: The last words that Wanda ever said to me, and I (could have) to her:

"Oh how *woeful* that we had begun this, this *pummeling* of ours—and our thinking that we-*needed*-it."

"Sometimes," I'd answered, "things just—well they-*tell*-you. You don't tell them."

"This hitting told and shouldn't have."

I said nothing. Whatever I'd have conscientiously ventured in the quest for "rightness" would no doubt have been wrong.

"You know, Alan, I very much did *not* appreciate it when you fucked me up the ass, in-and-out, in-and-out, *in-and-OUT,* as if I were a *sewer,* to be snaked, or a plank of wood to be augered. That *hurt.* I hope though that *you* enjoyed it."

I did; but I stayed mum. What I did hazard was—

"I did not think of you as a sewer, Wanda. And, you know, my *penis, you* took-out *your* worst—"

"But not the *ass,* the *rectum,* you could have caused *fissures and fistulas,* true *damage.* It *bled.*"

"Not that much, I remember." Had it been more serious I would have insisted on driving her to Emergency. I said: "On the toilet paper you showed me, I could see—"

" *'Not that much'.* You are so *cold,* you know. 'Not that *much*', you say. And now you're a proctologist?"

"But Wanda, you know I'm not cold; you hadn't complained or fought-me-off, and once you even told me that you preferred guys who had strong muscular rear ends who could really drive hard into your ass."

"I remember. I was being risqué, okay?"

"Well, If you had told me I was hurting you, I would have relented."

"I doubt it. You're trying to lay the blame on *me*—?"

"Wanda, I'm not trying to lay any blame. There was no blame. All there was was Us."

"No! The blame *you* won't admit, that is what it was; you put it not on yourself and your erotic male wants to *give-it-to-us-women,* you blame *that* on the women's obedience, it's *nature's way,* huh? it's *congenital? right?*—that which women despise but haven't got the gumption to give *up? right?,* that's what *you* say, or you *think,* and which women, you say, they won't admit they *like*."

"I didn't say any of that."

"Alan, you didn't have to. It's fuckingish *built-in*. You know what it is, what it *really* is?—it's *you*, you *men,* you getting-even with your *mothers.* Did you get too many enemas from your mom Ida, all-*powerful* then *she* was, when you were four years old?"

All these years, if not blaming Moe, then shoving-in my sympathy for my "brother-dad" in place of the 'get-even' for his explosive cuffings . Believe it or not, I had never once considered Mom's Enemas—and I *had* had them—and all the enema-substitutes in the forms of woman-to-boy diminishment: jailhouse-cloistering; dishwashing (we had no machine washer); short-pants; call-ins for (justified?) quarantine from my fun-in-the-street; etc. Not unconventional stuff which my mother had, I guess, in some subliminal way, taken some pleasure in? . . . Wanda was armed for bear: she had read her texts.

"Wanda," Troubled, I shifted gears. "You could have used your dildo on *me*. You know that—from how we were carrying-on with all we did."

Her "dil" was a shiny black weapon, large as a snub-nose '38—she had showed it to me on more than one occasion (I suppose as an ultimate, a be-and-end-all if called-for); it had an "app" on its other end, sort-of like an automatic trigger, for concomitant service on her clitoris.

I repeated: "You could have strapped that thing of yours on and—"

"Hah!" With her indignant jolting-up of her chin, Wanda's head rocked as if pointing the direction of my please-to *get-out*. "Alan, you may well have pussy-envy, I suspect it, I always have. But as if you don't know it, you would *not* have permitted me to *dildo* you, you *know* that. You would have *run*, like the *coward* you are. Like *all* men are—if women only *knew*."

"I would not have run. I would have allowed."

"Hah! 'Allowed' Women are submitted women. Men, in their kingly graciousness, 'allow'. Is *that* it!?"

"I would not have 'allowed', as you put it. Alright, I would have . . . submitted. Okay?'"

And I just then experienced the provative-demonstration impulse of wanting to drop my pants and bend over, over her wide gray kitchen sink, or her Formica kitchen table, or to just let her hold onto me at the waist as if she owned me, as I had (masterfully?) done with her. Her hard life had given her the requisite female strength.

"It would have hurt you bad," she said, her right hand unconsciously forming the shape and position of its insertion into me. "My 'thing', my *in*strument. *I* would have hurt you bad. I couldn't."

"Wanda, then I would have complained, said STOP, as *you* didn't do—and as you *didn't* do, Wanda, I would have fought you off—if I'd had to. . . I guess."

"Men are scum."

How many times did I have to hear that? or some variation on its woman-excusing theme.

"Wanda," I decided. "I'll let you have the-last-word."

"As if you don't know that you just-now, by saying that, *haven't let me have-the-last-word*: Men are scum. Manipulators by instinct and by the trickery born of instinct. Majestic kingly scum. QED and *QEF*."

"Okay, if that pleases you."

"Will you just *shut-up*!"

"Okay."

"I will have the woman's dignity to now *not-take-the-last-word,* which you men so pathetic-blind *desire.* Female noblesse-oblige."

"Okay." I was shaking my head in I-don't-know-what. . . "But Wanda, the truth is, I still and you still. . . "

Yes, we still wanted We. " 'Two lost souls on the *hi*-way of life/One with no sail, One with no rud-*derr*.' " But like the boy being ordered in from his fun-in-the-street, I ceased fun and I desisted.

3. I hadn't known it (but I had suspected it), that Wanda Handelmann Hardesty had most likely seen me as her last hope (if she even had a hope), just as—in the ultra-opposite way (I think)—I'd then seen her as mine, my last hope. . . But Wanda: It couldn't have been more than one month after our "break-up" that she had gone into her one-car garage, double-locked it and prevented any saving trickles or wafts of air from seeping in by meticulously spreading blankets beneath the long metal-clamped portal; then entered her joyous-looking small red Honda sports car (a poignant irony for her to own—and in the throes of her black humor she was definitely aware of that—it's why she'd purchased, used, the "adventurous happy machine"), she'd turned-on the two-bit (but roundly loud) engine and awaited her likely long-wished-for sleep—at which she was not found until the postman notified the authorities because, after a week or so, he could not stuff any more mail into her fully cramped mailbox. . . But *stop-it*, I did tell myself: *'You are no more to blame for this tragedy than*

Vronsky was for Anna Karenina's leaping onto the train tracks, nor Leonard Woolf for Virginia's leaping into the rapid river.'—one man a fictional selfish "heartthrob", the other a real-life literary grind who wouldn't move back to London to soon to suit his wife. Selfishness makes its perfect landings all over the place, onto victim as well as victor. It's air. The true fault-of-all lies, as always, with the one who has made of themselves the (supposed) fate-victim—as causation otherwise assembles-up far too many causes and inter-actions for even IBM's great Chess Champion to unravel: Wanda had made of her death a shadow, a mirror, even an apology, for all those of her People (and mine) who had died, not by Exxon's innocent gas-station pump but by Germany's Xyklon-B. And how do I know this—or suspect it? Because she had talked often-enough of how she had escaped non-existence due to her father's "escape" from the cattlecars to Auschwitz—and just by his being a good hotshot Jew salesman in The Soviet Union's Eastern territories. (Instead, in ensuing years, she had just gotten herself beaten-up by Poles).

Some guilt there! Some anger there! Wanda's father Zev's having been a shoe salesman (and socks) in The Eastern Territories. . . this life-accident had made of Wanda "ugly" (I believe she felt that) and a debtor to non-existence.

And I, *I*? I was a privileged American. A father who hadn't made the Majors was excuse as *nothing*! If I had a debt, a duty, it was to make for myself "an existence". No?

And I'm not even sure that that conclusion of mine,

weighted-down by Wanda's fate, is just too "American" to be right. . . As she had said to me when once, against all my wills and sanities I had tried to get together again—"There is too much water *over* the bridge and *under*." She had declared this Balthusian-evoking epithet employing her most adamant of East Europe accents.

In any case, twice of an afternoon I stood outside Wanda's beautiful red brick hills house and just stared at it, almost convinced that she still lived inside. In my penance (deserved or no) I stared until a neighbor asked me if I was considering buying the place. ('*I've already bought it,*' I considered saying.).

THE SAINT AUGUSTINE AFFAIR

His story is truth and lying-legend. After a youth of serious no-holds-barred debauchery, the rebellious Augustine experienced a conversion (and not of hysteria) and wielded his philosophical weight in the direction of the good gospel, preaching of sex-un-married as ingrained evil, its inherent sin. Procreation only, that was the Christian ticket. . . . Which, by the way, did make for the dangerous Atlantic-crossing to our America. Hell, it just about *caused* the "Puritans" to brave it.

Albeit a Jew, and considering the frustrated dimensions of my romantic failures (and the failures of the women who were my failures), I decided, what-the-hell, give Augustine—and the Puritans—a shot (albeit that so many of them [usually the leaders] were dyed-in-the-wool hypocrites): The shot: Abstention in the non-marriage, non-child-aimed-for, arena. . . But could I follow-through?—even as "wife" Linda—improbable but probable-possible (to save our marriage?)—wanted a child. Decisions are easy actions, action-actions require various sorts of nerves and muscles untaxed in simple good-folks interaction—thus their usage may well cause serious strain, they may well not be so healthy as church (and psych) advertised. Even John Milton, Puritan that he was, Cromwell supporter that he was, turned out, in the obverse of Augustine, to become quite the heavy-duty stick man.

Denial thus procreates the parade. (It always will do that!): The thralls, they mock you, unknowing (they've got their own rotten problems). The streets and avenues, such as Berkeley's historically famous (and infamous) Shattuck and Telegraph and University, these walkways for students and teachers and idling hangers-on headed with woolen caps (sometimes these beanies are topped by little spinning propellers, multicolored) and handed with their hawkable poetry (tons of it now in computer-printout times), they strike-back at your dumb Denial by becoming demo-boardwalks of beauties, nothing-but-beauties (luscious lures are all now that you see since your no-sex resolution), these ugly streets have now become model catwalks, Runways of Lady Liberties, and so of your captivity. What I'm trying to mean is: Your Denial mind, that friendly-enemy self-imposed, that salvation kit (of damnation), it transforms the average woman, whom you might or might-not care-for normally (*and who may well not care for You!*), your frustrated mind transforms her into a penis-fostered trollop. Oh, that ass, those hips, that taunting-daring walk (which may well be intended as neither taunting nor daring), and those despicably beguiling mile-long legs!—plus plain conventional average nothing-much breasts, these now become unbearable provocateurs, as sinful to myself as they must have once become to the new-converted Saint Augustine, who then in mortal Christian combat, no matter what encasing cover-ups the later Romans had deemed appropriate, he probably turned-round to despising them and their (supposed) blatancies. They would rot in hell. They *should.* . . Well, that puritanically loony twist of logic started to sound right to me. It did! Damned *females!* Them and their obscenist subtle *weaponry! What right have they, to Be!—those bitches!*—aside from birth-giving, of course. Despite all, I will DENY! . . . I will shut myself out; I will shut *their*-selves out: I will become, like Melville's Bartleby, the closed-off man—but instead of concentrating on nothing but, like Bartleby, the brick wall outside my window, I will expunge The Woman and hone-in, exclusively, on My Bikes.

It may be chalked-up to the effusions of my deluded ego, but in my Denial Mode I soon enough came to believe that some women who entered GEIST'S BIKES were becoming offended that I *did not* hit on them— *some* women, obviously not all—and perhaps they seemed to be commencing to the hating of my con- verted self, as some kind of nasty TaunterMan, just as I had already commenced to the (*justifiable!*) hating of Taunting *Them*; although, admittedly, the afore- mentioned may well have constituted nothing but an- other contorted Al Geist illusion, and one perversely prized (for that contorted reason that it was *my* illusion, and thus an undeflatable one). . . Still-to say, all this is not as bad as the beginning but persistent scraping of a rumor fantasy-fear that some of these women—while they overacted by scrupulously inspecting bike after bike after bike (as if they knew even one damned petty thing about these marvels)—they were now considering *me* as gay, and spreading the goddamned libelous word around. Now, as I say, this was *my* fear-fantasy, and after all in this "enlightened" age where one can thrive by dual identities and cross-purpose loyalties, sexual brandations of this specious type ought neither hurt nor help with bike sales—but *still*: Although I have been more than happy to attend the occasional Gay Berkeley wedding (and definitely experience the sadness of loss at one Gay funeral), and my sucking-off of my buddy Shel Sevenecker aside, *I was not overjoyed by that* (possible) *homosexual aspersion!*—it had me recalling The Great Moe Geist having once asked—or really having vigorously implied by his asking his son Alan— if his son Alan was gay. . . So I soon enough became aware that swearing-off interpersonal (i.e. intersexual) sex was not sufficient, and within two weeks, or three (but definitely not as longstanding as a month) I do find myself in the bathroom of GEIST'S BIKES pulling-away at my startled and recently unpracticed (but not unprepared and jubilantly ready-to-roll) pecker: Your doggie with whom you have, out of depression or sick-ness, not tossed a ball for it to fetch for quite some time, now leapingly jaunting after the pinkie you have wound-up and let fly. . . But as all men know (as *all men are onanistic*, despite the lies to-the-contrary of so many [vide Norman Mailer and Franklin Graham, Billy Graham's son]), whacking does not make it full-fledged. In spite of its producing the desired results (sort of), and even with its permitted fantasies that may well surpass the realities of action with most women, whacking-off is as ultimately disconsoling as is the hunting-down of and quickie-shoot-out with a hooker.

Frustrated but still not wishing intimacy, or even connection—is this remotely possible?!—I decide to let my limping libido lead me to the crutch (and eventually, yes, crotch) of Yolanda Sanchez, the twice-a-week cleaning lady of GEIST'S BIKES (who of course knows no one I know, not one soul but that expansive one of my "underclass"-devoted "wife" Linda) and is the reasonably attractive mother of four (I think it was four, who, unlike their mother with her broken-tortured English, do speak "my tongue" as well as do I). It is not a difficult task to seduce this woman who is perpetually staring my way over her shoulder while she is sweeping (yes, the hips do do their sweep-rotatory thing, as if this is a traditional Mexican dance) or she is on her knees ascrubbing? (with picturesque sunflare dress curdling above her ample thighs and cleavage uncleaving from her loose but also ample dress) or she is swabbing the deep-treaded tire marks dug in by all those bikes that have been tried-out by, sometimes, the "beauties" off of whom I have foresworn myself (which foreswearing has of course served to render them all "beauties" to my deprived (and, okay, begging-regretting) libido. . . Except, after three episodes of, I must say, a certain three-quarters-hard squishiness (my dick a doughy marshmallow), and while I contemplate the fourth, Yolanda goes and quits me—and her job. She simply telephones me and does not tell me why. Have I scarred her honor? (I don't even know if she is married). Have I perplexed her?—she did appear a bit cross-eyed at the sight of my attenuating circumcision? Have I empha-sized, by fucking her, my lone (and lowly) employee, a certain inherent slavery-slant that she can no longer bear? Yes, that must be it. (Perhaps she would even like to murder me—*I* would even like to murder me.). Well, I cannot promise Yolanda on the phone that the sex is done-with and she may return to her job unabused. What's done is done is done—and I find myself back in my GEIST'S BIKES bathroom, sorrowful penis in sorrowful hand, and begging for my imagination to make it hard again, as if I am the retinologist of a blind man beseeching him to return to him that sublimely glorious attribute he once had, his sight—which he is not even sure that he can explicitly remember. . . So, what can I do?—I interview; and I *hire* yet: a fat, and tent-dressed, hillbilly lady by name of Martha Hires (there was years ago an elegant actress by name of Martha Hyers, and it puts me nearby to nausea to have her name and image invoked for me by this hefty-hick Martha, she out of, she says, Lexington, Kentucky [she boasts "Lexington" all nostalgia-sparkle-eyed, as if that nothing-nowhere town is Shangri-La—I have no idea why she resides now in such an unSouthern region as Berkeley]), this abdominous Martha who in her down-time watches annoying daytime crap on GEIST'S BIKES corner TV (it's perhaps the last cathode-ray job west of the Mississippi), and who's got to "keep-up with what in this world is what" by gluing her eyes and ears onto Fox News—especially by way of the "smart insightings that the likes of that handsome Sean Hannity is not afraid like most to come-*out* with." (I've sneaked my looks at Sean: his eyes are too close-set, as if focus-challenged: how can they not border righteous evilness and conscious-thought-myopia?).

What to do? What to go and do? Get up off the floor and try another relationship? A real honest one, albeit another larceny of marriage-cheating creepiness. But I'm not ready, and I know it. I am in one way informed of my unreadiness by my infatuation with a woman, a good-looking person (but not even a beauty) who in her plain-day attractiveness resembles the accomplished all-purpose actress Julianne Moore; this woman who, as she is perusing the bikes (she seems to know a bit about them), she in her attractive plainness but insightful eyes, sees my, well, despite my hoodwink-diversionary moves (even stooping to watch fucking Sean Hannity over fat Martha Hire's ample shoulder?), oh this "Julianne", she perceives my interest. And is it that the maintaining of my sights upon her (and quickly snapping my sights away), and my approaching her to explain this about that bike, that about this, too many times, too too many, these feeble strategies communicate to her that the delivery of bike-info is not in the least what is interesting this Mister BikeMan—but *her*. As I say, this woman is no beauty (she cannot rate by comparison with my own "wife" Linda, nor with the exudatious Suzanne Thalbrucker, or even poor Sally Asher of years before), she is no draw-up-to-phallus-potent-woman from the deep well of my deprived eros; she has likely been hit-upon by a man now and then, sure, but, I imagine, not so frequently as to be "a stuck-up bitch"—but nonetheless she is unnerved by me and my uncamouflaged (enough) oglings, and after, say the fourth time I approach her regarding, this time, brakes, "excellent gripping but with computerized two-wheel balance", and shift-lever locations of the nature-trail favorite Surly, she smiles at my helping knowledge, says (curt-polite) "Thank you very much" (translation: "Get away from me, you *pest!*") and takes-off, likely for The Oakland House of Bikes, or for my chief competitor across the bay in the city of San Francisco, where there are many many more bikes on display and in stockroom reserve—and perhaps less-horny salesmen.

Meditation teachers and groups are like mosquitoes in Berkeley—they're all over the place abiding and abuzzing and abiting, and often, for some reason, near water—maybe it's that the sea, or even a creek, can draw-up one's soul, one's poetic innernesses—if one has such, or has such illusions of having. And, sex-creep or no, I had such illusions (although I also thought that the whole meditation deal was magnificatory bullshit—a kind of occupational therapy, or recreational therapy, or nothing-to-do vacuum therapy, or, worse, an Asian precursor of American-based, holy-hell, *Scientology*!?, like those ridiculous Zen *koans* that some schmucks see as so *right-on-skewering-into-the-IT*)—but wasn't it therefore, face it, not out of the universe re my greedy self and women? And just having had the privilege, as a child, of watching my father rear-back and pitch a baseball, and a batter whiff at his looping (beyond belief) curve or his (beyond plain gravitational instinct) slider, this was enough poetry for my own chord-kindling, and thus enough for me to justify conjuring something hopeful for myself, *something*, *still*, even if I did not own such godly physique-poetry as had my dad. What I had hoped for was, needless to say, something beyond Kierkegaard's *The Fear and Trembling Unto the Death*—was such really necessary for a deep-poetic sensibility? Well, Big Bad Moe, poet-of-the-physical, he had struck-out the Kierkegaard-shakes by way of that blast of his '38. Not wishing to follow *that* suit, however, I fought myself (and Moe) and, what-the-hell, I went and took myself (while fighting-off my going and taking myself) to a meditation group (in a Victorian *beside a fucking creek*)—Vipassana being the Berkeley biggie. And there, as the leader, the teacher, talked his "equanimous" theology, he mentioning that dread word at least twenty-thousand times—equanimous equanimous equanimous *equanimous*—I finally recognized that meditation headman as Leonard Raznick, a kid who couldn't play sports and who we kids used to beat up on, not because he couldn't play sports, but because he wouldn't talk to the rest of us kids who *could* play sports—so he was putting us down as louts and lummoxes, obviously because he was putting *himself* down; but as kids we couldn't be remotely spot-on to such psycho-right-back-atchaness, so we'd just gone and beat the everloving shit out of Leonard Rasnick; and now here he was getting-even in a way by being The Leader teaching us all how to pitch our breaths onwards towards The Equanimous and not beat-the-shit out of anybody. But if "pussy-wimp" Leonard Raznick was going to help ease me into "a balance", a "centeredness", heaven help me. And so, at this my first meditation engagement, I could not much concentrate on my fucking *breath*. I felt like the things I had come to this creek-abreast meditation place to get rid of, I felt it

even more: self-contempt, selfishness, envy, deluded-
ness, childish horniness.

But something else: I am making too light (and of
course too easy-harsh) of this meditation experience—
even this brief one. For there had come also a darkness,
and yet one that was worthwhile: I had seen my father
Moe. This vision of my father had taken place while I
had been trying to concentrate on my breath—and
although the dad-sighting was of short duration, it was,
as you might imagine, tremendously dramatic. There
was Moe the pitcher, with his straight brown-black hair
looping down his forehead as it always did and the part
of his hair a fraction higher than was normal, which
gave him a kind of offbeat crooked politician look (or a
crooked anything look), which remained until you (I)
would get that gander-glimpse of his raw cheekbones
and his strict jawline, which contributed a trace of a
touch that was avenging, ancient, Biblical—an Abraham who might sacrifice his son for God's word, that
God-word being *Throw that ball, throw and throw and
throw until you are a perfect thrower though your
family suffer as you have not gotten yourself a job!* . . . I
tell you, with that meditation breath bringing in Moe on
its inhale it was, or it might have been, like a feverish
unsteady Hamlet contemplating the skull of Yorick:

Alas, poor Moe, I knew him well.

Except, poor Moe, I did *not* know him well—and I
knew it. I did not know that he had got himself so tormented that he could not sleep, and he was seeing a
psychiatrist, a Jew psychiatrist, who he hated (he

despised those bearded skinny-shouldered "coreligionists" of his who kept saying the name Freud as Moe might say Bob Feller (a great pitcher), and they could not duke: *Toss a goddamn hardball at those pisherfaces it'll bounce off their saggy egghead noggins.* But yet, so miserable he had become that he had gone weekly to see one of those "shitasses". My mother Ida had finally told me that dad had been seeing a shrink, this just after everyone had left our house of *shiva* for the dead.

I had not known that Moe had once beaned an opponent batter in a Minor League game—an intentional brushback beaning to intimidate the hitter for Memphis, or was it Charleston? who was crowding the plate, so as to intimidate Moe, and who had recently been called up to the Majors and would be leaving for "The Show" (the Bigtime) in one week or so; and that (accursed) batter-with-a future had run out to Moe on the mound and clobbered him, beat him up unlike anyone, so far as I knew, had *ever* beaten-up my father, and of course this humiliated him—he couldn't pitch further that day, or really for more than a week. This told to me by his psychiatrist, that "shrivelly shitass kike" of five-foot-six who had become *my* psychiatrist. By default. What did *I* know?

I did not know that my father had done, once, what Jewish men (in arrogant myth) *never* did to their wives. He had hit her—blackened mom's eye, just like a *goy* would. Out of baseball frustration; out of, indeed, baseball itself, and now just sitting in their apartment while I was in, maybe first grade, and my mother had taken a job at Sears (at the sparkling jewelry counter), and Big Moe had become Big Bum Moe, and couldn't take it.

My mom was now, in effect, the boss of the house—
which had made my belittled father, a man who had
always spoken so softly (as a hero—of sorts [he loved
Gary Cooper's softspeak]), mom's now rise to family
bossy-spot got dad to bellow his voice to break his now
belittledness, just as he might have broken some
"faggy-creep-queer's" head.

And now, thanks I suppose to that meditation which
I have here belittled (but, can you believe this? I stuck
with, for a time anyway [even while feeling schmucky
as I did it]) I had gotten a glimpse of an education as to
why I had perversely given up on Medical School and
graduate school in lit. It was—ah, again, "in part"—
why, after the *shiva* we had sat for my suicided father, I
just could not conceive of Successfulness. Bizarre to
perceive, but Success would have betrayed my dad—
shoved "Winner" into his angry-hurting "Loser" face.
Does this make sense?—well, when you think of it just
about everything in Life makes sense. Not good-sense
necessarily, but Sense. Life being so damned Big.
Sense is as circumferential as is the Earth. Cannibalism
is Sense. Nuclear holocaust is Sense. My hetero sucking-off schlumpy hetero Shel Sevenecker is Sense. And
so: This brief Sense-junket with Vipassanna had given
me the gumption to admit to—well the only person I
could admit it to—my "estrangedish" wife Linda,
who'd hugged me when I'd told her, hugged me hard
too—told her of my having been in a mental hospital
after that self-inflicted hero death of Big Moe's. I had
signed myself in, and after five days I had signed
myself out. They had given me Valium. Which, to this
day, on a night of sleep-misery (awake-misery or

dream-misery) I take not the impotent whites but the spacey yellows, the 5 milligramers. . . Sometimes two of them. . . . Or three.

ALEXANDRA

Even the German woman's sovereignesque name
said it all: Alexandra ("And don't ever call me 'Alex'—
not if you know what is good for you."—comically
proffered with yet uncomic cruel-lipped smile and un-
forgiving stare as fixed as an unmelting glacier). But
Alexandra's name might have been Wretcheda and it
wouldn't have mattered, as I was trying to antidote, to
counteract, poor Yolanda and poor Wanda and poor all-
the-others—not to mention poor me, who had so identified with those distorted self-and-other-tormenting
women, poor me who had paired-up with all of them as
a kind of comradely salvation. And a salvation of de-
struction? Which, I had come to realize was, against all
earnest belief, why I had married "my" Linda, as moral
and intelligent as she was: I'd come to realize that by
pairing-up with "my" Linda I had committed (can you
believe this?) a masochistic act, a reduction of "my"
self by way of comparison with "my" achieving wife,
my *over*-achieving and over-salvational ministerial
wife—and I'd *wanted* this? Living what should have

been, but couldn't have been, considering who I was, the decent equilibrium of a give-and-take married life. A life with honorable upright charitable Linda with whom, (again, can you *believe* this?) I had just bought this clapboard fish-scale-shingled house (neighboring the Berkeley ghetto, of course—Linda would settle in no other area). And even more of the ridiculous—can you believe it?—I had simply in the beginning told myself that "things will work out just fine." What things? Really, *what things*!? The 'things' that were like the poison darts and arrows and emotional boomerangs of my own unconscious (and, sure, my own conscious). Those foreign art movies that Wanda had euchored me into, viewing slumped and backached and counting the slowest-passing minutes possible at Art House, bored yet worry-absorbed on top of the philistinish boredom: worried about life's awful ambiguities—those films (that probably never made a profit), they were unprofitably profitable to the glorious masochist who had set up shop in the cortex of Poor Alan Geist, and so they had said it all.

But Alexandra already. She was, for one thing, similar to the Swiss ex-model *Mar*-lies (they both being Germanic), but she was without the *Mar*-lies earnestness, nor with that *Mar*-lies gullibility (which was actually rather endearing [for a time]) and she certainly, remotely, was not Linda. Had, say, Martin Scorsese been the director on-the-scene he might well have instructed this German Frau (although she still considered herself a Fraulein) to "do everything the opposite of what right-minded Linda Miller Geist does." Alexandra was—as "The Germaness" would (proudly and sternly) say of herself—*gleichgültig*. Explanations shortly coming. But I can say here and now that Alexandra personified the sadism of indifference, which made me (as if I didn't make me myself) the masochistic personification of the eager-bleating goat. Or, okay, sheep. And she was a dancer with the dance in her dance, yes, but not—and I know this seems impossible—the dance was not in her soul. Not as I-the-goat saw it anyway. Alexandra headed a dance company, The (what could it be but?) Alexandrians. At age twenty-seven she had come to Berkeley from her *"Heimat"* (she employed that German word so damned frequently, to show how "the English language does not quite have a word for it, for what it truly *means*—not just 'hometown' but one's *origins of being, one's borne heart*, as the tree has its root and grounds and its distinct wind and air, and even as its leaves may fall *upon* you."), thus her *Heimat* of Heidelberg—"that wonderful *Shtadt* of what you Americans will remember as the home of The Great Castle, and the noble dueling, and 'The Student Prince'—who was it in your naïve movie?—Tyrone Power? Errol Flynn?" "You know of them?" I'd asked, "they are so far back in movie history." Alexandra had merely smirked, as if it would truly take a dumb American to ask such an empty-headed question. (Her contemptuous gibe: "What *are* you, doltish Heidelberg Man?—who existed even before did the Neanderthals."). Yes, Alexandra said all she said with no effort to conceal contempt, as if we Americans satisfied ourselves with but the simulacrum, the outer skin of appreciation; of knowledge; of, well—what I came to feel that *she herself* did not possess (and *Mar*-lies, and Wanda, and Georgie and Suzanne did)—soul.

"So why did you come here?" I'd once asked (no, much more than once).

"In the late Sixties," she'd answered "it appeared that the Bay Area was the new and brightest birth, of hope, of adventure. In life, you could say, it was dance."

"And it wasn't? 'Dance?' " As if *she* knew; as if that 'you could say' of hers were but another manifestation of her thrusting the sharp two-edged knife into America. And she'd added: "Its birthright, your country's, it was there, but it just fell and failed." But then she went smiling, in that deadpan (yet stark) way of hers, as if she were quite glad of our flat-fallen hope: "It failed because America happened to be, not your fool Reagan's 'The City on the Hill', but it was only fool *America*; what is it you say?—no silk purse from no sow's ear." Same critical scowl which had accompanied her soulless depiction of our lack of "soul". Same distance and indifference—feigned, I believe, but did not believe at the time, because I had as yet not come to know of what the Germans refer to as their *Gleichgültigkeit*: The indifference, the whatever befalls me, and you, and all the world for that matter, wellthen, *Let it Be*—Life is Life is Life, and it is no picnic—on your dumb-merry way, you (yuch) *optimist*. A kind of Badly Buddhism with an admixture of the diffident, the "sophisticated"; the sort of stance we Americans tend to regard as the exclusive arrogant property of, not the Mittle-European but the more Western (and more clever-snobbish) French. . . That (supposed) "Euro-cruelty" that we (in weirdest envy?) bow to.

*   *   *

Enough already. Alexandra came into GEIST'S BIKES—"direct from my studio."

"Your studio?" I'd asked. "You're a photographer."

"I suppose it would have been too much for you, *of* you, to think of *dance*?"

"I'm sorry."

She nodded an unaccepting acceptance of half-shut eyes.

She had entered Geist's Bikes as if she happened to be The World's Greatest (Female) Bike Rider, come to assess the joint for the locale of a TV commercial in which she would be giving her world-prized endorsement.

Beneath her pleated charcoalish (slightly stretchy shiny-patina) short skirt Alexandra wore her black dancing tights (with their own unusually shiny patina); above, a multi-striped gaucho with white collar (I was put in mind for an instance of one of those tough-souled and never-real portrayals of jerseyed French bar-women with cigarettes dangling from their lips in our musicals of the Twenties.). For a dancer—at least I supposed the 'for a dancer'—quite large breasts, the cleavage of which allowed not so great a distance between them and the elastic top of her skirt. All Germans, wrote Tacitus (I remember from schooldays when I'd naively considered graduate work), all Germans have red hair; and all Germans, assume all Americans, have blond hair. Both wrong: Alexandra's hair, tied over and round in a long mid-spine ("royalesque") plait, was just about as black and shiny as were her dancer tights—maybe blacker (but I did make out a few gray strands). Her face, with its thick eyebrows and looming blue eyes over a pale complexion, was, I suppose I might say, aimed, like a spy keeping watch from a hotel window, or (it now occurs to me) like Calder's wire Medusa: narrow nose direct almost to a point, thin lips in a kind of thin-pouted gravity; her face just did not, would not, waver (what *is* it about sharp Euro-bones?—why do we regard them so highly, even *revere* them? why can't a soft relaxed-looking cast get its deserved credit?)—at one moment you might see the strict challenging look that Elizabeth Taylor could assume; at other times, facing you was a coy-game, shocked-but-brave, Audrey Hepburn. Yet at still other times, it was the face that might remind you of that of a cocky rat. . . Alexandra was a woman who was thoroughly aware of herself. Which meant, of course, aware of her power. . . And she was aware too of her changeability. (Did I say 'aware'? Sure she was 'aware': After-all, she was the one who occasioned her checkered ways.).

"I have been advised by my phys*i*atrist—*not to be confused with a psy**chi**atrist!" (as if I were a just-hatched idiot-nincompoop)*—"that while dancing does provide exercise and good balance and extension, and running is too hard on the heels and the Achilles and the knees, biking can provide an enduring exercise for the dance, and safely as well—if done *rightly*, for it is so, in basic, *linear*."

"I did not know that."

Was I trying to be witty? Or modest? Or sarcastic? No, I just didn't know that "phys*i*atristic" stuff. I didn't even believe that it was true—especially the charge (I'll call it that) that biking was "linear". But I did believe enough of the body-word language that Alexandra was venting, near whirling into the air to tell myself, Now here's one super-hostile woman, a darer who loves daring, maybe lives by daring: a woman I, with all I have come to know about myself, and fear about myself, and lament about myself, and resolve to better about myself, would never get involved with. Even should she allow me—with all my straining efforts.

So: by way of exhibiting for me the basic differences between the flow of dance and the "straight-edged rigididity (sic) of 'bikery' ", Alexandra mounted an old German Hohentwiel that I disliked but kept for an accented display at the end of a long line of newer bikes (had there been something familiar, something reminiscent for her in that Hohentwiel?), and she first-off leaned forward and burlesqued a furious demon-pumping, as a dramatic dancer might do in caricature, and then she (her word) "overflowed" that demonstration with what she called—"and, sir, this naming is an improvisation" (she announced such without the slightest de-stoning of her face)—"The Stolidous Dance of The Bicycles", arching as if careening about a sharp corner, then standing high on the pedals (yes, I worried about breakage of the near antique) and letting-go of the looping Germanic handlebars to reach high for the "heavens" (my ceiling), and then circling her body about, hips and shoulders, while she "danced" both on and off the seat.

"I see," I said, now seeing her exhibitionism—she a dancer or not—as insane. And passionately mean-spirited.

"No, you do not look like you 'see' at all."

Snubbing might be the best medicine: I turned towards a perusing man who had happened to enter the store at just about the midway point of Alexandra's terpsichore.

"You're *ignoring* me?!"

"I'm trying to go and help a customer while you dance."

The fellow grinned politely.

"And you, let him try to do what *I* just did."

"I'm sorry," I said to the man. "She's a brilliant dancer."

"And I *am*," she said. "I-am-a-*brilliant*-dancer. You . . . mockingbird."

Mockingbird?

The customer had kept-up his obscuring grin, but it had come to seem mostly as a defense; and as a prelude to considering that perhaps he might do well to exit GEIST'S BIKES and drive down to Oakland where East Bay Bikes would not be so likely as to cater to potential witch-psychotics.

"And to prove my command," Alexandra now said to me, "I am inviting you to *enjoy* my Alexandrians Dance Troupe." She told me where the next local performance would be, and then she actually purchased the ancient German Hohentwiel ("*Ein Schtuck Gedächtnis*"[7]). "Perhaps," she said, "I will maybe employ this fond bike as a dramatic equipery in our dance. The use and drama of *contrast:* The old and the new."

I had no idea of her meaning.

Yes, despite myself and as you probably expected I did go to her performance—one week later. In a small auditorium on Addison Street, downtown, next to the folk music place (that calls itself a jazz place, for some reason). But: *I will not get involved with her!* I would

---

[7] Memory

not allow myself to get involved with this woman who suddenly appeared onstage in her super tights (but not in her surrealish French bad-girl jersey) with one leg held high at the ankle in what seemed to me a balletic exercise motion above the Hohentwiel bicycle I had sold her, then that leg subtle-snaking away from the bike (as if it, that old German bike, had bad-intentioned extrasensory perceptions), and she managed this move without benefit of her holding hand (*what balance!*), it was as if she were escaping the holding hand, *her own holding hand*, as if the holding hand symbolized (well, to me, as she had emphatically used the word with me just one week earlier) the "stolid" grip of society, of mud-like social norms (as I have said, to me, to *me*), then, with her somewhat arrowlike face aimed in a posture of what could only have been conceived of as *Victory!* (unabashed *Sieg!*) she pantomimed a quite graceful shoving-off of the German bike into the hands of what I thought must have been the only other dancers in The Alexandrian Troupe (at least for this particular performance?), who were all male and who went sliding and gliding with the Hohentwiel, passing it hand to hand, their faces in twists and fraught retractions (and/or no-expressions), as if none of them quite wanted possession of that fossilized German bike, that "stolid" *thing*, that (apparent) life-impairment thing which was trying to infringe upon the "freedom" of their living; except, these men were not professionals, they were not trained in ballet or in any kind of show-type performance—that was obvious in their stilted (and bouncy) clumsinesses (and I wondered why did they ever *volunteer* for this sort of humiliation: their girlfriends' coaxes and cajoles? [they certainly weren't

ALAN GOLDFEIN

being *paid*])—and really it did become somewhat comical—no, beyond comical, staggeringly preposterous—
to have been trapped within this captured-audience, all
of us forced to be *grinding-it-out with those men-boys*,
those *fools*, all their awkward-bumbly multi-thumbed-
and-foot-toed "dancing", even their "glidings" with
bike in hand (really, grip-grasp-fumbly hands) and their
steps not at all in unison (or, I've thought later, were
they *meant* [by Alexandra] *to be* chaotic?—men, most
men, they just seem not-born-to-dance, except for the
few men-dancers, and boxers and mimes, I guess; men
are just not graceable material for a rhythm that cap-
tures the observer with its flows and its undulating
swerves—and that's very interesting, no?—sure these
fools' girls and wives must have put them up to this, but
how did Alexandra get the wives in her "group" to
accomplish that?—sex-bribery? sullenness or scream-
ings?). And, perhaps because I was soon enough unconsciously imagining myself as one of the awkward-
jerkass man-dancers on-stage, or perceiving myself as
already having been one (The German Bitch's art-
intention for all males in the audience of perhaps one-
thousand?), I could not help it: one of those spontaneous demanding guttural-bronchial laughters broke from
me, and at first I tried heroically to muffle it, but I
couldn't, so it grew, and then it became a communi-
cable thing, like a blood transfusion or a virus, a kind of
Clique Comic Cackling Adversary of the Dance, for it
had worked its invisible subhuman way into the audience, through the audience, at least that wing of those
spectators in my area, and there came to be a kind of
insidious cabal of sniggers and snorts, whereby most of
the laughers might not have even known about what

they were laughing—but they laughed and they laughed!—and sure I felt miserable for having been the one, the pilot-light, who had, unintentionally, started it. Yet the dance had been choreographed by Alexandra, it had its planned-out steps and gestures and "scenes", and as she continued with her various devices and/or acts of allegory, reaching for the bike in slow dance motion and then fighting-resistant her own reach, and the men geekily gliding the Hohentwiel away, and as the audience, or my segment of it (and myself as well) began to gain control of ourselves and gain a respective silence, I saw—or I believe I saw—Alexandra glowering down at me (in those super-tights of hers, those dare-you-come-on defiers [which had me realizing that, as Wanda had said she loved a full-strong male ass as it could facilitate a superior penis's drive-on into you, so I could love a full-strong female ass as it could do a return drive-on-back *into you* [me]), and Alexandra now became an angling arrow from that rental stage of hers for my having ruined the whole Alexandrian performance. . . And then did come the denouement, the rhythmic dance-women, natural-woman-rhythmic, but by then those women, with their WOMAN message, this seemed too much a mere afterthought. An amateurish conceit.

Afterwards I went backstage to somehow combine a false compliment, a singular applause, with a discreet apology. What would I say? What *could* I say?

"You were wonderful."

"You lying bastard. How *could* you do what you did?!"

"But," I tried, "I meant *you*, Alexandra—*you* were wonderful. True, I did not appreciate the"—I started to say 'men' but I switched to—" 'others'."

"Have you no sense of the *decorum*? The civilized *respect!* Are you an *animal*!"

Her short black skirt whirling round her tights—how had even this adept dancer managed to so quickly slip it on?—she had spun round and fixed me not unlike how she had first delivered herself on stage from the supposed civilized symbol of the primeval bike, and how, when she had first shown herself in GEIST'S BIKES, she had used the Hohentwiel like an Excalibur to magnify herself. Only now her spin-on-me was with the speed of spite.

Aside from her repertoire of looks, however, I believe it was Alexandra's reprimand that most got me. For, although my mother Ida had suffered considerably with my father's failures and his depression (not to mention his blowing his brains out), and although she had succored me so often, on escalators, in doctors' offices, even on elevators failing to be equipped with rescue-phones (usually in doctors' office-buildings), she had also been an expert reprimander: "Alan, you may do well in school, but you have no common sense." I now recollect that I had taken one full year in Junior High Shops to shape-together a plaque upon which a heat-hardened clay-molded lion's head would be affixed—while other kids, mostly the "low-class goyim" from my poor neighborhood (who did not do so well in academics), were already busy placing the finishing dials and antenna-touches to the superlative radios they had completed. Or, as when I had, as Milton Berle used to say, "made a funny", my mother would not laugh but rather she might opt for hitting me on my bicep with a strange cut-me-down anger at my lack of seriousness—which meant she would hit with serious force—or she would say "Very funny", meaning of course 'Very *un*funny. You continue as you are, Alan, and you'll see what you are in your later life.' . . . But I've got to say the following about my mom: She, broken by dad's own brokenness, was not beating me over the head with my "lack of common sense"; she was saying, I'm pretty damn sure, she was entreating 'Alan, before it's too late and you've gone catatonic, *go get yourself some common sense.*'

So here I was in my later life at age forty-one being excited by a woman, a strikingly Euro-accented woman, who was perhaps in her mid-thirties, and being told by her that I had no sense of decorum and no *civilized* respect. And here I was, putdown-prepped, quite believing it. That amalgam of looks that this Alexandra packed—come-ons through-on to go-get-away-goes—these sure hadn't hurt: that natural ability to project herself as Elizabeth Audrey Hepburn Taylor—these were superstructure to my mom Ida's infra.

"Please," I said, "let me make it up to you."

"On your knees, slave."

Sitting on her dressing stool, satirically grinning, she had extended her right leg, pointing her big toe at beseeching me—message clear, but more reflexive, more dramatic, more ridiculous than actually intended (her way of being wryly humorous)—all for me to deep-knee-drop.

My best recourse was to smile in appreciation, just as I ought have at her performance onstage.

And recollecting this scene I do now believe that while bravely in the penitent process of asking Alexandra if I might take her to "dinner or something", I was at least halfwise visualizing my widowed mom Ida—who was now deceased herself (diabetes).

" 'Dinner or something' " This was further Alexandra satire.

My mother had often used the same technique of mocking repetition, from which, as I got older, I learned to just walk away. (Dad Moe had advised me to 'be a *man*, Alan, *free* yourself from her.'). But this walk-away from a Queen (who I despised for her queenery, but not near as much as I was daunted by that sovereign style), this exodus was out of the remotest question:

"Or," I said, "you know, like anything? A movie? Dinner and a movie, or . . . "

She raised the right side of her cruelish lip at my concept-paucity of entertainment.

Alexandra quite knew she already had me by the balls—and she certainly believed she deserved that (illegal) wrestling hold, my having "taken the torch to" (one of her colorful expressions at dinner) her Alex-andrian performance. And she no doubt knew that my laughter—even if justified by the jerkball performance of "her" men—my critical horselaugh cackle had been prompted as well by my confused intoxication with her. Her lips had now gone into the ever so slightest of triumphant (and sardonic) breaks in their usual tight pursings, and her habitual interrogatory wide-eyes had gone narrowing—angry Elizabeth Taylor taking leave of cute-skittish Audrey Hepburn.

"The Maryland Crab House," she suggested, surpris-ing me—as it was a beer mug and crab-mallet clamor-quarter of long boarding-house tables and (purpose-fully) rickety chairs just by the Berkeley pier which was crowded with Hispanic fishermen—buckets, lures and endless stink. Berkeley carpenters went there too—many of whom had PhDs in History and English. She would meet me there, said this European "sophisticate" who, when she did meet me there was blended-in by way of uncharacteristic jeans (loose ones too) and denim workshirt.

Alexandra sat at one of the long tables, surrounded by at least six men—perhaps her (awkward—but devoted) dancers? Had she brought them so that they'd take me outside to the pier and beat me up?—as I deserved? Was she trying to humiliate me? Was she just innocent, oblivious?—being German she was just replicating the non-sexual camaraderie of a Munich beer hall? Was I simply expected to join the crowd—*her* crowd—packed as it was with its shouted-out crazy-competing conversations *("The Bloomsbury Group could've whipped the shit out of The Algonquin Roundtable at volleyball!"),* was I expected to just order some Alaskan crab and crack-away like a crab-pro in the midst of her energetic admirers and sycophants? (Did they even know that she and I had agreed to have a one-on-one dinner here?). From my back seat in the audience of Alexandra's performance I had not been able to get a fix on the faces of any of her dancers, but I had little doubt that these guys clob-bering-away at their crustacean claws were those guys. This ridicule (and I *did* feel ridicule) had to be my punishment.

Screw this! What kind of pussy do you think I am? (don't answer that). I nodded to Alexandra and I took off. And not in any kind of pussy-huff. I just left.

*   *   *

But me being me, I called and saw her again: unbelievably she returned to GEIST'S BIKES, where by way of confronting me (which "pleasure" I had deprived her of by turning tail) she said:

"That Hohentwiel you sold me is a piece of shit. Hohentwiels always were. *Schtuck Heimat*, my ass, what they they are is *Schtuck Sheise*. But, just because they were *German* other Europeans always bought them like as they were special and endurable. Kept those *kerle* fuckers in business. Undeserved. My dance, which you *ruined*, it said all about all that domineering, conveyed it, about Germany and about society-in-general, *all* societies, this in my-own-head of course. I couldn't expect you peons to know, you provincials." She was grinning slightly, her usual subtly-supercilious, as if a reigning monarch were eternally amused at her god-given precedence which she had no reason on Earth to deserve and had no interest in ever yielding-up. She was being, whether she knew it or not, a Hohentwiel, and one of the undeserving Germans her dance had been constructed to mock. "No," she said, "no one knew what I was thinking, what I was up-to—not even here in 'Brilliant Berkeley' with all its Nobel Prize winners and its 'genius' *Jews*. They all thought, just like of the Hohentwiels themselves, my performance had to do with the staunchest of German brilliancies and with society's implacability itself."

Whew! I did not comment. I couldn't even make out if she were bragging or complaining.

Anyway, such was Alexandra, three days later, upon that next entrance into GEIST'S BIKES. In a flounceysprightly Spring-like happy dress, white and floral and wide-pleated, small white buttons down the front, permitting very little décolletage, as if she had just come from an art exhibition at the Cal Museum (to which I had not been invited), or an afternoon dress contest amongst the most well-to-do ladies of The Bay Area. The best modality that I can draw up with which to describe this woman just then was that she seemed born to be dressed as she was. In other words, as I never saw, nor *accompanied*, such comfortably sprightly women in my once rebel town—which it was no more—is to say, while still hating her, I loved *It*.

"You know," she said, "running away as you did from 'my men friends', you are such a child. So insecure. Do you *not* feel yourself like an equal *man*? So Sir, for that 'piece-of-shit' Hohentwiel that you sold to me I have had my usage, and I do wish now a refund, full."

That Alexandra stern, natural, instinctive—I doubt that she could ever have held it back, even covered as she was in her sweet Spring dress: all those appropriate feature-narrowings, bunchings, loosenings, tightenings, so natural to her, and then the intimations of explosion. God that perfect floral dress and the dancer-exhibitionist (but dancer-subtle) way she moved within it—a sheath one moment, then as loose, and yet still alluring, as a swept-about sarong.

Which (I keep saying, I know it, I know it) excited me. . . But not so much that I wouldn't contest with her. Rather, her "ways" excited me so as to have me contesting more.

"I sold the bike to you for fifty bucks. That's pretty cheap."

"I gave you a free ticket for my show."

But what my desire-enmity could not stop its returning to now—because I knew that she was the type who would do what she did again and again, one way or the other, was Alexandra surrounded by "her men" at The Maryland Crab House. I just knew that she was the type who would demean any man, every man, again and again—if he allowed her to. She was just plain lying-in-wait for me. Just readying to make me shrivel and squirm and become an awkward nobody.

I wrote-out a refund for her VISA, and I said, "Keep the bike."

With a pretty good Frisbee motion she threw the refund in my face.

Which (of course, again) excited me. As much as did her invitation, out-of-nowhere, unbelievable!—did I *hear* right?—to come visit her in her "castle home". Was she kidding?—would her dance-men be there?—just all set to guffaw-at-the-hopeless-hoping schmuck? But, well, the thought of all that, the challenge as much as the fear, what-can-I-say? it excited me straight-on to the nit-dimwitted notion that, Hey, she's just too surrounded by her-own-self, *that's* the problem and she wants out of it, it's suffocating; why she might be other than she is, nicer, softer, charitable, understanding, "giving", "loving"—she has all the equipment—she might try her hardest—she is after all so strong—she might make it, me being realistic, let's say halfway she might make it—should she meet "an equal", not a "follower": The Right Man. . .

Okay, I suppose I ought to add that such "nit-dimwitted notion" I did entertain, Chrissakes, not all the time.

Actually, her "castle home" was only the merest portion of a castle, the only one in Berkeley, so far as I knew. It was in the hills, approximately two-thirds the way to Grizzly Peak, the top; as the castle was in the old medieval knight style with turrets, a bit like the rook in chess, it curved round in a horseshoe shape, allowing for cars to enter the grounds. There was no moat. Within the horseshoe, surrounding the interior, were seven or eight small "house-apartments"; Alexandra's had a balcony and a late addition fireplace substitute, red: one of those metallic pot-bellied-bottoms-with-pipe rising up through the ceiling like a periscope—purchasable I imagined at, say, Home Depot. I also imagined Alexandra dancing round it (in a calculated conscious trance) in lieu of doing, say, stretches and calisthenics. Although half of one curved wall contained bookcases, there were no books—save an English-German *Wörterbuch* and a hardback of the thick *Infinite Jest* by David Foster Wallace, which I was sure she had not read, just as in my generation everyone had owned their hot-off-the-presses copy of Thomas Pynchon's *Gravity's Rainbow*, which they had not been able to struggle-through beyond twenty pages. And it occurred to me that this "superior European" most likely figured *Infinite Jest* for a joke book.

"So, you have got your great wish," said Alexandra. Meaning I had been invited to her *Zuflucht*, "my eyrie, my sanctuary". "We," she'd said, "we calm down, no? We owe it to each other for the revoking of our mutual worst behaviors."

Well, that sounded, if not only Germanic-superior in its croaky tone and syntax, promising.

Along with a pair of starkly new jeans, Alexandra

had been wearing a T-shirt that she must have purchased in Germany just before her first visit on Lufthansa. As so many Europeans these days wear Yankees
caps and pullovers and tank-tops that carry messages in
Americanese that these foreigners believe are hip but
turn out to be ludicrous, Alexandra's "T" portrayed a
confused-looking man peeking out from behind a
billiard 8-ball that was a good ten times larger than his
head. Its message, just beneath, was what else but:
BEHIND THE 8-BALL.

She asked, "Why are you smirking?"

" 'Behind the 8-ball'," I said, "it means loser. Not,
like, hidden, or groovy, or cute, or anything, like,
'good'. It means you are advertising, I AM A LOSER."

"I am *not* a *Loser!*"

"I know you're not."

"You laughed at my performance."

"I thought we were finished with that. Anyway, I
was laughing at the men—the 'dancing' men. Only at
the *men.*"

She now recapitulated her (annoying) look of wry
confidence, the narrowings of lips and eyes: essentially
she was throwing my 8-ball smirkishness right back at
me. "In that case," she said, again rather Germanic-
croakily, "I shall dispense with this shit shirt. It is a
Hohentwiel."

I laughed. In light of my horselaugh 'performance'
at her dance-show, I wasn't sure I should have, but I
laughed, at her drawing of the dual shirt-bike identity. It
made sense. It was intelligent. The intelligence was
sexual, and confident—at least taken as so by me.

—and now expressionless, she lifted the T-shirt
above her slender dancer body, making her dark plaited

and braided hair flip-rise in (what else but) a dancer's
sleek fluid motion, as did her large (and braless) breasts
(larger than I'd anticipated), her hair falling onto her
now naked back. She Frisbeed the shirt, now-revealed-
as-greenhorn-stupid, she threw it onto her eyrie's
hardwood floor. And naked, the second thing she did
(the first was to vehement-gracefully [and jokesque?]
stomp that goddamn Bozo shirt as if she were an Irish
dancer doing the Watusi), the second thing was to show
me how, hardly without trying, she could balance a
quarter, then two quarters, on the outreach of her (rather
high) perfect hips: "I can do this with a two-Euro piece
in Germany."

Alexandra performed sex totally on top, no changes,
no exceptions (she later swore: "On the bottom,
beneath, it has me feel crushed, smothered, anonymous,
a *nothing*."). So, top was the world to her. Top was Sex.
Top was the grandiose exposition, even egregious, it
was she taking hold of The Other's penis and inserting
it as if it were in the legal clutches of her proprietorship; it was (it came to me) bossing not only The Alex-
andrian Troupe of her male dancers (and carpenters? or
whoever those men seated round her at the oblong table
at The Maryland Crab House had been), but "top" for
her was the prone existence righted, finally stamped-
out, supine-pillow-headed-male come-face-to-high-
exalted-lady-face, the legitimate attitude of mankind-in-
the-world. Watching from beneath the arising jut-out of
Alexandra's chin as she leaned forward, the sleek poke-
out of her ass (available to me by way of the opposing-
walled long fleur-de-lis crowned mirror above her
dresser), the slightest writhing of her plaited hair (same

mirror-observation mechanism for me), the stark emptiness of her darkened-by-risen eyes, the nonexistence of
even the slightest grunt or groan or whimper or cry, and
I—well this says more about me than about her—*I
loved it . . . I loved it?* Her character fit tight to the skin,
within her harsh beauty. . . And what (superfluous?)
passions I might have experienced with this Alexandra-
woman were well-blocked behind that one-way mirror
of her glass case—and *I loved it?* . . . Well, yes, I've got
to say I did, sort of. I'd *wanted* it?

"This is your punishment," she did amuse herself by
saying (and you bet in her Germanic guttural, now slid,
no, slithered, to an attempt at the mesmeric) as we—I
think the best words would be—maintained our
operation.

"Punishment?"

"You will be obsessed by me. Obsessives live in the
houses that compulsives build: You are an obsessive.
This was *punishment.*"

I let that one roll-on by. It was less than opaque in
my case, I'll admit it, but I'd bet anything that she'd
likely seen the line delivered in a movie by some seduc-
tress and decided it was best adopted by herself. Obviously she'd uttered it a thousand times. No need to
think and rehearse.

No need either for Alexandra to exhibit even the
slightest of personal closeness: she was just "up-
there"—on the (fast becoming fragile) throne of my
pelvis; she might just as well have been straddling a
see-saw. And then, the woman's coup de grace: On me,
spanning me with those sinewy-but-smooth dancer's
thighs (like smooth baguettes her quadriceps), she
began with her corkscrewing. *Corkscrewing!* Now here

was a new one! Alexandra started-in with her winding-round and undulations, ribs, hips, shoulders, neck (but not head) as if she were on a surf-board in evasion of a board-biting shark, or she was choreographing a pre-lude—but a surreal prelude—to a religious eclipse such as occurs in the evangelical churches of the Bible Belt—just before the minister-enraptured collapses into the minister's waiting arms: "If you *feel*, you are *healed!*" In my case I did not respond to her as a holy-baptized, but I did, for an instant, see myself as being a twisted-open wine bottle.

"How long then before you come back here for more?"

Three days.

I was not welcome.

Worse than that, her words: " . . . and don't you come back again, no matter how crazy you get for me; and don't follow me in the streets . . . and don't *call* me . . . and if you *dream* of me, good, wonderful—keep-on *dreaming*—and don't *bother* me!"

Had she ever loved a man, truly loved? I had intended to ask her, but I never got the chance.

ALAN GOLDFEIN

ALICE

Denouement in some thirty pages: Hang on.

Alice Play Dough. That was not my perverse-wise-guy jokey name; that was the name *she* used, "I am Alice Play Dough", as her family name was Plato and she wasn't even Greek but Czech, by which the real original family name the family had gone-by for two thousand years (or so), until her anti-history American adaptation of it, had been Plaitczov, but this is The Land of Innovations (even if we do pronounce "entre-preneur", a good French entrepreneurial word taken originally into good English English in the correct way [*err*], we 'Murkins take it as <u>*ooer*</u>, which sounds stupid to all the world [not that *we* care, as we have, so to speak, entreprenoored thus with that good right correct "entrepreneur" word, as is our Great American Right (and determination) to be "innovative" but comes off moronic, and singularly so, while we continue believing we are geniuses [as good a definition of moron as one can come up with[8]]), and anyway Alice Plato did have these ambitions of being cleverish hot-shit, and Play Dough as a name might well provide that spark. . . But, as I came to learn, Play Dough really was a perfect fit— *the* perfect fit for Plato; and I'll now be telling you why:

Alice Play Dough was a film-maker (At first I hadn't liked her because she'd claimed—I'd thought bumptious-pretentiously—to be a cousin of the actor who'd played The Soup Nazi on *Seinfeld* ["He's actually a really nice super guy."]). Alice was in the process of making a documentary about The Bay Triathlon, which begins in a swim far more realistic than Clint Eastwood's in *Escape from Alcatraz*, whereby his character strokes across ocean and bay to Angel Island or San Francisco (it is never clear); then the Triathlon has its dripping survivors (not all in wet suits either) running along the Marina to the Golden Gate Bridge, then jumping onto their own aligned bikes, crossing that span and pedaling up the ten final miles to Mill Valley in Marin, where the few who have survived all this trauma gather in celebration (with what seems to be burdened with few recriminations or envies) outdoors of the coffee house-bookstore known as The Depot. The origin of this Triathlon, the opening scene in the documentary of Alice Plato (I feel silly constantly going-with the Play Dough), it was her genius to decide would be at a bike store, "a functionally authentic place

---

[8] Comp-troller—there is no such word, although we Americans believe there is, and of course we say it that dumbass stumbly way—and on the London Stock Exchange they do tend to be amused. The correct international (non-American) pronunciation is "controller".

with no ornamental glamour" (her phrase) with participants studying their "weapons". And, after looking-over
my two competitors in the East Bay (why she chose the
East Bay was not because the stores there [here] were
more to her taste—it was only because she lived there
[here: it was the most convenient]) Alice settled on Al
Geist's GEIST'S BIKES. She lived on Spruce Street,
some five blocks away.

So, with one camera-person, a speech-sparse man,
and this Alice Play Dough with an incredibly roundish
billowy face parenthesized by her short-cupping hair
style, and that face so pale (wasn't it necessary for doc-
filmmakers to occasionally film out-of-doors?), and
with so eager big brown eyes that seemed to keep
swelling and swelling, and with a nose like the dot-nose
of a caricaturist's little girl, say Orphan Annie (yet that
presence somehow managing to produce these sometimes fluted flaring nostrils that competed for dominance with the spheres of her swelling eyes) and a
mouth so wide it appeared that she was constantly
telling herself the brilliantest of dirty jokes—and with
all as framed by that rounded only jaw-length brown
hair with its too-perfect-snipped bangs (which made her
forehead beneath and beside seem by close-contrast
almost alabaster)—she showed-up. On her (unexpected
but) unbelievably-perfectly shaped body (great ass, but
serious-no-tits) she wore what might have been the
regulation outfit prescribed in *The Documentary Filmmakers Haberdashery Guidebook:* blue denim workshirt, two buttons undone at the neck, olive-drab khaki
workslacks that surpassed cargo jobs as they were
equipped (decorated) with more pockets (with humongous flaps) than might be required for a very industri-

ous and overworked mechanic at Boeing, brown leather hiking boots (or workboots—I don't know the difference, both go rising above the ankles towards the shins and have thick rubber soles and brass eyelets paradoxical in such no-monkey-business "gunboats", and both put me in mind of Gestapo boots—of course, me-being-me), these "Gestapos" overhung with thickest gray socks (that ironically now reminded me of golfers' shoes with their fancy-dancey tongue-like overhangs). And I thought I might have determined the slightest bit of a limp, a sort-of ancient remainder and reminder, a scar-in-motion from what might have been some operation, on a hip, a knee, the back. (The result of an accident? or a birth defect?—or an ongoing affliction like osteoporosis?). She asked me if I had any reservations about her filming at GEIST'S BIKES: "It won't take but"—she shrugged—"say one half hour. And I'll compensate you if you feel that I have chased-away any customers."

"No problem."

"After all, a side benefit is that it will really serve to also be an advertisement for your business—don't you think?"

"I said no problem and I meant no problem."

Why was I annoyed? I oughtn't have been (although I will readily admit to being Mister Easy-Annoyable). I suppose my chafing had to do with the brusque proprietarial (and demi-stomping) manner in which she had invaded my store—obviously doubting that I would reject her, and probably well-prepared to argue her way in—and even take-over—like an experienced, seasoned, pushy salesman-politician.

But then right-off she said: "Yeah, I know I

shouldn't elbow you around. It's a problem. I apologize. I don't mean it, not really. I'm a sweetie-pie, I swear it. Don't hold me against me."

"Okay."

"You know, you're all-right."

"Thanks."

That self-parodic smile—the kind that made you feel that it was also you who were being parodied.

Alice Plato also had the kind of sharp-edged female voice that projects a confidence compounded by annoyance; too much confidence—so that what it really sends-out is a struggled-with uncertainty, an inner-most wrestling-match. Which she covered with her self-deprecating humor.

But that was fine, as I was—it ought be obvious by now—frightened of women who were too sure of themselves.

Her cameraman went about kneeling and tiptoeing, making close-ups and slow arcs, and then bending to get underneath shots, even laying down on his back and shooting upwards. Why? Bikes were not automobiles, there were no hidden "undercoatings".

Alice now advised me: "You'll notice I have no mic. Just my I-thingie here for notes. I'll fill-in my wordage later, at home. If you want to hear what I say to make sure GEIST'S BIKES isn't compromised or run-down in any way, you can come to my place or I can come bring it here."

"No problem. Either way."

"You sure are the most amenable man in town."

Lotsaluck on that.

"Yeah, that's me: Mister Amenable."

She smiled that wide-mouthed swallowing smile of

hers, as if I had lain-on her the greatest whopper of a witticism she had heard in many months.

I chalked that up to her proficiency at—and love for?—the chummy-conning.

"I haven't met anyone as amenable as you," she said, "since I lived in India with the family of Shree Bamana."

Bamana yet!? Come now—she was pouring it on too much. How much faker could a fake name be!?

"You lived in India?"

"By which you insinuate I merely *visited*?" That stretch-smile again going with its elastic dilation. "No-sir, I *lived* there. I-*lived*-there. And not as some young impressionable thingy beside herself to be squatting-down in the land of Deepak Chokra, *that* phony-baloney, amidst the *kurtas* and the *saris* and *wearing* them. No, I went to *cure* myself, dear sir, and of a-*real*-thing, not that usual excuse, you know, jettisoning the Western ego. I went to *fix* myself, my twisted curse of my twisted back, through yoga, and serious *doing* it, *hours* of a day, because scoliosis is nothing to be laughed at."

"Scoliosis?" I had never heard of it.

"Wanna see?"

And with that rhetorical question, or inescapable demand, while her cameraman was still roaming GEIST'S BIKES, camera to eye, caught-up in his awkward bendings to catch all the bike components, shift levers, derailleurs, cranksets, drive trains, Alice Plato Play Dough unbuttoned her workshirt, pulled it back and down her lengthened arms, and turned her back to me. Having no breasts to speak of, she wore no bra, and there facing me was a naked back that was snaked to high heaven by a wandering-all-over vertebra that might be described as either a dollar symbol or a Euro symbol or some Sanskrit marking that no anthropologist (or orthopedist) would comprehend. *Jesus!* I myself had been tormented now and then by a bulging disc at T-3 that threatened to herniate, and "my" Linda was troubled by a lumbar stenosis that she refused to deal with ("It's mind over matter, Alan."), and true to the layman's eye (or the doctor's for that matter) nothing was there between Linda's pelvic pennings-in to be seen. But *this*! this Alice Play Dough *scoliosis*! This deformity of hers (and now I realized why she called herself in tormented-jest "Play Dough"), this gnarling asymmetry (no exaggeration), it reduced the average back problem, even the ones operated on, to the insignificance of a piddling hangnail. How could a human being navigate life with such a spine-shape more complicatedly curvaceous than a burlesqued S or the musical treble clef? Apparently, the life-route was by—and only by?—deep yoga. "And not the superficial stuff they do here in America," said Alice. "You have to commit yourself to living in India with a guru who *knows*—and *forces you to know*. And so I *did* live there, for two years: yoga morning, noon and night—until, even with that sigmoid of sigmoids wrapping round me like a Formula One race my torso became as flexible and easy as"—here those lips of hers went so wide as to push her rounded cheeks out into the cover of her arced parentheses of hair—"I hung-in there until my body melted into wonderful soft, well, Play Dough." For exhibiting her "stupendous success" at flexibility she now wriggled-away, as if her back were these days as pliant as were anyone's fingers and toes. But, as if she were superstitious that too much outsize boasting might rebound and re-break her back (was this caution too a part of Hindu theology?), she made modest caveat: "At moments anyway it's like this. Even yoga is not perfect, and I go back to India for whachacall touch-ups." Then her crescendoed smile narrowed for a reverse emphasis and her eyes lit, they did one quick-sparkle. "Of course, undercover, I had my *fun* there too."

Staring at her contorted frame I'd gone Wow—there was no other possible response. I mean, to live with, from birth, such a major defect, such an abnormality. I admired this Alice Plato who had indeed through yoga cured herself, at least partially, at least enough to be a full-fledged functioning human being. All this requiring what so few Americans would have subjected themselves to: Uneasy years in India. (She of course hadn't said "uneasy" or "difficult" or "fearful", but I imagined, because I was me, those first years had to have contained tough times—or started-out that way.).

I thought for an instant of beautiful naïve model *Mar*-lies and her Scientology, which was likely taking her money and was probably not helping one damn bit.

"Trace those curves of mine if you wish," Alice now said, as she went once again to wriggling her back in what was certainly a showoff pride that was deserved: She had de-handicapped herself.

I did; I ran my finger along the scoliated spine of this determined, undefeatable woman known as Alice Play Dough.

She put her workshirt back on.

As promised, some two weeks later, before the Tri-athlon was due to take place, Alice did invite me to her apartment on Spruce to listen to how she had voice-overed that small part of her documentary that had to do with GEIST'S BIKES. Interestingly, in a positive way, I heard her techno-film-voice as solid and mature, and even-leveled by a suggestion of easy life experience (which she obviously had not had, could not have had—perhaps, for special occasions, she had picked-up the calm control of her Indian guru [whose name, Bonano, or whatever, I still could not countenance without holding back the gusts of laughter I had displayed when ruining The Great Alexandra's dance performance); after all, in my bike store Alice Play Dough's tones had been spotted by a fluteyness, piped by a random squeakiness, especially when she had reached for that dread (and now reduced to illiterate) word "awesome". She had been a woman—or a girl—who displayed her excitement, or her frustrations and her anger, too readily. Now she was not that person. Well, electronics are so advanced these days: had her voice undergone self-correction by computer?

In her flat, Alice wore the same cliché work-clothing that had covered and (maybe) costumed her in my store. That consistency did annoy me, although what was she supposed to be attired in?—the sequined dinner linens such as wealthy connoisseur Richard Gere had selected for his naïve hooker Julia Roberts in *Pretty Woman*? or a nice casual-gray cardigan buttoned-over a fashion-ably-unfashionable greenly-pleated skirt?—and it did now occur to me that Alice's closets were probably chocked and strangulated to the brim with dozens of workshirts and multi-flap-pocketed khakis. . . And that, perhaps, her scoliosis troubled her more than she allowed herself to let on, such that self-possessed "smart" woman-clothing intimidated her.

"Tape sounds great," I managed. I told her that I was eager to see the documentary after the Triathlon. "Where will it be shown?"

"We'll do it here."

An interesting turn of phrase. To a perpetually horny man anyway. . . But a man who does not wish to exhibit his (weakass) eternal horniness. At least not right-off.

"I don't want to pester you, Alice. I can go to a public showing."

"There isn't any."

"There isn't any?"

"My agent hasn't found for me one stupid spot. And there must be hundreds, around Berkeley and Oakland."

Instinctively I pictured the small auditorium where Alexandra's troupe had presented their "masterpiece"... But I certainly couldn't ask the German Goddess how she'd wangled that location. I kept quiet.

"Agents," Alice opined, "are such assholes."

At least however I was impressed that this oddball girl did have an agent. I mean, anyone who can save her life by packing-up and not just visiting but *relocating* in exotic India. . .

I said: "Oh I'm sure she'll find for you some sucker."

I'd meant the 'sucker' as a joke (I hated the word, but yet I'd fallen to using it: why?); but Alice, after I suppose a great deal of effort trying to locate a show-place, wasn't joke-receptive. Or even joke-comprehending:

"Did you mean 'sucker'," she asked, "as a schmuck-loser with no taste, or just as, you know, illiterate people—I mean *Americans*—now use the word indiscriminately, for, like, 'thing' *Any*-thing?"

"Believe it or not," I tried, "I meant the word as being supportive."

"Some weird conception of 'supportive'. I don't *need* your support, okay?"

"Okay."

Suddenly, under her alabaster forehead, her huge brown eyes and thick (real, furry) eyebrows, inflated: "I *told* you, *didn't* I! I went to live in *India* for two damn *years*, while most suffering scoliosis patients just sit and wait passively and accept Western bullshit *surgery,* from Western bullshit *surgeons*—which usually makes them worse. I-don't-need-*support*."

"I'm sorry."—I said, uncomfortably, as it was a short sentence that I seemed to find myself using with too too many women. . . And—come to think—men too.

"And that '*she*'," she said.

"That what?"

"I didn't refer to my agent as a 'she', but *you* did: you referred to my agent as a '*she*'. *Men* can be agents, and they are. Men *are* agents. Just as women can be CEOs."

"I'm sorry."

Her fluted flaring nostrils went about what looked like the resolute and life-necessary, and immediate, vacuuming-up of air, as if she had just surfaced in a narrow scrape from from an ocean's undertow.

It was stupid and weak (and I will give myself 'sympathetic') but I heard myself say again: "I'm sorry."

I took an educated chance and asked if her agent was a man.

"He's a '*she*'—okay?"

Silence. Immobility. "You"—as if she'd just caught hold, meditative hold, of her frustrated anger and decided to detox it—"You 'sucker'."

She was grinning as prankishly as a child.

"Male agents are into the-*big*-time—they don't even *reply* to you and your inquiries. I *hate* them. *Fe*male agents can at least be complimentary, even when they reject you. They say 'you'll get better'. Stuff like that." Like a child caught lying, she stared down at the floor as if she'd espied a galloping herd of cockroaches. "I hate *fe*male agents too. Fucking *liars*."

"Yeah," I said, having no idea where I was heading, "I guess—"

"Agents *suck*."

That's right: she'd again used the stupid word.

Then, improbably, out of nowhere:

"You know, I've got the best ass in the business." She turned round so that her rear end faced me. As if her buttocks were both introducing themselves to me and challenging me. And she went on: "One might not expect my perfect female ass considering my other orthopedic 'deficits'; one might expect that the spinal crook-around would continue on down, just logically. You know, like that old black song, 'neck bone connected to da—" she wriggled and shimmied as if dancing or badly itching—"spine bone, now heeyuh da word of da lawd." Again she wriggle-shimmied. "But heeyuh ahma standin' with the ultimate ass of asses."

I grinned appreciative at the brief performance—it being so quick that I had no time to figure out why she did it. But, face it: She was a racist in the bargain. Or face the other: She was the least racist woman one might imagine in your neighborhood. But one thing was certain: despite her having conquered her severe physical problem, or having considerably alleviated the immobility and misery it caused, she was still wounded by it, emotionally, psychiatrically—as how could she not be. She was an angry woman, this Alice Play Dough, while she was a happy woman. She who had bravely fought birth's fate, but she who was still furious at the inescapable fact of fate's birth, for its having made her fight, forced her to fight, while she might have been, as had local girls her own age, canoeing along the Russian River or running marathons (and with her dogged determination she might well have won such a race—or the one which she was now relegated to bystander-hounding and *photoing*: maybe she actually *hated* the natural sideline passivity built-into photography; I myself had always considered it not an art but a form of reality-leeching, or even thievery.). And if you were furious at what DNA had done to you willy-nilly, even if you had resided in India with the world's greatest swamis and gurus who taught patience and understanding and all the multitudes of pacifistic whatnot, you were nonetheless fated to not go-about on total even-keel in life. You'd have your residues. You could rage. You'd *have to* rage—at times anyway. You could wickedly toss your ass in the face of a man, any man. What you wanted—and I know I'm projecting here (but that don't make the projection wrong)—you just wanted to get even, even as getting-even was impossible: All life, in a way, is a scenario of the too-late and the unfair random—and you understand that more than most, just as I understood, if nothing else, Alice's fluting flaring nostrils and how they accompanied her swelling eyes. Alice Play Dough was, it deserves saying again, an angry woman—I (the projector), I just sensed it and I knew it. What was unique, however, was that her scoliosis had taken the anger and transubstantiated it from the usual woman anger at being considered less than a man—at trades, at business, at doctoring, at sports, at pay, at almost everything—the scoliosis had buoyed and balmed her anger. Fate's diversionary can of worms.

Same with that can of *ass*. Even as it was sheathed in her multi-pocketed film-worker-girl khakis I could make it out in all its full glory, as if I were Michelangelo about to do it justice. There facing me was a rear end perfect-clefted, as if measured by compass, a sex-nectarine. Perfect rear-thrust. Perfect elevation and suspension, rise and fall. Perfect out slope, perfect in.

"Best ass ever on a white girl, no?"

Then she returned her front to me.

I answered what else?—"Yes. Best."

As she has chosen to display it (albeit in its khaki cloak), and well-aware of the dangers inherent in challengingly or playfully messing with this ambiguous woman (as justifiably ambiguous as she may be, and I knowing that the ass-thrust is her way of compensation), I go for it:

"I admit, I was smiling at the display."

"*Display!?*"

"Well . . ."

"I have *not* displayed, Mister Bike Boy." The blaring nostrils again in their fluted flare, two outspread (I'm uncomfortable to report) black holes on the grounding of that plain of a pale flat face; the right hand in abstracted challenge brushing up her so even bangs and then dropping to distractedly measure and straighten that selfsame forehead-evener. "And if I *have* displayed—as you so insensitively put it—"I have 'displayed', not for any *sexual* demonstration, but—"

Come now!

As, without further ado—and what further ado could there have been?—Alice Play Dough unbelts and drops her "worker" pants, and then her worker-no-bullshit white cotton panties that a man might wear (save for the little curlicue designs surrounding the elastic waistband), and there before me, like a flesh-colored floating kite-balloon, there levitates the proud Alice Plato ass, which is everything it predicted itself to be, every agony it has employed itself to roundly defeat in the poor buckle-bowed back above it—and more.

"My ass is as full-formed and sexual—and coveted—as Jennifer Lopez's, as *any* black woman's ass."

"Stipulated. Agreed."

"I hope you're not just *tolerating* me," she says with her ass out and her worker-pants about her booted ankles.

I considered a normal male response, such as, 'No, I'm not *tolerating* you.'

And I rejected it. Too stiff and stuffy, too wrong, considering her life-boldness; too senseless considering that here she was standing there, pants and panties dropped about her boots. She was now knuckle-rapping at her naked thighs in (intolerant) impatience; and I dropped my jeans, pulled down my black Haneses (black not for 'Fifties Swedish movie porn-appeal but to obscure the inevitable urine drops that used to stain my white Haineses [after the ripe age of about forty]).

She said: "This looks stupid. You step out of your

undies I'll step out of mine."

When we lay down on her bed, Alice Play Dough made immediately to turn onto her stomach. Perhaps to obscure her breastless boyish chest which had got me confused as to whether to stare at them or not: A too obvious looking away would have caused her embarrassment, as probably would have my sympathetic fixating there.

"I have a rule," she says.

Expecting the worst, I await the rule.

"Due to all the troubles I have seen—"

Yes? Yes? Yes?. . .

And as she hesitates to give-out with her "rule" I hear her preface of expected troubles that I *should* have expected, as something out of *Porgy and Bess*, and I can't help it, humor lives in everything (does it not), what I hear is a deep resonant black male voice like Paul Robeson's complaining that *"I'm tireda livin' but feared a dyin, but ole man ribba he jus' keeps rollin' alonnng."*

"Are you chuckling at me?"

"No, believe me, at myself."

"You want to hear my rule or don't you?"

"I want, I want."

Yet on her stomach, but with her head crooked towards me, and I not yet touching her (am I expected to?—I really am not sure: we seem more like partners, confederates-in-malaise), she postulates—

"Maybe if my film gets shown, and makes real money, and I get a career out of it, and a *name*, all of which I sure *deserve*, I'll let up on the rule I'm now gonna tell you, I'll eliminate it." "

What rule!? What goddamn rule!?

"But, as it stands at present, before I let a dude "do" me, especially up my out-of-this-world ass—god I *hate* that!—and before I intoxicate him with all the yoga-moves I have learned in the land of yoga, I expect a certain—call it a toll. Can you guess?"

I could—but, "No." I'm guessing that the toll is in the neighborhood of, say, licking up and down her spine, paying a respectful tribute to the emotional pain of her scoliosis—which I am more than willing to do. I even want to.

"Well," she says, "I would appreciate it greatly, especially due to all the troubles I've gone through, which I didn't deserve in life—"

"No you didn't deserve. But really Alice no one deserves what troubles—"

"Oh shut up."

And she is right to tell me to shut up. Who needs such jive bullshit-obvious preachments about what a person 'deserves'. Truth is I am even starting to go bored by my dull routine "compassion". 'Understanding' sucks.

She turns back to fullest on her belly, her rear end risen now as if she is a cat about to pounce on a blue-bird.

"My rule is, the fucker-guy has to show his commitment and his respect by doing a pretty good lick-job on-and-up my ass. (Well, so much for the religious licking of her scoliosis.) As, my shit, it is sweet—bitter sweet. It's Yoga Shit—there is such a thing, it's chocolatey. And, by the way, this act, being intimate, is well known in Yoga. You don't though have to go on up the full rectum: just ten millimeters, say."

But as she gives-out with her Rule, and she is

measuring out for me ten millimeters on the uppermost digit of her index finger, I am caught, as I have been so many times, within the remembrance of my father, and I am actually wondering if old Moe the tough-guy pitcher would have succumbed to licking Alice Play Dough's ass, or, rather, belting it—as he had, no few times, belted *me* . . .

As I kiss her ass, the great rear of this wounded woman, and I only *kiss* it, I don't lick up there (maybe one mm—by slipshod accident), I augment that act by simply saying, lying, as a lick-substitute, "I love you."

And her response? Not, 'I love you too'. But, "While you're at it, you can let yourself go."

"Come?"

"Come."

"But." To speak clearly with no mumble I have risen my face from her rectum. "But, I'd like to save myself for—"

Her response: "Oh *you* would. *'Men'*. You bastards, you always want what *you* want and *when you want it.*"

I went with a mumbled, "Alice, I—"

"And do I want to have sex, plain normal sex, face-to-face and all, all the rest—I'm no *pervert.* I'm *normal.* You just won't now let me *be* it."

Huh?

Sothen, what was I supposed to do?—face-to-ass, debate her on the nature of male selfishness?—it's ontogeny built upon the DNA that came from—from where?—the Big Bang and maybe even in the maelstrom before that! . . . And on my taking leave, in so many words, I suppose because I did not lick beyond the nice ass-kiss, Alice Play Dough seems to echo

Alexandra the Great (or The Raylettes) with her: . . .
"and don't come back again, no matter how crazy you
get whack-imagining my ass and all the pretzel yoga
things that I can do—and *believe me I can*—and don't
call me or *bother* me."

On the walk home it does strike me that, considering
her years of debility, and her self-image of being other
than normal, mightn't Alice Plato have wanted in now
time, and in such intimate circumstances, to have conquered her past and become then as normal as possible,
meaning not demanding from jump-street my tonguing
the channel of her rectum until my nose was thoroughly
plunged and flattened, but simply face-to-face loving,
as she'd promised that would only come later. Well,
people become slanted into an alternate way of being
when they are brought into the world in an alternate
way of being—and, by habit's becoming desire they
remain what they are, even when the need is no longer.
A former thief become rabbi may well yet experience
the licentious robbing urge and steal a *talis* from the
synagogue. A former rabbi become con artist may yet
temper his business conning with the soothing phrases
of the rabbinate. Such behavior is true, and that is the
human answer. But so what—I have done the same all
my life as has Mademoiselle Play Dough all of hers.
Leave it. . . At home, however, I do masturbate about
the ass-licking. I see myself going the deep-dive mms.
In the fantasy I can go at it for quite a long time. At first
I wish to bite it, bite the damned anal thing deep for its
demand of my labial reverence. But this is a hatred that
is also erotic and it is, also, a respect—for her troubles,
her spine-bent spine and her breastless breasts. My

empathy remains. More-than-her-share has slammed this woman, you could certainly say. And what I feel is also a kind of Love. In my jag-off fantasy I am tongue and Alice Play Dough is all ass (I can actually see the cartoon of this). In that whack-figment I have imagined Alice's enjoyment, I have experienced her feeling superior and even motherly. And I hear her say "I love you, Alan." What she wanted from me is a human thing that is part of *all* our human things. It belongs. It is exciting—without the smells.

EUGENIA

What happened had to happen.

"Want to see an owl?" This question was not the first put to me by Eugenia Damis ("I love my name, it's real-sounding, is it not? and it sounds so strong, damnably.") and I'd actually believed that as I lay beneath her in bed she was about to abandon our monkey-business and, for some perverse reason—a taunting divertissement? a unique mesmerizing?—rush outside to show me one of those winged wide-eyed weird-necked nighttime predators, perhaps squatting in its nest—or laying wait to take-off and pounce, or wounded.

"No!" I insisted. "No owls. Not now! I want . . ."

Unsaid went what I so did want to do: Continue laying beneath monumental Eugenia, taken-in by her sexual strengths which were so self-confident that they required no apocryphal attack-birds of the night to fortify them nor clever requests of any sort.

"My dearest schmuckie boy," went Eugenia, "Dionysian rites are therapeutic, and you are heading for the Dionysianest of rites." This as she widened her eyes quite owl-like, as if her pupils alone would devour me, or freeze me—they along with her sexual monkey-business. . . Of course, the Eugenia owl-eyes were her own eyes outspread and they were part and parcel of her mesmerizing sexual monkey-business. . . And they worked. Intimidated and overwhelmingly devoured by her double spread-out vision, sesames they were (that word had rushed-up to me from down-deep childhood tales), even maws were her eyes too (and *that* word had come to me from some bad novel I had read), my attraction to her magnified and magnified, and I dove down and passing-up her breasts—which were oldish— I immediately ate the pussy of this now (I really did think) owlish woman who seemed to be ordering me to do just that eating eating eating, she could just do it, *order*, with her inflated impact way of looking. . . . And then speaking: "No, not there, that's too low. *That's* not *it. There.*" For, surprisingly, it had been no picnic, no Easter-egg hunt, to locate Eugenia's wise clitoris. "Yes, *there—feel it?.*" . . . But the (nearly) unattainable "there", the soft succulent pulpiness of it (even mushiness, I've got to say), was such, I figured, because Eugenia—while imbued with a carnality that was miles beyond age—was the other side of the half-way mark between fifty and sixty (or sixty and sixty-five?, or even, I shudder, I'm sorry—seventy!); and when I did, following her precise directions, locate her pleasure—what shall I call it?—I'll make-up a word—

her pleasure-*schlam*—it was really a pebble that had so softened to the consistency of a clam or mussel, it was so beyond my experience of clitori that I considered it was really some new element, some female addition come by way of her years; and although Eugenia Damis did moan (from memory's respect? or from reality's?) her "erection" did remain in that doughy way. Not a bonbon, I think now in mixed recollection, but a (rueful haha) malmal.

Eugenia was my realtor, I was selling my house—as Linda and I had finally overcome our intricate and hopeful ties (and indifferences and passivities) and accomplished our split. And Eugenia the realtor was not Eugenia the Dominatrix, although she did dominate me. (Not the easiest to admit, even given my history of marginal dominations disguised as marginal submissions and vice-versa, so give me credit for swallowing that bitter pill I'd never ever swallowed before—and by now I too was on the cusp of, not my fifties but my forty-fives.). A good believing woman in her own stark way (she had her intact faith in "God"), Eugenia was however in a disbelief quite stark too ("I can't see for the *life* of me how Eve and Adam's eating the apple was a *bad* thing—if they *hadn't* bit their big chomps out of it they'd have been bored in no time and that place wouldn't have been called *Paradise*—*you* know what it *would* have been called: *Hell*—with a mountain-molehill of dull-bored fuckings and one impotent castrated frustrated snake."). (By the way, I admit to using Eugenia's name far too much, as, as did she, I love it, as it sounds strong with its central *geee* emphasis, and that name-repetition '*Eugenia*' reinforces [in my own mind] the tidal wave that she was). Now, as

I say, she was no confirmed dominatrix, Eugenia, hardly that, she was just a woman dead-set on experience (even in these her well-experienced years when most women would have been dead set *against* more 'experience'—*enough* already!); and she was not great looking, I've got to admit that, no overflaxened hair (which would have had to have started its desiccation to hay by now and fallen these days over her thickening strands of gray), no face nor boob nor neck jobs (she would consent however to wearing bright splashy sashes to cover the underchin wrinkle-crackles, and she surely wore no absurdly comical stockings such as older women had pulled-up to mid-thigh in the 'Forties-'Fifties; and her panties boasted no contemporary porn-film handy sex-slits at the crotch—but who past fifty, maturely past, and in confident mind, gives a shit about such artifice?—you figure what was for what it was and you wave goodbye-to-all-that, and then you take-to what sheerly shines now, the person in her personness, absolute—you pass the lengthy hallway mirror (that you once loved as much as you loved yourself) without giving-in to its original narcissist demands, it's now just furniture—it does *not* reflect. But, as I say—or did I? (I sure should have said)—Eugenia was larger-souled than your average—whether she did or didn't wage any large-souled dramatic efforts, these just came to her. Eugenia understood and loved cocky-stiff-smirkeasy-paranoid-untrustworthy-inspiring-trustable (and sure, handsome as Tyrone Power or Stewart Granger) Count Vronsky as much as she loved and understood (and identified with [and had unidentifying contempt-for) poor suiciding Anna ("two-facing is cruel and normal, Alan, it's *life, and so it's needed and it's to be expected"*); she envied the 'Fifties sweet-child Leslie Caron for what "those virtuoso hope-seals of her eyes must have once covered-up—'a torn plight'," said Eugenia, "while the girl was trapped in her own over-gamin essence—until she *aged*, she became *old* Leslie, and those eyes'-spirit, those *truisms*, they could no longer *be* or *show*—*I'm* like that, I *understand*." (I'd just accepted all that 'perception' of Eugenia's on Leslie Caron, or on whoever, whether it concerned love or envy-empathy or hostility, or all—the woman was impressive-paradox, "as is all existence, my old-new boy Alan."). . . . But here, amongst all the smart anomalies, is one damned Big Anomaly—ugly too: Eugenia despised music, I'm serious: for some poignant nutso angry ingrate disappointing confusing failure reason Eugenia, SHE DESPISED MUSIC!—and how do you despise *Music*!?—classical, swing, pop, folk (native folk, foreign folk)—you should have heard her go off on Dvorak for his use of "that sloppy hill-country Czech worthlessness", and of course "our American redblooded-redneck rock and rap and, whatsit? that 'superior' Pete Seeger with the 'He knows an old lady who swallowed a fly'—oh, hardeharhar*har*." "Music," Eugenia claimed, "it's second-hand, it, like, trample-trods (yes, she could speak that way—sometimes she could), it crushes-down the *pure* poetry." "Come-on, give me a break!" I'd answered, "Music is an expression of man's feeling God, it can be, if it's good it carries you, it has you thinking your good thoughts, feeling them, your best high thoughts, it has you wanting to make some of your own, music, and believing that you could." To which Eugenia had replied, "That's Pollyanna child *trash*—I don't know if I *ever* want to *see* you again, how's *that?*—*now* you, bend *over*." She had in her right hand my blue felt belt from my Levis (ironically, it looked like an Air Force pilot's belt), I'd turned round earlier in an accommodating slow pirouette to make it easy for her to slip off that copy of an air-hero's cincture—we'd done this lash thing before, she pulling down my pants, revealing my (her) pink panties with the waistline frills and dainty fleurs-de-lis (she permitted me access only to her pinks and whites)—"My balls feel so *imprisoned* by these soft-clinging things of yours"—I'd said this many times, and actually, well, loving saying it (*Why!?*— really *Why!?*), and she ruefully grinning; she had looped the belt, my "hero" belt, keeping the harmful buckle in her palm so it wouldn't hit me—but still there was pain, and that pain, I admit it, it had me feeling weakness and a needed-love for this woman who was my belter, and it made me (and this is no picnic to write, but it's honest) come—orgasm I am talking. . . Eugenia's grounds for all that unique, unreasonable, loony, music-distaste did have me wondering though what sort of melodious trauma had stricken the woman when she'd been a young girl, maybe in school she'd been a heart-wounded wallflower while other girls heard the dulcet strains of swing bands and got asked to dance? Maybe when Sinatra sang *I've Got You Under My Skin* she was achingly aware that she was under no boy's skin. But truth is, well, some people just don't have rhythm, they don't have pitch, that's it, these jewels, these gifted valuables that we accept as natural, they are buried, that variation of times and repeats and soundings of instruments that compel most of us to tap a toe and hear the subtlety of a brain wave's led emotion-change, so that we, us *hearers*, we might rock up-and-back like especially a blind man does, Ray Charles or Stevie Wonder, those "eye-deaf" with their super-hearing and their super smiling LOVE, and so its an emptiness for such Others, such "deaf" people, such depriveds, it's an inscrutable void, which, when they see Others so moved by this "invisibility", it then makes for as much reactive anger within them as over-whelms citizens of warring nations when they feel rage for each other—for no reason; and so, like crazy, they rationalize, these musicless ("music is phony, it's bull, it's *math*, it's just waves waving their disturbed air by horns and strings, ask any physicist, that's all music is, it makes you *feel* like you should *love* it and you're *freakish* if you *don't*—music, it can even be *evil,* like forced *marches*;" and so such people, girls or men, musicless, euphony-unaware, they feel inadequate, badly so, which makes them feel superior to save them-selves, but fake-superior and, as I say, quite hate-harried. In any case, despite my contempt and my be-littlement (to myself, *within* myself, and *not* towards furious Eugenia) and my distancing from her (I did try that, it was like quitting cigarettes, it's easy, you quit fifty times a day), and considering my awe for her (and, yes, I admit, those tits of hers which were monumental [DDs, and in right proportion to her physique—by Net she custom-ordered for these what she called "power-bazooms', this "lady-of-a-certain-age"]), and despite in-real-time (like outside, where I played, no, really *was,* the boss [she naturally knuckled under, *she wanted to*]), I knuckled-under with her when indoors. . . But I'll here in writing be good to her—because, *She was not normal, and I was.*

What a lie! . . . Even those who love music can be liars. . . Because Answers are so Hard.

Eugenia, what more can I say? (plenty)—she damn sex-dominated me, while not dominating me at all. And, damned if despite myself, despite my perplexed resentment (and pride?), the first few times, after I left Eugenia—well, in spirit 'left', for actually it was *she* who was the one who withdrew (daily), as it was in *my* house where we made our "love"—after we parted (yes, that's better, 'parted') I'd spit into the toilet, as if I had eaten bad-stinking too-old sushi and I wanted to prevent it from making its way down deep into my innards where it would cause its ultimate in gastro damage. Anyway, and here's the kicker: despite myself I yet grew to feel more than a mere affection for Eugenia, I'll call it a love—I can conjure no more accurate word— and I felt a responsibility (more of this later); as I've already admitted, I prized, I fancied, the voicing-out of Eugenia's Eugenia name, its ring-out emphatic *U* and its aimed (and blaming) *geeeneeya*, I heard the whole as one might, I don't know, I don't want to be pretentious (though I know I *am* being that) but I heard her name as a kind of Minerva's wisdom peal—and I wondered honestly if it, Eugenia, was her given name at all. "I'm avenging *O*," Eugenia had said, this was one of the first things she had said: "You could say it's my mission". "Huh?" I'd responded to Eugenia's *'O'*: "*The Story of O*," she said, "it's *French*, the progressive enslavement of a young girl." I'd said, "I never read it." She'd nodded with a sort of annoyed confirmation of her anti-man-brain prejudices: "Men are illiterate clods, idiots, even the *best* of them—I'm *serious*." I said, "What

about Einstein? Marx? Freud?" "Interesting," she
answered, "you should pick all *Jews*—but yes, *all* men:
those 'geniuses' you've named, they were idiots when
it came to the opposite sex, don't you think *Einstein*
had his exploitative dominances?" "I never thought
about it." "Well, *think*. And Thoreau, and Kierkegaard,
they just kept *away* from women—and I *do* give them
weird credit *there*. And I suppose you've never read *9½
Weeks* nor *Fifty Shades of Gray*". "No," I said, "but
I've heard of them." "What, you want a medal? Haven't
you ever considered," she said, "that there is a glaring
absence of female dominion in the 'wonderful world of
lit'?" "No. I'm sorry." "Yes, 'sorry', you certainly are."
"It's not rare among men," I tried, "feminism illiteracy
like mine. We have other—" " '*Other*'! Some excuse
going *there*. Change the word 'illiteracy' to 'hostility',
to 'prejudice', to 'enslavery'. You think female
domination is against nature?" "I know," I'd said, but
weakly, "there are dominatrixes." "Oh *do* you now?
You peek into the dirty magazines, do you?" "No."
(Though I had been guilty of that 'exploration' some
few times, and I did regard the existence of
dominatrixes as only a kind of release, not really real-
life real, as in a relationship.). "Well," Eugenia said,
"there was even a movie—French of course: *Maîtresse*.
Needless to say, it was X-rated in America. *Triple* X
rated, never shown—not for the decent man's
digestion—too bitter a pill to swallow." I ventured (and
I suppose not without a first-flowering antagonism),
"You seem to have made a study, what're you,
becoming a specialist?" "No more than the average
woman, it'll surprise you, Alan." "That," I said (again
semi-believing weakly), "it will, it will surprise me."

301

(Though, I've got to say, it didn't surprise me, not at all). Then she called me, "Asshole"—and, interestingly, we smiled, and this paired-up smile had a depth to it— an obvious agreement along with an obvious, and growing, antagonism—that we yet definitely seemed to covet. And although I knew she would belittle it, but because I yet wished to maintain some shred of male sophistication-muscle, about male recognition of woman-dominance, in this case in the form of literary knowledge, I reported: "I've read *Of Human Bondage*, by Maugham, where the man—I forget his name"— "Philip," she interjected. "The man, Philip," I inter- jected her interjection, "he's, well, 'besotted', like a slave, pretty much, to this woman, I forget her name"— "*Mil*dred," she threw-in, her features pinching in strange indignant triumph: "*Mil*-dred. And what a miserable dry sourish baptismal *that* was—even Maugham's giving the woman *that* dour *name*—it showed Maugham's prejudices, his contempts, even if he *was* gay and *not* depressed and *not* elated, and really not *anything*, no sympathies even for his "friend" Virginia Woolf." Defeated again (and loving-hating it) I said: "You do seem to know your English—" "and," she butted-in, "correct me if I'm wrong, sad-named low-class *Mil*-dred—and *you* probably just saw the Betty Davis movie and never read the book—(she was right, but I tried to manufacture an offended face)— *Mil*-dred applied no *physical* dominions onto Philip— and Maugham had to make him a *gimp*, didn't he, Leslie Howard, not a 'normal potent man'; *Mil*-dred applied no cock rings, no brandings or tattoos, no whipwork." With such voluble picturings I couldn't but cringe (internally) while Eugenia's right eyebrow rose up wickedly (just a bit too Thespian wickedly, I thought) and her lips hooked downward at the corners, and these two puppetlike hinge-lines formed slopingly towards her jut-out jaw, as if she were watching these love-tortures she'd just mentioned performed by Betty Davis upon Leslie Howard, and as if she were disapproving of Somerset Maugham's omissions of them (not to mention the American producer and director and Board of Cinematographers who might have wished a profit from their film and not an empty theatre except for geeks on Forty-Second Street [as it was then]) while Eugenia remained thoroughly approving of said tortures themselves?—for realism's sake? "Well, what can you expect," she concluded, "from a *man*. Not much in the way of sex-muscle allowance for the distaff. Genes are *genes*," declared *U-geenia* as cadenza. "Even, I'll tell you, a Henry Miller or a Lawrence. Even a Norman Mailer who knifed his wife. Even a William Burroughs who *shot* his wife. To *death*. You cannot expect *any* goddamn *give*-in." Her right hand—I watched this—it had now inadvertently forged-itself into a pistol-holding clasp, she hadn't even known her nerve-endings had gone and framed that killer grip. "And, how come Burroughs, *he* got off scot-*free*? Whereas, if *I* shot, say, *you*, I'd be cooling my heels on a cot on *death* row."

I'd been tempted then to make a twofold (pointless) argument: One: in California, the death penalty is hardly nowadays invoked; and two: execution is near never—even in our American Red states—a sentence dropped-down onto women. . . Of course I held my tongue.

Well, Eugenia did apparently know (and despise) her male-books, the ones that suited her male-derision; and for a well-read Eugenia (okay, wellish) there was no beating round the bush (that could be a pun, but I hadn't first intended it). And domination, I do hate that word, as when you come to think about it, domination is not domination, it's as much a servitude, a magnetized, galvanized, mutual-glue fidelity, an obsessive reliance on The Other, a faith—the dominator could be your slave, it often ends up that way, it often even *starts out* that way—and when the "dominator" loses his dominatee he (she) might well decide that he (she) has lost "it all" and so then end "it all" (or what he/she perceives is left of "it all"). Yes, I'm talking suicide. (Yes, I'm recollecting Moe. Yes, I'm not only recollecting by reliving the black hole into which he fell and into which I couldn't but live to pitch my tent). . . But all that's getting myself ahead. Eugenia, she was after all not a pro-dominatrix, no Internet was involved here, no pecuniaries, no staunch rigid impersonality. And anyway, in the usual sense of it I was not a submissive (I maintain it and I swear it!), and Eugenia did not believe that I was—had I been, the whole deal would have been killed, aborted. And of course following my logic, as I've said, a submissive could in any case be a dominator, even outright—this can't be said too much—it all comes down to that seesaw, it may even be preconceived as that—subliminally preplanned. Transparent and/or translucent. Or it may be unconscious—innocent is a tempting word but wrong. Sinister is a tempting word but wrong. Objective, neutral, these are just plain wrong. But this is getting way way too intricate, too complicated, it oughtn't be subatomic science—and it ain't. . . Occupationwise, Eugenia was not only a realtor but she was a stager

too—and this is not a wry metaphoric putdown.
Eugenia provided conventional vanilla show-off faux
furnishings for homes being sold ("in the best neighbor-
hoods," she'd lie with a saleswoman's straight face and
a coconspirator's elbow nudge), she decided what crap
was right for what even crappier house. As Eugenia
later informed me re sex (I believed it was re sex), "I'll
tell you what's what and what to do." Such while
holding my penis and flagging it as one might do with a
flashlight: "This may be attached to you, Alan, but
that's nature's half-assed foul-up; the thing, it's mine."
I couldn't help it but I just loved her giving-out with
those raunchy ladyship words, with her (kind-of
croaky-voiced) dictat-authority [which somehow
managed to be also mellow]—although later-on she did
honestly admit that "staging" was pretty much all
"whimwork"—"you get a bullshit notion and you go
with your bullshit, if you're a person who's confident of
her bullshit and who has not one idealistic second-
thought bone in her body, or artistic—and once you
start-out with a style, there's no stopping, even when
you know you're creating a piece-of-shit even worse
than the piece-of-shit you were there staging-away to
make a *better* piece-of-Shinola—and damned if it don't
sell.". . . My wife Linda, by contrast, was the idealistic
lawyer and public defender you've already met—and
she was bitter; she oughtn't have been, but bitterness
had always formed-itself into a cloud she wore, or wore
her, even when she won a (rare) case for some Alameda
County railroaded innocent (or guilty). Linda had met
this socially concerned and active Workmen's Compensation lawyer who also won (rare) cases for "the
deprived" (and talked endlessly about "achieving"

such) (and he also hated bike-riding, or he feigned that contempt), and so my wife and I were finally divorcing: A ten-year life-rupture of reliances and companionship and few arguments (and more support than I was even aware of until these ended), a home-beingness that was both nothing—or a kind of strainless strain—hardly even a hint of any Greek tragedy of will set against will; and that was, overwhelmingly, our world. Over. So, despite my infidelities (and Linda's) this ending did call forth for me as did so much else the ever-ready image of my dad Moe's life-ending, his withdrawal: For percipient (and prehensile) Eugenia I was— although I hate to descend to the pathetic word—prey ('Ready' is too weak. 'Ripe' is too ready.). . . And so there, in our "crappy-staged" house on that black ghetto border, two doors from a much-burgled Ace Hardware, Eugenia (well, true, not right-off) dominated me (my fleeting thought: she's treating me as one would our pathetic funky inanimate stageables); and, to put it bluntly (but, again, not right-off, rather eventually), I wore Eugenia's panties. And when I donned those "knickers" (she Brit-pretentious called them [some-times]), until she realized that I didn't find the name knickers at all erotic) the wearing became (again, not right-off) not just for the hours of our "interactions" but for the length and duration of our weeks of our *generalized* interaction, her underwear "clamped"-on me became a substitute for her herself, and, for me, I guess, (this is so hard to say) a *transformer,* a re-identifier—it was as if I were a dumb bear trapped and glad-and-sad to be so—I living within a sex-version of the infamous Swedish Syndrome (although, as I've said, out in the street, or at a bar or movie, *I was the boss* [Hard one to believe, huh, but the word 'wimp' here would be a misnomer.). Eugenia's last name was Damis. This was her family moniker, it was Greek (she lied too that it had been Aristotle's surname—sure she might have picked a more obscure classical Athenian) and the Damis was *not* made up (I checked the Oakland phonebook—there were others), and Eugenia did feel that her family patronymic fit well even soundwise her controlling ways at sex—*Dayyymis!* And as I've said, Eugenia did permit my wearing only her panties that were white or pink—a strict limitation with which I had zero problems (after a while—figure *this*!—I found that I *wanted* them, only those two "girlie" colors) this especially when we were engaged in our "enterprise".

And as I've also implied before by saying that Eugenia was in her late fifties or sixties (or even early seventies), her manner was certainly not advantaged by what you would call her looks, no way: Eugenia's features were plain okay—but you wouldn't stop dead in your tracks to eye-swallow her as you might have The Exudatious Suzanne or The Goddess Alexandra. Eugenia was, let's say, a B or she might have even been classifiable down in the C+/B- category—fine filaments of gray hairs swept back across the temples and above her ears like cat whiskers or scheister lawyer touch-up strands done by the latest local Max Factor. But that average (or low-average) normalcy, it did not apply to Eugenia's breasts, which were proportional to Eugenia's general proportions if you were not under Eugenia's sway, but were beyond that proportion, far beyond, if you found yourself under her influence: I know I mentioned this before, but Double Ds they were (She did not brag about these exceptional drawing-cards: I checked the labels in her bra's dresser drawer [and oft-times I found myself kissing them and fondling as if they were sacred raiments and arabesques un-earthed by Professor Alan Geist the archaeologist in Asia Minor, they hidden many meters beneath some distant neglected pyramid]), and it was a matter of tawdry (but smirk-controlled) pride with Eugenia that she had to special-order for them (she mentioned that required "mail-order" purchasing a lot—and, as I say, without the vaguest of taunting smirks or sardonic smiles). But her subtle pride was not the sum total of all the elements that Eugenia's psyche had going for it; she had this prehensile (I had to look that word up, and it does fit in this case) intelligence: "You want to be handled," she'd said of me to me—and this astute observation came pretty much right off the bat, right— as far as I could see—right out-of-the-blue, she staring her gray drillpress pinpointer eyes at me. And I hadn't thought of that "handling" thing, not in the, well, "prehensile", manner in which she spoke and looked when she let out with it. And what's wrong anyway with having a handleable-desire?—one's genitals by the way I'm talking, they grow-up learning the wanting-to-be-handled, don't they?—and as a boy you fulfill that wanting (Hell, you show me a man devoid of any hand-ling-desire and I'll show you a paranoid zombie-robot-hermit-sickie-monk: Perhaps the wooden-stiff types that Lawrence Harvey and Dirk Bogarde and [in America] Clifton Webb and Vincent Price used to play so perfectly and to such acclaim [in this acclaim-case just the Brits]—there must have been a great demand for such characterizations then in the movie world, *and in the movie audience?*). By the way, woman-

handlicization is applicable here as well—it's even
worse with women, as if you, even you women, didn't
know. So, with Eugenia, due to her perception and her
near-immediate acting-upon that perception, you felt
that you were in ultimate, savvy, good hands, über-
hands, you (okay, *I*) you were so flushed with craved
satisfaction (and anticipation) that you never noticed
the Eugenia-flaws, and I must say that they were not
unprominent: not the knuckle-wrinkles with their
oblong crease-warps and canyons (not unlike elephants'
elbows), not the varicose veininess, not the somewhat
clawlike tendons and bowing-arched-oppositionally
fingernails and/or the like—such as those corrugated
eye-corners that had you conceiving that this woman
had seen everything in human behavior that was to be
seen, and she wanted to see no more.

Eugenia first rubbed my back when I bent to sit on
the overly-plush quicksand stage-sofa she had provided
for our house-sale (it would have remained so deluxe-
saggy for maybe a month, through perhaps five subsequent stagings, and then collapsed into itself like a
sinkhole.). Anyway, not wishing to appear impolite, or
prudish—and quite flattered by Eugenia's bold back-
rubs—I went about rubbing Eugenia's back, shoulder-
blade-to-shoulderblade (and downwards a slight well-
judged bit [the kidney area is my best guess.]. . . But
what was this strange stager-woman's motivation for
her bold reach-out handling-out-of-nowhere, act?—
Christ, I had no idea. Was it client comfort and assurance? Client maintenance? Client entrapment? Sales-
lady psychosis? They certainly hadn't taught the
woman this overt technique during her realtor training—even were it advanced. No, it was just Eugenia's

natural way? her habitual way? no more outrageous nor
out of the ordinary for her than shaking hands. But then,
when with her average-looking (but penetrate) gray
eyes sizing me up (I call them 'gray' because I can no
longer recollect her eyes' true color, if I had ever even
paid attention to such), Eugenia went and performed
that aforesaid testicular cupping, and I was too surprised, too startled, and although well-pleased, too
cowed (too dignified?—nah) to perform a similar
grasping move between her legs (she was wearing a
skirt, although this wouldn't have mattered *to-a-real-
man,* and the truth is, as with her eyes, I'm not so sure
what her skirt was, it may have been one of those
imitation pants-skirts, and even just plain "breathing"
cotton pants (it was summer, definitely summer)—and
so this disequilibrium of my non-cunt-cupping just
made her penis-cupping the boss cupping (which,
having already sized me up, she'd known would be the
case: she admitted this to me in later days). Insert
thought though: Eugenia's ball-cupping might have
been due to my casual clamping onto her right shoulder,
and thus with my long male arms surrounding her in
near totality, which might have been female-offensive,
although I did consider it, as do all males (pretty much)
male prerogative with women, although male-on-male
it might merely indicate a pal thing, not an ownership
thing, a "You're my meat", as male-on-woman it could
tend to imply, and thus be counteracted or combated, or
sex-equalized, (by the offended woman, who might be
one of those ladies who eats nails) by a quick reply-
lurch to the available resort of testicle-cupping of the
shoulder-cupper. Sex can be confusing, as we all know
(and even too often hope-for), thus it shouldn't require

a Rubik's Cube-like brain to grasp that very inappropriate sex can be a very major-complicated thing
(and about as appropriate as can be)—up there, almost,
with forbidden sex (which, again, we too often hope-
for). "Would you like to worship my power bazooms?"
That's what Eugenia then went and offered. Yes,
'power bazooms' was her descriptive (it must have
been a fifty-year-old risqué phrase, even then in the
Seventies), and "worship" was the woman's chosen
verb. Yes, I said, only Yes, or I did manage to get it out
in a frail exhale—and I can hear my vowels now
already fallen into a votary's weak reverence, *already* (I
suppose the surprise of her worship-word did that), and
Eugenia said, calmly as a masseuse, "Lay back" (on
that stage-plush super-sinking sofa—which felt so alien
in my house), and damned if she didn't de-blouse and
de-brassiere (flip-tossing the "big girl bra" with intentional carelessness as one would a Frisbee [it landed on
the sales-pro-staged Kennedyesque rocking chair and
hung there as if some mid-life lady had been so surprised by, what? a rat? a raccoon?]—and so how could
I not find "the hanging bra" a stand-in for a defeated
life, and thus appropriate?). Anyway and thus and so:
why not lay back as this woman said (no, softly
ordered?), considering my divorce-draining life? Oh
now, you bet, I did love my separated Linda more than,
God, *anything in life*; and I did lay myself back (such
that instinct made me look-about this my leaving house
scattered yet with the few articles of our living that
Linda had left to me—the Melitta, a small red-stained
glass heart I had once given her for her birthday, my
childhood miniature doctor—in all white—holding his
dangling stethoscope [as if it were a de-frocked

brassiere?]; and then such that my instinct had my heart or soul or mind seeing what was *gone*—Linda's Everything, except for a few black law books with their purple-stained page-edges, except for Linda's electric by-the-bed clock that kept time by satellite, except for—oh hell, forget it!). And so I had lain back as ordered by Eugenia—and that damned realtor sofa-substitute-thing reverse-caterpillared me, triple-arching my legs my back my neck; and, as I expected, my mouth could not fully absorb Eugenia's supersizer breasts, and which failure on my part (I guess it was a failure, to take her weighty breasts completely in, like the world's greatest eucharist), that failure got her smiling in her patented Eugenia-power way, as if she had just accomplished a great female feat over the inadequacy of a little boy-man—who, by the way, couldn't help but be thinking then—I'm sorry, but truth is truth—thinking of no more Linda but his gone mother Ida—which smile of hers, Eugenia's, not my reconjured mother's, affected my expression into I guess (*I know*) an awed subservience (well, *more of one*) which had Eugenia then de-skirting (or de-pants-skirting), laying on top of me, and humping with sheer potency, as might a man—in a porn film anyway—my legs wrapping (naturally) round the backs of her thighs, as would a woman's—and I thereafter feeling a curious guilt and awkwardness and ignominy and impotence—*and excitement*, which last I made good use of in my subsequent masturbation fantasies about who else but Eugenia—which, for a time anyway, edged-out all (almost all) masturbation fantasies about other women, none of whom had actually (to that juncture) lain (male-ishly) on top and—call a spade a spade—fucked my brains out with her—what shall I call it?—"power vagina"? Which, honestly, was the expression that Eugenia, grim-smiled, had actually put into play: "I'm now going, sir, to fuck your brains out with my power vagina—any objections?"

"Uh-uh. . . No."

Though actually I had plenty of objections. I still had.

Though actually what I said was, "Have at it." I *said* that.

Absurdly, that mandate seemed to me, in these circumstances, objections or no, manly.

Manly? . . . What could have been less *manly*?! Me with my legs wrapped about her hamstrings just precisely as is the woman's natural way.

Eugenia's husband was Les. He was a landscape architect. " 'Architect,' he calls himself," she'd say. "What a glorified travesty on the title 'architect', what an embellishment, he's a fucking *gardener,* like a Mexican. (She'd smile-sneer). It's the same male trip as an accountant upgrading himself to a financial analyst, or a mechanic to an engineer." Eugenia's husband did the landscape architecting for my house-sale, thus gilding the lily, embellishing that shithole's salability (so Eugenia claimed [sneer-smile]). Eugenia's husband—I just forgot his name, from two seconds ago—ah, Les: Les would not "stand for" her domination—she said that; and "I," she said, "will not tolerate my submission, not to *him*." (Here she made a wasted face as if entering an abattoir.) "It's kind of like Jack Spratt who'll eat no fat while his wife will eat no lean." Eugenia was no female Don Rickles, but, as you must imagine by now, she was not *not* a humorous put-down specialist type individual.

"So," I'd ventured (making conversation?), "what's your sex like then?—the two of you."

"It's like," she'd answered, "bookkeeping calling itself accounting."

Which put me in mind of my Linda and myself, with reckonings and regrets of why couldn't it have been other. Which picturings, as always, cut me through my heart—I mean I could feel the knife, and this is not a stab that's figurative. I asked—

"So why do you stay married?"

"Because it's perfect, what we have."

"Huh?"

"God are you dumb. About relationships. Don't you understand *anything*?"

I wanted to clobber her. For Linda's sake, I suppose. Although at this stage in the game Linda could not have cared one iota what Eugenia meant about her or implied.

"Alan," she went, "why do I stay married? Have you ever heard of loneliness?"

Was she kidding? Just then, sex with Eugenia notwithstanding, I was the Tuscanani/Toscanini? of loneliness, wailing-away on the podium. (Or for others of you, the Elvis in his grotesque Memphis mansion, Ruger-Lugering at the big-screen TV, his enemy.). (Or for still others the isolated Lou Reed, whose denied real name was something like Louis Reznickoff—or something). (Or Moe).

"You know," she said, "I didn't know I was what I am until I became it."

I hesitated, then out of default I went with a "That's

weird."

"No it's not. That's the last thing that it is—weird. Did you know what *you* were?"

"Hey, I'm *not that*, what you—submissive?—it's just, with us . . . it *happened*." I was shaking my head then as if a cop had just pulled me over for surpassing a speed-limit by 3 mph. "It was just happening."

" 'Just happening'." She laughed, a glorious well-pleased cackle. "Happening shmappening."

At that moment, by the way, I was sprawled across the woman's thighs and she was in the intermittent process of spanking me, taking a breath, and spanking me again. . . My mouth—I just seemed to want it to be this way—my mouth now went huddled within one of the receptive cups of her big brassiere, which lay on the edge of the sofa, and, I guess for more inspiriting, I took in deep breaths of it—but it merely smelled of washing.

"Actually," she said, "I think you still don't know who and what you are."

And, between breaths and brassiere-sucklings I turned my neck as far as I could (managing to glimpse only the sidereal edge of great maternal breast) and I combated her declaration with an, "Oh, everybody's really in their hearts that way. In the dark."

"If it comforts you to believe that."

But surely it was—and is—true.

"And you, you're not 'in-the-dark' "?

"Not me. No. I graduated long ago. Painful process."

I didn't ask about her pain. I could be an empathetic man, I could; but I suppose not for a woman plastering-away at my ass. I did not want to know about Eugenia's conquered pain.

And she went back to her spanking—which now had lost considerable of its propellant oomph. The intervention of psych-debate on human consciousness had stunted it—though I've read that, smartly done, verbal debate can magnify it too. But really, in our case, the Eugenia punch, exhilarating for both giver and receiver (the fantasies! the fantasies!), it had drifted-off to a perfunctory pitty-pat.

"Eugenia," I said, "Quit acting. I could step out right now from this stage play we're playing, and it would be no big thing—I'd forget it in ten seconds."

"You're fooling yourself, Alan. About yourself. You still are."

True I'd relished that knuckling-under. But for my own self-dignity, I had to deny.

And what was to come: There came, without my fighting it, the diminishment (and pain, let's face it) of my being bent over the staged drop-leaf (plastic-mahogany) dining room table and fucked by Eugenia with her black strap-on (4-5 inches: she claimed she was "considerate", "I could have bought a longer one, and anyway I won't go all-the-way"), the back end of which entered her vagina and found her clitoris as she drove into me, thus feeding two hungry birds. When we performed this act I remembered how I had been the dictator with Wanda, who had screamed-out, and I did not move one inch, being fearful that this shifting would magnify the rectal pain—which (coincidentally?) I experienced in my penis when I fucked Eugenia in the "normal" way (we did do that, upon occasion), her diaphragm (I thought it was that causing my pain, even while being aware of her "advanced" age, but what else could it have been?), her "diaphragm" almost always seemed to sharpishly pinprick and jab at my penis, which pain did inhibit my driving-in on her vagina, my male-ish pumping-in—and if that pain-inflictor was her diaphragm that she just kept using as she aged (to feel young?), had she stropped and sharpened it? (to feel armed?—an armadillo diaphragm?), was there some S-M diaphragm on the sub-rosa market just made for such wicked recoil spiking purposes?—what otherness could it have been that hurt me so? But raising my eyes and watching Eugenia in profile in the oblong stage-mirror as she arched like an underwater swimmer or a dolphin coming up into me with that strap-on, that vision was incomparable—it reminded me (I have to say this) of my mother's having given me enemas when I was a child, and my wanting to get even but not having any clue (I certainly would not have given my *mother* an enema, at my age five—or, okay, of course, at *any* age—and yes I was guilty of wondering if my father Moe, that ex Jew-jock, had ever submitted himself to such stuff with my mom, such indignity—no, *never!*— *of course no, never!*—but with other women? Hook- ers?). Eugenia and I, though, we did draw the line at Eugenia's engaging in maneuvers such as peeing in my mouth or—Jesus!—shitting on my face. "I'll puke with that," she'd said, "and so will you, though truth is it would make you fully mine forever in your mind, I once heard a dominatrix lecturing about that." (Yes, of course, the question begs: *She went to a dominatrix lecture?* And where?—certainly not at the Tuesday night series at the Berkeley Y, where I had attended to hear Noam Chomsky, and also "the American Proust"—I've forgotten that guy's name, he's dead). But really in the final analysis I allowed Eugenia's entering me in that indignant doggie rear-end way (well, indignant for a "normal" guy) because (and this is not temporizing, it is true) I'd (half) convinced myself that I was doing my bit, my bizarre bit for sex-equality (now that equality-driven Linda had left me—yet by way of some spiritual Progressive grapevine she would *know* my "sacrifice"), and (also true) I suppose I feared that if I disappointed Eugenia she would quit doing her clever things to me like the erotic near-strangling of my neck with her potent bra—and also such as when she took hold of my cock on the third or fourth go-round, calibrating it, she being house-wise as a realtor-carpenter, she having extracted a leak-worn-to-be-replaced copper washer from the kitchen faucet, and she jerry-rigged that item (with heat-bendings, easy enough from the stove), and thus she adjusted that sink-washer to be a "fashionable", but plain-unencumbered, cock-ring, which with grunty elbow grease she jostled over and onto my penis (with little room for airy looseness) and then she said, "Alan, you're my wed-husband and my prized spigot." (I swear: I never wore the damn thing when she was not around—*but when she was around, I liked it*—its pressure clutched and it imprisoned [but unlike that pan-imprisonment that certain personages like myself can regard of legal mar-riage] and it reminded with its tight clench—I was adorned as *HERS*). And yes, in the state that I was in I was sure that had I not submitted to these "innovations" Eugenia would go off to find someone else, some substitute second-string abandoned man selling his-and-his-wife's dream house or buying one, there was bound to be another Alan Geist type in Berkeley, I don't know what the odds of this would be, but I'll go with a, say, thirty percent?—knowing I'm likely estimating high for self-justification, although why I need that I don't know, as truth is I grew to love Eugenia. *I grew to love Eugenia!* I loved how she had become—by reversal— another me: sure this sounds so ridiculously solipsistic, and it no doubt is, as much as it was with bi-physique Dale—although (of course) it also isn't that at all—no way: Eugenia had become the looming persona, acute, of my secret soul (okay, yet another one), she was like a lockbox, guarded in a bank's recesses, of my most hidden-protected me (again with the solipsism), and so of my unadmitted me. But there was also—and more importantly—how this container-banding of my self (*she _and_ me!*) did seem to showcase a *care* for me (again, that damned accursed solipsisticity), it reflected how she thoroughly watched me, how she held herself while watching me, as if struggling to maintain her power-image, how—I think—because of me, she was worried, really, that I had become *her* All, *her* obsessed-upon reason for being, her own transforma-tion of her own self into its truest destiny, its final-found, the most important best-change in her life, a dis-position that made her living larger. No, wait! now *come on*! Isn't this hyper-hallucination on my part, widest-screen delusion?—no, seriously, I just don't think so—I believe that it's the ultimate realism, crazy as it is. . . And yes, sure, it is *crazy*! . . . And, again, I have to repeat what I've already said, because in my mind it keeps reappearing, meaning in my masturbation fantasies: there was another act, which we talked about considerably—but we never did (and I am tempted to go here with a semi-sheepish 'alas'—no, a full sheepish—on that 'never did'): my crouching beneath

Eugenia's ass, which, by the way, hadn't undergone its female age-drop yet (very impressive, that, and she might well have reached by then already, I suppose, *seventy*) and—*out-with-it!*—my eating Eugenia's shit!—the tasting of this defecating Clytemnestra. Eugenia had declared that eventually it would come to that: earnest-faced, as if she had held her hand upon the Bible in a courtroom, she'd vowed "My shit is sweet, Alan, it's manna"—and I now picture her erotically meditating to come up with such simile which most folks would certainly find disgusting (Had she learned to say it at the lecture by that dominatrix?)—and I did too, I found it repulsive—when I wasn't, over its force-ful-thrust (obliterating of all else) image, whacking-off. So, of course, *we never did it. . .* Although, sure, yes, I still do picture it. . . I can't stop.

"Have you ever done all this with anyone else before?" I'd asked. This was, not unironically, just after Eugenia had sold my house, and so there was not necessarily any commercial reason for us to be together any longer. Not legitimately anyway. The buyer's furniture would be moving in, soon after Escrow cleared.

" 'Have I ever before?' You want to feel special—is that it?" She asked that just as she began to leave my house, and in overly rapid steps, manufactured steps, edited steps, walking towards her new-fashioned-old-fashioned gray VW Bug.

I ran after her.

"Hardly," I said re wanting to feel special, and she turned back towards me.

"Oh, 'hardly' is it? You lie and you know it. You know, Alan, I'm offended by your saying that 'hardly'." She bent and picked up a stone that her landscape architect husband had had lain to accentuate the curving path to my (once-upon-a-time) house (he'd had the path made of sandstone "rather than boring old-hat brick, brick's too logical, like geometry—sandstone's Now, where it's *at*; sandstone can hide lizards and garden snakes, and they'll come out now and again—it's charming; and the sandstone looks like the maps of countries, topographical, say in Central Asia, like Kazakhstan or any of the 'stans'." "This is a sales plus?" I'd asked—he'd really been annoying me. "Yes," he said, "it's a plus; people do like nature."). Eugenia now threw that stone she'd picked-up, threw it at me, at my midsection, and I dodged it (and, you bet, felt like athletic Moe). "And, by the way," she said, "I wouldn't call what we've done, what *you've* done, cuckolding my husband. As men do like to be cuckolders, don't they, makes them potent, unearned potent—does that statement hurt?"

I thought about it, weighing this and that. "I guess it does—some. Hurt. Yes. But, then again what you and I've done isn't what you and *he* have, so there's no parallel, like, to set against, so . . ." I believe I was wriggling my shoulders slightly in known worthless thought. "So I don't really feel as if I've cuckolded—"

"*God*, men really are such pigs. Child-pigs, you ass-holes." Eugenia reached her VW and comically, hostilely, pressed the red alarm button on her auto's remote, the *weee-ya-weee-ya* making for this un-perverse-perverse woman smile. "And, by the way, in answer to your question of my doing this before, the answer is a zillion times."

I knew it wasn't 'a zillion'. But still I was devastated—or nearso. I was Nothing.

Was I so inadequate, so squealingly narcissistic, that I had wished to gain the being of a Something, even at the risk of the mastery of the "kneeling art" of male submission?—which sort of did make you a Nothing.

I could not believe that I was that.

But don't get the wrong impression (I still don't know what is the right impression): Eugenia was no Green Beret nor Army Ranger nor brave FrogWoman of sex. Not hardly. Eugenia had her liabilities, her feeblenesses, her deficiencies, her hurts, and these were hardly endearing, even when you cared (and *I did care!*). For one, Eugenia housed this pest anthropomorphically-named irritable bowel syndrome (IBS) with diarrhea (IBS+D). You might mention another girlfriend, especially one *you* might be engaged in the (wished-for) domination of, and there Eugenia would be within moments hurtling off to the toilet with a groaned-out "Oh damn *no*!" or "There I go again" or "*Damn* this unjust *curse*!" You might "cast your dubes" on Eugenia's suggestions, similar to intellectual Wanda's, that we might, occasionally, "tear ourselves apart" and "go out, as to a club or a restaurant or a movie, so that our "dynamite sex" would not be "the be-and-end-all of our relationship" (yes, she could cotton-to this conventional complaint to this oh so conventional man), and with your slack dissents, your slumped dissents (you regretting your Linda-loss, you reminding yourself that you deserved that loss in spades), there Eugenia would be, holding her hurting "irritable" stomach and howling-out "*You stick-in-the-mud*, you're worse than my husband," while she went hurtling right back to that Emergency magnet of a toilet. Eugenia had once said to me that at a certain age, meaning *her* age, the world becomes a lost telos (she did not use that word): you are no longer in mid-ocean of life's waves of possibilities, you don't see the need to do things anymore, to achieve goals, to receive accolades—although what accolades she might have received for staging houses is another question. But Eugenia's point was that the nearer one came to death, the farther one went from dreams and drama—which really were the reasons for life; and perhaps the nearing-end was the reason why she instituted the sort of "sex-beyond-sex" with me that she had. If it was nothing else, it was exciting—at least for a time. So, although this is not an excuse for anything, passion has its own excuses, Eugenia's Lady-of-a-Certain-Age perceptions did have me fearing that if I ended our "relationship" she'd have nothing left but staging sofas and plastic-mahogany coffee-tables and fake Persian rugs from Home Depot and an indifferent husband who was hooked on sandstone as a miniature Kazakhstan— and, who knows, she might kill herself.

Is this being overly dramatic? Probably. But well, my father Moe did kill himself. He did it smack-dab right in the middle of our best bike-riding days, which I relished, which I had so so relished (and skipped-out-on late afternoon Hebrew School for [dad didn't care about that "candy-ass Jew hypocrisy"]), but dad's demise came also when it became obvious to him that he no longer had any interests worth an interest. He had been that dreamed-of pitcher, center of a team, but at best in the International League minors (America plus Toronto and Montreal), and he had never got over that league's holding him stuck within it—and I could always (almost always) see that sadness in his eyes as he tried to get over it, The Big Failure, The Big Never Begun, while, say, riding beside me (such that *I* got so that *I* could never get over it—as if *I* had never got past the Minors, and never would—so as to be (and this *does* make sense) to be loyal to my dad. Loving to my dad, I would not surpass him, on pain of—on pain of *what*!? My father Moe's bike riding with me, and I had come to realize this too, was Eugenia's riding me in a whole other way. . . Or—and this is a big Or: Was it really all *me*, Alan, leading *Eugenia* on?—innocent Eugenia with the million gurgle-demanding gastro maladies. The blame, if it should be tagged blame, was not only any-one's. The subliminal submissive is after all sublimi-nal—and what on earth is not!—it claws-up at the dominant. What about when with the exudatious naïve Suzanne Thalbrucker I tied her up good, which she seemed to love?—and which had me wishing also to kiss her sweet-girl ass. What about my more grotesque male-maddenings with vengeful Wanda? And is such a line of investigation hardly worth the effort? What does it say but that, like say Anthony Hopkins or Robert De Niro, this fellow Alan G. could play lots, enormous lots, of parts?—while convincing himself that all of them, at the desired time, were not play at all but real. Is sexuality really not sexuality at all?—but as mysterious as the origin of the universe, about which we will never gain more than speculations made by very smart men who, in this universe-case, are no closer to an answer than remain the rest of us, the dummies?

And the truth was—of course you've likely guessed this—I did come to arrive at the "stage" where I didn't enjoy very much my *being* bossed by Eugenia's *being* anymore. As, what was starting to happen was I would see myself *telling* Eugenia what to do to me: Bend me here, take your bra and—do this there, etc etc etc. Eugenia had become my boss-slave. Or slave-boss. And this would more than likely lead to the even greater revolution: my being the boss boss.

I didn't even really much like the name Eugenia anymore.

Maybe, like her, it was Staged.

There is such a thing, I think, as too much experience, if it has come by way of fighting-off The Too Much Emptiness. What you see then is that old expanding circle, Life, closing itself tight, contracting—back to Life. You see your house, Linda's choice on the ghetto's brim, it now an island in the Caribbean destroyed to near vacancy by the conjunctive Hurricane Linda-Al. . . And by a realtor's experienced *Stagings*.

ALAN GOLDFEIN

AH, LILY

I considered the giving-up of Geist's Bikes (Black Jamil had put up a sign ten years before: WE ROLL) and my doing something Worthwhile, like, I don't know, becoming a Nurse. Unlike Doctoring, Nursing might only take for a degree, what?—two-three years? Instead of obsessing about myself, I could help save people.

Nursing didn't save me, as I couldn't even bring myself to the nearest hospital—Alta Bates—to find out, from some passing-by Nurse, say, how to start the application process.

Don't even THINK in such SAVING terms!

Lily saved me. Irma Lilia Smirnova Poskus. Lily, who had been dragged across Europe post-war at age five, in the direction opposite from the route that had taken Wanda: from Lily's native Lithuania, which had been overrun by the Soviets, she to dwell for seven years in foreigner-hostile Schwabia (southwest Germany), that U.S. occupied land of Mittle-European peasantish-but-not-quite-peasant folk who wouldn't take even to a little blonde kid who could pass for mythical Aryan more easily than could these South-Deutsche "snotsters" (Lily's word) who looked more like Italians than they did Prussians or Saxons or Schleswig-Holsteinians. So quiet Lily, while keeping her distance from all those mocking Württembergian "schoolmates" of hers—which was no picnic I'm sure for a little kid—she despised Germans as much as did Jews and as much as she had Russians. And she did know how to handle adversity, that was her armor-gift from History. And, seeing that she had that capability (it was in her soft-strong face, that could appear, and at the same time, sympathetic and imperturbable; it was in her placid gray eyes that were pearlish and yet too a sturdy granite), seeing such abiding panoramic range in Lily, seeing those emotions that stretched the scale of emotions, I thought: *Don't lay your weary load on her!*—it's bullshit-nothing when you get right-on down to it, it's conventional garden-variety nothing-much Americana, she'll have no respect for you. . . In hopes then that not employing one's (my) weary load might mean, eventually, that one's (my) load would no longer keep growing to be so weary, I edged myself close to Lily Smirnova Poskus (pronounced *Posh*-kus).

And she and I did not meet by way of GEIST'S BIKES: Lily was a Vet. By that I of course do not mean a proud discharged member of the armed forces but a person who treats animals. After Linda had left me and I had moved back into my flat above the bike store (which reduced existence had provided me with yet

another opportunity for my habitual lookings into the
bathroom mirror and seeing my father Moe staring back
at me with serious mixed-misery) and Eugenia and I
had rid ourselves of ourselves, I had got myself what I
had begged my parents for a zillion times, to no avail: I
had got me a dog. A Golden Retriever, one year old—
affectionately (what else?) I called him Poopyhead.
Poopyhead was—and I know it sounds ridiculous to say
this—he was my Lily before my Lily became my Lily.
Poopyhead had the most sensitive dogface a dog might
have (I know, all Golden Retrievers are blessed with
such intimate-endearing-sorrow looks with under-
current flashes of instinct-jolly happiness), and I loved
him as soon as I'd seen him staring up at me (as if he
sensed my own miseries and was intimating *I am with
you, pal—you look at Me, not in the mirror!*), he
connecting his large deep understanding eyes with
mine, he washing me with those God-gift eyes like soft
lights come burning through the wire-bars of his cage at
The Pound (The Berkeley Humane Society), and all
that soft full auburn fur afollow. What asshole, for *any*
reason, would have let The Poopman remain rotting in
his cage!? (Well, apparently a shitload of assholes
had!). . . But The Poop had his problems: He was
ambiguous, as mix-minded as, you guessed it, me
myself and I—he had, in other words, no center. It was
as if out of either soulful eye My Poopyhead was ever-
engaged—and one engagement at the same time as the
other—in seeing the world differently, oppositionally—
which one could argue was a sign of his brilliant
(human-like) intelligence or his afflicted (human-like)
schizophrenia. The PoopMan could run alongside me as
I rode my bike, he in perfect parallel gallop, not

stooping to sniff or poop, until, truly poop-prepared, when he'd cock his head towards mine and alert me with a one single breakoff of a muffled brotherly bark and very meaningful no-bullshit eyes—and I'd quit pedaling and wait for him to do his duty. Unlike most Berkeleyites, I—well I'm sorry—I didn't bother-with a pooper-scooper but just pedaled-off irresponsibly when The PoopMan had finished-up—but responsibly he never did drop his load in the middle of the street, instead angling-off for clean-relief at the curb. As if he understood propriety. And decency—fellow mammalian decency. Regard for the-next-dog, even if he or she be human. But still: My Dog (God I love uttering that phrase, like some newlywed men [and overjoyed over-the-hillers] take their super-pride in alluding-to My Wife—my wife this and my wife that), but My Dog PoopyHead, as I said, he did have his problems: As I've described, he was an ambiguous sort, not canine-scatterbrained exactly but mix-minded: Sweet but with no strict control-center, out of nowhere as we rode-and-ran side-by-side, he'd eye, even, a Pit Bull, leashed and well-obedient, it strolling with its owner (thank Mercy this never happened to be Wanda with her Mister Winston), and My Dog would go into primitive wolf aggression: he might as well have been Hell-howling as he lurched towards that muscular ocean-mouthed Pit and jumped on that toughest-roughest of all mutts that could like-as-not take-on a wolf or bobcat—Poopyhead instinctively going on the suicide mission of lunging for the invulnerably thick Pit throat, as said (blameless) Pit would instinctively do the same, usually to my dog's bleeding-out, and embarrassment (his big brown eyes would ride-up hidden beneath his eyelids as he looked at me in shame's sorrow), such until the Pit owner would manage to yank his innocent blameless monster off, along with my apology for my dog's "attack". ("Geez, I don't know what came over him."). But that's not all: One might take-to thinking from what I've just revealed that The Poop Man would satisfy himself that he was at least number two among roughneck doggies—but that was not the way his mentality worked. At a walk confrontation with a mild black Labrador, or even a well-behaved Dalmatian or an evenly tempered beautiful Swiss Mountain Dog, The Poopster would inscrutably back off, usually not by just backing-off but by laying down on his back, paws retracted, in universal-known canine submission: *Please, I recognize your superiority to me, Mister Dalmatian, I beg of you to not hurt me.* And even I would be embarrassed at this slunk behavior of my partner, my new soulmate—it was so cowardly, seemingly cowardly anyway—I would now have preferred aggression, as ugly-bellicose as that might be. . . I didn't understand, not at all. I mean it was like Mike Tyson, say, after destroying some badass boxer with one noggin-punch, going down to the canvas from a weakish jab or two by an unrated (and white) Palooka with a pathetic record of one win, twenty losses.

And here is where all-feeling Lily Poskus makes her entrance—or rather I made mine. After an especially bad take-down by a faultless Pit who The PoopMan had attacked, and whereby he was bleeding from the throat, I took him to East Bay Vets (it was next-door to Bloom's pool room where I had been a regular years before, often playing with my father who with his pitcher-accuracy could make nine of ten spot shots [I could make, at best, say, four]), and at East Bay Vets it turned out that Lily was one of the three practicing veterinarians.

"What a sweetie-pie," said Doctor Irma Lilia Poskus as she, sweetly herself, but firmly, ruffled The Poop-Man's long auburn fur to get a good look at his wounds. "Many Pit Bulls are very nice, but if they have been trained to fight, then it's Cathy-bar-the-door."

The correct phrase-name was Katy, but hearing Lily's Euro-accent I let it slide.

"It was my dog's fault," I admitted, and The Pooper seemed to look towards me with his eyes narrowed, which I took to mean, "Alan, you are a great sniveling-snitch of a betrayer."

As she examined my dog, and dressed his wound, Lily's face had gone alongside his. They appeared as a portrait: communing, sensitive, mutual-understanding, twins.

"He has this problem," I said. "He'll go aggressive with dogs out of his league, and then with dogs he could destroy he goes passive. A kind of noblesse-oblige."

"I know the type," said a wisely smiling Doctor Poskus (and she had dimples). "What it is is he's what we call a Wise Protector. He lives with you, and he knows you, by absorbing you and feeling you, just almost by instinct. You must be the same Wise Protector that he has become."

That, I doubted. That, I wished were true. Ever Mister Negative, I said, "But look what it has got him."

"It has got him," this depthful Doctor Lily averred, "an owner who he reveres so much as to imitate, and so as a dog to have good sensile feelings, for doing the right thing—or what he believes is right—he has a sense of 'right'. Retrievers very do."

"Don't you think you might be anthropomorphosizing a tad?" I said to this (again for me, alas) blonde woman, she in her Vet whites, loose-fitting but still allowing the protrusion of her breasts (*ah, they must be considerable, luxurious Titians!*), she whose every motion seemed to reflect and project a calm and graceful easiness, as if she were dancing, and dancing alone, to, I don't know, a slow unrushed Chopin Polonaise? It was as if her touch could not hurt any being, it could only heal—and without really making any forced effort that might be false, her senses could not allow that. Yes, I am quite aware of the profuse romanticism of that description, but it is a true one, and likely that truth is one that Lily Poskus had adopted to survive early in her life, as an unwanted alien in South Germany. I will say, however, that in her motions and in what appeared to be her moods, even as she softly handled my Poopy-Head, there was something of the abstracting element, as if she were there and she were not, as if she might be dwelling as well in an alternate universe. But didn't it have to be a good universe, considering the so kind way she took care of my dog—I saw in his eyes his immediate love for her—and there was the tender thoughtful way she looked at me as she spoke. . . But I also believe that within herself, defending against human craftiness and manipulation, she might well have preferred that My Dog had been able to come to her on his own, alone.

Hard to believe—I didn't even debate it as a strategy, that great inner-wanting within me guided it and did it, told me don't leave this meeting with this special woman as a simple commercial passing—I touched her hand.

She nodded, near imperceptively.

I had no idea what this benign nodding meant, or even if she intended it to mean anything. No other woman I had ever known had so simply employed her oval face and pearlish eyes in that microscopic way while facing me, while, I guessed, addressing me— delicate-strong bones rising and descending so evanes- cently. Was this some sort of password?, and to whom? herself or me?—these infinitessimal motions had happened in a kind of ether that she herself had created, and they continued for a time, again as if she were there and not, and they were dwindling as gravity smothered them—she was again the abstracting universe. Which allowed me to hold my hand there on her hand. This did not even feel as if I were being bold. Nor did my, on instinct, tracing my fingers along her right wrist. Bizarrely, beyond her calmness, it struck me that she was behaving as if she were locked in prison, held in a kind of refugee camp or such where the jailers and overseers could do what they wanted to the refugees, the "residents"—and they, the jailers, would be pun- ished only by fate, or by God. I did not know it at the time of course, but this Lily was a person who had finally been freed from all such incarcerations at still a time in her life where her personality was yet reaching for formation, so that she might well have been or- dained to become something like a church cleric or a nun or a social worker (or, well, a conscienceless female mass murderer)—or a veterinarian at a pound. Stray dogs and cats were refugees. Powerless. Unable to talk back. Vulnerable to jailer whim or ecstatic at jailer kindnesses.

Slowly, as if to not offend, to not harshly reject, Doctor Lily Poskus slid her hand from mine. This with her strong pale gray eyes held on mine, firmly, unwavering.

I might have seen that steadiness as reproach but, surprising to myself, I saw it as a trust, a trust that was certain it could defeat any distrust—for certainly she knew in depth what human distrust was and she had learned how to handle it, or at least fight it—and with that quiet cool. She had perhaps even learned how to affect its change, reform it. Or, at least, to softly gird herself—to hard. All this, learned on her own. . . How dissimilar from the harsh antipathy that bitter Wanda "Hardesty" had built-up in order to react to not so dissimilar a childhood situation.

Really this stability of this Lily was more than surprising; it was in a way, frightening. To a cynic like me anyway. To one who has so thoroughly, so often (so consistently) misled himself. Until that moment of facing Lily my main trust had grown to be that things were never what they were and I ought *not* trust. . . Dogs trust. . . We all think.

And after all she had not ushered me out of the Pound with my PoopyHead for my audacious (and actually ridiculous) hand touching.

There must be more to her, I reflected. More to her ingrained ballast. Her transfixing. And I was right. It's coming.

And again, as with that hand-touching, I peeked-out and ventured from my hungry core, asking, "Could we meet?"

And again, it was her inscrutably calm-confident settledness that had allowed me to gamble this.

"A man was here with his Border Collie a few weeks ago," she said in the lightest of voices, "and he told me that I made his bones melt."

It was as if she were both reporting and asking what it meant. She was not boasting.

"And . . . ?" I asked. "What did you do?"

"I did not react." She continued that steady mooring of her eyes onto me. "I was not trying to 'make his bones melt'."

"Why," I asked, "are you telling me this?"

"In an nicer way, and I don't mean to hurt you, but you are reminding me of that man."

I wanted to cry out, *I am not that man!* Except that I believed I was.

"I just," I said, "I don't know what. But"—*you cad, you*—"I-am-*not*-that-man." Well, at least I had not cried it out, my lie which was not a lie. It wasn't only that she also did make my bones melt; it was that, in her near-virginal presence, truth or misleading, she made me feel, not guilty, but beyond that—dirty. Ulterior. Exploitative. Motives scrambling over motives. And, I'm serious, *contrite.* A Spanish intruder among the American Indians loaded with his deadly Euro-viruses.

"Of our meeting," she now said. "Please, don't make me make the decision." She was now tousling The PoopMan's mane, for—I thought—a defense-reflex thing to do.

I suddenly experienced the ridiculous vision that she lived in the Berkeley Pound, in a back room, alert to any dog or cat's cry of need. That she was content, as perhaps Thoreau had been at Walden and all through his life, and he'd died a useful virgin.

Come now. Ridiculous. Certainly she did not live at the Pound.

Maybe she did? Stranger things have happened.

At a loss I turned round and looked at the dogs in their cages (this was of course the doggie section). If they were not claimed they would be put-to-sleep, I believe, in two weeks. The "fellows" had pleading faces, or wised-up already given-up faces, or they lay inert, or asleep (titillated by hopeful dreams?—I doubt it). They were mind-readers better than Houdini—but unfortunately they were not his equal as escape artists. They understood life, fate, they understood existence, and I believe they knew that I provided no hope for them as I already had Poopyhead standing at my side— Poopyhead who, it was obvious, understood what those poor canine souls understood. I noticed that he could not stare them in the eyes, his fellows, his brethren; he'd intentionally look away: away from the Pomeranian and the Wire-Haired Terrier and the sweet-faced Beagle who was ludicrously gaining an erection (Lily and I smiled at his growing penis, enlarging while he was yet closeted in the crisscrossed wires of hopeless adversity); and there was an alert Poodle who looked so ridiculous in captivity, and a German shepherd-and-something mix, who seemed to stand and lie and then stand as if trying to find the best posture for attraction and obedience and showoff; and there were more fellows in the cages lodged behind the cages in the front. . . It was not possible to not experience allegory in this captive bare-hopeful place.

I said, and wanly—with, I'll admit a wan intentionality: "I'm lost here."

"I too am." Still, her eyes held, Lily's did. "I do not work here to meet men."

"For godsakes I know that."

Her smile appeared tied, wrapped-up, impossibly flaming with shyness, disallowed excess by the watchful warden within; yet sending, unmistakably, a gratitude.

For what?

Has she ever been married? She wears no marriage ring, but that is not necessarily absolute proof. And it strains my imagination to picture her as a wife; what seems to be her goodliness—it just cannot be an act—her goodliness would have me as her husband screaming within myself, I can see it, I can see my discovering more of my badlinesses than even I am aware-of now, I would not be saved, I would be remanded more than ever to the deepest furnaces of Hell. (Well, maybe not quite *that* deep—we all know who would be the characters consigned way down there.). I am old enough to know of course that stranger things exist or have existed, than a marriage to such a woman, such a model of the angel-opaque (and stranger things than a man like myself *already* imagining such a marriage for myself with such a woman, after but a few moments' meet, my being so desperate), and I am working on my oxymoronic analysis when Lily is now rescued from my lost attentions by the next patient, a beautiful Malamute running what the female owner (she is not particularly attractive, so I pay little interest), the Malamute running what that owner says is a high dog fever. And what is a dog's normal temperature?—I doubt that it is 98.6, but who knows. What I do know is that this wonderful veterinarian Lily who is like no other woman (I really feel that this is true [again, my desperation-hollering, as if it is the screeching-silent voice of the doggies captive here in their cages]), this blonde doggie-doctor who is perplexed that she makes men's bones melt—human men's as well as those of pets—she is saved by that beautiful feverish Wolfish Malamute, saved from me and my cravings borne of inadequacy and loneliness. As, by her, I am saved from myself, or rather, wish-to-be—I could not take any more rejection, even when it is clothed in a sick acceptance such as, especially, that blasé one of old Eugenia. . . And on the way home with The PoopMan beside me, he strolling so obediently (a lingering love for this Lily Woman?) I find myself concocting canine illnesses that will have me bringing myself back to her in shortest order (but believable order, acceptable order), back to this new and best-possible since "my" Linda, my "ex" (and I am so certain of this Doctor Lily bestness), this "new but rightful" (and "insightful", and, alas [yes the "alas" creeps in too] *wrongful*) object of my desire: Sothen, Dog Diseases to "use" for my purposes—Doctor Google's got 'em, in spades: But there, even with Google the Vet, and after some serious searching, industrious investigation, I cannot find a malaise that is both not-so-serious yet is Vet-visit-worthy: that is, one *I* could bring about on-a-dime, beyond mild (quick-correctable with an easy anti-tox) poisoning; and/or one that Doctor Lily Poskus would not ascertain as obviously concocted and trumped-up—and cruel. And criminal. So, forget it. . . But brainstorm! As criminally insensitive and colossally selfish as this new idea is I will now go to leashing my boy and taking The Poopster for a number of walks, moreso than before, and ulterior creep that I am I am hoping (sort of) that we will encounter an ill-humored Pit Bull or, say, a relatively toughass German Shepherd, and being who he is, the protective Poop will try to save me, and/or other dogs in the neighborhood, by challenging that vicious dog, and I will tug him away before any real damage is done beyond the superficial (although if you have ever witnessed a violent dogfight you know how impossible this might prove to be for a mere human—and you will in all likelihood end up at your own Internist yourself.). So, this intention, this plan for again seeing Doctor Lily, is unworthy even of me, it is admittedly ugly, it is beyond ugly, do I not seem to comprehend even the intrinsic fixed rudiments of love?—love now for The Pooper I'm talking—*but damn I must see Lily again!* and it does occur to me that under the aegis of this doggie fight-promoter concoction *I do not DESERVE to see her again,* or *any* woman, *ever*—and I even stoop to praying to "God" to understand my motives, the desperate loserly sad-ass needs of a *loser* who seems to believe (while not-believing) that HE is the whole world; I even say to The Lord that I do not *really* intend what I'm intending, it's all just a sort of pretend-act, a misfantasy—I really do go through all this, as I am, like many uncertain frightened foxholed men, a Believer—uncertain as my Belief might be. . . Anyway, as I really did recognize at the start, the plain truth is, *I cannot go through with it—* wreak harm on my sweetie Poopster? How could I even entertain such a . . . Just *Stop-it!* . . . And indeed, as fate would have it (fate, it is such an interesting, taunting, thing), a few blocks from GEIST'S BIKES on the very next day we do come upon a possible victim (or victor), a black Labrador minding his business with his civic-minded owner nearby equipped-with a proper Pooper-Scooper; but I hold the leash tight and The PoopMan's instinctive attack-strength is no match for my own defense—I hold him in check and I do feel good about myself for the final eventual win-out by my morality. . . But what then am I to do?—just wait until my beloved healthy Poop, on his own stick, gets sick? This might take a year. Years. What a thing to wait for—and with, yet, *anticipation*?

Chrissakes, will you, be a man! Finally then, after about one month's rock-sturdy vacillation, I bring my-self—and *only* myself, no PoopMan—to the slat-suffused shack that is sandwiched between Le Bistro jazz-restaurant and Bloom's, my old poolroom hang: East Bay Vets. I had eaten many times at Le Bistro, with Linda, with *Mar*-lies, with Suzanne, but I'd had no idea at those times that unwanted animals were being fixed-up or "put-down" on the other side of the fancy brick wall of the restaurant's kitchen. (Food for thought).

"You are alone?" said Lily when after an hour's wait it was my turn (after a Beagle and an Afghan and a clutter of restless-confused-to-befuddled dogs [and sleepy-slumped indifferent ones too] who had come here before me with their owners). "Is your, Poop-Man?—no?—so indisposed as not to come?" She added that she was not making a joke although she said that she did make jokes sometimes—and she did make home visits when necessary.

"You have a wonderful, caring, memory," I said, and I was impressed. "Yes, it's The Poopman, that's his name. But he's fine."

"Then why . . . ?" Her gray eyes skirted into a kind of bright-open narrowing that endearingly wrinkled-up her rather longish (but thinnish) Euro-nose—a scrutinizing nose. "Why?"

I couldn't, and can't, believe that she did not catch onto my motivation. Thus I go bold and I reply, "Well I would like very much for you to make a home visit."

Her smile is pure her: It is a smile extended and spontaneous, a smile of loving when she cannot possibly (yet if ever) love—I mean with untrustworthy *me* as the object, old selfish Alan Geist?—and her smile is one of calm withdrawal into self, as if she is hearing what other humans cannot hear and she is diagnosing what she hears right on down through its many weblike Byzantine avenues. Such a complicated smile—for, I suppose, a woman who, as a girl in unwanted and unwanting Europe, had to smile a lot, and well-raveled, and thus protect herself.

"I'm kidding," I say. "I mean, oh hell *out*-with-it—I would like to take you out."

I can't tell now if her smile has transmuted into a frown or if that frown is indeed part and parcel of her smile. A frown of hidden-blatant sympathy? . . . She says—

"You have waited a quite long time."

"Yes."

"I understand."

She does? What, what does she understand? That I have never in my life, with all the women I have known, all those multi-varied exemplaries and screwballs, I have never met anyone quite like her (an illusion I have had before, as of course have all men), and yet I really have no idea what that convergence of ours means?—that seeming convergence. Does her web-scrutinizing 'understanding' find depths that are not there, or are there but remain mud-clear to me? Was she actually waiting for me to come calling?—no, that's ridiculous! Has she the portentous ability to see into the future?—to our inevitable quirked-up relationship (no doubting that one), beginning-middle-end. Who *is* she?

"I have," Lily looking all about, "many waiting dogs."

It's true, that she does. But could she also be speaking metaphorical?, in riddles meant to protect herself— for there are, which I had not noticed earlier, these two dimples which have appeared just beneath her cheeks, these dents of what appear to be total (and pleased?) (and *sexual*??) (and divergent too) (and certainly phantom-invoking, because of hidden fears) comprehension.

How can I trust her? Simple. Because, unlike even my gone Linda, my "ex" woman who cared so greatly about "the uncareables", this Lily is impossible to not trust. Trust reverberates about her, sound waves, sight waves, honings-in and hums.

And look at this me, Mister Trust, he who is wondering if he can trust. Ultimate chutzpah.

I'll just take my cues from all these little cats and dogs who seem to perk-up when she calls-out their names—these "Fluffies" and even "Spikes"—monikers that I suspect she herself has given them. And all of us, when we are not being too Darwinian, do trust that "the animals just sense in their beings" who are the best amongst us. No?

So, brash-but-nudnik, I can't stop myself from going with, I've got to say, 'My bones'—but then I collar myself before I can come up with anything super-tender-profound (and insipid) (and asshole wry), as my words would be identical to those poesies that that man's who Lily had told me about, that bone-melted man who had brought to Lily his Collie; or my words would just fall in default to something as inane as, 'Oh what I feel is throbbing within me.' How pathetic. So with a head-shake and a hand-waver-off, I dismiss any reference to any of my dumb bones.

All of which confusion of start-stops she doesn't appear to have even listened to, or paid the slightest of attentions: "I have got," she says, "to get to dear Billie."

Billy? Her husband? Her girlfriend—or wife? She must ask his/her permission for our 'going out'?—she remains so swaddled in The Old World?

She is waving-in the next patient and his owner. A patient (reluctant?) mixed-breed of moderate size she calls by, of course, Billie.

"But what about . . you know?"

She knows:

She hands me her East Bay Veterinarians card and quickly scribbles at the bottom her private phone number—just in time, as the eager Billie, no-holds-barred, leaps into Lily's waiting extended arms and licks her well-pleased face (as protection from Billie's tongue she does not—as do most people with licking dogs—shut tight her eyes). But Lily's number: I cannot discern the 4 from the 7, for she uses the European crossbow seven. No biggie. I go home to my flat above GEIST'S BIKES beside myself: mission accomplished—three-quarters, anyway. At "home" I speculate: this Lily, she is the calmest, nicest, most feet-on-the-ground, least assuming woman I have ever been with (even though I haven't yet been "with" her)—and this is not without (yet) the exception of my ex-wife Linda. But then, you guessed it, creeps creep into the creepable caveat: so why then did Linda and I end anyway?—and she with good old me?

Oh stop it: That's obvious. So you are not worthy of this so so worthy Lily.

Don't call her.

I call her, Irma Lilia Smirnova Poskus. After an appropriate and strategic three day wait—although I am sure that the last thing she has been doing is counting those days.

"Aha, Mister PoopyHead Man."

Terrific, she does have a sense of humor. At least I try to grant that her greeting tells me so. It does not tell me, however, what I learn when I show-up at her small gray shingle twin-wood-pillared house on Rose Street—which is that she, Lily, is what we used to call in the Sixties, a "head". The "shack", she refers to it—and it does not from the outside bear no little resemblance to her small Vet "hospital"—including by the existence of one doggie, an energetic Border Collie named Jonas (pronunciation *Yo*-nas; and of course super-affectionate and peering-eyed) who she claims can discern nouns from verbs and adjectives. And the house smells with that particular giveaway, to me anyway, of stale dirty-underpants redolence, like a "marijuana factory". But, not quite fitting—no not fitting at all—this good Lily is not dressed in doper clothes. She has been waiting for my arrival in what one might call "dress casual": a green-red pleated plaid skirt, knee length, a plain blouse with collar, not athletic shoes but loafers. As if she is about to attend a business meeting,

or go to church. Sad?—is this sad? Marijuana has not
yet at this date (the Eighties) been declared legal in
California. So is Lily trying too hard, for a simple house
visit from a dog-owner? Or showing respect, for *me*?
No, okay, maybe not respect, but regard, as a proper-
brought-up-woman would show—for anyman. We sit
on a curved-back sofa (with a fleur-de-lis peak) so
rock-firm it must cause any visitor backaches and ass-
aches, but she sure seems not to mind the hardness. The
coffee table is beige, simply lathe-made with its uni-
form ribbings, bands and clefts—there is scarce more
furniture. On the coffee table is a VCR that has written
on its spine Mekas, and there are a few books, elegantly
bound—I recognize the names of Milosz and Gombro-
wicz, Lithuanian exiles I have not read? although I do
know of their themes of ethnic displacement and ethnic
cruelties ("my" Linda had taught me to a frustrated
distraction). Knowing next-to-nothing, I do not mention
the authors and the apparent filmmaker—nor does Lily.
But I am impressed that she reads poets, intellectuals,
and absorbs weighty movies, all the solid sensitives.
And I am relieved and I am in deference and admiration
for her, for while observing that I have not the minimalist knowledge of the desperate wisdom these men have
earned and preached about lost homelands (she can see
that in my averted glances at the books, as if they are
conscious and can stare back at me), she, Lily, sees my
lack of wisdom and knowledge of the men, and she
does not ask of me anything about them—she feels, she
knows lostness and discomfort enough, she has been
sentenced before to the world of absence and cruelty,
and she does not wish to embarrass this callow American who has had it easy. Expertly as fingering doggie-

fur she rolls a joint and offers me a sharing. I have not inhaled in years, not since the days of student-actress Suzanne Thalbrucker (I do not count my doped-up "homosexual" suck-mutuality "experiment" with my pal Shel Sevenecker), but disappointed (and, face it, already a trifle hostile), as she is not to my mind The Perfect Unflawed Woman I had dreamt-of, I still in-dulge. But: I cannot resist coming-out-with a petulant wiseass (although croaky-voiced from the reefer), "Is this how you handle being with dogs and cats all day every day?"

"That is mean," she says.

"It is," I say. "I'm sorry."

"And anyway," she replies, and tokes. "Also parrots, I have here. And mina-birds. And one pet raccoon, who is brilliant but he is opaque—you would not believe, the patience—he is trying."

The raccoon is her?

"And so then does this smoking dope mean that you need it to do your work?—that you don't quite love all the animals."

"No, please don't you *say* that."

I could shoot myself.

"I didn't mean it. It's the grass."

Would that it only were the grass. What am I to do with my untrusting self!? Especially of someone so Other. Seemingly she is beyond such conventionalities as trust or distrust.

"I love them," she says. "I love them all very much."

"Yes," goes Mister Makeup. "I do admire that."

She tokes (and is it my imagination, my discombob-ulated fraughtness that has her appearing more sophisti-cated, more poised, more unflappable—and perhaps less lovable?—when smoking-up than when she is just nicely lacking marijuana?). "Oh well yes," she says, "there are a few of them I don't really care for. They are work."

"That sounds normal, I would think."

"Oh I guess. But what is 'normal'?"

My sentiments exactly.

Her huddled-inward eyes, the grays obeying it seems the dope-shrinking, the diminishment of her pupils, almost denying their gray color. "I don't like to say anythings I don't like."

But her voice, so normally now dope-croaky, has gone whispery: she's embarrassed at not loving every-all animal she nurtures? As if such is a religious viola-tion, a silent pledge evaded.

Al Geist the psychoanalyst: Is this grass-ingestion of hers, is this overpowering simplicity of her gentle pet-attendance, the great conscientious pathos of it, is all such quiet intensity but the aftermath of how she has (and had) handled her imposed orphanagerie in Europe?—that prescribed instinct-menagerie of the human animal, the Euro-tribe all once being dead-set against her. Maybe she doesn't even know that there is such a connection. And maybe it isn't even true, maybe there isn't such connection, it's just my excusings and explainings, my wished romanticism inflating, billow-ing, gone once again crescendo. . . Oh Come on, Al, *cut-the-crap, will you!*—she is just a person, this Lily who makes men's bones melt, grab onto yourself, your non-melt *hard* bones, you have them *somewhere*—she is just *a person,* that is *all* she is. . . I watch her toke and toke and toke, three-five times my (loyalty-imposed) frequency—she employing now a rheostat to clamp onto the smallest smoken-down roach imaginable—and her precision-handling of that rheostat looks expert, so admirable, as if she is operating on the tiny delicate larynx of a parrot or mina-bird, or plucking the hurled-bunched quills of a porcupine out from the tormented jaws of a Pit Bull. And then—"gulp"—and her Adams Apple bobbles, it goes inverse, *it's not normal*, and her head rocks back, as if she has been hit—or had a stroke.

"What? *What?—Lily?!*"

Even Jonas, her Border Collie (who no doubt has been reveling in his usual [counted-upon] contact high), semi-stands to an alertness of shepherd concern.

"I believe I swallowed it."

She's announced this in the quietist of alarm, Lily alarm—in dope-compressed voice rasp.

"What do we do?" I am thinking Heimlich Maneuver—where do I press-in hard with my tight linked hands? or do I reach for her telephone?—*where is her telephone? Damn these modern people without land-lines.*

"It's no problem," she now rattles-out. "I've done this many times."

"Swallowing a roach?"

"Yes, the swallowing. I am quite used to it."

"Oh. . . Ah."

Even Jonas has settled down, albeit to an at-the-ready canine crouch.

Damnit, oh damnit, in the blinking—or rather in her gagging—I have changed. Romanticism, you fool, be gone, you! I want to get away from her—that suddenly; I respect her, still—there is no way not to; but I want to go home. Just like that. Or to a bar. Or to find "my" Linda—as impossible, as implausible, (and as pathetic) as that confrontation would be. Oh why must this woman, this sweet generous lovable Lily, be so addicted, so *needy*, so Euro-antiquated (as if this day today is still just after the devastating poverty of World War Two), why must she be so miserly as to conserve what need not be conserved, to smoke her cache of easily buyable grass straight on down to the last inhalable smidgeon of a gasp?—but *damnit, look-you, no one's perfect*, I also tell myself—and I tell myself—as I, obligingly I guess, supportively? and politely—damned if I don't!—I guest-toke beyond my self-warned limit. And, to myself, I then go on: *Can't you learn that adult-wise fact of imperfection, universal fucking SHORTFALL! Search the world, Big Al (because Little) Geist, search the universe, no perfect woman or girl. Nor man. Wise-up to your age, now forty-five—how did I get here so fast? Chrissakes, <u>adjust</u>. Accept. Make concessions. If this grass-gobble is the worst of Lily's reactions to her deprived former life, it's nothing! Your self is not so unblotched and untainted that you cannot fucking COMPROMISE (that's for sure)—especially for a connection with this so good woman who is, after-all, seriously super-nice and gentle (mostly, I guess) and who certainly knows in spades life's suffering. . .*

But can I compromise? I took a stab, I ventured—

"Lily, why do you like me?"

She closed her eyes, which had me feeling that she was ashamed. She said, again in near a whisper, clouded clear-through by its sibilance—

"How do you know I do?"

Because I didn't wish to give-out-with any words that might indicate arrogance, I shrugged—in a way befuddled-but-affirmative.

She knew why I knew: She knew that I was aware, deeply aware, of her handicapped self-image, just a mirror to my own. Magnified mirror too. This woman who did what I could not (and could not want to do): draw animals' yearning leaps into her arms?—this woman who in her waiting room had drawn the accentuated praise of pet owners who seemingly would bring their Billies and their birdies to no one but their caring, embracing Doctor Lily?

"I see you," she finally admitted through her marijuana smoke and haze (and once her gulped-down dope-roach had at least partial-cleared her bronchia, and she still held the clutching rheostat as one might hold, what?—a mic, or a ring to be placed upon the finger of another), "I see you, not, no, not as I see my animals, but—well, maybe, as *with* them, in their . . . pack?"

"I think I should be offended."

"No-no. It's, it's the . . . the . . . atmosphere? Of you."

I'd squinted, I recall that: to be comic, humorous (laughable?), my squint of pain-camouflage.

Her own ambiguity now worked further onto this gray-spreading of her eyes, and ironically it made her face so direct, unshifting (so un-American, male or female, I couldn't but see that)—and by contrast I was being turned into a sort of shy doggie? "It is there all round you," she said. "*You* are there all round you, you are written all *over* you. It is so sad, Alan, no cover-up. It is what you cannot *not* do, yet still-so it is brave, and it is honest. Instinct can be brave and honest—even coward instinct. Even though it is not the fault of will."

My comic squint again, again of pain-camouflage. And of not-knowing-what-the-hell-she'd-meant. . . But she was doped—to the marrow.

She said: "I don't know how else to explain—and I am drawn into it."

Into *me*?

So honest, I thought. So undevious. No woman-wiles. I hadn't the faintest notion of what to say. She'd said I was like a friendly furry creature, and, I guess, like a woman; but in a way, really, that settled and bolstered me—while of course unbolstering. She might just as well have been stroking Alan the BikeMan's bending doggie neck. . . Just now her sincere face has seemed to lengthen, her eyes become more silvery than gray and her arms have extended out, not as if so much to take hold of me but to touch me, or come so close to touching that those arms, they touch without touching, so much the stronger in that projected way, all antici-pation, they graft onto me without the pain of graft, they are all-reach, they transmit through air—and her voice has grown huskier, as if more girded onto the earth (or trying to hide that her basing, her foundation, is really less-based, less girded [just as I have so often done]). "I see animals all the time," she says, "they who are hurting and they are hurting so bad, and they cannot tell me what it is or where—"

"I know," I say, I suppose to show her that I am with her, I understand pain's soundlessness—that curse.

"They cannot point, the animals, you know."

"I know," I repeat pointlessly.

"They cannot tell me what they think, their own diagnosis of themselves—and I just *know* that they have such, I *mean* that—and so I have to look and I have to sense and I have to contemplate and then to compre-hend—as if I have some sixth sense within, a *seventh* sense of language—and that is why I *know* you, Alan."

Lily is explaining on, or pointing: her perfect lips in only the slightest of motions, her beautiful eyes in a kind of intelligent sorrow—and I, I am hearing nothing, no longer, no words, no meaning—I am only observing that her tones are being entrusted to *me*, a stranger really, even if in spirit, or even if *not* in spirit—a stranger sitting in an unending seat in which we two seem to think that we are near-one—while we are not nearly one. Maybe we are even the opposite.

I so *despise* my polarity! I so despise the world's.

"So," I say, "the marijuana helps, with your—I don't know—. . . your intuiting?" (Of myself and dogs and cats and etc. of the lower-lives.). And I observe that I have unconsciously drawn-in, my legs are bent partially beneath my thighs (as often women may tend to sit— women in skirts, that is), my back is bowed, somewhat, like an old man fighting-off the scourge, the displayed scourge, of old-manism. I am protecting myself—and from someone who herself has conquered such and so projects no protecting needs.

"The marijuana helps, yes," she says. "It's catnip, for us human cats."

"Ah, you make a joke."

"I know I do so seldom."

She actually exaggerates the 'joke' and its 'wrongness' by taking thumb and index finger and pressing-in her smile. As if she has been warned: *You bad girl, never smile.* She says—

"But maybe I have become addicted. I worry. The prescription is not so nearly as much as I now ingest." Suddenly she holds to her side, as if a stitch of pain has drawn its deepest lightning line. "Oh, my, liver?"

Should I say something?—something wise and male? . . . I should.

"Then how do you get the quantities that you have?"

"The quantities?" She seems confused. This is weird.

"The marijuana. That you seem to have."

"Oh," she goes, lowering her narrow chin (and exhibiting without intention the perfectly precision female skeletal line of sparrow neck and jaw); the way she looks up at me now, it is as if I have implied that she is a criminal or a bad-behaving child. Or that is how I fear that I am seeing the last thing that I want to appear to have seen, of this sweet good unselfish woman. And *damn! I am sure she is these things*. . . Except, as I perceive (and make so much of) these wonderful qualities of this wonderful dope-smoke-woman, I realize that years ago, before we fell apart, before we lost each other out of boredom and idle brush-by-ness and non-recognition of what our good relationship had once contained, and yet even in ignorance we should have stuck-to containing, fought-to-containing, I and my ex, Linda, we'd felt that sweet good wonder that I am feeling now, and with greatest warning. Which alternates, mixing with the wonder—and magnifying it.

Doctor Lily Poskus, she is now wearing this subtle smile, perhaps not unlike the one she might have worn when she, without trying to, made that Man-with-a-Collie declare that her soft presence made his bones melt. . . But it is also so subdued a smile that it could easily be too a guilty one, and that childishly proud one that tries its best to hide; and she says—

"Acquiring the marijuana, that is not a problem, you must know. Not in our East Bay."

"I know, but—" take-the-bull-by-the-horns—"well,

could you, like, you know, cut back?" And why do I ask this? What right have I to advise someone to even stop scratching their ear? The woman has a painful disease, *la malade du* Alan Geist—*must I keep thinking this way?*—she has the syndrome of life's transience, life's home-abandonings, which had become escape for gain of one's own life-saving, and it is, in a way, auto-immune, human turning-in upon itself. And so it is dug in. It is *her*! So, what am I asking?—that she should cold-turkey the diazepam of marijuana, risk more soul-based pain?, and the implication being *For Me. For Me?* For, face it, you GeistMan, you lowly bike sales-man; and she should not give-up the dope (sure I know it's mild stuff, but still—), not give it up for a doctor or a lawyer or a professor, all of which *I* might have been (I have told myself so often, berating, the internal scold, the, face-it, maternal scold), but for this strange twisted loyalty-son who keeps shoving himself towards being like his dad Moe the Jew ballplayer, that muscle-rarity, that Hebe-tough who was tough as a hic-goy (and to what end? *to what end!?*). She, this Lily, she should give it up for, for good or ill, this struggled mirror of herself? And thus of, she has felt it, and dare I say it, that abused word, that too-often faked word—*sensitivity*? . . . Gene Kelly singing not *I've got Rhythm*, but *I've got Sensitivity*?

A oneness, Lily and myself, not with kissing, not with embracing, not with making love, not yet.

And that Yet—its discovery—how can it not come, not delay for cause of its ever "distortionness", not weigh on what we already have, and maybe wrongly-weigh, you know it can do that, *does do that!*—we know that it will do its telling too:

And so of our Sex I will say only this: Lily—Irma Lilia Smirnova Poskus—she, in a soprano that is almost breathed-up to low-alto, and an alto that near reaches up to a tenor-alto (and how can I not hear Coltrane crying-lyric as he did this?), she coos to me, while I am within her, "Oh mah honey." And her voice, it does not contain its straightened Lithuanian-whimpered caste but rather that of—at least to me—a black woman, a strong one, trying to please, trying to put-at-ease. And with Love—I decide. Though Love based on so little. Love urging this tightening, this muscular squeezing of her vagina about my penis, a holding-onto that I have never quite experienced before, for it seems mirrored in her avowing lips, and so this act, it is therefore speaking, *pointing*—as if, in her earlier life, she had held-onto much (much within her) in other ways, many ways, like maybe huddling stray animals, white rabbits escaped too from peasant hutches as she had done, cats that resembled Charlie Chaplin and did not know that they looked funny, doggies as begging wounded wolves not knowing that that bold-wildness is what they really were. Her vagina, those muscles, holding me, possessing. . . Asking.

For we do not know each other.

And at least we recognize that this sensitized "intense-but-not-inane" might, maybe, hold-out for good.

FOR COMMENTS TO THE AUTHOR
PLEASE CONTACT:

americaneditions@aol.com